Sands of Ruin

BOOK ONE

R. M. MULLER

WILLOW
HOUSE
— Publishing —

For my girls,
fight fiercely,
love with everything you have . . .

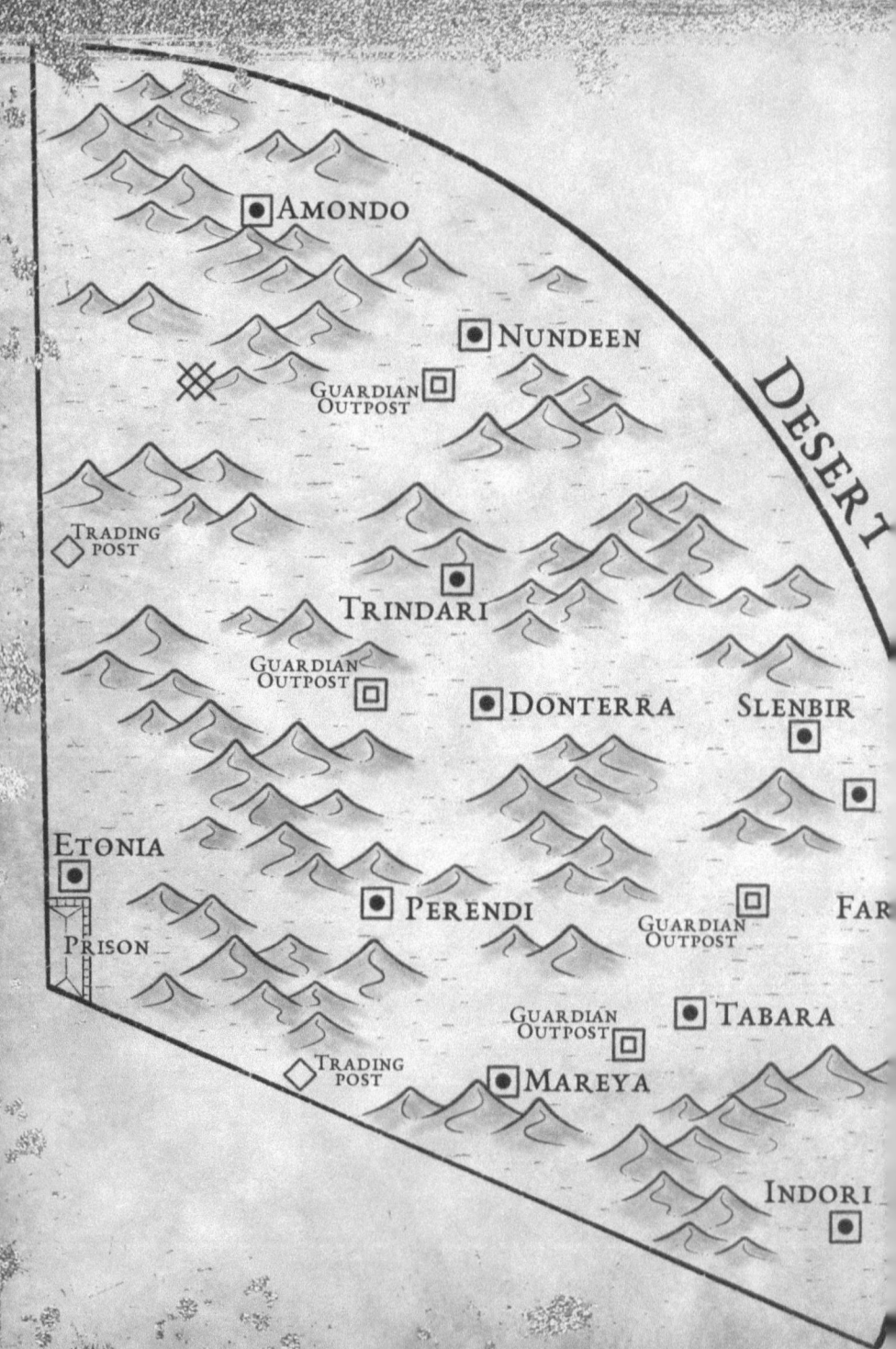

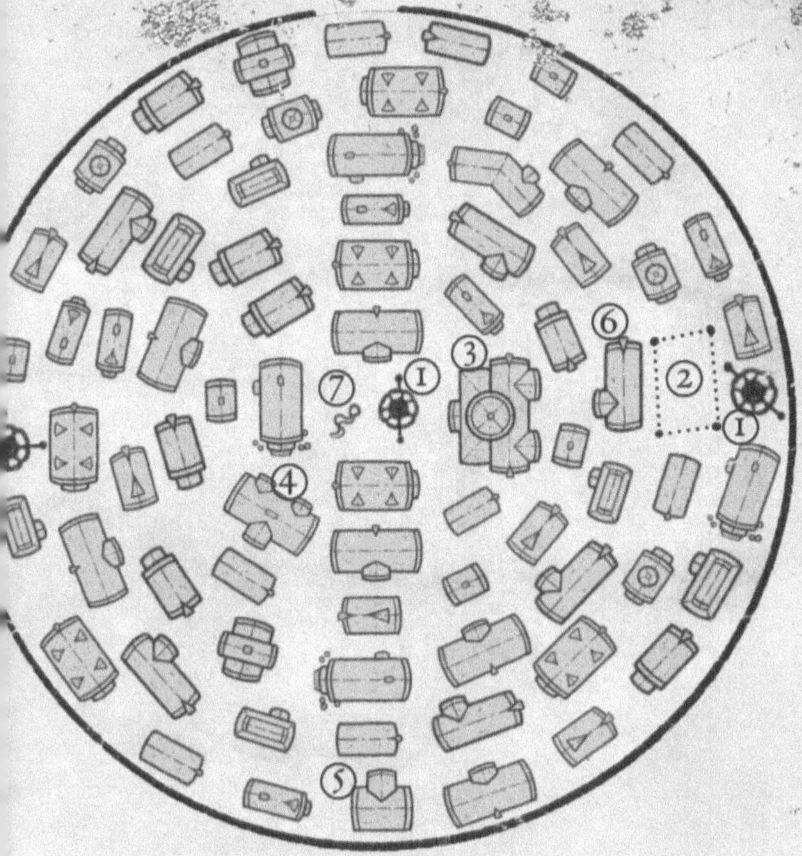

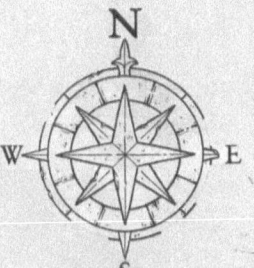

1: WELL
2: GOATS
3: HEALERS SHELTER
4: HARM'S HOUSE
5: ARLO'S HOUSE
6: MASON'S HOUSE
7: HANGING POLE

RUINATION CAN ONLY BE REDEEMED BY THE HANDS OF COURAGE.

Sands
of
Ruin

CHAPTER I
HARM

The midday ground burns through the soles of my boots. Past the last ring of houses on the southern side of our home between the dunes, I stand in the shade of a spindly, grey-leafed tree. Waiting for Arlo, I whistle to pass the time. Sand stirs amongst the patches of rocky outcrop to my west. Harsh, thin grey plants hide from the suns vicious rays between granite stones at the edge of our village. Soon he appears from behind the last building, his hunting gear slung over his shoulder. Mid-melody, I smile, losing the tune, and he returns the gesture. He plows through the sand, dropping next to me.

"Hey, Harm," he says, bumping a fist to mine, as I sink down beside him.

"Hungry?"

"Always." His grin fades.

I open my cloth of food while he does the same. His lunch is miserable, a tiny portion of dried meat and a pickled fruit that drenches the cloth in its briny liquid. I tear my bread and hand him half. The corner of his mouth tugs upwards, and we hook into our lunch. Arlo's bony knees poke through his worn trousers, and the

1

dirt that has been there for many days makes his skin appear much darker than it is. A knot grows in my stomach.

We eat until every crumb is gone before I stand, offering Arlo my hand. He slaps his hand in mine and pulls himself up. Collecting his gear—wires, small cages he handmade, and a bag of something that reeks like bait—we wander out to the rocky crops, where the white meat hides between the hot, jagged stones. He kicks small reddish pebbles along as we walk.

"Don't fancy Marla, then?" His smirk follows his not-so-subtle dig at me.

"Not at all. Why's that?"

"She came asking about you yesterday. She really seems to fancy you." The stupid grin on his gaunt face makes me screw up mine.

"Yeah, I caught that part."

"Girls scare me. They're like the wind, always changing their minds about something." He laughs. "Felicity is different, though. I could be around her without losing my mind." His face curls into simper. He has had the same goofy look on his face every time he sees Felicity since he was twelve. Almost a year younger than me at sixteen, he has another year before his parents start trying to match him up with a village girl. He drops his load next to the cluster of hot rocks. Small desert flowers claim the hard ground between every mass. Rock daisies and desert anemones compete for the spaces closest to the rocks' bases, hunting moisture. I pluck a snare from the pile and rig it behind one rock. Arlo does the same.

"What would you do if they selected you?" I ask, gently releasing the taut snare and stepping back.

Arlo holds my gaze before returning to his trap. "Refuse." He grabs the bag of bait, pulling the cloth over the cord to open it. I wince at the horrid smell of whatever he has decaying in there.

"That's not a choice, Arlo."

He hands me a small chunk of rotting meat, and I dump it into

2

the loop of the snare like it's burning my fingers through. Arlo grins. But my face is tight, concerned that he's not kidding around this time.

"I know, Harm. I wish it was." He sets another snare and grabs his leftover gear, wandering through the patches of rock. I follow him, keeping an eye out for lizards and jackrabbits. He bends down to grab his trap from yesterday, a lifeless jackrabbit swinging in the loop, and his eyes light up. "What about you? What would you do?"

"Nothing, I guess. If we fight it, they'll make life miserable for our families. I wouldn't do anything to hurt my family, nor would you." Stepping over smaller stones, I weave my way toward the old man cactus in their center, covered in fruit. Folding my shirt up, I twist the fruits from its gnarled, spiked branches, only taking what I think Mother will need for the next few days. I toss a few to Arlo, and he shoves them in his tattered pockets.

"What if we could prevent them from taking boys somehow?" he says.

"Like how?" My gut twists thinking about him rebelling, and what they would do to him when they caught him.

"Maybe we could pretend the boys had an illness, or we could say they ran away. I don't know, we'll think of something, Harm." He pulls up another trap, another rabbit, throwing it over his shoulder with the last one.

"That would be punishable if they caught us," I warn. My brow deepens, and he punches my arm, trying to lighten the mood, but the amusement drains from his face.

A huge rock lizard, almost three feet long, swaggers over the top of a rock near Arlo. His eyes go wide. He slides his spear from his back with slow movements. Lifting his arm over his head, he creeps toward the giant length of lizard, every step slow and calculated. I don't move, not wanting to scare the lizard off. Arlo sucks in a breath and hurls the spear into the belly of the lizard. It topples sideways, landing in the dirt with a thud. Arlo tosses his bounty onto the ground and jumps over the rocks. The lizard thrashes, sending up sand and dirt. He whips a small blade from his boot and ends the old lizard, watching as the life drains from its body, its claws curling up and eyes turning white.

We lean against the hot rocks for a while, tossing pebbles into the sand, talking about the projects I'm working on. The hot winds glide past as the sun above warms my body. Arlo pushes off from his spot, gathering his bounty. His face is solemn. "You want to take one of these jackrabbits, Harm?"

"No, buddy, you take them." I hold my shirt full of fruits and bend down to pick Amaya some flowers.

He leaves, wandering back home. "Thanks for the food, Harm," he calls over his shoulder, walking over the rough ground and then through the sands, back into the village.

"Any time, Arlo."

He is out of earshot already, and guilt washes over me for so many things: having more food, having a useful trade ... having a better existence, period.

I push up from the hot sand and make my way back through the rings of homes. Almost back at the village center, I run through possibilities of how to help Arlo's family. Lost in thought, looking down at my shirt full of fruit and Amaya's flowers, I run headfirst into Mason. He stands with his chin up, arms crossed over his chest, face twisted with hate.

"Stay away from my sister, Travesci."

"I have no intention of touching your sister, Rayner."

He steps toward me and I let out a long sigh, tired of the whole Marla issue. "Do you really care who Marla flirts with, or is this just another reason to annoy me, Mason?" I doubt he even cares about that. More likely he's dirty that this is our last selection day, and they still haven't picked him. He has been waiting to be selected for the regime from the day he turned fourteen. Heaven knows why.

Mason's lip curls into a snarl, and he draws a fist back. I push my shoulders back, balling up my own free hand. His fist slams into my face. I stagger back, and the fruit in my shirt falls to the ground as I crush the stems of Amaya's flowers between white knuckles. Blood seeps into my mouth, running from my nose. I hold the back of my hand against the flow, releasing a growl.

"Simmer down, you two," Father calls from the village center, now in our line of sight.

Mason's gaze flickers to my father and back to me. "Daddy still fighting your battles, Travesci? Pathetic," he seethes, then turns in the sand and stalks away.

I stem the blood from my nose momentarily before picking up the fruit, bundling it back into my folded-up shirt and stalk home, red-faced. I push through our front door and flop onto my chair at the table. Mother stops chopping and walks over, taking the fruit from my shirt.

"What happened to you, my boy?" She places the fruit in a bowl before returning with a wet cloth.

"Rayner," I growl.

The corner of her mouth turns up. "Well, you two have never gotten along. What was it this time?"

"Nothing, forget it."

Her eyebrows lower for a second and sighs. "You two better patch things up and at least be friendly to each other."

"He doesn't deserve my friendship."

"In this family, we forgive others. We don't hold grudges, and we certainly do not retaliate." She takes the flowers from my hand, popping them into a mug of water at Amaya's place at the table.

"Even if they nowhere near deserve forgiveness?"

"Especially then, Harmen."

5

CHAPTER 2
HARM

Blonde curls bounce around Amaya's small shoulders as she busily arranges scraps of wood and dead twigs into a makeshift hut, alongside Father's weathered outbuilding where he stores tools. Her little hands carefully prop up a worn rag on the top. The spitting image of our mother, with green eyes from Father, she is small for seven years. I sneak up behind her and lift her up. With a squeal of delight, she wriggles out of my arms. Her feet meet the ground, and she spins around, flinging sand in a flurry. She jumps up, and I bend down and scoop her up into a cuddle, wrapping my arms around her.

"Harmie." She places a hand on either side of my face. "Are you worried about being selected today?" Her excitement fades, and her face twists with concern.

"A bit, May May. Nobody wants to be taken. But it's the last time I have to line up. Fingers crossed, hey."

Her warm forehead presses against mine, and her eyes close. I run my calloused thumb over her soft cheek, and Amaya inhales a long breath.

"Please don't leave me, Harmie," she whispers as her tears plop onto my shirt. The moisture soaks through to my skin, and her hands work into a tangle in the opening of my work shirt. My heart hammers in my chest, and aching fear runs through me. My mind reels through the devastation that will consume my parents, but most of all my little sister, if I'm taken. The sweet honey scent of soap and the tang of dirt flood in. Her soft curls against my face, her small frame in my arms, and the rise and fall of her ragged breathing envelop me. I close my eyes, ingraining this moment in my memory, just in case. The brotherly urge to protect Amaya swells in my chest. A moment passes before she wriggles in my arms, and I put her down. She grabs my hand and pulls me over to her small structure.

"Right, Harmie, you assemble the supports for the back frame with these materials here," Amaya instructs, pointing to a pile of sticks and rocks she has gathered into a messy pile.

"You sound just like Father," I chuckle, "ordering around your building crew."

Amaya beams. "One day, Harmie, I will build you a new home, just like Dada does, when you're Blended." She holds my gaze.

"Sure thing, May May." I pick up twigs for the back frame. "You'll have to keep practicing until then." A grin splits my face. She pokes her tongue out at me and returns to the roof rags. Suspended at its apex, the sun marks midday, and the call for selection interrupts our building. I stand and sink my hands into my sore lower back, my heart racing in my chest. Hands shaking, I pick up Amaya and carry her to the back door of the stone house my father built. A timber roof, angled to the south, sits over our home, dotted with windows on every side, cloth draped over them, flapping in the desert winds.

Amaya's arms wrap around my shoulders, and she clings to me every step of the way to our back door. Mother waits in the doorway, her face solemn. She reaches under Amaya's arms, pries her

7

from my chest, and sets her down next to her. Amaya cuddles into Mother's skirt. Her worried eyes follow me as the three of us make our way through the center of our home to the front door. Mother offers a brief smile of reassurance that sends an aching tightness through my chest, ripping a hole in my heart with each step I take into the sands of our village center. They hang back with the crowd and watch as I trudge through the sand toward the small line of boys forming near the village's center well.

A hooded figure bumps into me as I near the lineup. She turns instantly, the scowl over her face fades into something friendlier as she meets my gaze. Her brilliant blue eyes study me briefly, dark wisps of hair slip out from under her hood and face wrap. "Sorry," she breathes, dropping her gaze to the sands before turning away from me.

A heartbeat later, I push through the sand, coming to a halt beside Arlo in line. I whip my head around, trying to catch a glimpse of her. But agitated bodies are moving about in the heat, and I lose her in the crowd.

A single Guardian stands unwaivering in the dappled shade from the lone tree in the village center, hands clasped behind his back. Dark-grey pants rest over his standard-issue heavy black boots. His light-grey starched shirt, trimmed with black epaulets of a second-rank officer, a black belt, sand goggles resting on his chest, and grey felt hat trim his disciplined stance. His eyes are vacant.

Boys I have grown up with stand in the selection line before the motionless officer in front of the crowd. Arlo shoots me a grave smile, and our low-hung fists knock together. His clothes hang off his large but bony frame—just what the Guardians look for during selection. At the far end, full of his own importance with chin up and arms crossed, stands Mason. He runs a hand over his mousey blond hair, oblivious to the dirt that streaks his oval face. His light-blue eyes study the officer waiting under the tree. *Please take him this time.* I don't think I can take spending the rest of my days with him tormenting us. Besides, he would make a fine Guardian. The only person who would miss him is Marla.

Our mothers stand in the hot sands of the village center with the other villagers. Their quiet sobs echo through the waves of heat while we stand under the unrelenting sun. Wisps of hot wind play around our feet, tugging at the worn rags the seven of us pass off as clothing. My skin burns from the vicious midday rays, and sweat trickles down my back. Through my boots, the undersides of my feet sting from being immobile on the burning sand. Some of the boys beside me stifle sobs. Every inch of my body trembles, my heart thumps against my ribs, and I force air in and out of my lungs. No one wants to be chosen today. Not for this.

Three Guardians return from this quarter's tax collection, alone. My body relaxes slightly at the absence of distraught people being dragged from their homes. Everyone has paid their taxes this quarter. They will throw no one in the center well today.

Two officers take up position under the tree, with legs apart and hands clasped behind their backs in the shade, while their commander saunters over to us, his three-foot cane rotating menacingly through his fingers. Inspecting each boy, he moves along the lineup.

He halts in the sand in front of me, causing a small wave of sand. I suck down a breath, holding it in my lungs. He inspects me from head to toe. Fear courses its hideous way through my chest, creeping through my arms. Heart hammering, I swallow, watching his expression. He scans every inch of my face, as if noting every detail: my tall, lean frame, the brown tufty hair I got from my father, my deep-brown eyes, and the square face of my mother. What is he looking for? Finally, he looks at my hands and arms, strong and well developed from building furniture for the last seven years since my schooling finished.

The Guardian gestures for me to turn around. Hesitant to move, I oblige with almost numb legs, my feet heavy on the sand. No, this is not what I want. I will not leave my family. I will not be drafted into a regime that takes away your every freedom, along with your soul. A lump rises in my throat as images of my freedom, a life of travel and excitement, carousel through my mind—a life with love and meaning, all about to be ripped away.

Marla gasps, and her gaze finds mine. I drop my eyes to the ground.

With a flurry of sand, my father comes to stand beside me, and I stare at him with wide eyes. His face is stone, eyes drilling into me, telling me to keep my composure and hold my tongue. I turn to face the commander.

"The boy has a weak heart, and a healer has confirmed this." He speaks confidently, despite his trembling hands.

"You have *written* confirmation of this?" the Guardian asks. The cane in his hand comes to a halt. His deep-blue eyes pierce my father with an accusing look fit for the low-life filth they consider us to be.

"Yes, sir." He pulls a tattered paper from his trouser pocket, handing it to the Guardian. He turns it over in his hands and looks me up and down.

"Name and age, boy," he demands.

"Harmen Travesci, seventeen next month, sir." I train my focus to the ground.

A grunt leaves his chest and he folds the paper and shoves it into his trouser pocket. Moving along the line, he hesitates a few boys down. My heart slows with every step my father makes back to my mother. She grabs his hand and my little sister's.

He passes by Mason, who puffs out his chest and looks the Guardian in the eye. Courage and arrogance melded into a single gesture. The Guardian pauses, maintaining eye contact for longer than anyone expects. He scans Mason up and down and asks him to turn around. Mason's obnoxious grin beams as he does as instructed. The Guardian taps him on the shoulder, signaling he has selected. Mason steps forward and stands with the lower-ranking officers, hands clasped behind his back, chin up.

Moving on, the commander peruses Arlo a second time, and he stiffens beside me. I hold my breath, silently urging the Guardian to move along. He gestures for Arlo to turn around. My stomach plummets. Arlo remains planted in the sand.

"Turn, boy," he demands.

A sour look twists Arlo's face before he obeys.

"How old are you now?" the Guardian asks.

"Just turned sixteen."

"Fine."

Arlo shifts around on the spot, as if desperate to flee. The Guardian taps him on the shoulder. I hold my breath, watching Arlo's every movement. My heart hammers in my chest, sending thunder through my head.

"No," Arlo says.

My stomach flips.

"What did you say?" The Guardian's eyes narrow over his curled-up mouth.

"No, I won't go with you. My family needs me here."

"It's not a choice, boy." His tone turns malignant. "You are coming with us." He gestures for Arlo to fall in line with Mason and the other officers. Arlo glances at me, his eyes apologizing and pained. Thundering against my ribs, my heart races faster. I know what is coming next. Pleading with every inch of my expression for Arlo to not do this, I choke back the strangled breaths that claw their way up my throat.

"I said no. I will not go with you, mongrel," Arlo spits. His words send electric pulses through my veins. He is as good as dead if he refuses now.

No, Arlo. Don't do this. Please.

The Guardian steps into Arlo's space, wearing a vicious look. "Fall in line, boy." He spits out each word, pointing to the line of officers behind him. Arlo holds his ground, chin high, face defiant. I force myself to breathe, hoping the man in front of us takes Arlo's defiance lightly, knowing he won't.

The Guardian grabs him by the arm and pulls him towards Mason, whose face is a cross between disbelief at Arlo's audacity and amusement at seeing the Guardians denigrate him for the entire village to witness.

Arlo pulls back and breaks from the harsh grip of the Guardian. He teeters for a moment, trying to regain his balance, his thin, fatigued frame working against him. The Guardian strides back to him, stopping only inches away. Without hesitating, he slaps him across the side of the head. Arlo crumples, hitting his head on the stone well before landing with a sickening thud on the scorching sand.

Every villager stands immobile, their stunned eyes locked on Arlo. The Guardian hovers, cane held up, waiting for Arlo to rise and retaliate.

He doesn't move.

A piercing scream rises from the crowd, and Arlo's mother pushes her way through the frightened villagers.

Arlo's breath is gone, and mine stops. The side of his head is caved in. Blood soaks his hair, a flood of crimson seeping into the sand. My legs fall away from under me, knees hitting the ground. Sand rises up in waves from the impact as I crawl over to Arlo, arriving beside his lifeless body at the same time as his mother. I stare into his vacant eyes. His mother shakes him repeatedly, calling his name through a torrent of tears and choked sobs.

"Arlo, buddy, come on, wake up," I plead. His body is limp. "Arlo, open your eyes for me, please." I grab his shirt. "Arlo, no!" I choke. My hands move to Arlo's shoulder, and I slam my eyes shut. Salt and moisture sting my cheeks. I shake his shoulder, and his head flops to one side. Murmurs rise and fall.

I push to my feet, turning to face the commander. The crowd falls silent. Not even the Guardians speak, standing with arms across their chests and faces hard as stone. Rage thunders through my veins, stealing my better judgment. I fly at the commander. His powerful arms hold me at length while I throw fist after fist at him. His expression is impartial. Barely tolerating our grief, he stands staring at me lashing out at him, waiting it out until business can resume as normal.

"Get back in line, boy, unless you want to meet the same fate as your friend over there," he spits, pushing me backward. I stare at him, numb. I stagger back to my position in line with tears streaming down my face, dripping onto the sand. Whimpers from Arlo's mother haunt the crowd, her head resting on his chest.

"You have all just witnessed what happens when people disobey the laws of our counties!" the commander yells. "We will not tolerate resistance or outbursts. Any person who tries to retaliate after the events of today will meet a similar fate in the well, accompanied by their entire family!"

My hands ball into fists, and fire rises from my core. The lives of my parents and sister are all that hold me to his order. I stand rigid in the sands, every part of me wanting to flog the Guardians down to their last breath and see the sands reddened with their blood. Still, I stand planted in the dense sand, unmoving.

CHAPTER 3
HARM
ALMOST THREE MONTHS LATER ...

Tendrils of steam ascend from the warm water in the washbowl. The sharp edge of the blade slides across my skin, each pass removing a few days of growth from my face, chin, and neck. High winds rattle the bathroom mirror. Running a wet hand over my now smooth, angular face, I check for nicks and rinse off over the washbowl. Banging on the door hurries me along.

"Harmie, hurry up! You can't hog the bathroom all the time," Amaya says, her impatience growing like the heat outside. Pulling one of Father's shirts over my head, I open the door.

She rolls her eyes at me and lets out a sullied groan. I land a kiss on her forehead and sidestep a blow before a groan escapes her mouth, twisted up so as not to show her amusement at her big brother.

"The teacher won't wait for me if you make me late. I only have a few years left, and I don't want to miss a day," Amaya moans.

"He wouldn't dare start without you, Amaya. Who would answer all his questions if you're not there?" I suppress a chuckle, and soap hits the wall beside me. Letting out a laugh, I turn with a grin. Amaya screws her face into a pout as she slips into the bathroom.

My cluttered workspace attached to the back of our home sits strewn with various projects. Gone are the days of just making one thing when people needed it. I run a finger down the list of items for this quarter's traders. My calloused hands, rough from long hours and many splinters and mishaps, turn over the paper and mark off the pieces that are complete and ready, leaving seven pieces to be completed before they arrive. Too many pieces and not enough time. I let out a ragged sigh and bend down to hunt for some timber to finish my current project. The piles of scraps and offcuts threaten to fall and cover the stone floor. Grabbing two smaller lengths of timber, I shove back the scraps with my foot before sitting down to continue working on yesterday's piece.

Barely an hour goes by before Mother raps on my door. Looking up, I wipe the sweat and sawdust from my face with my arm. Pulling up a small stool, she sits next to me, her mouth pulled into a thin line, her arms crossed. I put my work down.

"I need to talk to you about a match. The Blending ceremony is only nine months away now," she says, searching my face for a reaction.

"I know. It's not something I've given much thought to, to be honest," I lie. My mind wanders to the girl I saw at the selection, her dark hair and brilliant blue eyes, and I wonder what happens to those who don't get matched. What if there is something more than domestic village life? I have daydreamed about leaving Amondo. What happens to those who refuse to be matched by their parents? Captivated by the girl from selection day, I can't bring myself to settle for anyone else.

"Do I have to be part of the ceremony?"

"It's the time for you to be matched, Harmen. It would break my heart if you ended up alone." She squeezes my hand.

"I just don't want to spend the rest of my life with someone I hardly know, or don't feel that way about. I want what you and Father have. Not an obligation."

This is as honest as I can be with her. If she knew I wanted to leave and how I dream of a girl I met once, she would scold me to no end over it.

"Your father and I were a match, and what we have has grown. It didn't start out this way. What we have now has taken years of love and compromise and learning. Not every match is instant."

"I guess so," is all I can say. She pats my hand and takes a deep breath. I brace myself for what comes next.

"Marla's parents have spoken to us about a potential match with her. You are both capable people. You would make a good match and be able to build a suitable home from that."

Marla's name is stuck in my throat.

She waits patiently for me to respond.

"No, please, not Marla."

My mother looks to the stone floor as if what she needs to say lies there. "If you're worried about Mason, don't be. Guardians hardly ever return home. He would not be a problem for you."

"It's not that. I really don't enjoy being around Marla. I don't think I could ever ..." I hesitate, images of being betrothed to Marla fading in and out of my mind as my hand grasps the back of my neck and my face twists to get the words out. "... be what she wants in a match."

"I'm not sure who else in Amondo you could match with. There are only a few girls your age left that have not already paired up. I could approach their parents," Mother says with a sigh. "We will work something out, I'm sure. The women of the village are

16

meeting again today." Rising from her stool and returning it to its place, she walks out.

Relieved, I pick up my work again and start moving the planer roughly with each pass to shape the wood in my lap. Without the pressure of potentially being matched with Marla, I feel lighter. Content, I work for hours without realizing I need to break for lunch. I pad back inside to the kitchen. A plate of bread, dried meat, and a few pieces of cut fruit from the desert cacti fill my plate, waiting for me in my place at the table.

I wander around the kitchen eating, trying to imagine how and when my parents got to the affectionate point in their matched relationship. The items around Mother's kitchen, neatly placed, are some gifts Father brought home for her after trips away for supplies, tokens of his affection and monuments to the home they have built together. Amaya and I settle into our reading chairs in the living room lit by candles after dinner. Her reading is brilliant now, and she reads to Mother and Father every night.

They lay back in their chairs, listening to her words dance around the room. She tells a story of a beautiful queen named Cassiopeia, whose daughter was just as stunning. The queen bragged about their beauty to the sea god, Poseidon, who punished them. Amaya reads the notes in the margin about the constellation named after them and the heart- shaped nebula in the night sky that sits amidst the Cassiopeia stars, undetectable to the eye, but always there.

Far too comfortable in my worn lounge chair, I sit listening. The ease and familiarity of the chair threaten to lull me to sleep as images of clusters of stars hanging in our desert sky drift through my weary mind. The moon is high in the sky by the time we retire to bed. With a half-conscious bid goodnight to all, I amble down the hallway to my room.

Laying my weary body flat out on my bunk, a long yawn

escapes before closing my eyes. My muscles relax, and my head fills with scenes from today until sleep takes my consciousness from me.

Thumping startles me awake, and I bolt upright. A silhouette crouches in the corner of my room. My pounding heart sends me hard up against the wall next to my bed. I strain against the darkness.

Silently, it rises and stands tall. I make out the outline of a skirt, and two arms move up, releasing a mass of wavy hair that was wrapped up. Still, with no sound, she steps forward into a slim beam of moonlight, her hair bouncing around her shoulders. She turns towards the window, and the curved shape of her chest heaves under the ribbon of light filtering through my window.

My heart leaps into my chest as I recognize the features of her face. Marla. She turns back to me, and her thin hands start pulling her shirt over her shoulders, one at a time. Her eyes lock on mine, making sure I am watching. For a moment, part of me wants to see what she wants to show me. Then flashes of my life, decades chained to Marla, snap me back to reality. The obligation, the regret ... There is no way I can let her do this. This is a part of her that belongs to someone else, not me.

"Marla, stop," I whisper.

"Why?" She doesn't bother to be quiet.

"Because this is not happening. *We* are not happening."

"But we could, if you gave me a chance to show you all of me."

"No, Marla, we couldn't—and please don't."

"Why are you so stubborn about this? I want us to be Blended, Harm. You are the only boy I am interested in."

"I noticed."

"So, why not, then?" She moves to stand over me. Her top is so thin that it only just conceals what lies beneath it. A strap hangs precariously from her thin shoulders. Her chest sways in front of my face, and the fragrance of her freshly washed body fences me in. Her hand drags the thin strap over her shoulder, leaving it bare. I search the floor.

"No. I'm not interested." I stand and push past her, heading towards my door.

She freezes, her face contorted in the soft light.

"Please, leave."

"That's what you really want, Harm?" Fire twists in her words.

"Yes, please go."

Marla steps towards me, stopping just inches from my face, hair jerks to a stop in front of her shoulders. "Big mistake, Harmen Travesci."

She pushes her strap back onto her shoulder and stalks back through my room. In a moment, she is back out the window. *How many times has she done that?* Waiting until my heartbeat returns to a normal pace, I settle back down on my bunk. Her smell still lingers in my room.

Awake for hours, I replay Marla's words over in my head. *"Big mistake,"* she said. Just like her brother, resorting to threats when they don't get what they want. The thought of being Blended with Marla sends a shiver down my spine, and I shake my body to dislodge it.

Dreams find me as soon as I fall back to sleep, but the horrors of life imagined with Marla haunt me for hours. As hard as I try, there is no escaping the dreams of the well and a meager life. Desperately, I try to imagine a life somewhere else, but darkness has my mind entrapped tonight.

CHAPTER 4
HARM

I lie awake, legs tangled in the blanket that hangs halfway off my bunk, as if a brawl happened on top of it. Tossing and turning all night ruined my chances of any sleep. My head throbs like it's been pummeled with an enormous stone—the kind you use to put the small, ailing livestock out of their misery. The way Mason's father does to dying goats. The look of satisfaction on his face made my stomach turn as a child.

The moment I sit up, Marla and her vicious words fly into my mind. Pushing the image of her angry face out of my head, I sit down for breakfast. Amaya is bouncing around the table with her dolls, while Mother gives her a look of amusement.

I have an important task today: selection day. I finish my breakfast quickly and make my way to the house of the first boy I will hide from the Guardians. The door opens sharply. His mother's flustered face greets me as she shoves her son toward me. I push down the knot in my stomach. I'm doing this for Arlo.

"Thank you for doing this for us, Harmen. We didn't know what else to do. Your parents are fortunate you are seventeen now, too old for selection, but we just can't lose our son," she whispers, her trembling hands holding mine. Then the pleading in her eyes softens.

"Someone needs to do something against the Guardians. We can't let them continue to rob our village of its sons," I offer, and she releases my hands. I guide the boy to my side. "But please know, this can't get around to the rest of the village, or they will punish both our families."

She nods, forcing a smile for her son. With a last look at her boy, she shuts the door.

At the next two houses, I collect more boys, gathering six in total. The seven of us head to the healer's building, making our way around the back. A figure startles, running from their concealed spot beside the wood box. I watch them disappear for a moment before lifting the lid off the wood box and check for desert vipers. Making a step with my knee, I help two boys into the box.

"It's so hot in here," one moans.

"Shut up, you want to be taken?" the other snaps, hand holding the lid up.

"Hold the lid up slightly to let air in. Make sure you're quiet," I warn.

The next hiding space is easier. Under the back benches of our old tool hut, two boys crouch and give me a nod before I close the door and lock it with the old brass lock my father's father fashioned to protect his tools. The remaining two boys and I hurry to the western side of the village, where the second well sits. The two remaining boys give me horrified looks.

"No one will use it this morning, as most villagers are staying close to the center, awaiting selection time," I say, leaning over the stone perimeter of the well, tugging on the ropes that hold the platform above the water. It's small, but it should be enough space for the two boys left, who are the smallest of the six. The rusted old mechanism screeches in protest as I wind up the platform. The ropes, I notice, are still mostly in working condition. A wisp of panic whips past at the thought of the platform failing. Swallowing the fear stuck in my throat, I am conscious of the limited time we have before the Guardians arrive.

The first boy climbs over the stone edge and carefully tests his weight with one foot, glancing back at me. I nod, and he lifts his remaining leg over and places his full weight onto the old wooden platform, crouching with his arms folded around his legs. We hold our breath collectively for a moment, as if testing our theory, before I gesture to the second boy to move into position on the platform. He climbs over the stone edge, and the wooden platform groans. Eyes wide, both boys grip the ropes tight.

"It will be fine, you will be okay," I offer. I wind them down towards the water level.

Next, I jog back to the center of the village, where people are gathering. Tension lies suspended in the hot air around us while boys line up, some for the first time, having only just turned fourteen in the last few months. Every person in the village stands waiting for the selection, a reminder of our place—that they take our own kin to enforce the harsh laws that govern us into a life of mere existence.

The sun is high in the sky before the Guardians return from collecting the taxes, and I fidget with the stray fibers on the insides of my pockets, praying the hidden boys are surviving their hideouts. Heat bears down on us all, more intensely for the boys lined up in the sun. The usual number stands under the tree: three Guardians. This time, one of our own accompanies the commander. Mason.

As I school my face into one of indifference, every muscle in my body tenses. I force breath in and out of my lungs. Shoving my hands into my pockets, I tangle my fingers around a stray thread. *Please don't let Mason realize there are boys missing.* Why would he be here? They never assigned an officer to their home village. Mason must have requested it. He would take great pleasure in tormenting those he deemed inferior, left behind on selection day.

My gaze finds Marla. The smirk plastered across her face runs chills down my body. For a mere split second, I consider retrieving the boys from their hideouts, but that would risk exposing our rebellious behavior, which is punishable, putting their families and mine in danger. Eyes trained firmly on Mason's face, I wait for any hint of realization that the number of boys is too low.

He stands to the right of the commanding officer. His uniform is painfully neat, topped with a look of superiority that he has held his entire life. The dark-grey trousers sit over his shined black boots. His light-grey shirt carries the black epaulets of a second-rank officer already. That was fast.

The commanding officer gives the same speech as always, before he scours the lineup for the pick of the boys. He walks up and down, looking for something that is not there, willingness.

Mason gestures to his commanding officer, who walks back and collaborates for a moment, before slowly turning back to his baited audience. Mason's eyes scan the crowd before him, looking for what I can only assume are the missing boys. My heart thunders against my ribs. The frayed piece of cotton in my pocket snaps between my fingers. Everyone is waiting, not daring to look at one another, for fear of being accused of something.

The commanding officer comes to a halt in front of the lineup and gestures for the boys to sit down.

"My name is Fletcher, commander and officer of the fourth rank of the Guardian regime." He pauses, making sure every person is listening. "It appears today that some of the village members have been concealed. This is a direct act of rebellion, punishable under the laws of our county." He stops and marches back and forth in a small stretch of sand. The sun glints off his silver epaulets as he stops and spins, facing us again.

"We will return in fourteen days to deal with this act of rebellion. At such time, the person or persons responsible for this act will be punished. If this does not occur, it will force us to reconsider the privileges this village carries, along with an assessment of the resources allocated to it. This affects you all, so I suggest you have the culprits ready for when we return in two weeks," he finishes, and signals to the officers to move back to the dune buggy.

Mason slides into the driver's seat and clicks over the ignition. Nothing happens. Fletcher tilts his head up, gesturing for Mason to check it out. He climbs onto the side of the buggy, fiddling with the wires that connect the solar plates. Fletcher turns the key again. Nothing. Mason jumps down and walks to the front, stepping up onto the hood of the machine. With three swift twists of his fingers, the wires come loose. He kicks the plate from the roof, and it lands hard in the back, next to his comrade. He jumps down, pulling the hood up. Sun glints off the surface of the new plate he pulls out. Fastening it to the roof and twisting the wire in place, he hangs over the side. "Try now, sir." Fletcher twists the ignition, and the buggy roars to life.

After the last of the sands fall in their wake, I sprint to the wood box behind the healer's building. The lid flies up, with the two boys' faces red as they pant from the heat. Pulling them out roughly, I tell them to make themselves scarce, before running to the tool hut behind our house. The two boys have already come out from under the back benches and made themselves at home, playing with the tools and some scrap wood pieces.

"Time to go, make yourselves scarce," I say as they burst through the door and back to their homes, pushing and shoving like it's all a big game.

My pace quickens as I make for the well. Those boys will hopefully be just where I left them. Niggling thoughts push me faster across the village. What if the rope broke? What if the wooden platform didn't hold the boys' weight? My heart races faster the closer I get to the well. With trembling hands, I grope the rope and try to pull them up. It's too heavy; it slips, burning my palms.

"Boys, are you alright?" I call down.

Inside, the well is quiet.

Dammit.

I grip the stone edge of the well, and try to think through what to do next. Snatching the metal handle to wind up the platform, I make sluggish turns. The platform is heavy, and the rope strains under the weight. Good; at least they are still on the platform. But the well is dark, and I can't see the boys. The underground water tables rise and fall during the day and night, with the lowest point at midday and the highest water level at midnight. Little by little, the platform winds up, much slower than its descent, from the water's low level.

With every turn, my arms burn and my hands cramp. I slip the metal rod into the spokes of the mechanism to hold the position of the platform and look over the edge once more. One boy—lying motionless. Throwing the pin out, I wind as fast as my arms allow, and fire rips through them. Tingling spreads in my hands, and heat fills my lungs. The platform groans under the force of the ascent. Every turn feels like forever. Muffled sounds from the boy on the platform echo up through the well. Another three turns, and the top of the cradle hits the stopper below the winding mechanism.

He is alive, eyes open, but he's drowsy. The metal grates as I shove the pin back in place to hold the platform up. I pull him out and sit him up against the side of the well on the sand. His head bobs from side to side, and I shake his shoulders.

"Hey," I coax.

His head bobbing around, he doesn't answer.

"Hey, where is he?"

He looks up, eyes glazed.

"Where is the other boy?" I plead.

"He fell in," he rasps, and his head lolls down to his chest. Panic courses through my core as I wind the platform back down with haste, the heavy wood jumping back down with the swift release of the rope. When it hits the water, I jump onto the rope and shimmy down to the bottom, feet landing on the platform. The waterline of the well is around seven paces in diameter. I search for the other boy in the dark waters.

Against the far stone curved wall floats the body of the boy. Water slaps my face as I dive across the well and reach out for his limp figure. I drag him back to the platform, barely keeping us both afloat. Pushing his wet body onto the wooden platform, I kick my legs to stay afloat. With what little energy I have left, I push up with my hands and propel myself onto the platform. Hands trembling, I shake him hard. Water flies off his wet clothes. His chest is still. His face is grey. Instinctively, I roll him onto his side and thump his back over and over. Nothing.

With one hand, I pull him back to lying flat. He remains still. My head falls into my hands. What have I done? Nausea swells, blurring my vision. All our fears of having the boys taken by the Guardians, and now I have taken one's life. How could he have fallen off? Why is the other boy so groggy? The thick heat of the air in the well envelops me. Letting my hands fall from my face, I look back down at the boy; his lips are blue. His wet clothes hang from the bones of his small body.

"Please, wake up, dammit!" I curl my fingers around his shirt in the center of his chest. I tug at him, every muscle strung tight, and the blood pounding through my veins is deafening. "Wake up, dammit!"

Don't let them win. Please, don't let them win ...

Lifting my hands, gripped together high above him, I pound them into his chest; the low thrum reverberates off the curved stone walls around us. Water gushes from the boy's mouth and nose. Again, this time even harder.

More water.

Again.

My arms pump up and down, thumping his chest like a lever on a waterspout. With every thud, more water spills from his blue lips.

Crack!

Bone breaks. Holding my breath, I stop and wait. Shallow breaths move under his wet shirt. Rolling him onto his side again, I thump his back. This time water and blood come out, followed by a cough.

"Yes, breathe. Wake up!"

I throw another thump on his back before cries and gasps rack his torso, echoing around us. My legs wobble as I stand and step over his body, crouching down in front of him. His face is still grey. He looks at me through vacant eyes and blinks. After a few moments, I sit him up. His shaking hands rest over his now broken ribs, and he breathes shallow breaths, his wide eyes fixed on me.

"Is it over? Are the Guardians gone?"

A strangled sigh leaves my chest. "They are gone."

For now.

CHAPTER 5
IMANI

The heavenly scent of spiced game hovers around me, tormenting my empty stomach. Every few houses, I find pickings left on sills or out on back patio tables. Spoils for a sand rat with no home. Amondo's people seem to be more generous—or careless—with their food supplies. I'll stay here as long as I am able to keep eating well without being caught. I shove a handful of meat strips into my pocket from a tray of jerky left out to cure.

Hood down and face wrap over most of my face, I head for the home where the boy who hid those boys lives, on the off chance I can find out more about him. The steady hum of a dune buggy carries on the scorching winds—my cue to make my way to the shadows.

I pad down the side of his house, careful to not draw attention. Banging comes from the back of the home, and I walk toward it. A workspace is attached to the back of his house. A window is open and I flatten against the wall of the house, beside it, listening to what is happening inside. Hammering, a low grunt and something heavy drops onto a table. Rhythmic scratching starts up, continuing for a time, and I roll off the wall and peer through the window.

His corded arms push a wood planer back and forth over a piece of timber. His focus wholly on the work in his hands, his mouth pulled up slightly on one side. A half built chair sits on the floor beside him. And I watch his arms flex, his body tense, as he works with sweat dripping from his brow. The buggy engine shuts off and I spin to see who is in it. I swallow as the familiar figures remove their goggles and pull on their hats.

"Harmen, Guardians are here," his mother calls. He drops the tool and timber instantly and jumps from his seat. He pushes through the door of his workspace, rushing back inside.

Harmen. His name is Harmen.

I loose a breath, pushing down the butterflies that soar through my stomach at his name. Time to make my way to my usual hiding spot. I round the last building before the well, the healers' shelter, and shuffle in beside the wood box. I keep an eye out for anyone approaching, not wanting to be caught out like last time. Having to backtrack and hide amongst Mason's goats was not what I had planned. It took two days for the smell to leave my clothes.

From here, I can see the village center, the well, Harmen's house, and the commander. I double-check each way before dropping my hood, relishing the almost cooler air now that I'm out from under the stifling robe. Sweat runs down my back and between the rounds of my chest. I yank the wrap away from my head, letting it fall around my shoulders, and run my fingers through my long waves of dark hair, fanning my neck, desperate to cool down in the slim shade that covers my hideout.

Heat ripples down from the midday sun, and mere moments after the commander's feet hit the burning sand, commotion spills out of the village center. Harmen and his mother hurry through their front door. Cries ring across the village. A woman kneels in the sand holding onto her daughter for dear life, begging the Guardian who stands over her, grip tight on her shoulder, to please make an exception. The crowd has gathered now, and the expression on every face reflects his answer.

We all know he won't.

They never do.

Mason and his comrade burst through the front door of their family home, fresh paint on their front door, a red X, dragging behind them the husband of the crying woman.

"No, oh no," Harmen's mother falters, grabbing onto his arm as she watches with wide eyes. The woman twists in the sand, her gaze searching before locking onto Harmen's mother. They must be friends. "Hannah!" she screams, trying to pull out of the Guardian's grip. Harmen holds his mother firmly beside him, both arms wrapped around her shoulders. She strains against his hold briefly before going still.

"Miranda!" Hannah cries, lifting her hands and covering her mouth. The man flails around, attempting to break free from their grip. Unrelenting, they pull him through the sand on his knees before dropping him at the feet of Fletcher.

The pain on Miranda's face as she clings to her daughter sends my stomach into a rapid descent. I scan the faces of the three Guardians. Mason stands tall, with no signs of conflict. No pity, no empathy, no whisper of sadness for the people he grew up with. His face is emotionless, blank. He stands over the quivering man, who is now also pleading for the lives of his family.

"For failure to pay taxes on repeated occasions, the Milfrey family are sentenced to death by drowning," Fletcher reports to the crowd.

"Please, no!" Hannah cries, tears streaming down her face. She drops her head onto Harmen's shoulder. I swallow the lump in my throat as he responds to her, tucking her in tighter. Fletcher nods in the well's direction, and as per routine, Mason drags the girl to the round stone wall, the only small barrier left between life and death.

"No, please, not our daughter! Just us. Just us!" Miranda cries. Her fear and desperation run through every one of us like a bolt of agonizing lightning. The village carpenter crew have put down their tools and file in beside their families. The man leading the crew and a small girl file in beside Hannah, Harmen's father and sister. Everyone is waiting. Hannah grabs her daughter's hand. I already know how this will end, despite the desperate pleas of the family. The same as every other family I have watched the commander take. It ends with death.

"Momma, that's your friend," his little sister chokes. Hannah's husband pulls her trembling body from his son's hold and into his, enveloping her. He sets his jaw, training his eyes on Fletcher. Mason lifts the screaming girl up to his chest and throws her into the well in one move. I cling to the side of the wood box with white knuckles, forcing my body to stay frozen. Every part of me vibrates with hate and adrenaline. But if I interfere now, I can't help others. I can't help them unless they survive until midnight, when the water level rises.

Tortured screams pour from Miranda, and her husband thrashes against the two remaining Guardians standing to hold them in place. Muffled sobs come from the crowd, for the family and for the realization that it could have been any one of them.

Another scream.

Lightning rips through my core. Mason and his comrade drag Miranda to the well's stone wall, tossing her after her daughter. Too many seconds pass before her body hits the low level of the underground water in the well. Hannah looses a long, painful wail.

Miranda's husband sobs in the sand, quieter now. He no longer fights, sitting on the sand with his hands on his head. The worn clothes on his back show the bones of his frame. They can barely feed themselves, let alone pay taxes.

With the last gesture from the commander, Mason and his comrade lift the man to his feet. He shakes his head, and they let him walk unaided to the well. Mason gives him an impatient shove, and he lands on the side of the well wall like a sack of grain, looking back at us all. Defeat and sorrow distort his face. He stares at Hannah. Harmen shifts on his feet, and his arms hang by his side, the corded muscles flexing in time with his jaw. With despair and hatred turning his eyes to fire, his gaze is fixed on Fletcher. He stands, rocking from foot to foot.

Please don't move.

Stay where you are.

"Please, don't," I utter. Briefly, he breaks his gaze from Fletcher and meets mine. I duck down quickly and slump my shoulders, as if that will keep me hidden from view. He scans my face with swiftness. My heart kicks up the pace, and I release my hold on the box. I will intervene if I have to, even if it gets me thrown into the cells. It wouldn't be my first time locked up.

Don't move, Harmen.

"Get on with it!" Fletcher yells. Harmen's gaze swings back to the commander. Mason shoves the man backward, and his head hits the inside of the stone wall on the way down, echoing with a sickening *thwack* seconds later when he hits the low water, dozens of feet below ground level. Harmen growls, and his father claps a hand on his shoulder, pinning him to the spot.

I toss my hood over my head and tie the wrap around my face. I round the box and lean against the shelter wall, eyes burning into his face. His chest is heaving as his fists curl and uncurl over and over. Fletcher glances in his direction before turning on his heel, walking back to the dune buggy. I relax slightly.

As if something has snapped in his mind, Harmen shakes his

head and follows his family home. Who is this boy, who was seconds away from retaliating? I wait a moment before following. I sit on the sand between his house and the next. With my hand on my chest, I will my heart to slow its ragged pace.

"Stay with your mother, Amaya," his father says and leaves to return to his construction work. Amaya—Harmen's little sister.

Clanging and shuffling spills out from inside as I imagine she sets out their lunch.

"Amaya, eat something, sweetheart," Hannah says.

"It doesn't feel right, eating, when your friend and her family were just executed," Amaya replies.

Tears burn their way into existence, as I realize they have lost their friends today. I twist the ends of my robe between my fingers. The smell of stew and grains wafts through their front window. My stomach groans with the constant ache of hunger.

"I know, my love, but I need you to be strong. Eat up."

"Oh, Momma."

Moments of silence, broken by cutlery moving on the wooden kitchen table, pass before a chair slides out.

"I'll be in my workspace if you need me, Mother," Harmen says.

"Okay, my love," Hannah returns, her words wobbling.

Still shaken.

CHAPTER 6
HARM

S itting down at the bench, I try to focus on finishing the piece of furniture. The work my father and I do and our ability to offer products for the traders keeps our family out of the well. To distract my mind from the screams that insist on replaying, I switch my thoughts to the girl from yesterday. She looked right at me, her dark hair and brilliant blue eyes imprinted in my mind the second her eyes met mine.

Imagining her face rouses something inside me. Continuing the sensation, I imagine what she would sound like when she speaks, and I try to dream up a name for her. Nothing sounds good enough. Before the hour is up, I have constructed a real- life girl with a personality that sucks me right in. Her sarcastic demeanor keeps things interesting between us. Some of her is still a mystery to me, but one thing I know: she is not Marla.

Daydreaming can be dangerous—clear now by the grin on my mother's face when she interrupts my musings midafternoon. Heat rises through my neck and covers my face. Determined to appear busy with something on the bench, I avoid eye contact.

"Harmen, can you help Amaya and I with the well?" She hovers in the doorway.

"Of course." The wood falls from my hands onto the bench and I rise, following Mother and Amaya. At the front door sits a large crate, with lime powder, salt, and bunches of desert flowers stuffed into it. I pick it up and trail after Mother and Amaya, who huddle together, walking through the sands to the well. I place the crate on the stone wall, handing Amaya the flowers. Mother pulls the bag of salt from the crate and drifts around the well, pouring the salt over the water below. The last of the salt leaves the cloth bag, and she drops it into the crate.

"You know, if Marla is not a suitable option for you, perhaps one of the other village girls? Some mothers that meet at the well every week have asked me if we intend you for anyone. I know at least three of them that have daughters, almost of age for Blending."

Could this conversation get any worse? But however awkward it is, I know she has a point. If not Marla, then who? The girl with the dark hair—that's who. Whoever she is. Not that I answer my mother with this. She will think I have lost my mind.

"We don't have to talk about this now, if you don't want to," I say.

"Life goes on, my boy, even if it feels like it shouldn't."

"Who are you talking about, then?"

"Well ..." She swipes up the lime and unties the bag. "There is Heidi's girl, Sara. She was born a few months after you and is very skillful with weaving."

"And the others?" I recall the brutish way Sara treated the small children in the village one time when they spoiled one of her weaving projects by using it as a pretend magic carpet, burying it in the sand.

"Next, Wilhelmina's daughter—but she has no interest in

being Blended, as her mother puts it. However, her father has insisted. Maybe she wouldn't be suitable. I imagine that would be a hard relationship to foster."

"Who else, then?"

"That only leaves Felicity, the healer's apprentice," she says, checking for my reaction.

I take the lime bag from her, half empty, hanging over the side of the stone wall. "Oh," is all I can say. Felicity was the girl Arlo had his heart set on for two years. The thought of being Blended with Arlo's girl makes my stomach sink, twisting into knots.

"You know I can't do that. Not to Arlo."

"I thought you would say that. But Harmen, she will be alone if nobody wants to be Blended with her because of Arlo. She shouldn't have to lose that too." Mother's tone is almost reprimanding. I try to imagine a life with Felicity, but even out of kindness, it still feels off. She is a healer, and I respect her greatly for her work, but she has always been off-limits to me, out of respect for Arlo.

"I'll think about it," I lie, wanting this conversation to end. Amaya is plucking the heads of flowers from their stalks, tossing them down the well, humming to herself. I know she is listening.

"That sounds reasonable to me," Mother says, pulling the bag from my hands and sprinkling the last of the lime into the well. "Harmen, please know that we all loved Arlo, but he is gone. You are still here. That matters. Life is too short to walk around with ghosts as your only companions. Please consider Felicity seriously. She would make a good match for you."

Nodding, I take the empty lime bag from her. I try to mesh together the parts of a life with Felicity that don't involve Arlo, or the memory of him, at least. There aren't many. Would thoughts of Arlo come up in everything we have together? Would she always be comparing me to Arlo?

Mother hangs by the stone wall briefly, whispering a last goodbye to her friend. Amaya leans into my side. I wrap an arm around her, and she rests her head on my chest. Mother turns from the well and comes to stand beside me, hugging me the best she can.

"Let's go home, my loves," she says. We walk home, holding on.

Absentmindedly, I pack up the tools and place the pieces on the bench, laid out for assembly tomorrow. Dusting everything off, I briefly sweep the sawdust from the floor. It whirls around before landing on the sand outside, almost indiscernible from the golden granules that cover our village lands. Amaya is busy helping Mother bring in washing from the morning. She rips the pegs down, tossing the clothes into the woven basket. At the sight of me, Amaya throws the last item into the basket and stalks off.

"What's with her?" I ask Mother, who is corralling the clothing back into the basket and off the sands after Amaya's tantrum.

"Amaya is not happy about you being Blended and starting your own household."

"Oh."

Following my mother back into the house, I decide not to pursue Amaya and instead opt for the bathroom, feeling the need to wash away the unpleasantness of today—both the execution, and the expectations held for me by my parents and this village. After taking longer than I should have in the bathroom, I appear clean and dressed for dinner. The smell of bread and stew hits me as I walk through the hall, matched by an eager protest from my stomach. Amaya sits at the table and refuses to look at me. Mother offers an empathetic smile, and I sit at the table.

"You okay, Amaya?" I ask, not expecting a reply. She grunts something inaudible, piercing the boards of the table with a fork like a small game, before a hand covers hers, followed by a look of reprimand. She drops the fork and shoots up from the chair, knocking it over before running out of the room. From the table, her sobs echo through the hall before her slamming door mutes them.

I rise to go after her, but Mother tells me to sit back down, placing a steaming bowl and spoon in front of me. Before I can protest, Father comes through the door, dusty and weary, dropping his tool bag to the floor by the entrance. His face is grim. He sinks into his chair, and Mother places a hot bowl in front of him, followed by a kiss to his stubbled cheek. For a few minutes, they don't speak, but I can tell by the exchange of looks that something is up.

"What's going on?" I ask, looking back and forth between their worried faces.

"The Guardians are coming back tomorrow," he replies. Mother sits down with her bowl and starts eating, taking in only small sips of the hot broth. Father eats in silence. Keenly aware that my fourteen days are almost up, my whitens around the spoon.

Amaya has come out of her room by the time we settle in the living room, and she picks away at a piece of bread while she reads to Mother, still not talking to me, nor looking in my direction. It seems I am to pay for even having thoughts about starting my own life, one under a different roof than hers, even if that is not the life I want.

Despite the hard day and the looming fear of the Guardians' visit tomorrow, I enjoy the story Amaya reads aloud, one of courage and love—something we all cling to when our reality renders us inert to choose the former. The latter, however, they could never take away from us. The harder our life gets, the tighter we hold on to the ones we love, as if our hardened circumstances make our love, loyalty, and kindness grow exponentially.

My head falls to the side, slipping off the hand propping it up. I say my goodnights and lay a kiss on Amaya's head, who has long since fallen asleep beside Mother. She mumbles something in her sleep, and I amble down our narrow hallway to my bedroom, shutting my door behind me. Wishing for the dreams of the girl with the dark hair, I fall into bed. Dreams find me the moment I slip into the darkness of unconsciousness.

Trees stand before me, as far as the eye can see, tall and evergreen—like nothing I have ever seen before. The smell of the timber carries on the breeze. The ground underneath my feet is layered with crisp brown leaves. Each step sends a resounding crunch through the canopy. I wander past the tree line into the trees. My shirt flaps against my chest with every step and tendrils of wind tussle my hair.

At the end of the passageway through the trees is a girl. I freeze. Standing just inside the forest, she is flanked by two silhouettes, her dark hair whipping her face and jumping around her shoulders. She is watching me, as if assessing friend from foe. A hello leaves my mouth before I have time to hesitate. Her gasp echoes back through the tunnel of the trees that lie between us. Her voice is as sweet and elegant as it is desperate. But no sound leaves my mouth in response, and in an instant, the girl and the trees disappear. The wind dances around me before it too disappears.

I can't breathe.

My heart lurches in my chest, and I sit bolt upright in my bed, torn between her existence drifting away and my current reality. Sweat runs down my arms and neck as if mocking my parched throat. I stagger out of bed and shuffle to the kitchen. In the darkness, I fumble for a tin cup and scoop out some water from the enamel jug my mother keeps covered with cloth, and I gulp down the entire cup.

Exhausted from the dream that felt more real than this present moment, I slide down the cupboards and hit the floor. With my knees up, I bury my head between them, trying to remember the sound of her voice. The soft scuffing of my mother's feet on the stone floor entices my head up from my lap. Her face is pale in the moonlight, cut through with worry.

"Can't sleep?" I ask.

"No, I was asleep. You were calling out in yours, Harmen. What's going on? Was it just a bad dream, or do you need to talk about it?" She lowers herself to the floor beside me.

"I can't Blend with Felicity. It isn't right." I hesitate. "She isn't right."

She is silent, but her eyes drift to the floor. "Harmen, sometimes you must do what is required, not what you desire." Pain breaks up her words. For the first time, I understand that those words mean more to my mother than I realize. The moonlight that pierces our kitchen window lands on her face, exaggerating every line it holds, illuminating the evidence of her hard life. Every hard day. Every impossible choice. Life in Amondo, our small and impoverished desert village, is no place for weakness or doubting your choices, but she would never trade it. Every day with her family and her village is precious to her.

"I know this is not just about me. Felicity deserves to be happy, and I'm not sure I can give her that," I utter.

"Arlo would have wanted you both to be happy. You two were like brothers, but if you ask me, you would be his next choice for Felicity, if he couldn't be hers. I know you two would do a fine job of taking care of each other. You know that too, Harm."

It is the first time in as long as I can remember that she has called me Harm. Her softness makes me reconsider my decision— almost.

"Is there something else bothering you?" she asks.

I stare at the sands crawling along the stone floor, pushed along by the draft that drifts under the front door of our home.

"I'm not the person you all think I am," I choke out, so quiet that I am not sure she hears me.

"I thought you may have taken those boys; it's something I would have done if I were your age." She closes her eyes and leans her head against the cupboard behind her. "Your father would never approve."

"I just couldn't stand another selection day, watching boys being taken from our village to be used against us. I had to do something, with the Guardians coming every quarter now. Some of the boys' parents came to me a week before and asked if there was anything I could do to help them keep safe, having been through so many selections myself and never being picked. They don't know about the forged healer's letter. Apparently, they thought I had some ploy to never get selected, and they wanted my secret." I force a huffed laugh.

As she opens her eyes, my mother's face curls in amusement, but concern underlines her expression. "So, you agreed to hide them?"

"Yes, just for the hour while the Guardians were here."

"I am proud of you for standing up for our people, Harmen, but I'm afraid of what the consequence may be if they find out it was you."

"Who's saying they will ever find out? Even if they punish the entire village, we have been through tough times together. We'll make it."

"That's true. But I hope for your sake, and ours, that they do not." Rising to her feet, she secures the light cotton robe around her thin body. With a sad smile she leaves me sitting on the cold stone floor in the half-lit kitchen.

CHAPTER 7
HARM

For fourteen days, my mind has been elsewhere. Every task, while a distraction, is not quite enough to remove the fear and agony of guilt. The conversation I had with my mother replays over and over, until the first slivers of dawn's light announces its arrival through my window. Despite my efforts, shoving my head under my pillow, I can't descend into unconscious slumber. Today, the Guardians return. My actions may cause the entire village to pay the consequences—or if I am found out, may cost me a lot more.

I pick at my bowl of food. My stomach is in no state to receive food, churning and butterflies keeping it well occupied. Pushing the oatmeal around in front of me to make Mother feel better, I only manage half a dozen mouthfuls. Amaya is giving me a sideways look, and I almost forget she was mad at me.

The gathering for the Guardians' return will happen around ten this morning. Two hours to go before they arrive. I head to my workspace, trying to carry on as normal, but my hands take longer to perform even the simplest of tasks. My mother busies herself, but her anxiety is plainly visible to anyone. Father has gone to the construction site, the same as any other day. When he left for work, I realized she hadn't told him.

The wood pieces tremble in my hands, like an earthquake of tiny proportions. Time drags on. After what feels like an entire day has passed, the call of a small child signals the Guardians' arrival. I rise from my bench and set the wood down. Every movement feels as if someone else makes it—involuntary.

Taking a moment to straighten my clothes, I join my mother and Amaya in the kitchen, and we walk out to the village center together. But this time, unlike every other time, my mother holds Amaya's hand and wraps her arm around me. Just before everyone has assembled, my father slides in beside Mother and throws her a brief look of concern. Fletcher, Mason, and the same Guardian that travels with them stand in front of the crowd assembled in our village. There is not a sound made while we wait. No one dares to speak.

"We are here to locate and punish the guilty person or people for the crime of the interference with selection day and the conceal-ment of village members. If no man or woman steps forward to claim this act of rebellion, I remove the village of Amondo from the privilege of trading with other villages and counties!" Fletcher yells. The look of pleasure that spreads across his face makes my skin crawl.

For an age, nobody moves, either from fear or ignorance, and my heart pounds hard in my chest. The parents of the boys will find it hard to speak up without placing blame on themselves as well. It almost seems we have arrived at an impasse—when Marla steps forward.

My heart sinks.

Her words to me when she visited that night replay in my head:

"Big mistake, Harmen Travesci." The weight of the four words crush my chest. Frantically, I flick my attention between her and Mason. Without a single word from Marla, Mason points to me. He already knew. Mother grabs my hand tight as whispers and gasps filter through the crowd. Mason and his comrade storm over and grab me, one arm each.

"No, you leave him be, Mason Rayner!" Mother cries, clinging to my hand still. She speaks to him like he is one of the village children. A risk.

Force from the two men shoving me forward breaks her grip on my hand, and my father's stare burns into my back as he lets out a low growl. One look back, and their pain rips through me like I knew it would. Amaya whimpers, her head buried in Mother's side. Betrayal is etched across my father's face.

"What have we here?" Fletcher circles the three of us. Holding his leather whip in hand, he taps it rhythmically on his palm. A smirk curls up on his face. He signals for me to be turned to face the village. Every set of eyes I know stares back in disbelief. One pair, though, is lit up with delight: Marla. I glare at her with all the gall I can muster.

"For the crime of interfering with selection day, misleading Guardian officers, and inhibiting procedures from being carried out, I sentence Harmen Travesci to thirty lashes and two days and nights confined to the hanging pole!" He turns on his heel to face me after his theatrical announcement, sending sand flying in the crowd's direction. Meeting his twisted stare, malice dressed in a smirk, I stand tall.

A quick wave of his hand, and Mason and his comrade drag me to the hanging pole. They tie a rope around both wrists and hang me over the metal nail above my head. Mason rips my shirt from my back. Fletcher stands behind me and the tails of his whip fling loose and gasps come from the crowd.

"No, stop this!" Amaya flies from Mother's hold into Fletcher, fists raised, and lays down blow after blow with her small hands. They make no impact, and he chuckles at her distraught state. Pushing her with one hand backwards onto the sand, he looks back to the crowd.

"Does somebody own this heathen girl?"

Craning my neck, I bend my head around as far as I can to find Amaya. My father steps forward and picks her up. She screams in his arms, her body flailing around beneath his grip. My mother's gaze alternates between Amaya and me, and she sobs where she stands. She raises her head when she notices me looking back at her, and nods, setting her jaw as tears flow down her face. I turn back to the post and rest my forehead on the wood, letting out a long breath.

I wait.

Crack!

Fire rips through my back and spreads sideways as Fletcher lays the first lash down.

Crack!

Skin on my back tears apart, and the sting steals my breath. Teeth gritted, I wait for the next blow.

Crack!

Another wave of fire. I grind out a growl. My entire back feels like it is burning under the rage of a thousand suns. My legs start to tremble around the fifteenth lash.

Crack, crack, crack ...

Lashes land, one after the other.

My body jerks with every blow.

I lose count.

Blood trickles down my back and saturates the sand beneath my feet. I stare at it. Red sand. Smoky currents waft past my vision. The rope around my wrists has burned through the skin, and blood runs down my arms. My head lolls from side to side as another lash rains down on my ragged back. Points of light creep in from the sides of my vision.

Crack!

Darkness.

Dark tangles of dark hair blow behind her as she walks through the sand. Her eyes fixed on mine, she wanders towards me. I hold my hand out, wanting her to reach me so desperately. Urgently, I strain my hand towards hers. She smiles, reaching for me.

But something heavy is holding me back. Stopping mere inches away from me, she waits for me to speak. My mouth moves, but no sound escapes. I reach a hand to touch her face, and blood runs down my arm from my wrists, dripping onto the sand. Blood streams down her cheeks from her eyes. Sorrow pulls at the elegant features of her beautiful face.

A shadow creeps over me from behind. She stares at the coldness that was not there before, and she reaches out to grab my hand. Mason tells her to stop. Just as our fingers touch, she disintegrates into sand. Panicked, I turn around. Mason stands in the sand, laughing at me. He looks me over before turning and leaving, every step away from me loaded with insults.

Somebody touches my shoulder, and I jolt backward.

"Harmie, wake up." The soft, scared voice of Amaya reels me back to the hanging post. The darkness surrounding us is cold. The pain in my back cascades, wrenching through me with every breath, and tears slide down my filthy face. I suck in my breath, trying to hold in my cries for Amaya's sake, but fail. She holds the tin cup to my mouth, and I sip. Felicity is standing behind her.

Amaya's face is red and swollen from crying, and her hands shake as she holds the tin cup.

"May May, you shouldn't be here. They will punish you for helping me," I choke.

"I couldn't leave you out here by yourself," she whispers, releasing a fresh stream of tears. Felicity wraps an arm around Amaya, her eyes scanning the darkness of the village center for signs of life.

"You need to go." I meet Felicity's gaze.

"I know," she says and turns to leave, pulling Amaya around with her. Felicity ushers Amaya back to our house, and she bursts through the door and into my mother's arms. The sight of me draws a painful expression to my mother's eyes that now meets my gaze as she stands frozen over the threshold of our home. I suck in a deep breath. The wooden pillar connects with my head as I slump towards the pole, letting it out.

When the first warm spears of light jut over the horizon, my body relaxes from the coldness. Limp with fatigue and fear of any slight movement sending ripping pain through my back, I beckon sleep to me—just until the village awakes, at least. My eyes hang from their anchors in a smoky daze, and my body slackens as sleep carries me away.

Cold water blasts my face. Disoriented, I choke back the small amount that made it into my mouth. Every cough sends searing pain through my raw back. Shaking the water from my drenched hair, I raise my head to look up at a Guardian. My gaze snags on small brown shoes, then a skirt, followed by the clean but tattered shirt held in place by an overly tight brown belt. Then to the smug face of Marla.

"I told you. You will pay for not wanting me, Harm. You should have just taken me up on my offer. Could have saved yourself a whole lot of suffering."

"You would have made a fine Guardian, Marla."

"Pity they only select you filthy boys."

"You done?"

"That depends. Are you going to change your mind about us?"

"There is no 'us.' No amount of torture is going to get me to want you."

"Suit yourself, Travesci." Her eyes linger on my bare torso as she recedes from the village center, back to her house, bucket swinging, satisfaction plastered across her face.

I shake my head again to rid the last of the water and her words. The cool trickle of the water runs down my searing back, stinging every inch of broken skin. Balling up my fists, I draw deep breaths to stave off the fainting feeling that is creeping its way up my insides. As the sun rises higher in the sky with each hour, the stinging turns into a raging fire, and waves of shudders rack every muscle.

Desert sun burns even the toughest skin if it is left exposed, and it will damage my raw back beyond repair after two days. The smell of burning flesh twists my stomach into a clenched knot, and my mind wanders. White balls of light dance around in the sand, waiting to be caught. A half-baked simper briefly splits over my face as I hang lifeless against the pillar. The sand beyond the pole moves, and a silhouette drifts cautiously toward me. The sun glares behind her, inches from where I hang. I shake my head. She is still there. A small, soft hand touches my face, and a weak groan trembles from my lips.

"I'm so sorry," she whispers.

Only just making out the words, I shift my hanging arms to look at her. Pain pulls at my back. I slam my eyes shut and open them again.

She is gone.

I drift off again after the midday sun falls.

Someone is shouting. Snapping my head up, I squint to focus. Mason is standing over me, carrying a cane. Trying to wedge herself between me and the vicious cane is the village healer, Enora. Felicity stands beside her.

"Let me pass, Guardian," Enora spits, her face fierce with anger.

"Nobody is to interfere with the punishment handed down."

"He needs water. I have no intention of interfering with your sadistic plans, boy."

After a time, Mason lets her pass. A small cup with cool water touches my lips. The burnt skin on my face all but cracks as I put my mouth around the tin cup to sip. A sad smile escapes her concerned face, and she sighs heavily. "You could very well pay a high price for trying to protect others, Harmen." Her words are soft, but her tone is serious. I muster a small croak.

"You are a very brave young man. You must get through this. There will be other things for you to do one day, others that will need you." She pats my hands as they hang from the rope bonds suspending them. I try to show my appreciation, but I can't. The sun has turned my skin to stone, which will surely crack if I move.

Mason retreats to his family home while he is here on watch. No one else is game to interfere with the punishment handed out by the Guardians—at least, not in broad daylight. Hanging from the pillar, I shiver through the night.

At dawn, I stare at the sun's splintered rays poking over the dunes, the bile in my twisted stomach dripping from my mouth. Every retch sends ripples of searing pain across the lash marks on my back, triggering more sickness. By dusk, I sway, hanging in my bonds, somewhat conscious. The dark, bloodstained sands that were below me have all but blown away, and a sound beside me rouses my head. Mason is standing over me. How long he has been there, I am not sure. His eyes wander up and down my body, lingering on my back, as if he is making a mental note of the damage.

"Time is up. Collect your wounded!" he yells over his shoulder. The cries of my mother and Amaya follow his words. Within minutes, they are beside me, holding me up. Something tugs at my wrists. A blade runs back and forth on the rope. As it stops, I collapse onto the sand, half held up by the arms of my mother. Soft whimpers come from Amaya, followed by the heavy footsteps of my father.

"Gently now," Enora says as two large hands move under my arms, lifting me to my feet. My mother positions herself under one arm, my father under the other. Mother's shoulders shake with sobs with every step. Streaks of tears that have escaped his control mark my father's face, running in rivulets through his stubble. We move ever so slowly towards the healer's shelter.

Across the threshold stands Felicity. The healer greets her at the door with instructions that send her rushing to the supply cupboard. The bunk closest to the door greets me as I am laid down. New cracks fracture along the rigid scabs on my ragged back, sending fresh currents of agony over every inch. Someone is squeezing my hand. I turn my head to the side to see Amaya.

"Hey, May May," I croak.

She bursts into tears. "Why did you do it, Harmie?"

"Someone had to do something." I breathe out and squeeze my eyes, hoping the pain will lessen.

It doesn't.

"Come, Amaya, let the healer do her job now." My mother has

found her composure. The footsteps of my family fade. A cool, wet cloth falls onto my back, and I flinch. Coaxed into my mouth is a paste, vile and green, followed by chewing instructions. Only a few moments pass before the room goes dull and my breathing slows. Before I can call out, the heavy, oppressive lure of unconsciousness drags me under.

CHAPTER 8
HARM

I try to rise in my half-conscious state, and a firm hand holds me down. I strain against it, and another presses down.

"Don't," a soft voice says.

Felicity.

Sitting with her warm hip up against my side, her hands go back to work on my injured back. Warmth rises through my chest into my face with the touch of her hands on my bare back. She tends to the deepest of the lash cuts, and the sensation fades, replaced by fierce burning. I cry out. Grabbing the legs of the wooden bunk, I hold them as tight as my burned hands allow. Burying my head in the thin pillow, I scream with each pass of her hands over my back as she applies the thick balm.

"I'm sorry, Harm. I will do this as quickly as I can," she whispers.

Tears soak my pillow, and I am glad my face is sunk into it. Rhythmically, I push deep breaths in and out. It is all I can do to stop my heart from bursting with the pain. Then, her hands stop. The bunk creaks, and the warmth from her hip against my side disappears. Exhausted from the treatment, I turn my head and rest.

Felicity and Enora are talking while they work on the wooden bench I made years ago. Felicity's thick, wavy, light-brown hair is tied up, a cloth wrapped around it, strands escaping to frame her lightly freckled face and hazel-green eyes. Her apron is stained with my blood, and she stands hammering the mortar and pestle against each other. Enora notices me watching and offers a small nod before I drift off.

Three days pass before Enora allows me to leave the healer's shelter. I can move enough to go back home, but I am on bed rest for three weeks until the scabbing has healed and is not in danger of reopening. The slightest task sends out sharp pains from the firm scabs that plate my back in lines, showing the many bloody tributaries cut by the lashes. Father has not come to see me since I came home and keeps himself scarce, only attending meals. We exchange no words—only the pained looks my mother gives him, which he returns with a deadpan face.

The only thing worse than my flogging is the rift that has taken up residence between my parents. By now, I figure Mother told him what she knows, and now she is paying for my actions as well. It is the first taste of betrayal our family has ever felt, and I caused it. That hurts worse than any lash.

Gingerly, I sit up in my bed. In an old notebook, I write, trying to think of ways to fix what I have broken in my family. Not one thing I scratch on the paper feels good enough. Could I tell him that I made her promise? But he would argue that she shouldn't have made such a promise. Maybe I should tell him that Mother only found out from one of the boys' mothers, and they threatened to tell the Guardians if she spoke of it. Everything I write seems like I am blaming everyone else but myself. I broke the laws we have abided by for so long. I paid the price set by the Guardians, and now I will pay the price set by my father, if only to save my mother from paying it for me. If I take the brunt of my father's anger, maybe then he will forgive her.

With blood thrumming through my veins, I push up out of bed. On my way through the door, I grab the cane Enora gave me to help support my torso. Ignoring my mother's pleas for me to return to my bunk, I shuffle out the door and trudge my way to the building site on the other side of the village. I take three times as long to hobble through the hot sand and arrive out of breath and full of anger.

As I round the side of the home, the men who work with my father look up from their tasks. Wide-eyed, one of the crew calls for my father. A moment later, he comes around the front of the building, wiping sweat from his brow with his arm. His frame is alive with the force of hard labor, and he wrings a rag through his hands, removing sweat, sand, and sawdust. Stopping dead in his tracks, standing so much taller than me at this moment, he stares at me for a time, looking back and forth from the stick to my face. He has no words for me either. Good. I will speak first.

"She has done nothing but try to protect her son," I spit out, deciding on a full-frontal attack on the man who has raised and loved me for nearly two decades. He throws a glance at his men, and they make themselves scarce. My resolve waivers slightly as he steps forward. I lean back on the stick, pushing my aching frame to stand taller. The hurt in his eyes makes me understand what pains him most: that Mother thought she had to protect me—from him. It hits me like a slap up the side of the head, and I swallow back the lump in my throat.

"Then tell me, Harmen, what were you thinking, hiding those boys?" His words are calm, not fiery as I had expected.

"I was trying to help, trying to change the way things are. Their parents were desperate."

"You just put everyone in danger with your foolishness." He gestures to the village as he steps closer again. "And your mother kept it from me."

"Then hate *me*. Make *me* pay. She didn't do the wrong thing. I did!" His eyes widen. "Imagine if it were the other way around. She would never treat you like this, ever! You are breaking her heart!" Tears I am trying desperately to hold back, prickle. Heat rises from my neck to my face. My weakened legs shake, and I clutch the stick in my hand, straightening up before turning to leave.

"Harmen!" he calls after me.

I can't stop.

Now, I hate *him*.

My mind plays the tortured face of my mother over and over as she looked at him so desperately, only to be met with indifference. Worse than her receiving a reaction from him, he has shut her out.

I am almost back to our house when the cries of a villager summon all to the village center. The Guardians have returned. To inspect their handiwork, most likely. Falling in with the crowd, I join Mother and Amaya. Father comes to a halt on the other side of my mother and stares at me with a perplexed look. Amaya slips her hand into his as we wait. The three Guardians stand, hands clasped behind their backs and eyes fixed on the horizon behind the crowd. After a moment, waiting for all to quiet down, Fletcher steps forward.

"By order of the governing laws of this county, the people of Amondo are prohibited from trading with or in any other village or county, from this day forward until duly notified. Anyone caught trading from the village of Amondo will be sentenced to death by hanging." Fletcher's face is stone. Father curses under his breath, and the village goes into an uproar.

55

What?! I paid the price!

My hands ball up, one a white grip on my stick, the other a fist by my side.

"No! We paid the price, as per your terms!" I hobble to the front of the crowd with my stick. Fire still lingers in my veins from moments ago as Fletcher steps into my space, his frame overshadowing my weakened state.

"You don't make the rules, boy. We do. The punishment dealt was not received with the earnestness it should have been. My word is final. Trading will cease." Fletcher's eyes are lit up with eagerness, as if waiting for retaliation, and I push up on my stick, rising tall to meet him.

"You mean because I didn't die on that post, you will punish the rest of the village anyway?" I seethe, eyes burning into Fletcher's.

"Think what you want. The order stands." He spins away from the gaping crowd and leaves. His officers follow behind in step. Before they load into the buggy, Mason shoots me a cursory warning glance. This was his village too; his family will suffer now too. As the buggy pulls away from the crowd, Mason's look turns to hatred, as if he has only just decided that this is all my fault. Not Marla's. Not his. Nobody's but mine. I uncurl my fists, and my hands tremble as the buggy plows off through the sands.

Hobbling through the thick sand, I turn back to the crowd—only to be met with more anger. This time, almost every face seems to strip me down, all except the families I helped, and my own. Villagers yell out all the ways my actions will cost them dearly, and how stupid I was to interfere with the way things have always been. They move towards me like a swarm. Like a trapped animal, I stagger backward.

My father steps between me and the crowd and crosses his arms, standing firm. My mother and Amaya follow him. Father's crew and the families of the boys I hid join him. My chest swells, sobs and hot tears threaten to spill over. My gaze is fixed on the back of my stoic father, who stands between me and the angry, growing group of hecklers. A heartbeat later, there is a small gathering between me and the crowd. Finally, after nobody wants to budge, the villagers return to their tasks, and my parents escort me home, Amaya triumphantly leading the way.

Back in my room, my mother sits on my bed, my father standing in the doorway.

"Get some rest, Harmen," Mother says.

"What will happen to the village without trading? For who knows how long?"

Mother forces a small smile and pats my hand, looking to my father.

"The people of the village will make do, son," he says. "They have done it before. Do as your mother says: get some rest." Father leaves the doorway, followed by my mother. Never have I felt this much like a small child. Not only have I made things worse for everyone; they are protecting me from it. Awkwardly, I ease onto my side to face the wall and let my mind wander.

The wall stares back at me when I wake up hours later, a blanket covering me. A board creaks near my door, and I struggle to roll onto my other side without putting pressure on my back. Mother walks into my bedroom with a tray, setting it on my dresser before helping me sit up. The smell of her stew and grains makes my mouth water. She fetches the tray from the dresser and sits it on my lap before shutting the door and sitting beside me. The spoon in my hand hangs suspended halfway to my mouth.

"Harmen, I need to talk to you."

Offering a slight nod, I shove the spoon into my mouth, eyes fixed on her face. The stew makes my stomach growl. I barely chew the mouthful before throwing another spoonful in. My mother watches me eat for a moment.

"Your father and I understand why you were trying to help those boys. We are not angry because you were trying to help, but because disobeying the Guardians never ends well. Not for you, not for our family, and not for the village." She takes a deep breath. "Things have been this way for a very long time, and people are not used to standing up for themselves anymore. For most, life is easier and less risky if they just conform to the rules, no matter how uncomfortable things get." She holds my gaze and hesitates. "But things weren't always like this. Decades ago, people were free. That may be the case again in your lifetime. However, until that time, you must stay safe. You need to stay alive for it." Breathless from what has turned from a conversation to a plea, her eyes are fierce, as if she is trying to tell me something without saying it.

Carefully, I put the spoon down. "You told me stories like that when I was young. But what do you mean, I need to stay alive for it? What difference could I make?"

"They are not stories, Harm; they are our history. And now, every person counts, especially the younger generations."

"Enora came to see me while you were in the shelter," she adds.

"Oh? What for?"

"Felicity was taking care of you while you were under their roof."

"I was there." Returning my focus back to the food on the tray, I hope this isn't going where I think it is.

"Enora was watching the two of you. She thinks you make a good match." She waits for me to look up, "and so do I, Harmen."

"We've talked about this already. I can't."

"That was before you disobeyed the Guardians. You need to

settle in and live a normal life—one that doesn't see you getting strung up at the earliest convenience. At least if you have a match to be responsible for, you are less likely to do anything else so reckless."

Her words are firm. At last, the reproach she has been holding in for days comes into play. It is my mother's version of recorrecting my path, a much more subtle approach than my father's, but no less effective.

"So, you want me to be Blended with someone I didn't choose, and then live under tyranny, never hoping for anything better? A better life is not for us, ever?"

"That is not what I meant, but for the immediate future, it would be your wisest course of action."

This time I change the subject. "Why was father so angry at you? You didn't disobey the Guardians. All you did was keep my secret, which hardly deserves the treatment he gave you."

She hangs her head low for a while, and I don't push.

"The Blending of the Sands ceremony between two people declares their love, or the promise of it, and respect for each other. But it also swears each person to honesty and commitment above all. When you turn eighteen, you are eligible to be matched and attend your ceremony with your chosen partner. You are to be matched with someone of your own year. That's the way it has always been; this you know. What you may not know is that the vows you make to your match bind you to them, for as long as you both live. If one of you does not uphold the vows, the other takes this as a sign of not only disrespect, but," she closes her eyes briefly before continuing, "betrayal. When I didn't tell your father what had happened, he felt betrayed. Not just because of the vows we took years ago, but because we have never withheld secrets before. We are an open book with each other."

"But he hurt you so much, shutting you out and treating you

like the enemy for days!"

"Imagine how hurt he felt. I was the one who broke what we have had for so long. Fear stopped me from telling him. I was afraid if he knew, things would be harder when the Guardians returned, that he might try to interfere, trying to save you. I was afraid for you both. I should have trusted him; you are his son. He would do anything for you, Harmen—anything at all."

"I hate the way he was with you. I hate him for that. You were just protecting me. Maybe I should have told you both. But there was always a chance I would get away with it, right?" I quip, trying to lighten the mood.

She clips me playfully behind the ear before leaning over to kiss my forehead. "Eat up and rest. We will have more work now; there will be fewer resources. I will let Enora know we agree to the match for you and Felicity." She walks to the door. Her hand rests on the knob, and she turns back.

"You take after me, you know. I would have done the same thing once, had I been in your position. It's in our blood." She smiles weakly, opens the door, and leaves.

Finishing the stew, I push the tray to the side of my bed. With difficulty, I get onto my side and slide my hands under my head and pillow. With my mother's words drifting around in my mind, I lie on my bunk. Felicity. My stomach sinks, and I shove a groan into the pillow. No. Not like this. Not Felicity. I loose a breath and press the pillow into my face.

The image of my dark-haired girl in the trees wanders through my mind. Now, she will only ever be a dream, lost to memories. Heaviness pulls my chest tight. Hard as I try, I can't let her go. My heart aches with every beat. After an hour of trying to create a place for Felicity in my heart, I give up. Instead, I attempt to string together an apology for my father ... but I have no idea where to even start.

CHAPTER 9
IMANI

A hard shoulder slams into mine, and I pull my gaze from the sands to the face of the officer in front of me. His ruffled sandy hair sticks out from under his grey hat. His blue eyes burn into mine. The hair on my arms stands, and I shake down a shiver.

"Officer Rayner," I croon, pushing up the most insincere smile I can manage.

"Imani," he grunts, before running his gaze up and down the ragged clothes that hang on my too-thin frame. Briefly pausing around my chest before looking me in the eye, he offers me something between a simper and a smirk before catching up to his comrades. Filthy ingrate. If he thinks being part of the regime gives him privileges with women, he has another think coming. I brush my fingertips over the knife in my belt and shake off the sick feeling that claws its way up my spine. The dune buggy drones to life, plowing away from the village through the sands.

The day I first met Mason, he was different. He sat on the outskirts of the village, watching his herd of goats, eating his lunch from a cloth. He watched as I staggered in through the waves of heat. Stuck out in the desert for three days before reaching Amondo, I was so hungry that even the taste of the sand that coated my face was starting to appeal to me. Something about the way I eyed his food must have clicked, and when he left, half of his food was wrapped up and sitting out for me. At least, that was the story I told myself three years ago—one where not all men are bad; some are good. I almost chuckle out loud at my own naiveté but stifle the sound. Being unseen is the only defense I have left.

People hang in a line at the well, and I fall into place at the end and wait with the many others needing water. Harmen arrives with two buckets. He flips one over and sits on it, drawing in the sand with his stick. Marla stalks up to him, hands on hips, empty buckets swinging from each.

"You couldn't help yourself, could you, Travesci? Now, look at us all. We're all paying the price for your stupidity!" Marla snarls, hate plain on her face.

Eventually, he lifts his gaze to meet her eyes. "At least I don't hide behind my brother. Coming back here only to torment and order around the people who loved and raised him, who grew up with him. He's no better than the rest of us, Marla." Most of the people in the line are staring at them now.

"Mason is the only reason we are not all strung up!" Her face is twisted into something vicious. I stifle a sarcastic chuckle and suppress the urge to comment.

The line moves, and I reach the well, filling both of my canteens before shoving one in my rucksack and one around my neck and over my shoulder. I wander to the village center, sit on the stone bench and watch them, hood up and wrap over my face. That despicable girl is the real reason this village is suffering. Her whispering to her brother is what put Harmen on that pole, and why the village is now unable to trade. If anyone is to blame for what is happening, it's Mason and Marla.

Harmen fills his buckets and hobbles toward the first ring of homes. Marla watches him from the doorway of her home, and the smirk on her face makes me sick. Before I even realize it, I am only a handful of feet from her front door. She gives me a once-over, just the way her brother did. Heat flares up my neck and through my face, the blood in my veins thunders, and I inch closer to her, aligning my gaze with hers. She falters back slightly and crosses her arms over her chest.

"Can I help you?" she snaps.

"How about you help yourself, you two-faced wretch?"

She squares her shoulders, dropping her arms to her sides. "I'm sure I have no idea what you're talking about." She tilts her chin higher.

"Mason is a coward. A cruel one, who has no influence over Fletcher. Stop kidding yourself, Marla. Your family is not safe because he became a Guardian. None of you are."

"Our family is none of your business, whoever you are." She looks me up and down, curling her hands into fists. Like brother, like sister.

"At least Harmen tried to help. All you have ever done is cause trouble for other people. You're a despicable human being." Heat races through my core, and I lean into her space without thinking.

Her mouth gapes, preparing to fire back, but I turn on my heel and make for my hideout. *What the hell am I doing? I'm supposed to be staying inconspicuous.* I grind out a curse and stalk my way through the rings of homes. Sinking into the sands, I lean against the healer's shelter and remove my hood and wrap. This village is making me crazy. Or maybe it is the people—or one person. I should leave. It would be the smart thing to do. In a few days, I will head south to find the gypsies.

Harmen's voice drifts through the back window of the shelter. I straighten, listening to his words. Enora is asking him to wait. I slide up the wall and slip around the side. With a flick of my wrist, my hood falls over my face. I lean against the corner of the shelter. His face is blank as he stands holding a bucket of water. Why didn't the healer take it from him? Shuffling from inside floats towards the front door, and he stands taller, pushing up on his stick. He sets the bucket down and runs a hand through his messy brown hair. A flicker pulses through my stomach.

"Oh, hey, Flick," he says, reaching for the bucket.

The healer's apprentice steps outside, hands running over her apron repeatedly. Crimson flushes her neck and face as she steps toward him.

"Where do you want me to put this?" he asks.

"Um, inside. Thanks, Harm." Her words shake like her hands. "Okay. Can I talk to you for a minute though?"

Her gaze drops to the ground. "Uh, sure." She twists the fabric of her apron through her hands.

"Enora and my mother have matched us," he says, almost a whisper.

Flick swallows and nods shyly.

She is his match.

My grip on the building turns white. It's none of my business, but a weight sinks in my gut regardless. I peel myself from the building and creep back to the spot by the wood box. *This is what happens when you get stupid ideas in your head, Imani. What the hell was I thinking? I shouldn't have even followed him home. I don't stay in one place, ever. I'm no village girl. What did I think was going to happen?*

He will be fine with Felicity staying out of trouble. It's time for me to leave. No more Harmen, no more Mason, and no more pity. To stay alive, I need to be smart and not form attachments, no matter how drawn to him I feel.

CHAPTER 10
HARM

Hauling water and sharing supplies keeps me busy, and the scorching sun reminds me that the work is self-inflicted. The glares of the villagers who surround me reflect the sun's sentiment daily. Briefly releasing the buckets in hand, I knock on the door of Arlo's house and wait. The sweat runs down my corded forearms, dripping into the buckets of water. The door cracks open, and I lift my gaze to meet Arlo's mother. She opens the door this time and offers a reserved smile, looking down at my hands gripping the full buckets.

Pushing the door back, she allows me into the front room. The house seems empty now without Arlo, and I head to the kitchen. His brothers are playing out back, making a ruckus. Setting the buckets down, I lift the lid from the ceramic water jug. The water left over from the previous day is dirty. Around the kitchen, there are empty baskets, no bread, and no pot of stew bubbling on the cooker. My gaze meets her sunken and weary eyes. She is pale, despite living in the arid desert.

"You have no food?" I ask over the lump in my throat.

"We have a few things left, but with no trading, we cannot make supplies last now."

My stomach drops into a low pit. This is my fault. They are starving because of me.

"The children seem okay?"

"Yes, we give them the food first. All three of them are growing like desert thistles, lankier every day."

"I can bring you some more food, so you can eat too," I say, not meeting her gaze. Picking up the remaining bucket, I stride out, not leaving any time for her to turn down my offer. The next house I visit is our neighbor's. I knock and wait. No answer. I knock again. After a few minutes, she comes to the window.

"Get out of here, boy! You've done enough damage. I won't be seen with the likes of you. Go on, off you go!"

"I've just brought water. Should I set it down by the door?"

"No!" she yells, drawing the curtains. Hesitating, I try to decide whether to leave the water regardless, but with a heavy sigh, I take it with me.

A few searing strides later, I reach our front door, set the bucket down, and fall into Father's outside chair, relieved to be out of the torturous sun. A small breeze finds me, and I rest my eyes. Many others in the village will struggle just like Arlo's family. His mother's hollow face is the first thing I see, evidence of my actions plain as day on her face. Arlo's heart would break to see his mother like this. My mother's voice drifts through our house, like the fine sands that float just above the dunes at sunset. The kindness that she usually possesses is absent. "Things are getting tight; we're down to our last lot of supplies. What happens when we run out? We just starve, like the rest of the people in the village?"

"I don't know, Hannah. Everyone is finding it hard. Trading will start up again soon, surely. It's been weeks. We just need to ration ourselves," Father says.

"You can't ration nothing, Andrew." Her words are pained.

"There are others worse off than us. We will get through this." His words slightly muffled, and I imagine him holding her while he talks to her, his head buried in her hair.

"What do we do when they come to collect next month—give them bags of sand? We have nothing left to give, and we both know what that means." She sighs, as if the words are a sign of her giving up.

For minutes, he doesn't reply. No other sounds come from the house.

Before I have time to think otherwise, I rise from the chair and amble into the living room. Mother is sitting in her chair, her head in her hands, her lap stained with her tears. She looks up with a pained expression, but forces a wobbly smile. If only there was something I could say that would fix all that I have done. But words don't come that big.

"I will leave. If I leave and go south and find your family, that fixes the problem, doesn't it?" I ask.

She touches her throat, her breath hitching as she looks away from me, staring at the shelf of books and trinkets. She sighs and fiddles with her handkerchief. "I don't know, Harmen. I don't think that's a good idea. We wouldn't be able to send them a letter explaining either. That's too dangerous. I haven't spoken to my family for over ten years; it was just too risky. I know they're my family, but it would still be a gamble. Not to mention the journey across the desert." She leans back, closing her eyes, taking a deep breath.

"I'll be fine. I can read a map and compass."

She doesn't respond, her eyes closed, head resting on the chair behind her, thinking.

"This is my fault. I leave, and that fixes it," I offer.

Her eyes open, emanating sorrow as she stares at me. Her face softens, but more tears come.

"Oh, Harmen, nothing about our existence is your fault. All you tried to do was fix part of it and save a handful of families from having their sons taken. Thanks to that, those boys are safe for now. If you didn't do it, someone else would have tried eventually. Nobody is blaming you, but every action has a consequence."

"The village people blame me. Many of them. It would be best if I left."

She closes her eyes again, and I hope she is considering it. "That's what's happening, then. I leave. I will go south and find your family. You and Father and Amaya will be safe."

I move to leave, and she grabs my hand, squeezing it. The warmth of my hand wrapped around my mother's sends torrents of guilt and remorse through me, and I choke back my own emotions. She releases me, and I walk down the hallway to the back door.

Standing behind the flimsy screen door, I watch Amaya and Father work on a small cage, held together by thin twine at each intersection. She is filthy from the sand and dirt, looking triumphant in her efforts. They step back to look at the cage. Father nods his head in approval at her build, and I push through the door and step into the backyard, chest tight as a lump forms in my throat.

Wandering around my workspace, I look for items that I should take with me until I realize that not only would their weight and bulkiness slow me down, but I may also never build again. Finally, I grab my project notebook, leave the workspace the way it is, and close the door. Standing between me and the back door, with her arms crossed and her features scrunched up in a pout, is Amaya.

"What's that look for?" I ask.

"Why are you just giving up?"

"What do you mean? I'm leaving. It's not about giving up."

"Isn't it? You're just going to leave your family and throw in the towel like a coward?"

"You wouldn't understand. You're a child."

Instantly I regret my words. Amaya's face swings from annoyance to pure hurt.

"May May, I'm sorry." I stretch out a hand to stop her, but she rips away from my grasp and storms into the house. Following, I pause outside her door, the echo of it slamming still ringing in my ears. A few breaths pass before I turn the knob and bunt the door open. Poking my head around, I wait for her to retaliate.

Nothing. She lies on her bed, sobbing. My stomach plummets as I walk into her room and sit down beside her. She is facing her window with her back to me.

"I'm sorry, Amaya. I didn't mean that." I choke on the first few words.

She lies next to me, her body shaking from crying. After a minute passes, she sucks in a breath and rolls over. "I just thought, if anyone in this horrible place could make things better, it would be you, Harmie. I really thought things could be different. Better. You've always been so strong. If things were different, you could do it. I know you could. Maybe if we went away and came back in a few years?"

"Right now, I need to focus on keeping you, Mother and Father safe and alive, and me staying in Amondo is not an option."

She sits up and examines my face before hugging my chest and I sink my head into her curls.

"I'm sorry," I whisper.

For so many things, I am sorry.

Amaya nods her head against my chest, and I wrap her tight in my arms, releasing a ragged breath.

The dark of nightfall crawls in while we sort and pack what we can carry. My parents have decided that all of us leaving would be a better option. Amaya is happy about it. But I'm not convinced. The sounds of nightlife in our quiet little village do nothing to quell the restlessness that threatens to rise and swallow me whole. Four of us traveling together will be harder to conceal from the Guardians. I know I should fight them on this, but I can't. I don't want to leave them. Part of me is glad I will not be on my own, but my gut drops at the thought of us being discovered. I should leave tonight. That way when morning comes, I will be gone, and they will be safe.

Amaya hums around my feet, helping me find things we want to take. Noise from the kitchen echoes through our home as Mother cleans and packs the kitchen away. For whom, I don't know. No one will occupy our house once we are gone.

Father has been on the building site all day and has just returned. His face is grim from a long day, saddled with the strain of leaving his workmen to fend for themselves. They won't know it until we are long gone. Studying the lines on his face, I can't even imagine how his heart must feel right now, torn between loyal friends and his family.

Outside my bedroom door, I stand, eyes fixed on my parents clinging to each other, as if their connection is the only thing holding them up right now. If they lost that, they would both crumble. Mother is sitting in his lap, on top of the wood box by the front door. She wraps her arms around him. It is the first time I have seen my father really cry. My mother, who has already shed her tears in solitude, comforts him. Another act of strength, one of many she has already undertaken since the day I was born. Her thumb wipes away the tears that wash his face in his moment of despair, and he gifts her a small smile, returning the love.

Amaya stands beside me, taking in the scene of her parents' despair for a moment, before padding her way down the hall. She nuzzles her way under Father's arm and wraps hers around his neck, resting her head on his chest. Mother lowers an arm around Amaya. The three of them stay huddled.

Retreating into my bedroom, I close the door behind me and slide down the worn-out wood. Coming to rest on the stone floor, I sink my head into my bent knees. The agony on my father's face and the pain reflected in my mother's eyes from seeing him this way tears me to pieces. Watching my father break shatters the last of my resolve. An ache grows in my chest, so fierce I can't breathe. As I take stock of all the things I have done that have made this happen, drowning under the truth, the rise and fall of my chest comes with ugly groans that rip me apart.

CHAPTER II
HARM

An hour later, we are reading in the living room. I stare at my book, not following the words. Instead, I am entranced by every likely scenario for this journey we are about to embark on. We will get away in the small hours of the morning, then make a clear run to the south without being noticed, hoping that by the time they discover our abandoned home, we will be far enough away that they won't find us. Finally, I pray Amaya will keep up with us. Dread temporarily fills my bones at the thought of being caught, before I crush it down with the rest of the worries that circle me like vultures.

Father's feet appear beneath my gaze. I lift my head to meet his eyes. In his hand sits a small leather case. His eyes are tired, and I see the fears that I hold in him as well. He hands me the case, and I reach up and take it, eyes locked on his.

"This was my father's. Just in case something separates us on the journey, you need to know how to find the southern villages and your mother's family." Opening it, I tilt the case, and a brass compass slips into my palm. It's smooth and cold in my grip. I flip open the lid, revealing the face, a needle, a glass cover, and an elegant symbol etched into the flat underside of the curved lid. It looks old, but works perfectly. Turning it slightly left and right, I watch the thin needle flick, possessed by its magnetic ruler.

"Thank you, but I already have a compass."

He releases a breathy chuckle and folds my hand around the brass piece. "It's a gift, Harmen. It is the only heirloom I own to give you."

I swallow the lump in my throat. This is in case we don't make it—in case *he* doesn't make it. Leaping up from my chair, I throw my arms around him. It's the first time I have hugged him since I was a young boy. I don't care, his words feel so final.

Mother sits in her chair, absently playing with Amaya's wispy hair as she continues to read. The tears that well in her eyes tell me my parents have thought of every outcome as well— including one where they don't complete the journey with us. Breathing out, I slam my eyes shut to hold back tears.

"We leave before sunrise. We should all turn in." Mother breaks the moment, helping Amaya up and enveloping her in a hug. I slide the compass into my trouser pocket as we amble to our rooms. Our packed rucksacks near our bedroom doors wait patiently for departure. Mother tucks Amaya into bed. Amaya whispers her worries, and Mother follows with calm answers. Lying in the dark, I say a prayer that, one day, I will be as strong as my mother, and as gallant as my father. Then maybe I will be the person my little sister thinks I am.

When the house has gone quiet, I push up off my bunk and pad down the hall. In the kitchen, I find bread wrapped in a small cloth in my place. Flinging it off, I tear into the bread, washing it down with some water from our enamel jug. Moonlight streams through our windows on the eastern side of the house, illuminating the hallway and half of our living room. Pain twinges in my chest as I pass the room where we have sat as a family for as long as I can remember, reading to pass the time in each other's company. Speckles of dust and fine sand play on the stone floor, dancing in the moonlight, the cool desert breeze their willing partner.

I stand outside Amaya's room. She sleeps like a doll, tucked into a neat cut of cloth, motionless, waves of her breath rippling across the light coverings. She looks so small. Her stillness now is an acute contrast to her waking hours, full of energy and happiness.

Soft steps carry me to my parents' door. At the foot of their bed, moonlight hits the floor. The bed my father made for my mother was a Blending gift, and she has always treasured it. Now, I catalogue all the ways that leaving her home behind will bring her pain. Memories of the day I was lashed return. My mother was strong and unbending, lending me what I needed to get through it. Again, I am the reason she needs to use her strength. Defeated, I return to my room and sit on my bunk. I have to go, it's the only way to keep them safe.

I pick up my rucksack and swing it over my shoulder. I am leaving. I will leave. I pad toward the hall, and my heart thunders with a growing ache I can't dislodge. I reach the front door and rest my hand on the knob. Breath comes so fast I almost choke out loud. Beams of silver stream through the kitchen window, lighting the space where my mother spends her days. Amaya's dolls sit neatly on the shelf, their tiny black eyes watching me. I swallow the lump in my throat, and I let my hand fall from the knob. I will never see my family again. Never hear Amaya's laugh. Never see my mother smile at me, or feel her warm, gentle hugs. Never see the love and pride on my father's face again. My body trembles.

I can't.

I can't do it.

Moments later, I am curled up on my bunk. Exhausted from the onslaught of damning thoughts, I press the heels of my palms into my eyes, until unconsciousness finds me.

She is there. I stand at the edge of the trees, while she is immersed in the depths of the forest. The wind whips her hair around. She calls out, but I can't make out her words. An invisible tugging bond pulls me in her direction, closer, step by step. Another call leaves her mouth. This time, I respond. Instantly, she drops her belongings and calls my name, over and over, and it is the most familiar and sweetest thing I have ever heard. Desperation and excitement thunder through my veins as she runs toward me, tentatively at first, then at a sprint. My breathing staggers as I try to close the distance between us. I can almost see her face. My breath catches.

"Harmen, wake up. Time to go." My father's sturdy hand shakes my shoulder. The girl slips away as the darkness of my room falls in around me. Father is leaning over me, dressed and ready to move.

Running a hand through my hair, I check that I am decent after the dream before I throw the cover off and jump out of the bunk. A quizzical expression washes across my father's face, only just visible in the dimness.

Out in the hallway, Mother and Amaya are ready and waiting. Amaya huddles into me, warming herself against my side in the coolness of the predawn hours. Through the eastern window, the first splinters of light mark dawn's arrival. It's a little later than I thought we would leave, but still dark enough to conceal our movement out of the village, in case Marla has any other hateful ideas; her first has caused enough suffering for the entire village. And there would be others who would feel no guilt in notifying the Guardians of our timely exit, with tax collection day just past the next sunrise.

Tomorrow will not be a good day for many of our village friends. Arlo's family cannot pay the full taxes they owe. Tides of guilt course through me as I flick through the assorted means of punishment they might face, and our plan is to just run away.

Father gestures for us to move. He takes the lead, me behind him, Amaya, and then Mother, our traveling order. The only thing left is to slip on our traveling robes and rucksacks and sneak out the door.

"Wait—I forgot my journal from under the bed with my family's information in it." Mother turns and rushes down the hall. Before she reaches her room, a wet sliding noise starts on the other side of the front door.

Chalky fumes from ocher paint reek, seeping around it, followed almost instantaneously by hard knocking. Mother freezes, and I watch as the color drains from my father's face.

We are too late.

CHAPTER 12
HARM

"No," Mother whispers, her face twisting in panic. "They are a day early!"

Somehow, they have found out. We should have been a day's journey away before they arrived. Someone has ratted us out. Marla. My hands ball into fists, breath heaves out of my chest, and Amaya's wide gaze swings between the faces of our parents. Fear blanches its way through their features. Tears fall down Amaya's face, and I tuck her under my arm and hold her tight. Father takes Mother's hand. There is no point in trying to run now. The barter items we would need to pay our taxes don't exist after the last month's meager takings and sharing with other families. Our fate will be like others in the village, but there is no doubt in my mind that my actions will cost us now. Amaya's sobs course through me as I press her shaking body closer, tighter.

The door rattles again under the pounding of the Guardian's fist. Mother grabs our travel wraps and robes and shoves them inside the cooker. The embers from last night are still alight. They catch just as she clicks the door closed and pulls down the outside lever to seal it off. Father motions for Amaya and me to move to the sitting room, and we take up our regular seats and pick up our books. This would not be our normal routine, but how would they know that? Mason might.

Mother hovers behind the sink, her hands trembling as she tries to make it look like she has been tending to some unremarkable morning chore. Grabbing our rucksacks and tucking them under the kitchen bench, Father sucks in a deep breath before turning the doorknob. Amaya weeps from behind her book as three Guardians breach the threshold: Fletcher, followed by Mason, then by their constant comrade.

My father stands tall, asking the meaning of such an early visit. Fletcher takes in the scene before him, his gaze lingers on the rucksacks under the bench, and a smirk covers his face. Someone sold us out. My breath stops. Behind him, Mason stands, his face blank, as if he is removed from what is happening. For a moment, I hold onto the hope that he will try to help.

Fletcher demands that my father turn around, and Mason does not move, not even a flinch, still unmoved. Fletcher binds Father's wrists with rope behind his back. With a subtle tilt of his head, he sends Mason after my mother. Fear flashes in her eyes as he corners her in the small kitchen.

Father struggles against Fletcher's hold, desperate to get to her. "Hannah!"

Her slight frame compared to Mason's now pressed hard against the hot stove. She tries to slip past him. With one hand, he shoves her into the wall. Her head hits hard. She lets out a pained cry, and my father almost takes Fletcher down, straining against the Guardian to get to her. A sharp tug on his roped hands, and he stumbles backward.

"Andrew, I'm okay," she whimpers, and pain and fear exchange between them.

"Don't struggle, it only makes things worse," the third

Guardian says as he grabs my shoulder and pulls me towards Amaya, who is sobbing, almost breathless. A glimmer of sorrow dances behind his glazed-over eyes. He's not like Fletcher and Mason, as if he is still part village boy and not all Guardian.

It is only a few moments before they shove us out of our home and across the sand to the center of the village. In the chilly dawn, they have already corralled the village people like animals, with six Guardians flanking them like herders. No one speaks—no sounds from the crowd at all. My father is first, followed by Mother and then Amaya and me. At the sight of Amaya, small cries start.

Guardians swing their canes into the closest people. Moments drag by, and every movement is sluggish. Every part of me shakes, and I try to find a familiar face. Felicity stands next to Enola, her face wet with tears, her hand clutching the thin dressing gown over her chest. Some of the boys' parents I helped are looking at us now with eyes full of guilt and sorrow. One mother mouths, *"Sorry,"* and turns her head into the embrace of her husband.

We reach the village center, and they shove us into a line before the pitiful crowd, who huddle close, holding onto their families, helpless.

"For the act of rebellion against the regime of the Chancellor, complete disrespect and disregard of Guardian leadership and the laws of this county, I sentence this family to execution by drowning." Fletcher draws out the last word, as if it alone could steal our last breath. My mother goes weak, and Father moves closer to help her stay standing as she struggles to breathe.

Amaya's eyes widen, and she cries into my side, her breath rasping rapidly. "Momma!"

I grab her, tucking her under me again as hot, wet streams run down my face. Using my shoulder and sleeve, I wipe away the tears. As the sleeve leaves my face, Marla appears, snaking her way through the crowd. She stands at the front, watching, arms crossed, her lips turned up in a smirk. My gaze swings to Mason. His face is still stone. He looks straight ahead, his eyes are vacant. Heat sears inside me, and I return a look of hatred to Marla. If this is the last thing I give her, it is the least she deserves.

Fletcher taps the ground with his cane. Responding, Mason moves to my father first. He takes a firm hold of his roped hands and propels him towards the well. Prodding with their canes, his comrades make us follow. Every step takes enormous effort as fear burns up my throat. Amaya clings to my side, and her terrified body trembles against mine.

We reach the well, and Mason kicks my father's legs out from under him. He pulls him back up to a kneeling position by the collar and motions for us to do the same. They bind our hands behind our backs, like Father's.

Beneath us, the sand is not yet warm, the day is so new. Early rays of the eastern sun poke over the top of the well before us. Amaya shuffles closer to me in the sand, but before I can lean into her, trying to offer some small comfort, Mason tugs her up and drags her to the well.

No, May May!

The air stills in my throat, the heat of fear floods my body. "Amaya!"

I strain against the Guardian's hold, growling as I twist and pull against his grip. He holds me down tighter, his grip on the rope burning my wrists.

"No! Let me go, please! Please, Mason!"

Mason's chest heaves, but his gaze is vacant. My parents are both struggling against Fletcher now, who holds them from behind.

"Amaya," Mother calls to her, her voice calm. Amaya's gaze meets Mother's, and she quiets down. Up against Mason, she is so small. He prods her along, stopping just short of the stone wall of the well. Amaya pulls back, her focus on Mother lost. She screams again, writhing against him. Mason smacks her across the side of the head, and a small gut-wrenching cry rings through the village center.

Flying off the sand and to my feet before the Guardian holding me can react, I slam into Mason, hands still tied behind my back. His broad, muscular frame falters slightly, but remains standing with a tight hold on Amaya and his position. His fist lands across my face, and I flail sideways toward the well, blood gushing from my nose.

Seconds after, my head connects with the stone wall of the well and sand rises to meet my face. Sideways bodies of the village people blur in and out of focus, and nausea rises in my throat. My father's growl rips through the village center. Mason's boot slams into my back. Each sickening, painful thud radiates through my body. I lie limp in the sand. Bile burns in my throat, and I choke it back. The stunned looks of the village people burn into me.

Moments later, the *thwack* of Amaya's small body hitting the foul water below echoes up the wells stone wall.

"May May," I choke, air gone from my lungs.

Somewhere, a girl is screaming. Raw. Devastated.

My mother's face is still, her expression distant, lost in the depths of her mind. Father's eyes are closed, and a river of tears cuts through the stubble on his trembling chin.

Mason pulls me from the sand, and I battle to stand as he drags me to the side of the well. His eyes burn into mine. For a small second, I see a flicker of something less than cold and heartless. It is so quick that I am not sure it was there. Holding me at arm's length with one corded arm, his chest heaving, eyes slightly widened, he stares at me, like he has only just recognized me. Another split second whips past, and I pray he's torn, not wanting to carry out his orders.

"I can't help you, Harm," Mason utters, so quietly that I barely hear the words. His eyes strain slightly wider. He said "Harm," not "Travesci."

"Now, Rayner!" Fletcher growls from behind.

Mason's eyes fade back to emptiness. His gaze switches to his commander and then back to me. A trickle of blood runs down the side of my face, and a smirk pulls up on his. He hangs me over the side of the well. The stone wall is relentless on my bony legs as I try to contort myself to stay standing against his wielding arm.

"Mason, please don't."

A sound somewhere between agony and annoyance escapes Mason. He spins me to face Fletcher, his hand tugs at my wrists swiftly and he shoves me sideways.

I fall, eyes closed, pleading with the desert winds that I land on warm sands.

CHAPTER 13

HARM

The gut-churning feeling of falling swells up around me. My wrists burn, but they are free. The rope is gone. Mason.

Screams ring through the village center, chasing me down the well.

A girl is screaming.

I can't make out her words.

Silence.

Falling.

Finally, I hit the glassy cold water, and pain sears through every inch of my body, then waves of prickled agony. Water jumps up the inside of the well in waves. Thundering in my head splits me apart, and I descend into the water, arms and legs stretched out above me. Greyness floods every inch of my vision, only broken apart occasionally by the air that escapes my lungs, small bubbles above tracking my descent. I close my eyes, and the darkness is the same. There are no shadows, no light. White pinpricks creep in from the sides. As my lungs burn, my arms and legs jerk in protest, but I don't fight it.

She wades through the darkness in my mind. There are no trees, just her and the darkness. Behind her, light flickers to life, a halo surrounds her body, her hair, and finally I see her face. Her blue eyes are deep and fierce, her jaw set, her lips pressed together. She reaches out a hand to me.

She isn't real. I don't reach for her. Her face remains unchanged. But just after the last ounce of air leaves my body, her expression changes. Her face is pained as she begs me, pleading with me. Screaming. "Fight, Harmen, fight!"

It is the first time I have heard her say my name. Her words echo down the well walls, landing on the water's surface that ripples above me. A shape moves past me in the dark water, then another. A pale reddish cloud trailing behind them. My chest is squeezing for air so hard that the fire splits me in half. I thrust my head up and claw up through the water. Every second below the surface turns into hours. The water clears, and I see the rippling surface mere feet from my face.

I break through the plane of water and gasp for air. The air feels like shards of glass in my lungs as I suck in ragged, quick breaths. Adjusting to the dimness inside the well, I search the water and stone around me. On the other side of the water, blood and scratch marks cover the well. The blood is red, fresh. I look below, wading with my hands outstretched on either side of me. Only a small distance below, I see the peaceful bodies of my family, drifting downwards. The red cloud is their blood. They were gone before they hit the water. I stare at them, helpless, as they move further and further away from me.

Irretrievable.

I have lost everything.

There is no way out.

Hours later, small sobs tumble down the tunnel of the well, broken occasionally by whispered pleas for me to fight. Despite the water having risen, I still can't reach the top; my body is too weak. I have nothing left to give. All around me, there is darkness, cold water. Above me in the small round opening, stars lay suspended in their inky blanket.

The world continues, regardless of death. Every breath is heavier than the last, until everything goes black. Exhausted from hours of trying to stay afloat, every inch of my body rung out, I go still. I hardly notice my descent into the dark water; my body is already numb. I exhale, and try to accept my fate.

As the water curls in around me, pleas fall into the well.

"Fight, Harmen!"

Fire rips through my chest again. I thrash my arms and legs. I'm out of air. My face stiffens, and my hands cramp up. I break through the surface for air, just to ease the agony in my chest once more.

Suddenly, large hands grip my shoulders hard and tug upwards. Water rushes down my body, and I slam into the side of the well. The air is knocked out of my lungs, and I cough and gasp in one excruciating motion. Feeling returns, burning its way through every limb. Stone tears through the skin on my injured back like a razor as I am dragged up the side of the well. One hand releases my shoulder and grabs my shirt. The cloth tears, and I drop back down into the water. A small gasp.

"Dammit," a man growls.

Shuffles echo overhead, just over the well wall. Something light and long snakes down the well, hitting the water. Rope.

"No, you stay where you are. I'm not hauling the both of you out," he growls at someone. The rope slides up the well, disappearing over the edge. There is a small grunt, and the crunch of steps around the well.

Again, the hand grabs me, this time under my rigid arm. With one quick motion, I feel myself landing on the dry sand, still warm from the hot day. I flinch as something warm and heavy drops over my whole body. I move my mouth, but all I can manage are incoherent sounds out of my contorted face. Around me, shadows and silhouettes hover. I stare at the night sky, seeing nothing but darkness.

Light persistently invades my eyelids, and I gingerly force them open. Nothing is familiar. This is not my house. The small stone room has tattered curtains, a jug of water, and a chipped ceramic cup. The tang of oil and grease is everywhere. The small, roughly made wooden bunk underneath me creaks as I try to move my aching limbs. The tang of old blood washes through my mouth when I swallow. Soft conversation comes from the next room. The torn flesh on my back stings to life as I try to move again.

A man and a woman are talking. They sound similar in age to my parents. Fear and determination resonate in their voices. I try to make out what they are talking about. Then they say my name. Do they know me? I try to think why I might still be here. I struggle with the bunk and push myself to sit up, trying to hear them better. They are speaking about my parents and Amaya just the way I would have. The voices are not familiar to me, but this man and woman seem to know my family well.

"She was still there when I went to pull him out. I think she had been there since the Guardians left."

"Did she run when she saw you?" the woman asks.

"No, she stayed. She was going to go down there herself to pull him out. Wasn't until I picked him up to leave that she took off." The man sighs. "Strange behavior, even for her."

Footsteps draw toward the little room I am sitting in, and a woman appears in the doorway. Her face is old and lined, tanned by the fierce sun. Her eyes are kind, but look as if she has seen too much in her lifetime. She is tall and thin, and her shoulder-length auburn hair is all but invisible through the volumes of grey. Standing motionless, she looks me over, assessing my condition.

"Harmen, rest. I will bring you something to eat shortly."

I nod in response slowly as she glides out of the room. How does this woman, a stranger to me, know my family so well? I sort through my memories, quickly searching for anything that would connect to the tall, wiry woman. I am at a loss, and I can't figure out who these people are.

I still have on yesterday's clothes. The rotten water has turned them putrid. I slide my hand into my pocket, still slightly damp. My fingers find the smooth, flat surface of the compass case.

Footsteps move toward my room. This time, she holds a tray of food. Setting the tray carefully on the bed in front of me, she sits on the end, pushing the grey blanket aside. On the tray is soup or broth of some sort and two slices of bread. The smell fills the room, and my mouth waters.

"Do you know who I am?" she asks.

"No," is all I manage.

Disappointment briefly crosses her face. "My name is Maryanne. Christopher and I have known your family for a long time." She closes her eyes.

"Where am I?" I force out in a half whisper, holding back the sobs in my aching chest.

She opens her eyes and looks into mine like she is looking at an old friend. "You're safe. All that matters now is that you regain your strength." She pauses, her mouth opens and closes again. "We are very sorry about your family."

My body slackens, throat choked with unshed tears. "I need to leave."

She nods and leaves, pausing with a hand on the doorjam, her head bent down. She turns back and studies my face.

"We know."

CHAPTER 14
HARM

Christopher and I start the slow and cautious trek to the outskirts of Amondo as the sun starts its descent from midday. Similar in build to my father, he stands a head taller than me, his hands stained from working with grease, his hood pulled down low, as is mine. My mind races as we trudge through the scorching sands in silence. I can just see Christopher's face under the face wrap, and I catch a glimpse of the worry consuming him. He looks my way briefly and comes to a halt, motioning me toward a side alley between houses. He lowers his face wrap, and I do the same.

"I'm not sure if you're aware of why things are the way they are in our county." He pauses, waiting for some sort of response from me.

Is he referring to the Guardians? Why are we talking about this now? I need to leave.

"You know—the way things are with the desert we live in, the Guardians, and the rules we all live by?" He pauses again, searching once more for a glimmer of recognition of what he is talking about.

"I understand that the Guardians take what they want, leaving

89

the village people to suffer." What could be so important that we need to stop in the middle of my escape? I know these things.

"Sit down, Harmen." I hesitate, but he waits for me to sit and then does the same. "This desert environment is not the natural state of the land. It was once a magnificent place, with rainfall and rich, fertile soils. The people of Amondo were prosperous and had more than they needed—so much so that some thought this prosperity caused all our crimes. Now, there is very little crime. Everyone is just trying to survive, and no one has the riches we once did. It wasn't always like this. There was no desert, and people didn't just survive, they thrived. There were no penalties, such as the one your family endured for simply not paying taxes. What do you think that would be like, living in a place with trees and grass, rain every other week?"

I know most of this—but what does he mean, the desert is not the natural state of the land? How can that be? The trees he speaks of, I can imagine them very well. I have dreamed of them.

"I see them in my dreams—trees, hundreds of them, green and enormous," I tell him, leaving out the part about the girl.

"Before there was desert, there were trees and rain, grass and animals—and then one thing changed, and we lost it all. The Chancellor is responsible for the desert we live in now. He has the power to alter our weather to create either prosperity with rich, fertile soils and rainfall, or no rainfall and the harsh desert conditions we live in now." He stops talking and gets to his feet. I do the same and follow Christopher as he replaces his face wrap and picks up the pace.

"Wait—what do you mean, he changes the weather? That's not even possible." I march beside his quickening pace.

"We should get you gone, before we're spotted," he mutters.

"No, tell me, please."

He stops and turns to face me. "This desert," he waves his arms around, "was created. We live in this environment that keeps us from prosperity because the Chancellor made it that way. He has the ability to manipulate the dial, creating the environment of his choosing. People live in poverty, starve, and are thrown in the well when they fall short of things to offer, because *he* made it that way."

"Then why hasn't anyone tried to stop him?"

"Someone did, and paid the price for it." His gaze is stuck on the horizon.

"Who?"

A moment passes before his focus returns to me. "Your father."

"What?!"

"Your father, he tried to put a stop to it, to defend our people against the regime—and they tortured your mother, right in front of him." Christopher's face twists.

My stomach roils in a flurry, sending a lump into my throat.

My parents tried. They never told me. "How ... how do you know this?"

"Never mind, I just do," he utters, walking on, tugging his face wrap tighter.

I grab his arm and spin him back to me. "How do you know all this?"

He stares at me now, his face twisted, his mouth pulling down, and moisture swells in his squinting eyes. "Your father was my brother, Harmen." Christopher holds his gaze to mine, and the silver that now lines his eyes sends prickles of tears into my own. I release his arm, dropping my own to my side. I scan his face and build, noting the similarities between my father and the man in front of me. We stand, staring at each other, the sands playing around our feet, oblivious to the storm in both our eyes.

"What?... Why have I never met you?"

"It wasn't long after you were born. He and a few others tried to rally rebels to take down the Chancellor. I tried to talk him out of rebelling. It wasn't the right time. He never spoke to me again—not even after they hurt your mother." He sighs and clears his throat. "I'm sorry for that. Always will be."

Unable to move, I watch as he takes a few more steps toward the outskirts.

"Wait," I murmur. He halts in the sands and turns to face me. "I need to get my mother's journal. It has information about her family."

"Now? That's in the opposite direction!"

"Yes, now." My knuckles turn white on the straps of my rucksack.

He looks around, as if deciding whether it is worth it. "Let's go," he finally says, stalking toward the center of the village.

After what feels like an age, we finally reach the village center, squatting beside the well. Our small stone home is mere feet away, empty. The front door is wide open. Laying my hands on the stone of the well, I rest my forehead on my hands. My family are in there. As I caress the sand-smothered stone, tears slip down my burning face. Christopher goes still beside me. His brother is in there too. He swallows, resting his hand on my shoulder.

Goodbye, Father.

I miss you, Mother.

Bye, May May. I love you, kiddo.

I clench my fists, forcing breath past the lump in my throat. I need a clear head to make it back to my house. I press my knuckles into my eyes, and white spots burst forth from oblivion. Sucking in a deep breath, I refocus.

A Guardian is strolling towards the well. Christopher's hand holds me down. He curses under his breath. I press myself flat against the stone well, sinking into the sand. Part of me wants to stand up. Part of me wants to yell, *"Here I am, put me back in the water with my family!"* But my body doesn't move, and no sound makes its way through my lips. Someone calls out, and the Guardian changes direction, fading into the shadows between homes.

I stretch, peering over the well. The path is clear. We walk as quickly as we can without drawing attention. The wind whips around, tugging at my clothes. Sand flies up, hitting my face, and I protect my eyes with my hand. The village people move about, and I pray nobody talks to us. I need to get inside now.

Skittering across the threshold of our home, I scramble to a halt and grab the door. Christopher files in beside me. Heaving through every move my limbs make, I close the door with heavy arms. I slam my back against the door, sliding to the floor. The overwhelmingly familiar smell of my mother hits me. The agony of loss saps every bit of energy I have left. I didn't think about what it would be like to come home. Now, I wish I hadn't. I sit immobile, pushing breath through the immense pain in my chest. Christopher stands watching as I fight for breath. He pulls down his wrap, looking around our small home.

"Where would the journal be?" he asks.

I slow my breathing and meet his gaze. The stone floor under my hands has a thin layer of rough sand over it—evidence that my mother really is gone. She would sweep this house out every day to rid it of the sands that persistently blew in. Outside, the wind howls, whipping sand into the air. As if in time with the storm in my heart, the weather outside dances with a fury of wind and sand.

I drag myself up the door, legs trembling. "It's under Mother's bed in a tin box."

He tracks down the hallway, familiar with his brother's home. In a morbid trance, I walk through the kitchen to the living room, then to my parents' room. My mother's things sit organized meticulously on the small dresser table my father built for her.

I bend down and stretch out my arm, feeling for a solid box. Nothing. I lower down onto my hands and knees and reach further. Christopher stands in the doorway, eyes scanning for movement outside. My fingers hit metal and I scramble to get a hold of it. It is larger than I remember and takes me considerable effort to slide it out from under the bed. I sit back onto the stone floor and pry open the tight lid. Inside are precious items my mother had kept. One tin box is all that's left of her.

Rummaging through the items, I hunt for her journal that holds the information about her family. So many small things clutter the box. Impatience gets the better of me, and I toss the box over, dumping everything on the sandy floor. A necklace with a blue stone sits on top of the pile. I pluck it from its tower of treasures and turn it over in my hand. Her Blending necklace. Folding my fingers around it, I slide it into the pocket of my trousers with the compass.

A loud noise from outside echoes through our empty home. I freeze. Fear prickles over my sweaty body, and I hold my breath. The wind has picked up its pace. Amongst the pile of treasures sits a leather journal embossed with the initials H. M. S. in gold print. I briefly flick through it, and maps and names cover the pages. Gripping the journal in my hand, I jump to my feet and hurry to the kitchen.

A shadow of a man passes by the window.

"Time to go," Christopher utters, ushering me through the hall and out the front door.

CHAPTER 15
HARM

The village is quiet now with the wind up, and we make our way easily to the outskirts. The drone of an engine reaches us before we can make out its position. Christopher grabs my elbow and pulls me in between two buildings. He points to the dune buggy carrying three Guardians as it approaches the village. "Fletcher, back again."

The buggy carries the usual crew: Fletcher, Mason, and his comrade.

I need to leave. Now.

Waiting until the buggy has entered the village center, I run through the sand to the last ring of homes on the outer perimeter, Christopher behind me. I lean against the wall of the last building, drawing deep breaths.

"Go, now! Don't look back, and don't stop," he says, eyes scanning the sands to the southwest.

"Thank you, Christopher. I hope we meet again." Pushing off the wall, I run like hell into the sands, not looking back.

The paths to the south used by travelers and traders are worn and easy to follow. Every dense stride through the sands sends my heart racing. I increase my strides to cover more ground. The wind picks up, and dense sand swirls around me, offering me cover while I run. No engine drones from behind, and I keep my pace until my legs burn and my chest is ready to explode.

Dropping back to a walk, I swallow. My lips are dry. It's going to be a stretch for the small supply of water I have in the rucksack to keep me going for three days in this heat.

After powering through the sands for over two hours, the village I grew up in, the only place I have ever known, is now a speck in the distance, getting closer to the horizon behind me. The abandoned Guardian outpost that Christopher spoke of should be an hour away. I should get there before nightfall. The desert gives unrelenting heat during the day, only to freeze you while you sleep through the wee hours of the night.

Checking my map, I line up the few landmarks that are visible to double-check my position. On the horizon in front of me, I make out a small, tall building that I can only assume is the outpost I am looking for. To my right, the sun sinks slowly behind the rocky outcrops that are preceded by continuous low dunes. In the low light, three figures move in the distance from the northeast.

Dammit.

I pull the rucksack down tightly on my back and run for the building in the distance, continuously checking over my shoulder. They are closing in on my position. Through the thick sand, my legs burn. I push harder. Sand flies with each stride, and sweat runs down my face. Closer still, the three figures close in. Breath catches in my throat, and I force myself through the dense sand.

Completely out of breath, I barge into the outpost building through a narrow wooden door and slam it behind me. I slide the rusted bolt into its hole, locking the door. I hold myself up against the wall near the only window in the lower half of the building and scan the area I have just come from. Every breath burns through my heaving lungs.

Two figures move to the east. Am I so exhausted that my mind is playing tricks on me? I am sure there were three. Paranoid still, I crack the door open and peer through. Nothing—no movement in the sands. I shut the door and relock the bolt.

Darkness sets in quickly, and I walk around, checking every corner of the building. One last look through the jagged remaining glass proves to me that nothing moves outside in the creeping darkness. In the furthest corner from the door, I settle down. I grab the rucksack and search for the smallest of the food parcels Maryanne packed for me, leaving the larger ones for the days I haven't eaten yet. I unwrap one. A large chunk of bread and some hard cheese sit in the cloth. Biting into the bread, I relax, and I devour the homemade bread. I pick off a small bit of cheese and pop it into my mouth.

The door rattles, the bolt jiggling in its hold, followed by a muffled curse. Knocking hard and fast hits the door. I drop the cheese back down onto the cloth and freeze. I slide the cloth to the floor and rise, stepping over to the window.

A small figure stands waiting outside the door, shuffling from foot to foot, glancing behind themselves every few seconds. I close my fingers around the handle, and it rattles in my hand with another round of fierce knocking. I breathe out and tense up, thinking through the best way to defend myself.

"Let me in! I know you're in there!"

"No."

"Hurry, dammit, let me in!"

"Go away," I call back with a stronger voice, leaning against the door.

"Please." Something light hits the door, and a sigh breathes into the old wood. Light knocks echo through the door. "Please, let me in," they beg, their voice muffled against the door. I slide the bolt from the catch, press the tight handle down, and crack the door open. A figure, smaller than me by almost six inches, stands, arms crossed, blue eyes staring at me through a face wrap and hood. I move, letting him over the threshold.

"The last thing I need is those Guardians trying to rack up favors with the commander, or worse," he says, voice strung high as he walks a small circle before wandering around the decayed front room of the outpost.

"You know the commander?"

He ignores me, walking around still, checking every window and abandoned room before turning back. "No."

His gaze lingers on me before he disappears into a room.

CHAPTER 16
IMANI

I pace around the small, ruined officer's quarters, tugging at my robes. Why is he here? Of all the places he could turn up, it has to be in the only place that I find refuge, away from the Guardians and the villagers. Something low in my belly flutters. It's fine. If I don't talk to him and keep my wrap over my face, he won't bother me. I can wait until dawn and keep moving south. I smooth down the sides of my robe and ensure the wrap covers most of my face.

I make my way to the door, sucking in a long breath. All I have to do is not get involved. It's none of my business anyway. I push the door handle down and walk into the large front room. He is wandering around, looking at my things, touching the items I have left scattered around the ledge where I sleep. My breath catches, sending lightning through my veins.

I clear my throat, and he spins on the spot, going still as his gaze reaches mine. Nothing in his face shows recognition. I let out a breath, relaxing slightly.

"So, you're not a guardian?" he asks.

Heat creeps up my neck the second the words leave his mouth. "Are you daft? What did I just say?"

"Sorry," he utters. He looks at me, his face twisting in concern. "I don't think it's safe for a boy of your age to be out here on your own."

I school my reaction a second before amusement can fill my face and feign a cough. At least I won't have to worry about him recognizing me. I suppress the urge to roll my eyes at him. "Who I am and what I'm doing is none of your concern."

Letting out a long breath, he slumps his shoulders. "I'm traveling south."

"This is where I stay when I come through this part of the county. There has never been anyone here before," I say before turning away from him. I wander over to the ledge covered in my bedding, checking that all my possessions are still here. They are.

"I'm just passing through and don't want any trouble," Harmen says.

"Fine. You stay on that side, and I'll stay on this side, but I'll be watching you, so don't bother trying anything." Sitting down, I take off my rucksack and weapon belt. I noticed he doesn't carry a weapon. Typical conformist.

He moves to the opposite side of the room and slides down the wall to the floor before rummaging through his own rucksack. He picks up some cheese and takes small bites. My stomach growls and my mouth waters at the thought of tasting cheese right now. Hunger pangs low in my belly, and I swallow. With a last glance at his food, I make up my bed on the ledge.

Shifting on my dusty space to get more comfortable for the night, I close my eyes. The pain in my stomach intensifies, and my head aches. Losing a sigh, I sit up and dive a hand into my rucksack, hunting for the leftover cured meat strips. I find one last leathery morsel and pop it into my mouth. The bitter brine makes my mouth twist, and I force it down.

Harmen pulls out a chunk of bread. That's it. He is sharing with me, whether he likes it or not. I jump down from my bed and stalk over to him. He looks up from his food, crumbs on his fingers, the smell of the bread turning my mouth into a watering mess.

"You want half ?" he asks, tracking my gaze to the bread in his hand. I almost fall to the ground beside him, but slap a hand against the wall and nod. He tears the bread in half, handing it up to me. My hand trembles as I brush my fingers against his holding the bread.

His eyes are locked on mine, and for the first time in a what feels like a lifetime, I see no malice or anger, just kindness. How can someone so good have such terrible things happen to him? My heart cracks a little. He smiles shyly as I pluck the bread from his hand. I shove the sentiment down. Forcing out an utterance of thanks, I pad back to my bed. I fight back the urge to change my plans to accommodate him. I am not getting involved.

Sitting cross-legged on the bedding, eyes falling shut, I savor every bite. It is so good. When I open my eyes, he is watching me, still smiling, as if seeing such a simple joy in another person is the best thing in the world. I ignore him, sending my gaze around the outpost, checking that my only home is intact, trying not to think about the boy who is sitting in it watching me.

Content with the absence of hunger pains, I lay back after chugging half of my canteen. With an almost full belly, I roll onto my side, knees up and hands under my head. I watch as he tidies up his food, wrapping up the remaining tidbits and shoving them back into his rucksack.

An hour passes, and he stills, his breathing slows, and his eyes slide shut. He topples to the right. Jerking awake, he sits back up, eyes drifting shut instantly. I close mine, desperate for sleep.

Light fights its way through the opaque sand-blasted windows, and for a heartbeat I hold my breath as I piece together where I am: my place, or at least, my temporary place. I roll over. He is still dozing, so I let sleep take me under again.

Footsteps creep closer to where I lay. They stop next to me, and I keep my eyes shut. With the ruffling of my rucksack, I hold my breath, giving him the benefit of the doubt. I owe him that much. The clasp on my weapon belt clinks, and I snap my eyes open. He doesn't notice, and I spin, shoving my foot into his chest. He flies backward, landing hard on the gritty stone floor. Breath leaves his chest, and he gasps for air, tears lining his eyes as he scrambles to roll onto his side. Harmen grabs his chest, coughing.

Slowly, I stand and walk over to him. Hands on my hips, I press my boot into his chest, flattening him back to the floor. The filtered morning light illuminates the brown and cream rags that wrap around me like a curtain—baggy long trousers and a plain cream top that has seen better days, sporting several rips. I freeze for a second, praying my head wrap is still secured around my hair and face. I can see a wisp of dark hair that has escaped out the side. I whisper a curse.

"What do you think you're doing?" I demand, holding his gaze.

"I was just looking, honest. I wouldn't take anything."

"Right."

"You didn't have to kick me in the chest." He tries to rise, but I hold him down with my foot.

"You shouldn't have tried to steal my stuff." I sigh, now feeling guilty for overreacting, especially after his kindness to me. "Got any more of that food?"

"A little." His face crunches into a frown as his dark eyes scan my frame. Feeling instantly self-conscious about my too-thin body that I can barely feed, living the life of a wanderer, I pull my robe around and hold it tight.

"Would you like some cheese?"

I lift my foot from his chest and stand up straight. It has been an age since I have had cheese. *Would I like some cheese? More than you will ever know, Harmen.* I nod.

"You can have some cheese and bread. That's all I have." He motions to his rucksack. Standing, he dusts himself off. He hesitates for a moment, standing almost a head taller than me, he is so close. I track my gaze up his body, meeting his eyes. He stares back momentarily before heading to his side of the room.

Grabbing the remains of his bread and cheese, he makes his way back over to my side of the room and hands over the portion. It is gone in seconds.

"Where are you going?" he asks, washing down his half with his canteen.

"South. Where are you going?" I watch as he returns to the other side of the room and packs his rucksack.

He turns back. "South, also. Do you know how to get to the south villages?"

"Yep."

I shove my things into my rucksack. It would be a good idea to check out what I can see from the lookout of the old outpost. I climb up the stairs with the rucksack secure on my back. The stairs crumble under every step, sand and desert winds curling their way down the ruins of the stairwell. Standing on one of the broken pieces of structural stone, I peer out over the highest point of the tower.

Desert flanks the outpost in every direction, reaching the sky to form the horizon. Nothing for miles. A small patch of desert trees with their thin grey leaves, which just look like a lump of grey from this far away, stands amongst the sands.

Harmen files in beside me. "Not many landmarks," he says, pulling out a compass from his pocket and checking the orientation of the clump of trees. It is a perfect reading for south.

"We'll manage," I say, ignoring the war inside me, the voice telling me to leave him behind. He smiles at me before descending the stairs.

Checking the path is clear, we step out of the old outpost and start the walk to our landmark destination. The hot wind hits my face, and the sun burns my back, even though it's early morning. Walking in silence, we are making good progress, and I am appreciating not having to do this alone, at least today. My traveling companion easily keeps up with my quick pace. Without stopping, I reach for my water canteen and take a few sparing sips. This water must last me until I get to the gypsy camp.

Impatiently wanting the shade of the trees, I pick up the pace, and so does Harmen. Heat waves float above the sand, covering the last stretch, before we finally reach the trees and step into their sparse, cooling shade. I take off my rucksack and sit down, my back leaning up against a skinny tree trunk. He does the same. Wetting a small rag with my canteen, I wipe it across my forehead, removing the sweat and dirt. Harmen stretches every limb, joints cracking. With one hand grasping the side of my wrap, I undo the material and pull it off to one side, shaking out my long hair.

Harmen freezes beside me, his eyes wide. I move my gaze to the waves of heat that hover over the sands, stretching my neck from side to side before lifting my hair off my neck to fan myself.

"You, you're—" he gasps.

"A girl?" I snort. "Clever one you are." I shake my head,

sending waves of dark curls over my shoulders. The cooler breeze it makes is so satisfying. Harmen sits watching me, his mouth agape. I suppress the urge to roll my eyes at him.

"Sorry, I—It's not that, I ..." he stammers.

"You just thought I was a boy because I'm out here alone." I return my gaze to his. "Typical." I sit in the sand next to him, completely still, and his eyes study every inch of me. My heart thunders in my chest, and I fight the urge to cover up again, feeling way more exposed than I am.

"And who are you when you're not running around hiding in Guardian outposts?" I ask, schooling my face into an expression of ignorance. His stare is still frozen on my face.

"H-Harmen. My name is Harmen."

"Mm-hmm," I agree with him. "Imani. My name is Imani." I raise one eyebrow.

"Oh," he utters, a simper grows on his face and he studies me. I hold his gaze as long as I can before breaking away to rummage through my rucksack. I swallow, remembering to breathe.

"Why are you out here? And why are you by yourself?" he utters tentatively.

I draw in a deep breath. Blood thunders through my neck. I grip my hands around my canteen. "Do I have to answer your questions? What happens if I don't?"

He stands and readjusts his robe. "Nothing happens. Do as you please." His are eyes fixed on mine again, as if I will vanish out of existence if he takes them off me.

"Fine by me. Just keep out of my way, and you won't get hurt." I rest a hand lightly on my belt.

He takes a sip of his canteen, closing his eyes. Sweat drenches his shirt and sticks to his back. The water in his canteen is low, judging by the swooshing sounds that come from it every time he lifts it to his lips. I stand and grab my rucksack, swinging it over one shoulder. I look up at him, standing by his side. The veins in his neck pulse under the sheen of sweat coating his neck. A trickle of water runs down his throat, over his chest and disappears beneath his shirt. I jerk my gaze away and twist my dark curls around and wrap them up again, hands working the cloth with precision like I have done a thousand times before.

Digging out the map from his rucksack, he traces a finger along the line between Amondo and our current position, then to the next village, Trindari.

Not a place you want to go, Harmen.

"That will be my next stop," he says, circling the dot on the map with his finger. "I calculate it will take a half day's walk from this small patch of shade to Trindari. I've never heard of it before, but I need to find water."

Who hasn't heard of Trindari? "You don't want to go there."

"Why not? I need water." His eyes narrow, and irritation lines his voice for the first time.

I hold his gaze. "It's definitely not safe for someone like you."

"What's that supposed to mean?"

"Just don't go there. It's not a place for clean skins like you." I hope he is getting the hint. You don't go to Trindari unless you're looking for trouble or you *are* trouble. Harmen does not belong in either of those categories.

As he stands beside me, my smaller frame is so obvious next to his now.

"What's your plan, then? What about water?" he asks.

"We travel southwest to the gypsy camps. They are always willing to help fellow desert travelers."

"That will add extra traveling to my plan. I'm going to Trindari." He fixes his wrap around his face, highlighting his dark eyes.

"How long have you been out here? Trust me, I know what I'm talking about." I adjust my head wrap in one clean motion.

After all he has been through in the past week, the last thing he ought to do is go stumbling into Trindari. Heat rises in my face. He treads into the hot sands. Briefly, he fishes the compass from his pocket and checks his heading. I trudge through the sand behind him.

"Stop! Where are you going?"

"South, like I told you before."

"Are you stupid? Don't go that way!"

He keeps walking.

"Don't expect me to follow you!"

"Fine by me!" He throws up a hand as his voice fades into the waves of heat floating across the sands between us.

"Stubborn ass. Get yourself strung up, then!" I doubt he can hear me with the winds that careen across the desert plains, and for a minute I regret my decision to go my own way, but it doesn't last.

CHAPTER 17
HARM

Every step away from Imani was devastating after dreaming about her for months. But I can't afford to be distracted. I have to get to the south and find my mother's family. Being out of Fletcher's reach is the only thing that will save me. I'm sure of it.

At least two hours have passed. My water is gone. I can just make out the outline of a village on the horizon. Other travelers are moving towards the village from the west. My clothes are now drenched with sweat, and I long for some shade. I increase my stride, each breath searing through my lungs. Similar to Amondo, the village houses are organized in rings, with the water source on the outskirts of the village, a functioning well. I pull my canteen from my rucksack and lean over to find the pulley rope.

The stench of decaying bodies hits me, and I turn around and drop to my knees. With the smell embedded in my nose, my stomach revolts, and I stay there on my hands and knees, dry heaving. Horror floods through me, thinking about the bodies of my own family. I try to breathe, realizing I can't bring attention to myself.

I move over to the side of a building and scan for Guardians. Legs shaking, I stand and force myself to the center of the village, still concealed by my wrap. The waves of nausea peter out slowly. With a hand pressed to my chest, I let out a long breath, waiting for the stench curling inside my senses to subside.

I find a functioning well with clean water in the center next to the village hall, and I fill my canteen. A young boy walks around me like a curious animal. He looks about eight years old.

"I don't know you. Where are you from?" he asks.

"I'm just traveling through."

"Where are you going?"

"South."

With a grin, he moves closer, and I stand taller, fixated on his movements.

"Okay," he says quickly with a grin, and runs off. Stashing my canteen back into the rucksack, I dig out my mother's journal, checking the map. The next village before the southernmost village is Donterra. If I can find the outskirts of Trindari and track my direction from there using the compass, I won't lose any more time. I trudge through the village, heading south.

The village of Trindari is reasonably quiet, and only one or two men are out and about, attending to various tasks. The women and children are inside, staying out of this heat. A tavern lit up by rowdy noise sits to my left, and I duck down a narrow lane, searching for the way out. Three men are loitering at the end of the lane.

"Excuse me, I'm trying to get to the southern outskirts. Can you help me?" I ask.

They turn as one to consider me, and a prickle creeps up my spine.

"Did you hear that, boys? 'Excuse me.' What a polite one we have here," the tallest man says in a mocking tone.

"'Can you help me'?" the next man says in a squeaky voice.

"What you got in that rucksack, boy?" the last man demands as he grabs my rucksack, ripping it from my back. The other two men lurch toward me and grab my arms with a rough hold.

"Let go of me!" I growl. But they grin and laugh, looking at me like prey.

"I think this one needs to be toughened up, lads," the man with my rucksack says.

"Looks a little soft, if you ask me!" the next man sneers, sinking his fist into my stomach. Breath rushes from my lungs, and I crumple in half. They laugh, their rough hands holding me on my feet.

"We'll do you a deal, peaches. You give us the rucksack and your clothes, and we won't kill you."

I realize they are not grinning anymore, and a shudder creeps through my body. No. I need those things to find my way south. My heart flogs against my ribs in a wild dance. I open my mouth to beg, but I can't form the words.

The man in front of me nods, and the two hands gripping me release. "Take off your clothes and hand them over," he snaps. My father's compass weighs heavily in my trouser pocket. Rage ignites low in my torso. I lunge for the man. Two hard hands grab my arms, ripping me backward. I struggle against them, but the hands only grip harder. In mere minutes, I lose everything. They have the rucksack, my clothes, my father's compass, and my mother's journal and treasures.

My bare feet drag through the hot sand as the two smaller men pull me towards a solitary post standing in the desert sun past the outskirts of the village. Old, bloodied ropes dangle in the hot winds. They force my arms up over my head and tie my wrists up to the top of the post. The sun is already burning my skin and the rope cuts into me. With every part of me exposed, the heat burns into my bare skin.

I tug at the ropes and they tighten, searing my wrists. My chances of getting loose are not good. Even if I do get loose, how am I going to get to the next village with no clothing to protect me, and no water, no map, and no compass? Heaviness sinks in my chest, and I swallow back the lump choking me. Tears roll down my face. Imani was right. I won't survive on my own.

I hang lifelessly, half asleep as the pain from the agonizing heat takes its toll on my bare body. My skin is tight and burning. My lips are chapped, and my arms and hands hanging above me are numb. The sun is descending, and I wait impatiently for the relief of nightfall. With heavy eyes, I drift off, bobbing around the threshold of consciousness.

Shuffling through the sand fades in. Eyes wide, I twist from side to side, but the post blocks the view directly behind me. *Please don't be a desert viper.* They bite you twice. Once to paralyze, once to kill. I scan the sand for their black-and-white pattern. The ropes burn into my wrists while I fling around in my bonds with ragged breaths.

The shuffling comes closer, and I tense every muscle. Something bumps into the back of the post.

"Get away!" I scream. "Leave me to die in peace!"

Thud.

The post shudders.

Thud.

Thud. Over my head this time.

Again, the thing hits the back of the post. A small grunt comes from behind me. Vibrations on my wrists sting with every jerk of the rough fiber. A blade saws back and forth ...

Snap!

I tumble into the sand face-first.

CHAPTER 18
IMANI

His shoulder burns under my touch as I tug it, rolling him over. His wide, brown eyes burn into mine, and I hold their focus, acutely aware of his corded and very naked body at my feet. I throw his clothes and boots onto his bare skin. "You're welcome."

Heat rises in his face, and I chuff out a laugh before turning around. But the flip in my stomach kicks up my pulse, and I stifle a moan.

"Next time, you'll listen to me, clean skin," I say, sheathing my knife in my belt, half turning back. He grabs at his clothes, which I scavenged from the village. But the rope around his wrists is still tied tight.

"A little help here?" he says hoarsely, sitting up. The clothes rustle, falling into his lap.

I turn and lean down, looking him straight in the eye, and a sideways grin splits across my face as I slide the blade from my belt. With one swift move, I cut his wrists loose, not breaking eye contact.

"We need to get a move on before anyone notices you're not hanging on your post anymore," I point out, eyes still locked on his.

He scrambles to his feet and shoves them into the legs of the trousers. Sand hisses down into the legs, but he doesn't seem to notice. He's in a hurry. I spin and stalk into the dunes, briefly looking back to see if he follows. Tossing the shirt over his head and arms, he jogs barefoot to catch up, pulling the shirt down as he goes. I turn back into the darkness and head west.

"Where are we going?" he asks, slightly out of breath, filing in beside me, hopping from foot to foot as he pulls on his boots. "To the gypsy camp, about two hours' walk. Hopefully, we can get there before the cold sets in."

"Hold on—what about my stuff? Those thugs stole everything! I need it back." He stops in the sand. Heat fills my core. If he had listened to me in the first place, we wouldn't have ended up here. I stop and spin around, my glare meeting his and step into his space, letting annoyance curl my lips. Eyes wide, his arms drop to his sides, and he falters backward a step.

"And risk our necks for a few trinkets? I don't think so. I've already wasted time having to save your neck," I grind out, barely tempering the surge of anger. I turn back, walking on.

"They're not just trinkets, they're valuable, and I need the rucksack and everything in it to continue my journey to the south." He grabs my arm.

I turn, slowly, heat now rising through my core and chest. I grunt and rip my arm from his grip and walk on. He draws a long breath, blowing it out. I turn back, waiting for whatever is about to come out of his mouth. Arms crossed over my chest and my mouth a tight line, I fix a heated gaze to his.

He slackens and runs his hands through his hair. Sand falls, and so does his gaze. I can feel the defeat from here. The heat in my body ebbs as his eyes lift to meet mine again. Losing a breathy curse, I spin and push through the sand to the west. There is no way I can leave him out here by himself. So much for not getting involved.

As the cooler air sinks down to meet us, we approach the gypsy campsite. Lanterns sit in the sand, flanking a path toward the camp with flickering flames. Music, laughter, and fragrant spices fill the spaces between colorful wagons and large cream-colored tents, and people drift and weave between them. A large fire sits in the sands in the center of their temporary village, with pillows and rugs set out around it. Rowdy, colorfully dressed people are scattered throughout. Children run around barefoot, rags hanging off their bodies instead of proper clothes, squealing with delight as they careen through the sands playfully. Women wearing gold bracelets and long colorful skirts watch their children, and smiles bloom on their faces as they see us arrive.

My cousin greets me with open arms, and I relax instantly. "Imani, it has been too long."

"I know, Indie. It's good to be back."

Harmen looks around the camp with the wonder of a small child. I school the grin from my face and shift so Indie can be introduced.

"Who is this young man? Where is your traveling robe and wrap?" she asks, one brow raised.

"Long story, but this is Harmen."

He offers her a shy smile and holds out a hand. "Hello."

She takes his hand, shaking it, returning the smile. The delight on my face grows as I move through the camp, exchanging greetings and hugs with women and children. Harmen follows me, a few steps behind, only slightly awkward.

"Come on, I'll find you a place by the fire before you freeze," I say, gesturing to the center of the gathering. He follows me to the fire, and we find an empty rug. I dump my belongings on it.

"This will do for now. I'll ask Indie about a tent for you later. You can—"

"Look who the north winds blew in!" a voice booms from behind us.

My heart skips a beat, and a grin splits my face before I spin on the sand to face the large man. He stands with his arms open, eyes lit up, wearing a grin that could light up the sun itself. Jonah. I spring towards him, throwing myself into his arms like a little girl. They wrap around me, holding tight. He drops his head next to mine, and I swallow back the lump in my throat. I draw in his smell. Home.

He releases me, holding me at arm's length, looking me over, despite only a month having passed since I was last here. The weathered lines on his face are the same, and his eyes shine as he studies my face. "I have missed you, my girl." His gaze drifts over my shoulder, and his expression fades. I step out of his hold and turn towards Harmen.

"Jonah, Harmen." I gesture to him with a wave. "Harmen, Jonah." Returning the wave in my uncle's direction.

Harmen stands and shakes Jonah's hand, before letting his arms fall to his sides again. "Good to meet you, sir," he offers and leaves, dropping onto the mat.

Jonah's mouth compresses into a thin line before he clears his throat. He wraps an arm around me and kisses my hair. I fight off the rising heat in my cheeks and turn into the hug.

"Great, well, I'm starving. What are the ladies cooking up tonight?" Jonah says, releasing me, and I drop onto the mat beside Harmen. Jonah watches us before finding a seat with the men. Indie and one of the other women pass around plates piled with steaming grains and meat. We eat in silence, washing down the food with my canteen.

The cool night air rolls in, and we move closer to the fire. Children are falling asleep beside their parents on their woven mats. One of the older men tells a story about a great forest. He talks of masses of trees, and the man who controls the desert counties. Harmen listens to every word, enraptured by the stories I have heard a hundred times before.

The children are all asleep, and the adults, who have heard this story many times, disengage from his smooth words. Indie lowers a hand, I take it, and she leads me to a tent.

"This is yours while you're here. It's so good to have you back, Imani." Indie pulls me into a tight embrace. "Jonah was so worried about you. You need to come home more often."

"I know. I just have things to do." I sigh, holding her tight before letting her go.

She offers a sad smile and tilts her head. "You can't save everyone, cousin."

"That's the hardest part, Indie. If only I could," I utter, the lump in my throat blocking the last word. She grabs my hands and rubs them with her thumbs. "Hey, you do more good in this world than all of those so-called rebels put together. Don't you ever beat yourself up for not being at every godforsaken village every time."

I nod and swallow back the burning in my throat. She sets her shoulders back and tilts her chin up. I do the same.

"Any luck finding someone with the ability to change the dial?" she asks.

"Nothing. It's like it doesn't even exist. Maybe it doesn't."

"Jonah says it does, so it does. Don't give up, and when you need my help, you know you only have to ask." She holds the tent flap open, and I glance towards the fire. Harmen is laying on one side, curled up like sleep has already found him. The magnificent carpet of stars shines so brightly that they almost drown out the flicker of the fire.

"Night," I offer.

"Good night, Imani," she says, walking to her caravan. I slip inside the tent and sink to the soft blankets. *One.* I helped save one, this time around. It isn't enough. But I am glad he is here. I lie down and run through the last four weeks in Amondo. Before long, my breathing is ragged, and tears stream down my temples, soaking the pillow.

I only saved one.

Harmen has lost his whole family.

The moment he handed me the bread back in the outpost plays in my mind. His dark eyes, still full of kindness, even after all he has lost. My chest aches like it will split in half at any moment. I choke through stifled sobs until sleep finds me.

CHAPTER 19
HARM

A sharp cry echoes through the slumbering camp. I sit up, breathless. Another cry, full of so much pain that it transforms into a scream. It comes from the tent next to Indie's caravan.

Imani.

I rush over to her tent and pull back the flap. She is tossing and writhing in her covers. Hesitating, deciding whether to enter her tent, I hover at the entrance. She screams again. I drop to my knees and crawl over to her. I grab her shoulders and shake her gently. She doesn't wake up. I put my arms under her small shoulders and lift her up to wrap my arms around her, hoping to protect her from whatever is going on in her head. Her eyes fly open, unseeing. She reels backward and slaps my face. The sting bites my cheek instantly, and heat sweeps up from my core and into my cheeks.

"Get off me!" she yells.

I release my hold, and she inches away from me.

"Imani, it's Harmen."

She thumps my chest with both fists.

"Cut it out. I'm trying to help you," I growl.

Her hands pause, resting on my chest. "What are you doing in my tent?" She drops her hands to her lap.

"You were screaming in your sleep. I was trying to help." I move back to the doorway of the tent, a good two feet away from her. Imani's chest rises and plunges, but her eyes soften as she takes in my face, now fully awake.

Indie appears between the tent flaps. "Imani, are you alright?" She looks between the both of us.

"I'm fine," Imani breathes.

"You should go back to your mat." Indie motions for me to go. I leave the tent and start heading back. Indie grabs my arm, and I turn around, ready to explain that I was only trying to help. Her face is twisted with worry. She releases my arm.

"Imani went to Amondo, around four weeks ago. I don't know what happened there, but this is the first time in years she has had a nightmare like that."

I stand in the dim light of the dying fire, staring as she retreats to her caravan. I lie back down next to the fire and replay what she just said to me. Imani had been in Amondo for four weeks. Was she there when Fletcher executed my family? I roll onto my side and lie in the glow of the leftover embers, tears trickling down my cheeks, thinking about my parents, and my little sister.

I miss them.

I miss Amaya.

My chest twists until the pain steals my breath. The flickering embers dance their way through my pain until my ragged breathing pushes me into oblivion.

Clanging jolts me awake. The roaring fire that had kept me comfortable all night has died down to ashes and wisps of smoke.

Breakfast sits on the mat beside me, a bowl of last night's meal. Around me, men are packing up the caravans and tents for the next stretch across the desert. Sitting up, I grab the bowl and shovel breakfast in. There is no movement in Imani's tent. She must be still asleep. I stare at her makeshift bedroom while I eat breakfast.

"She not in there," Jonah says, watching me for a moment. "She took off before dawn." He goes back to his packing. I stand up to get out of the way of the woman who wants to roll up my rug to pack it.

"You can travel with us for the day. We're going in the same direction. She mentioned you two are headed south," Jonah offers.

"Thanks." I nod in appreciation. Without my rucksack, my mother's journal, or my compass, I have little choice but to follow them. Despite last night in her tent, heat rises in my throat, remembering Imani's complete disregard for my possessions. Now she has ditched me here with these people, knowing I have no way to navigate my way south.

I get to work helping the men pack the caravans. I fling the rope around the sleeping mats, tying them to the side of the caravan. The knots tighten under my white grip, and I let out a growl.

The wind plays in the sands once again, creating micro-sandstorms for us to wade through in the intolerable heat. The trek is slow, and I have more than enough time to think about Imani ditching me with these people. They are kind, just like she said, but I am trying to get to the south without getting captured by the Guardians or dying in the desert. And every step takes me further away from my possessions that are essential for my journey to the south and to find the family my mother wrote about in her journal.

By the time the sun is high in the sky, I am fuming and have a few things lined up to say to her when I see her again, whenever that will be. She will go back to Trindari with me to get my belongings back. I won't give her a choice.

The caravans stop for lunch. We sit in silence, sheltered by the shade of the large vehicles, and consume our pickings from the food bags. Jonah sits with me and two of the men, chatting idly about the chance of a sandstorm. The children are playing on the other side of the first caravan, shouting and whipping around like the wind in the hot sands.

Suddenly, the yelling between the children changes. Something is wrong. A woman screams and calls for Jonah. He rushes to the other side of the caravan. I jump to my feet and jog after him.

The women and children are standing around in a circle. The woman in the center tries to part the crowd. Heavy breathing cuts through them, followed by the tang of blood. The children are sent back to the caravans with two women, ushering them away quickly, making way for Jonah.

Urgency fills the air around us, and I push past the others to get to the center of the group of people. Jonah steps into the center of the circle. The small figure dressed in rags sways with exhaustion, blood trickling from one arm. I push past the last person. Blood drips onto the sand from their fingertips. The cut is deep, and I lift my gaze, scanning their body. The clothes are familiar: worn trousers and a ripped cream shirt. With their head covered, only their eyes are visible through the wrap. Brilliant blue eyes wander across the crowd.

I walk forward. "Imani?"

My rucksack hangs from her shoulder. Her eyes find mine. She collapses into the bloodied sand, eyes on trained on me. I grab her under the arms, holding her up. Jonah steps aside, making a path through the worried crowd. "She needs to be attended to immediately."

I scoop her up and carry her to Indie's caravan. Inside, there is a small bunk, and I lower her onto it. She is now unconscious. Indie peels off her headdress before ripping her sleeve open to assess her wound. Her head is fine, but her face and lips are pale and chapped. The second woman has a bowl of water and a rag. She lifts Imani's torn shirt where the blood has stained it, but pauses. They both look at me simultaneously.

"I'll come back in a little while and see how she is." I descending the stairs. Indie offers a brief nod before returning her attention to Imani.

My rucksack lies in the sand where she had collapsed, and I walk over and retrieve it. Inside is every item I own. Guilt courses through every part of me, remembering the thoughts I'd had earlier. The men are checking the caravans, and Jonah is talking to one of the young women, who is sobbing. Imani is clearly more familiar with these people than she has let on. They are her family.

Indie steps out of her caravan and walks over to me. "She's dehydrated. I would say she has been running for hours."

"She went to Trindari," I murmur, staring at the caravan.

"That explains the injuries. The cut on her arm is deep, but it's taken care of for now. She needs to rest for a couple of days to recover from the dehydration. Stay with us. Jonah could use the company."

She walks back to her caravan, and I make my way over to Jonah where he stands adjusting straps on the caravan.

"How's my girl?" he asks.

"A deep cut and dehydration, but Indie says she will be okay. But ..."

Jonah looks from what he is doing to me. "Imani can't travel with me for now. Can I stay with you for a few days?" I need her to get to the south villages if I want to survive the desert.

"You can bunk with me in the first caravan. My traveling companion left a while ago, so it's just me. It will be nice to have some company again."

"Thank you." I throw my rucksack into the caravan and head to the front to sit with Jonah.

"How did you meet Imani?"

"In an abandoned Guardian outpost. She kicked me in the chest for touching her stuff."

Jonah throws his head back and laughs.

Not the entire truth. I had seen her in our village twice before, but never actually met her, just dreamed about her. I keep that part to myself.

"I have known her since she was a little girl. Her mother is my sister. Indie is her cousin. They have always been very close." He forces a smile, but then his face drops. "Imani comes to us from time to time. She hasn't lived with her mother and father for some time now." His hazel eyes are kind, but sadness hangs there.

"I don't think she tells anyone much. I have only known her for a couple days, and for the first day, I thought she was a boy."

Jonah shakes his head, letting loose a chesty laugh. "Imani doesn't like people to think she's weak. She'll be the first one to tell you her mother is, but that's youth talking. She will see it differently one day."

"She ran away from home?"

He meets my gaze. "Yes, I guess you could say that. She didn't see things the way her father did. It was a problem for her, and she left." He sways with the moving caravan.

"Indie is your daughter?"

"Niece."

"So, you never Blended?" Curiosity surpasses my manners.

"I was, but I lost my wife in childbirth, and my son Luca to the regime nine years ago. He would be twenty-two now. I never saw him again after they took him."

"I'm sorry," I say, and mean it wholeheartedly.

"Not as much as I am." He glances at me before turning back to the sands in front of us.

"The story about the man who controls the weather—I have heard of it before, and I've been told it's the Chancellor, but how do you know who else has the ability? And what is that, exactly?"

Jonah's eyes widen slightly. "Sometimes I forget that your generation has such a limited education. It's a shame, really. Only those who have the ability can manipulate the dial. Why do you ask?"

"Father used to get books from the traders. He said they weren't allowed anymore, but I never understood that. Schooling until you're ten never felt like enough learning for me. We were lucky my parents made us read everything they could get their hands on. How would I find the person with the ability if I wanted to?"

He looks at me and smiles. "Even if someone were to find a person who can change the dial back, they would have to be brave enough to try. We have lived under this rule for a long time. People who are oppressed for that long are not likely to rise and succeed. And who's saying that this person would be young enough to survive the journey through the desert, anyway?"

He stops the caravan and stares ahead at the waves of heat that float in front of us. One hundred feet out a Guardian outpost sits in the sands. In a few moments, the entire convoy has come to a halt.

"You need to hide. If you've escaped, like Imani told us, you're not safe to go through that outpost. Hide in the caravan Imani is in, under her bunk. They won't lift the long blankets with the women there," Jonah says, gesturing for me to hurry.

"Aren't the outposts abandoned?" I climb down the steps. How does Imani know I escaped the regime?

"This one isn't. It is the last before the southern villages, so they always man it as a sort of border control." He motions for me to go. I jump off the last step and jog back to the fourth vehicle, where the women and Imani are. I scramble into the caravan.

"I need to hide. Jonah told me to get under the bunk." Indie nods and lifts the blanket closest to her. I slide down under the bunk, and Indie adjusts the blanket, concealing me. The tang of blood from Imani's wound fills the small space. I lay still and try not to move as the caravan makes its way through the sand again, swaying from side to side. The two women continue talking. Above me, the bunk rocks side to side as well, and the rusty, stretched wire springs dip under Imani's weight.

The caravan crawls to a stop. The door opens, and polite exchanges take place between the two women and three Guardians. One of them must have noticed Imani and speaks to the women. "What happened here?"

"Dehydration from the heat," Indie says.

"She'll have to be more careful next time," the officer grunts.

"Yes," Indie replies as the Guardian moves back down the steps. The caravan starts up again. With the rocking, something drops from above me. Imani's fingers are bending and stretching, searching for something. I place my hand in hers and she squeezes it. She lets go and lifts her arm back onto the bed.

By the end of the day, we reach the last village that stands between us and the south, Donterra. We make a campsite on the outskirts of the village, and I help the men to set up the fires and makeshift tents for the night. The women are preparing the meal while the children buzz around them, blowing off steam from being cooped up in the caravans most of the day.

A handful of the men go into the village to barter for food and supplies, while others go about their evening chores. The sweet smell of the campfire smoke inhibits my senses as I wander around the arid landscape to find wood to burn for the night. The desert has changed since we have come further south, with less sand and more rocky plains with dirt and heat-loving plants that sport sharp spines, keeping you from trying to steal their leaves.

Arms finally full of firewood from the meager pickings of the rocky plain, I turn back to the campsite. A small figure walks toward me. The last of the sun's rays blind me, and I raise a hand tentatively. Squinting, I make out Imani. She is shuffling through the sand, holding her arm. She stops a few feet away, watching me with the wood.

"You should be resting," I say flatly.

"I'm not tired."

"You know what I mean."

"Did you get your rucksack back?"

"Yes, thank you. You didn't have to go off and try to get yourself killed for it."

"I didn't—and I thought you needed it."

"I do." I hold her gaze.

We make our way back to the camp in silence and sit next to the fire after I dump the firewood. Everyone eats in silence. Tension that wasn't there last night fills the spaces between us. Imani sits next to me and Jonah as we finish our meals.

No stories tonight. The children go to bed moments after the stars fill the night sky. A marvelous quilt of shimmering points hangs above us now. Sleeping under the stars with the gypsies makes me feel free. Lying next to Imani, it is the perfect moment, looking up at the stars, campfire smoke dancing around us, with the soft calls of the night animals.

"Jonah has told me we can stay with him until the south villages," she says. "Our next stop will be Perendi. It will be safer for you, and I know he is worried about me after today. He worries too much. I can take care of myself."

I study her face. She doesn't look happy about going to

Perendi, eyes hunting the night sky. What is she thinking? "Once we reach the south villages, I will find my mother's family and leave you be. What are you going to do after we reach the south?"

"I have no intentions of going back north. That's not where I need to be. If things are ever going to change, someone needs to find a southerner with the ability to change the dial."

Right hand under her head, and her left arm lying supported on her stomach, her eyes are closed. My heart thunders in my chest and I roll over to face her. "The ability comes from the south? Do you think you could find them?"

"Guess so. I mean, there can't be that many people in the south villages, anyhow. They have a birthmark on their head—pretty obvious, from what I can gather." Her eyes are still closed.

"Jonah said they may not want to help."

"He did? You spoke to him about it?" Imani's eyes open, now searching mine.

"When I left Amondo, I was determined to find my mother's family, to start a new life in the south villages away from the Guardians." I suck in a breath. "But what would be even better would be if the Chancellor were overturned, removing the regime. If I can help with that, I am all in." I think of Arlo. If he were here, he would be right along side me. He would like Imani.

There is a long pause. "So, we go together, then," Imani says.

"Okay, but you have to promise not to run off trying to get yourself killed again."

"As long as you stop being so naive and actually listen to me when I tell you something, or you'll find yourself strung up some-where." A grin spread across her elegant face, mischief flooding her gaze. I imagine she is remembering my bare state when hanging from the pole, and I let out a low groan. She chuckles and thumps my arm with her good hand.

"Imani, you have yourself a deal." Silence falls between us and we lie looking at the stars. Before long, Imani sits up.

"There's something else," I say, and she looks back down at me.

"What is it?"

"You can call me Harm."

A smile lights up her face. It might be the most beautiful thing I have ever seen. She rises from the mat, but her legs falter, and I scramble up to grab her good arm to help her. She grabs my hand tight and pushes to her feet before bidding me good night. I watch until she reaches her tent, then I stretch as I make my way to the first caravan to climb into my bunk.

CHAPTER 20
HARM

Dozing lightly, almost asleep, screams pour out from someone's caravan and I jolt awake. I fly out of bed, slamming into Jonah. We rush down the stairs towards the noise. The screaming continues, and we track it to Indie's caravan. She stands in the corner of it.

"Jonah, please help him!" she pleads, her shaking hands clasping her paled face.

Jonah does a brief assessment of the boy lying stunned on the floor with a desert viper wrapped around one leg. He disappears, returning with a large chunk of firewood.

Striking the snake multiple times, he finally crushes its head into the wooden floor. The child convulses.

"No, Isaac," Indie begs, dropping beside her son and the mangled, limp snake. Jonah rips the snake free. It hits the floor, and I grab it and toss it out of the caravan towards the fire. Scooping up the boy, Jonah runs down the caravan stairs toward the village. I follow close behind.

As we reach the village, the people of Donterra come out of their houses to see what the commotion is about. In no time at all, a large crowd has formed for such a little village, and a short, old man steps forward to look at the child. He stands in silence, assessing the limp, pale boy. He points to the second house on the right, where Jonah and I follow him with the boy. Inside, the desert home is dark, and the old man hobbles over to the table to light candles. Herbs and glass containers of concoctions line the shelves of every wall. He is the village healer.

"Put him on the small bunk," he says, pointing to a free bunk to the left of us. The room flickers to life from the extra candles he lights. The other bunks hold sick people lying there, some asleep and some watching, as Jonah lays the boy down. He shivers, but his body is dripping with sweat. A shadow covers the doorway. Indie stands there with Imani holding her, tears streaming down her twisted face.

By the dim light, the healer works on the boy, pressing vials to his lips to force the anti-venom into the boy's system. He places a hand under the child's neck and raises his head and neck from the bunk, tilting his head backwards. He grabs the last vial from his wooden box and pours the remaining contents into the boy's mouth. Anti-venom trickles out of his mouth as it overflows. His mother comes to a standstill by the small bunk, her hands wringing her nightgown. Imani stands with her arm around her cousin's shoulders, brows lowered and chin wobbling.

"He's lucky," the man says. "You got here fast, and the anti-venom is very effective. He should be alright but will need to stay here for a few days to make sure there are no other side effects from the viper's venom."

The heat from the candles is stifling, and I walk outside into the moonlit village center. Walking through the crowd, I feel relieved that the boy will be fine, and my thoughts turn to my journey south. Lost in thought, I amble through the dense sand. The crowd has almost dispersed, the people returning to their beds. I follow the peaks and valleys of the sand underfoot for a moment—until the golden sands meet dark, black boots planted in the sand. Jerking to a halt, I hold my breath. Every muscle in my body tightens, and I raise my gaze up to the immaculate uniform, the familiar hands, the smug expression I have known my entire life. Mason—flanked by two of his comrades.

"Aren't you supposed to be dead, Travesci?" His smirk grows as he watches my face pale. Every thumping beat of my heart rings through my head. I choke on a strangled breath. He nods, and his officers grab my arms. I pull back, fighting them, heat surging through my core. I have become so comfortable with Imani and the travelers that I have forgotten my reality.

"Let me go, Rayner."

He snickers and gestures to a house across the village. "There's a search warrant out for you. How long did you think you could run around in the sands before you were caught?"

How did they even know I was alive? Was it someone in Trindari? I struggle as they wait for Mason's command.

"You're not happy unless you're hurting someone, Mason."

For a moment, he meets my gaze. His hard stare waivers only slightly before he flings his hand out in a command. The hold on my arms gets tighter, and I'm escorted away from the waning crowd. I turn my head, trying to glimpse Jonah, but I can't see him for the crowd of people. I try to drag against the two Guardians, and a fist smacks the side of my face.

"Imani! Imani!" I pray she hears me from the healer's shelter. "Jonah!"

Mason's brows lower, and he stares at me briefly, then does a visual sweep of the village. Moments later, they shove me through the door of a stone building. More Guardians lounge around inside. One has his feet up on the desk that sits in the center of the room with cells lining the four walls. Five Guardians, including Mason and his men.

My feet drag behind me as I am forced along. Mason tugs the barred cell door open, and I hit the sandy stone floor of the last unoccupied cell. The door slams behind me. Spluttering, I roll over. Mason stands on the other side of the cell door. His face is stone, unreadable.

How had they found out I was alive? My thoughts turn to panic as I realize Christopher and Maryanne would most likely be in trouble for helping me. I pull at my hair and sit with my knees up, fearing the worst for the kind people who gave me back my life. I don't even have a way to find out if they are okay. Lightheadedness washes over me and I force air in and out of my chest. I push onto my feet and rattle the cell door violently.

"Simmer down in there!" a Guardian yells.

"Let me out of here!"

The Guardian closest to me walks over with a smirk on his face. "Not likely, Travesci."

Around the stone building, men sit in the cells on either side of me. They are all considerably older than me.

Sudden yelling from the village center sends all five Guardians to their feet and out the door. Moments later, a small body slinks through the doorway and hides in the shadows. They cross the floor, stopping at every piece of furniture, searching for something.

"Where are the keys?!" Imani hisses.

"I don't know. Try the desk," I whisper.

Mason's voice drifts back toward the building.

"Hurry, they're coming back!"

She rummages through the contents of the desk but brings up nothing. Five Guardians stroll back into the building, and Imani flings herself under the desk. A Guardian seats himself there,

132

thrusting his legs underneath. Imani whimpers, and he jumps up, knocking the chair backward.

"What the hell," he utters. Bending down, he grabs Imani and yanks her out from under the desk. She twists, recoiling from his grip.

"Who have we got here?" he sneers.

She spits in his face. He slams a hand around her throat. She gasps in his hold. I grip the bars, watching her eyes turn from fire to fear.

"Another cellmate for our friend from Amondo." He grabs her bloodied sleeve, and she screams. Balling my hands to fists, I slam them into the bars. "Leave her alone!" Fury thunders through my head.

He grabs the wrist of her injured arm and twists her arm behind her back. She cries out and drops to the floor. My white knuckles shake the cell door violently. He turns slowly and laughs at me. Imani holds herself up with her good arm, knees on the floor, breathing erratically.

Mason, who has been watching from the shadow of the doorway, saunters over to the cell door, driving a fist through the bars and into my chest. I stagger backward. He opens the cell door, and the Guardian holding Imani shoves her inside. She rises from the floor, her face pale, and turns to the three men. Imani lunges for the Guardian who hurt her and he slams the barred door in her face. She screams at him. Swaying, hands clasping the bars, she lets out a low growl and crumples to the ground.

Arms still shaking, I scoop her up and lay her on the bunk. Mason leans against the desk, keys clenched in his hand, watching. Her breathing is too fast, and sweat has saturated her clothes. The pain in her arm must be bad.

"She needs water," I say to Mason, walking to the cell door. He puts the keys on the desk and walks out, a stony expression fixed on his face.

"You'll get some when we're ready," the closest Guardian says, smirking as his eyes run over Imani's unconscious body.

"We need it now!"

"Shut up, filth!"

Moments later, Mason reappears with a canteen, his face still stone, gaze fixed on Imani. He hands it to me through the bars. I stare at him for a second. What's going through his mind? I rush to the bunk and sit Imani up. As I tip the canteen, small dribbles of water run into her mouth and some down her chin. She rouses, coughing. Her gaze is distant, but the corner of her mouth turns up when her eyes meet mine.

"Trying to drown me, Harm?" she jabs, but her face falls. "Sorry, that wasn't funny." Grabbing my shirt, she sits herself up fully. Mason stalks out the front door.

"What do we do now?" I ask.

"Wait, I guess."

"Where will they take us?"

"To the prison near the great wall most likely."

"Great, I've always wanted to go there," I say dryly. A smile breaks out on her face, and she chokes out a small laugh.

"Popular destination for the unfortunate, I hear," she banters back.

We spend the night in the cell. Imani sleeps on the bunk while I lie on the stone floor. The cell is dark and cold, and I am relieved when the desert sun pokes its way over the morning horizon. The three Guardians from yesterday enter the building, followed by another. I wake Imani, and she sits up, yawning. A Guardian stands at our cell door, face hard.

I sit bolt upright.

Fletcher.

I grab Imani's hand, and she looks up. Her mouth gapes as she stares in disbelief. Fletcher's gaze falls to Imani, and a muscle twitches in his jaw. My gaze swings between Imani and Fletcher. Her shock turns to anger. She has had a run-in with him before, no doubt. He stands motionless. Imani gets up and goes to the door. He looks at her clothes and then back at her face.

"What are we in here for?" she snaps.

Fletcher ignores her.

"Travesci knows," Mason says, eyes burning into mine.

"No," she breathes. Does she know I was to be executed? If she was in Amondo for the last four weeks, she must.

"You don't have any say in the matter," Fletcher growls, eyes burning into hers.

"No, don't do this!"

He ignores her, again and takes the keys from Mason, opening the door. Mason grabs Imani by her good arm. Fletcher walks into the cell, stopping inches from my face. "Let's go, Travesci." He grabs my arms and spins me around. Rope burns into my wrists as he flings it over and over and ties it off.

The steel cage rattles, tugging along behind a busted old dune buggy. Fletcher sits at the wheel, staring into the endless horizon of sand, never glancing back at us. Imani sits next to me in the steel casing, her head between her knees, hands clasped over her bent head. We hit a rock, and the cage lurches to one side. She raises her head, then stares at nothing, lost in thought. She wraps her arms around her bent legs, hugging herself.

"Imani?"

"Don't talk to me, Harm," she whispers.

My heart twists in my chest. "You know Fletcher?"

She shoots me a wild, pain-filled glance. We have been getting along so well for the last couple of days, ever since she returned from the village with my rucksack. I look at her, as if to hold her there. She is glaring at me, like she can hurt me if she only looks at me hard enough. In an instant, a tear slides down her hot, flushed cheek. I swallow the lump in my throat, and she turns her head away. I don't understand.

The blistering sun sears us from above while the metal underneath burns through my trousers. The rags we are both wearing are not sufficient cover. Imani's skin has already blistered.

After an hour of traveling, the buggy comes to an abrupt halt. Fletcher jumps down from the driver's seat and strides back to the door of our cage. Without a word, he swings the door open and pulls Imani out. Struggling against him, she tumbles into the hot sand. He turns back to me, disgust marking his usually stony face. Then he slams the iron door shut, throwing the lock closed. Imani leaps up from the sand, throwing herself at him, fists landing on his arms and chest. He pushes her backward into the sand with one quick move and returns to his place at the wheel.

"Stop doing this!" she screams at him through clenched teeth, hands curled to fists by her sides. Fletcher looks at her, annoyance contorting his face and he slams the buggy into gear.

"You can't leave her here!" I bang on the hot cage.

Fletcher's gaze does not waiver from Imani. He intends to leave her behind, alone and injured. One hour in a dune buggy is a long way on foot. She may not survive out here in these desert conditions without water or shelter. Ragged breathing turns my clenched hands white, and I rattle the cage, the metal burning. I barely feel it.

The buggy surges forward in the sand. Imani jogs after us. Fletcher turns his head and looks to the horizon, as if nothing else exists.

"Please stop! Don't go there, let him go!"

Fletcher presses the buggy faster. Imani falls behind and sinks to her knees. Her small figure shrinks through the bars.

"You can't just leave her here, she'll die!"

"I very much doubt that." He doesn't look back.

Imani becomes smaller and smaller as we get further away. She hasn't moved since she fell into the sand. Her dark hair has fallen around her shoulders. She looks so small. I watch until I can no longer see her, only sand and dunes. Every minute we careen towards the west, my chest tightens.

Another two hours in this broiling metal cage, and we reach the prison, on the edge of a bustling village. Groggy from the intense heat, I force my head up as we stop. A solid wall towers over us, belonging to an enormous grey stone building.

No windows.

My stomach plummets, and the thundering blood in my veins almost drowns out the shouting officers as the gates fold back to allow us in. My trembling hands grip the cage underneath me.

Prison.

Please, no.

CHAPTER 21

HARM

Fingers curled around the hot metal, my still-vibrating hands sting. Fear prickles its way over my body. The dune buggy moves through the gate. The stench of dead bodies hits. I hold my breath. Lifeless bodies wait piled onto two wooden carts lining the entrance, ready to be taken away. Guardians handle the desert beasts strapped to each cart.

Fletcher barks, and three Guardians appear from a side door, one carrying a leather strap and chains. The vehicle comes to a rough halt, and the door to the cage is unlocked and flung open. I hold tight to the bottom of the cage. Two officers grab my arms, pulling me out of the cage and face-first into the sand. I lift my head and spit out sand while they hold my arms. They secure a leather strap around my neck, while Fletcher attaches the chains to my wrists behind my back. A hard tug on the chain attached to the collar, and I stumble forward. Another swift one, and I am yanked back to my feet, choking for air.

We walk across the large open courtyard towards the one open door of the repulsive building. Inside, the putrid smell of stale urine, filthy men, and feces claws at my stomach. Bile rises in my mouth, and I gag on the thick air.

Inside, a long hall gives way to two rows of cells with iron bars, and barred doors flank the large room. A large barred wooden door completes the space. Recessed windows near the top of the external walls let in a pittance of light. The inmates are the most miserable men I have ever seen, bodies of skin and bone crammed into the cells. I count fifteen in a cell made for half that number. It is as if time has slowed down, and their faces are presented to me one at a time, their eyes begging for relief, one way or another.

We come to the fourth cell on the right, and Fletcher unlocks the door. The Guardian unclips the chain from my collar and wrists and shoves his boot into my back. I slam into the revolting stone floor, and the door thuds shut. Coughing, I push off the floor onto my knees. The officers retreat, leaving only the quiet moans of the half-dead men around me.

Eleven sets of eyes watch me before going back to whatever they were doing before I was shoved through their door. It is then I notice that most of the men are bald.

"So, what did you do to make the Chancellor feel the need to square you away?" a voice says.

"Uh, stole some things," I lie, turning to face a boy not much older than me.

"That'll do it. Doesn't take much, I'm afraid." He goes back to scratching what appear to be shapes on the stone floor.

"What's your name?"

"Gillian," he says. "What's yours?"

"Travis." Almost the truth.

Gillian is scratching shapes on the floor. They create what appears to be a round item with a triangle on one side, pointing to the center. An odd thing to draw, it occurs to me. And I have seen it somewhere. Next, he draws two straight lines from the circular shape and then a wavy line under them. Instantly, I know where I have seen this before, a sketch in my grandfather's notebook. His version was neater, but they are the same.

"Do you know what this is?" I probe.

"No, but it keeps appearing every night. Usually, it's just this image all in gold. I've never seen it before. That's why I think it's worth remembering," he finishes.

"Possibly," I say, leaning against the cool stone wall. A clanging sound reverberates through the chamber of cells. The men around me hurry to grab a tin bowl from a pile in the corner at the front of the cell. The plates are just as filthy as the men scrambling for them. A large, wheeled steel trolley, making a horrible din, crawls between the cells to feed those with their vessels held out through the bars. Pushing it from behind is a thin boy, not much older than fourteen.

The men line up, begging for what smells like gruel. My thoughts drift to my mother, how she would be beside herself if she knew where I am now. She would be terrified for me. A lump forms in my throat. The men devour the contents of their bowls. Gillian returns to sit next to me. He wipes his face, and I realize I am staring at him. I school my face into neutrality.

"You take what you can get in here," he says.

I nod in response and examine his drawing. "Why do they shave your heads?"

"Looking for anyone who has the ability to change the dial—something about a birthmark. Like anyone with that would be stupid enough to end up in here, anyway. It's a wasted effort on their part, if you ask me."

"So, they'll come and get me sooner rather than later?"

"I reckon they will. They don't wait for an invitation."

I run my hand through my hair and feel the remnants of sand and debris in it from the last couple days' events. Not willing to part with my hair or receive a beating, I scan the cell for anything useful. The window is ten feet above the floor. There is no way I can reach that. Nothing else remains in the cell, only the bowls. I take in every corner of the filthy square cell, running a hand through my hair again.

"It's not worth trying, you know," he whispers.

I turn around, fixing my gaze on his.

"Even if you get out of this cell, they'll catch you before you get anywhere near the main gate. The last man who tried is still hanging up outside." The strung-out eyes of a boy who has seen things he cannot unsee stare back at me.

"So, what? We just sit here and wait to die?"

"Alive is still better than dead, especially if the tables turn one day and the Chancellor is overturned ... or better," he whispers, eyes flicking erratically, monitoring the faces of the surrounding men.

"What if we don't last that long?"

"You have to. That's the only thing we can do from in here."

He sighs and turns back to his drawings. There is no way I am staying in this place. Surviving until the Chancellor is no longer in control is not a plan I will sign up for. I go back to looking at my surroundings. Every cell is the same. Every barred door, the same. There is no way out of here—not from within a cell, at least.

The stone underneath me has changed from warm from the midday sun to the cooler feel of the sun setting for the evening. Exhaustion creeps over me. I lie down next to Gillian and place my hand under my head. Closing my eyes, I think of Imani. I can only imagine what she would say right now. There's no way she would sit here and wait. No way. Relaxing on the stone floor, the darkness around me drags me into the depths of sleep.

The sand around me rises in a flurry of winds, torn in every direction. The storm folds in around me, but my gaze stays fixed on hers. Hate fuels the fire behind her eyes. Intolerance and annoyance are plain in her clenched jaw and curled fists.

"Don't talk to me, Harmen," she spits. She drags out my name, like she is hauling something revolting behind her.

"I don't understand," I utter.

She laughs.

Fletcher steps up beside her, his face smug. Mason flanks her other side. The look on his face guts me.

I jerk awake, and Imani's face fades slowly. The foul smell of urine and musty stone hang heavy in the air. I breathe out slowly, trying to compose myself, one hand on my hammering chest. Gillian is still asleep near me, and the others stir. Every bone in my body aches at once. I rise, stiff and slow.

One man is relieving himself in the stained and permanently slimy corner. Sparse sunlight pushes through the small window high above. In every cell, men are waking up to another day destined to be the same as the abysmal one before it.

Metal wheels split the soft sounds, and the clanging starts again. Thin, dreary bodies hurry towards the piles of tin bowls, eager to satisfy their hunger. The same boy from yesterday absent-mindedly pours slop into each bowl before pushing on to the next cell. He arrives at the barred door of our cell, and I grab a bowl and stand in line for sustenance. I wait as each man before me takes his bowl and sits to eat. I approach the door and hand my bowl out through the bars. The boy looks up and fills my bowl.

"Morning," he offers. His tan shirt is buttoned up to his neck. Dark trousers rest over tattered boots. A smile wraps around his young face.

"Morning."

"I haven't seen you before." He lets go of the cart. "I'm Toby."

"Travis."

"They'll come for you today to shave your head. If you're lucky, they may send me to fetch you."

"Alright." I hold his gaze and he leans into the bars. I do the same.

"It's better that way. I can help you, if you carry the mark," he whispers, eyes widened, his lips draw into a thin line.

"I don't have the ability, or the mark."

Toby's expression softens. He probably hears that from every man who stands on this side of the bars.

CHAPTER 22
HARM

Eyes watering, I force down the gruel. Every mouthful wrenches a gag from my throat. But it is this or starvation. I need water. A dirty brown canister made from clay sits on a small wooden bench on the left side of our cell. The water is clear and has no odor. I drink sparingly, chasing down the filthy aftertaste of the gruel.

Keys clink near the cell door. Standing next to a Guardian is Toby. A warning lies in his eyes.

"Travesci, you're coming with us," the Guardian says, unlocking the door.

Hanging in the open doorway, he grabs my left arm as I get close enough. Toby hooks the chain to my neck collar and tugs me forward. We walk between the cells. Men to the left and right of me stare. Fear and sadness shape their faces. My hands shake, heart flinging against my ribs, blood thunders through my head, and dizziness creeps upward. We turn left, walking a short way to a door on the right. Toby tugs me through it, stopping me next to an old table covered with a collection of short blades. I shove my shaking hands into my pockets.

The Guardian rummages through the stash to find a sharp blade. Placing the blade of choice against the sharpening stone, he moves it back and forth with fluid motions. The blade snaps, and the handle hits the floor. "Hell," he growls, examining his fingers before shaking out his hand. Blood drips from his palm.

"Stay here. I'll be back in a second." Throwing Toby a stern look, he stalks out the door.

Toby grabs my head and yanks it towards him. Frantically, he brushes my hair off my neck. He won't find anything. He steps back, still holding the chain attached to my neck. He starts to undo the buttons on his shirt, his fingers trembling. Brows turned down, he runs an eye over me. I breathe out. He grabs my shoulders with one hand, pulling his shirt aside with the other. A small bird with its wings spread is tattooed on the left side of his chest, no bigger than my thumbnail.

"Do you know what this is?" he urges, eyes darting to the door and back to me.

"No, what is it? Do I have the mark?"

Eyes straining, he scans my face. "It's too early for this," he whispers to himself.

"What? What are talking about? Do I have the mark?"

"You are the two hundredth boy I have escorted to this room. They took some of them from their villages under the guise of being selected. But we brought them here to check for the mark. Half of them ended up back in the cells, the rest weren't that lucky. You need to get out of here. Now."

"What? Why would they do that? I can't escape! It's too dangerous. And you didn't answer my question."

His eyes slide sideways as he studies the line of blades and other equipment in the trays. "No, there's no mark," he utters, gaze hitting the floor.

I run my hands up the back of my head, swallowing the lump in my throat.

"I can get you out, but we have to hurry," he urges.

"Why are you helping me?"

"Because." He sighs and shuts his eyes, pinching the bridge of his nose. "It's the right thing to do." He drags me to the door. We listen at the door for a moment before opening it. Rapid breathing triggers tingling in my hands. Toby pushes past the door and turns right into a long dark hallway that bends to the left. "Follow this hallway until you reach the door at the end. On the left of the door is a false panel. Pry it open with your fingers. Make sure you replace it. Inside is a passageway. Don't stop until you see sunlight." He's almost breathless.

"I won't. I mean, thank you."

"Wait." He grabs my arm. "Hit me."

"What?!"

"They'll think you overpowered me and got away. Otherwise, they'll accuse me of helping you. Do it!" Refastening his buttons in swift motions, he sets his shoulders and nods.

I ball my fists and look him up and down, assessing how to do the least damage. Letting loose a breath, I swing and connect a fist with his face. Toby's eyes waiver, and he falls sideways with a grunt. He nods to the dark hallway, holding his cheek. Reluctantly, I run down the dingy hallway, not daring to look back.

The door appears where Toby said it would. I run my fingers around the panel to the left, tugging until it gives. I slip past the panel and pull it shut with two small wooden handles on the inside. The passageway is dark and musty. Damp air swallows me with the first step into the dim space.

My legs jerk forward heavily with every burning breath I take. Imani would pull me along with her if she were here. I pull memories of her to the front of my mind, something to fuel me as I go, if not a pleasant distraction from my exhausted body. Her brilliant blue eyes and dark hair. A deep ache in my chest takes over the fire that was there before. My legs speed up almost on their own, and the chain whips into my side with every stride.

I race through the passageway on my second wind. Imani's sweet smile spurs me on. Blood runs in torrents through my veins now, and sweat saturates my hair and the back of my shirt. The darkness of the passageway makes it difficult to gauge the time I have been down here. The collar wound around my neck makes every breath harder. Running my fingers around it, I search for a buckle or clasp. Smooth metal meets the tips of my fingers. I yank on the clasp, coughing as it tightens slightly. I slow to a jog. With a tug that smarts my fingers, the collar comes loose. I toss it to the side and run.

Village noises echo down the tunnel. Around a bend, sunlight peeks through a small arched door. Its frame, studded with rusted bolts, is the only thing still holding the door together. A long wooden lever over a metal rest secures it shut from the inside.

I pry the wooden lever up. The door creaks and sags back towards me. Holding it mostly closed, I listen, steadying my breath. Happy conversation drifts inward, the smells of spices and meat cooking—some sort of market.

Squinting against the searing sunlight, I set one foot onto the warm sands. Villagers in their usual desert dress wander around lines of stalls. Women and children hustle around in groups, while the men are trading goods in loud voices. A handful of Guardians poke around the market, talking and joking, looking off duty.

I slide out of the doorway into the closest stall. Amongst the ruckus of the morning's trading, no one notices. This stall belongs to a lady selling robes. Rows of robes, heavy, light, hooded, and plain, take up the floor of her stall. The brightest, colorful ones, like Indie and the other women wear, hang from a rack at the back to my left. I grab the plainest one from the rack in front of me. But I have nothing to offer her for payment. Everything I own is back in Jonah's caravan. She watches me as I move about her stall with my head down. With natural movement, as if she is gliding around checking wares, she moves to where I am.

I freeze.

Please don't alert the Guardians, lady.

Bunches of metal bangles slide down her arm as she plucks a robe from a rack beside me. With an oval face highlighted by the lines of age, eyes of blue-grey, and a wide mouth, perfect for laughter and smiles, she stops only inches from my face. Her breath touches my skin. She tilts her head to the side, scanning my face before she speaks.

"I recommend a robe more suitable for your current needs. This one with the hood will serve you much better, I think," she whispers, pulling the simple robe off my shoulders, holding the hooded one up for me to slip on. She stands in front of me, running her bangled hands down each side of the robe, assessing for fit. The robe is heavy, with two large pockets. She stands back, looking me over.

"Better. I'm Saraya. If you ever need anything—anything at all—just come back to see me." She returns to her counter. Once behind the wooden table, she tilts her head for me to go.

Throwing the hood over my head, I weave my way through the crowds and stalls, not really knowing which direction to travel. I didn't even have time to thank her. I make a mental note to remember that favor the next time our paths cross.

By the position of the sun, it is midmorning. The markets are on the edge of a small village, not unlike Amondo. They too have a well in the center of the village, but theirs appears to be functioning as a water source instead of a place of death. Women carry pairs of small buckets to the well and then turn around and head home. Children are playing in the sand between the houses. One young boy throws a ball in my direction, then nods, asking me to return it. I pick it up and take it to the three boys, who are now staring at me.

"What do you call this village?" I ask, handing them the ball.

"You don't know? It's Etonia," he replies with a half-hearted laugh.

"Thank you."

If this is Etonia, then I am at the northern end of the prison. To get back to the gypsies, I need to go east-northeast. How far, I don't know. Only one small village lies on a rocky outcrop between the east villages, Perendi—not a place you would volunteer to visit, if you believe the traders who visit Amondo. Unfortunately, beggars can't be choosers.

I start off east to Perendi. I have around seven hours before dark—plenty of time, but not enough if you get caught in a sandstorm. Head down, I shove my hands into the deep pockets. Cool metal touches my fingertips. Pulling out a single piece, the gold glint of old currency reflects up at me. I reach into the depths of the pocket again, a cluster of coins tangle through my fingers. I do the same in the other pocket, and more coins touch my fingers.

My chest tightens.

She gave me money.

CHAPTER 23
HARM

S qualls of hot air burst around me. Head down and with my hands in my pockets, I make my way east as fast as I can. The wind whips my robe behind me, clawing at my hood. I hold it down with both hands.

The last time I saw Imani, she was kneeling on the hot sand, stranded and wounded. I half expected her to be hanging around the prison when I got out. She has made a habit of showing up. If Jonah had seen what had happened, perhaps he went out to find her. They are good people. I resign myself to that thought. I hope she is safe.

Gusts of wind are becoming more frequent—a sure sign of a sandstorm developing. I break into a jog. After almost six-and-a-half hours of traveling through the hot sand and wind, I arrive at rocky outcrops. Sitting behind them, nestled between golden dunes is Perendi. Lips chapped and throat drier than the sand at my feet, I trudge the last hundred feet to the village outskirts. The sun sinks low, and faint lights pour from the rings of small homes in the village. The usual sounds of people going about their evening routines drift outwards to the sands, and the smells of the evening meals along with it. My stomach growls.

Passing the first ring of homes, I scan the houses, surveying them for any sign of trouble or Guardians. Every curtain is drawn, with only silhouettes moving past them. For a place supposedly so treacherous, I cannot hear or see anything amiss. I need to ask around for Imani and Jonah. They could have made it here by now if they had kept going.

My empty, twisting stomach pangs for food. I search for some sort of inn or tavern. There I can eat and ask around. A small building, squarer than the rest of the homes, has two half-sized arch doors. The smell of meat and the savory aroma only produced by a hearty meal lures me closer. I continue towards the building.

Inside is low conversation and the clinking of tableware. At the threshold, I peer over the top of the small arched doors. Men eating and drinking occupy the tables. Pushing one door open, I take a step forward.

"No travelers are welcome here," a man's voice calls from the side of the room. He stands, cleaning a mug with a cloth. Every person in the place stops, knives and forks in hand, waiting to see my next move. Now, I understand the rumors. I nod and back my way out of the doorway. My stomach pangs, and I trudge to the next home. If I can't get a meal honestly, I will have to beg. Standing in front of the next house, I rap on the door. Nobody answers.

I move to the next.

I knock and wait.

Shuffling from inside moves towards the door. "Can I help you?" an old lady asks through the small gap. "I'm looking for some food, and for my friends."

"Your friends are not here, boy. Steal someone else's food." She slams the door. I stand motionless for a moment.

The next door, no luck, no charity.

An hour later, I am at the last door of the second ring of homes. I loose a heavy sigh and raise my hand to knock. A little hand tugs on my robe.

"What are you doing?" a small voice asks.

"I'm starving," I whisper back, bending down to meet the gaze of a small boy, around four or five years old.

"You can follow me. My momma welcomes travelers."

"How do I know I can trust you? Maybe you're the one I need to look out for?" I wink.

He drops the hold on my robe. "My momma would would be sad if I let you go hungry." He grabs my hand, dragging me behind him.

His small house is lit up inside. The smell of food that greets me from the open window is divine.

"Are you sure this is okay?" I ask.

"Uhuh. My name is Miles."

He pushes through the door and calls to his mother, taking my robe. Standing on the wood box, he hangs it on a hook near the front door. A petite woman appears in the kitchen. She looks at me and then at Miles, then smiles at us both.

"Mother, I found this fellow going door to door for food. Can he eat with us?"

"You are most welcome in our home," she says, her hazel eyes lit up with friendliness. Her dark, wavy hair frames her oval face.

"Sit here," Miles says as he pulls out a chair for me and plonks down beside me. He fiddles with the cutlery on the table. I study the small home. It is very similar to the home my mother kept in Amondo. Few possessions, but immaculate, with a warm feeling of space. A shelf sits above the stove, a set of ornate, blue glass vials in a small tray with one bottle missing.

Meat, grains, and some sort of greenish-grey vegetable sits in the bowl she places in front of me. It smells like heaven.

"Thank you," I say. Her eyes meet mine, and she nods, her dark hair bouncing around her shoulders. I dig into the bowl like I am burrowing my way to the opposite side of the desert with my fork and spoon. It is delicious. My mouth waters as I eat.

Next to me, Miles is eating too, at a more civilized pace. He probably eats like this every day, the pleasure almost lost on him. In a few minutes, I clean my bowl. I sit back and wash it down with a small tin cup full of water. She refills my cup, and I drain it. Miles's mother sits across from me and starts her meal. I look around the home again, trying not to stare at one place too long.

"Where have you traveled from?" she asks.

"From the west."

Her expression does not change, but she nods gently in acknowledgement. I can tell she would like to know more, but is too polite to insist. I haven't even told them my name.

"My name is Harmen," I volunteer, hoping to make her more comfortable after such generosity.

"Hello, Harmen, I'm Petria." In retrospect after the past ten minutes, it sounds slightly awkward. But she just offers another smile and continues to eat. "Where are you traveling to?"

"To the east, to find a friend of mine. Actually, Perendi was their next stop. You haven't seen a gypsy camp come through here, have you?"

Miles looks at his mother and then back to me.

"We were traveling together and then got separated," I say.

Petria's eyebrow raises. She pauses, spoon halfway to her mouth, but continues after a heartbeat.

"My sister—" Miles starts.

"Doesn't live here anymore," Petria interjects firmly, her eyes locked on his. Then she turns to me. "Sometimes that happens, getting separated. But I have had word that they're still traveling, so if you need to find them, you could most likely catch them up by heading southwest from here."

That's all she says to me, moving from the table to clean up. I push my seat back and take my bowl and cup to the sink. A hall runs through the home, with a bedroom opposite the small living room. A large bed sits in the center. On the far wall is an open cupboard, grey uniforms hanging inside. Leaning against the cupboard are two canes. This is a Guardian's home. A streak of fear creeps up my spine.

"Thank you for your hospitality," I say, swallowing.

"It's nothing. We're happy for the company. My husband's work takes him away most of the year."

I relax slightly, looking back to the cupboard, and the uniforms that hang there. She sees me staring. I move toward the door. Her kind expression doesn't change. Miles is looking down at his bowl of food, half eaten. The burden of his mother's words alters his expression.

"Is there anywhere in the village I can sleep for the night?"

"You can camp out in the village rest area. People are always there. Some of them are travelers, some are without homes." She gestures to outside. "It's across the village center and to the left. You can't miss it."

"Thank you." I pluck my robe from the hook and throw it on, flinging the hood over my head with one hand. With a little playful punch to Miles's arm, he rises from the table and follows me out the door.

"Thank your mother again for me, will you?"

"I will," he says, deflated.

"What's wrong?"

"I wish you could stay." He kicks a foot through the sand.

"One day, someone will."

He nods, but his eyes are sad, and he shuffles back inside. I cross the village center and head left to find, just as Petria said, a rest area with people settling down for the night. I pick my way through the bodies and find a clear spot near the fire on the edge. Across the fire, three men sit chatting quietly. I lie with my hands under my head and look up at the stars, eavesdropping on their conversation to pass the time.

"You know a fellow escaped the prison at the great wall," one man says.

"He won't last more than a couple of days before the Guardians catch up with him," another man chimes in.

"Don't know, they're stretched pretty thin these days, with all the people failing to pay their taxes, and the uprisings going on in the smaller sectors," the third man says.

"At any rate, I wouldn't want to be him when they eventually find him. Rumor is he was already on the run before they threw him in the prison," the first man says.

News travels fast in the desert. Breath catches in my chest. If these men know about my escape, then surely Imani and Jonah would have also heard. I gaze at the flickering stars a while longer, trying to imagine what she would decide to do next.

Uprisings? Could there be a rebellion? Rebels? If we continue with the journey we had spoken about, to the south, and if there are rebels, we could find them.

Mild seams of panic subside under these welcoming thoughts. If I am caught now, the Guardians are sure to see the job through. They won't relent until they are standing over my lifeless corpse. I swallow the lump in my throat. I can only hope that when the sun sets tomorrow, I am closer to Imani, and miles ahead in our journey to the south.

CHAPTER 24
HARM

I awake before the first splinters of pale light split over the dunes, and the darkness hangs around me like an unwanted swarm. Cold air rolls in from the desert. Every inch of me aches from tossing and turning for hours. The men opposite the fire are gone. If they were on the move so quickly, surely the Guardians will be just as active in their pursuit, if not more so now.

I wrap my robe around tight and start for the outskirts of the village. If I am to stay alive long enough to find Imani and get to the south, I am going to have to keep moving and lie low. I need water. I toss the hood over my head. Towards the edge of the village, a small trader is setting up his wares, ready for the dawn hagglers. Canteens hang from one end of his cart. I track directly to him. I pick up the largest of the canteens, and he pads over to me.

"Traveling somewhere far?" he asks.

"Something like that." I hand over a gold coin. He startles at the currency in his palm. The first rays of light dance around my feet as a lady in a dark brown robe appears beside me. To her left, behind the trader, stacked in a small tin drum are maps. Without my rucksack, I have no map or book to guide my journey. I need something. Steadily, I make my way over and look at the goods near the stand. Her hazel eyes follow me. I grab a map, checking that it is what I need. It's clear, and as far as I can tell, accurate. With this map, I could make my own way south. I snap another gold coin down on the counter and head for the center well to fill my canteen.

I look up to make sure nobody is following me. No one seems to be, and I fill my canteen quickly. I have to decide. I could go southeast and find my mother's family, and start the arduous task of finding someone with the ability to change the dial. But without Mother's journal, I am not sure who I am looking for. The fewer questions I need to ask when I get there, the better. Or do I head southwest, diverting to avoid the prison and Guardians and find Imani? It is an impossible choice. I must choose between the girl who has saved my skin twice, and my own journey. I slide down the rough stone wall behind me and shove my head in my hands.

Moments later, I lift my head and stare at the stone wall in front of me. If Imani were here, she would tell me to get on with it. If it were her stuck out here and on the run, she would do what must be done. I will go southeast. My insides twist like a mangled rope. I desperately hope Jonah found her and that they are on their way south. I am eager to see both of them again. Finding someone with the ability will be much easier with her help. I feel better around her, like the weight of losing my family lightens just a little.

It is almost a day's hike to the next village in the south, Tabara. More sand, more walking. Head down and hood covering my face, I start out toward the desert, winding my way through the last of the outbuildings. The woman in the dark brown robe from the trader's stand walks toward me. "Wait," she says, her hand held out, her eyes bright.

Petria.

"Did you get what you needed?" she asks.

"Yes, a map and a canteen."

She steps closer to me, her eyes searching mine. "You need to keep moving. Do not stay in one place for very long. Disappear to the south villages and keep your head low. You should find your friends in that direction." She pushes a parcel of food into my arms.

"Thank you."

She touches my face with her hand. Something familiar in her expression sends a bolt of warmth through my chest. With a squeeze of my hand, she walks on. I do the same.

A wooden rail skirts the last two buildings, and I duck under it. A dune buggy catches my eye, covered in sand from probably the last six months' worth of sandstorms. There is no one around—not that I can see from doing a slow three-sixty turn. I hurry to the buggy. Swiftly I brush some of the sand from its surfaces. The keys dangle from the ignition like pure temptation.

My father used to tell me how these machines worked, and I saw how Fletcher made it go on the way to the prison. So, I have a basic understanding of how to control them, but not much more. I used to dream of having one of these machines when I was younger, knowing full well that was never something that would happen. Only the Guardians have buggies, and only they may operate them. I slide onto the seat, sitting the food parcel and canteen next to me.

I turn the key.

Nothing.

Looking up, I check to see if anyone has noticed. I turn it again and slam my foot on one pedal. Still nothing. I turn the key again and slam the other pedal. With a roar, the buggy bolts. Gripping the steering wheel, I lurch backward. The buggy takes off. I turn the wheel left and make a fast turn, the wheels leaving the ground in protest as it careens away from the village outskirts.

Looking back, not one person seems to have noticed. I press

deeper on the pedal and drive towards the landmarks of the south-east. The humming buggy drifts along the waves of the desert sand effortlessly. It will only take a matter of hours now, not an entire day. Excitement and adrenaline course through my body, and for the first time in weeks, a brief wave of happiness.

The landscape of sand, dunes, valleys, and peaks spread out around me. And as if that feat were not great enough, they continuously change. No two days does this place look the same; the winds make certain of that. Dotted throughout some of the rockier areas are sparse trees and shrubs. The odd lizard or snake makes its way across my path. Desert life is hard—not just for the villagers, but for every living thing. The desert doesn't discriminate.

Alone with my thoughts is a dangerous place to be. Memories of my family. Mother in our home, surrounded by the things she had collected and made herself, and gifts from my father. My little sister playing on the sandy floor close to my mother's feet. Father, tired but happy, back from another long, hard day. The everyday dullness of chores is almost too comforting to bear right now. Memories of my work, the wood in my hands.

Giggles from my little sister float around me as the hot wind flies past my face. I miss her—her little ways, her soft cuddles, and her gentle, small hands that would slip into mine when she was scared. Tears stream down my face, flying off into the wind that whips past me. The pain in my chest that claimed me in our house in Amondo shoots through my body once again. Sobs rip through my chest. My beautiful, sweet Amaya ... My heart breaks a little more with every ragged breath.

Buffeting winds push the buggy around. The landmarks around me signal that I am getting very close to the southern villages. I wheel the buggy in behind a cluster of spiny trees and turn off the ignition. My hands tingle from holding the wheel over rough terrain for hours. Sand falls from my clothes as I step out of the buggy and stretch my back, bending backwards. I unfold the map. One Guardian outpost to get past to the west before I make it to the southern villages.

The buggy will draw far too much attention. Head down, I take off south on foot, gauging my direction by the sun going down to my right. The last Guardian outpost illuminates, settled in the sands with the sun now sinking behind it. Raising a hand to shield my eyes, I search for movement around the outpost. It is around two hundred and fifty feet away—far enough not to be recognized, but close enough to be caught if they come out in their buggies. My pace quickens.

To my left rises a crop of basalt, craggy rock, as high as two men. The ground in between and around the rocks is sparse with pathetic-looking shrubs, almost too withered to bother dying. These patches of harder terrain make ample homes for desert vipers. I keep my distance and move at a good pace to pass the threats on either side of me.

There are recent footprints in the sparse sand, traveling in the same direction, south. Two sets: larger prints, and a smaller set. Not heavy boot prints. Not Guardians. No caravan tracks either.

As the Guardian outpost recedes behind me, I pick up my pace. Perhaps I can catch up to these people and get some information on the southern villages. Chances are they are returning home or visiting a place they have been before. They will most likely know more about the south than I do. Or maybe they have come across the caravans. I run, the robe proving to be a nuisance again, slowing my usual pace, with the rhythmic clink of the coins in my pockets.

I negotiate my way around a large dune. The sand is getting

thicker, filling my boots as my feet sink deeper with every step. Another dune, another slight turn left. This time, I slow down. The footprints are harder to see in the deep sand. I stop and search for their next patch of prints. They travel over the top of the next big dune ahead. Not knowing who I am following, and not wanting to expose myself before I do, I take the left side of the dune at a run. Water sloshes in my canteen, hitting my side with every bound. Sweat drips down my back. A handful of paces are left before I round the dune.

Two figures stand ahead of me. I drop to my knees, trying to quiet my breath. Between them is a map. They are looking from the map to the desert in front of them towards the south. Straining against the wind, I listen for what they are saying. I can make out the voice of a man over the winds. The other person doesn't speak. They are dressed in village clothes, with commoner robes and wraps. The man carries a large rucksack. A lighter one is strapped to the smaller person, covered in sand.

Reaching into my pocket to find the map, I assume they are deciding between the two villages on the map near this location: Tabara to the south, and Farno to the northeast. The smaller person nods toward Tabara. The man rolls up his map and slides in into his rucksack. They trudge down the dune. They gather speed, and I do the same, right behind them.

I wait for them to reach the peak of the next dune before I start up the incline. I cannot hear anything over the sounds of my own harsh breathing. My legs are on fire. I swear this is the biggest mound of sand known to man. I reach the top, lungs burning and head throbbing. My breath catches in my throat. They have stopped just on the other side of the dune in silence. I squat down, hoping they haven't heard me.

Head down, I wait.

Please don't see me.

A hand touches my shoulder. My heart skips a beat. Slowly, I raise my head to see the man, the smaller figure standing behind him. He gestures for me to stand. My legs are wobbly from the climb, but I push up to my feet. I leave the hood of the robe half over my face. The man leans towards me, lowering his wrap slowly. A look of excitement takes over his face, and he drops his rucksack on the ground.

"Harmen?"

I raise my gaze to meet his.

"Jonah!" I huff out a strangled laugh. He steps closer to me in the twilight, a wide smile across his face. His companion walks three steps away and drops to their seat, swinging their head between their legs.

"What are you doing out here? Why are you not with the caravans?" I ask.

"We have been traveling south, to the villages, hoping to find you."

"We?"

He looks behind him. "You didn't think she would give up on you, not after she—"

"Imani?" I swallow the lump in my throat. She sits on the sand, her back to me. "Is she okay?"

Jonah tilts his head to the left. "Ask her yourself."

Stepping around Jonah, I plow through the crest of the dune and kneel on the sandy ground next to her. She doesn't look up, hands over her face. I place my hands over hers.

"Imani," I whisper, my voice now raw. She goes still, breathing unevenly. Jonah sits down beside her a pace or two away and starts digging through his rucksack.

"Imani," I try again. Her wrap is still covering her head, and her hood is half over her face. She raises her head and drops her hands to her lap. Her bright blue eyes are lined with silver. I sweep my hand over my hood, pushing it off so she can see my face. Sand falls out of my hair and runs down my neck. I push back her hood. Wisps of her dark hair frame her face. Fire courses through her blue eyes. I drop my hands into my own lap.

Without a word, she stands. I follow her lead and stand in front of her. Her fists slam into the center of my chest, and I stumble backward. The dune slips from under my feet and I land with a hard grunt, almost upside down on the steep side. A foot lodges in my side, and I let out a primal growl as I slide further down the dune. I come to a stop at the bottom and sit up, shaking off the sand from my now filthy robe, face, and hair.

Imani storms down the dune towards me. She slams to her knees next to me and lands one fist after another into my chest. "You rotten, stinking, filthy commoner!" Her hands thump into my chest repeatedly. "I thought you were dead!" She loses a moan. "You bloody clean skin! I thought I got you killed!" Her fists come to rest on my chest, and she scans my face. I stare back, not moving. Jonah's chuckle echoes over the dunes.

"How are you alive?" she gasps, sinking to her heels on the sand.

"I got lucky, I guess." I sit up next to her. "There was a boy, Toby. He helped me escape."

She looks at me and then stands. Jonah, who has only just made it down the dune, hands her a rucksack—my rucksack. Her face remains unchanged. She hands it down to me. "Part of me never expected to see you again, but I thought you might want this back." She looks past me to the dark horizon. Standing, I search for any signs of damage, only finding it in her eyes.

"If you thought I was dead, why are you out here looking for me, traveling south?"

She stares at me and swallows before pushing her shoulders

back and crossing her arms over her chest. "Holding up my end of a deal."

I don't reply, just stand on the spot, eyes burning into hers.

"Well ..." Jonah's voice breaks the silence between Imani and me. "Are we going to Tabara or not, you two?"

"Yes, we are," Imani says, pulling down her hood and setting off towards the southwest, leaving Jonah and me to follow. Jonah laughs, staring at me for a handful of heartbeats before tugging his rucksack tighter. "Good to have you back, Harm."

We follow Imani's swift pace into the darkness. My chest swells at the sound of my name, and I watch Imani march into the gathering twilight with new determination.

CHAPTER 25
HARM

With nightfall only moments away, the spectacular sunset to our right pushes us faster. The faint iridescent lights of Tabara hover over the desert sands like a beacon. Warmth and light radiating from the village homes draw us in like moths to a flame.

"Look alive," Imani growls as we enter the village past the first ring of houses, giving me a warning glance.

I toss the hood over my head, pulling it down low. "Do you know where you're going?"

"Do you?" she hisses. The old Imani is clearly back. I let out a breathy chuckle.

"All we need to do is stick together," Jonah cuts in. "The last thing we need right now is you two at each other's throats. Imani, let's find what we came for. Harm, you're going to need that journal of your mother's soon. I know a fellow who has lived here for over sixty years. If your mother's family lives here, he will know." He nods to the center of town to an area of communal use, the well.

Hesitating, I follow Imani and Jonah and walk towards the

well. It's surrounded by stone seating, and the ground is tiled with flat stone. The large circular area skirting the well looks well-kept and clean. People sit chatting and eating simple foods in the light from the six posts with fire lanterns. A gathering place. We take a seat at the closest bench, and I rifle through my rucksack and grab the journal. It looks as if everything in my rucksack is still here, untouched.

Flipping through my mother's worn journal, I run a finger down a page, then another. The old blue cover, tattered, still holds. Passages about the home they are making together and the people in the village cover the pages. An entry about missing her family. No names; she only writes "Mother," "Sissy," and "Father." I flip through more, then I halt on a page revealing a spread, a map of the lands, like the one I bought in Perendi—except this one has a handful of unfamiliar markings on it. Some blue and brown lines run through the map. That's new. Or ancient, perhaps.

The next page has a drawing of a pendant. I dig around in my rucksack, pulling out the glinting gold chain and bright blue stone it encases. It's the same pendant. I hold it up to the light. The soft lantern light barely splits as it hits the stone. Imani sits motionless on the stone seat, wide-eyed. Dropping my hand instantly, I shove the pendant back into the rucksack.

Next page: a phrase written in a language I don't understand.
Next page: names.

Enid Starling
Howard Starling
Tabitha
Layla
Rupert Barlow

My grandparents' names are on the list. Could they still be alive? Their last name is not that common, or so my mother told me once. I remember her telling me stories about them. I'm certain my grandmother's name is Enid. Jonah lingers beside me, shifting from foot to foot.

"We should ask about Enid Starling," I say, looking up at him.

"Who is that?"

"My grandmother."

"Well, that's a start, at least," he says.

Imani is quiet sitting next to me. Her head is down, eyes closed, lost in thought. Jonah's gaze alternates between Imani and me.

"It's been a long day," he sighs. "We should find this friend of mine before the evening gets on."

Readjusting his rucksack, he gestures to move, and I follow. Imani stays still. Glancing back to Imani, I hesitate. Taking a breath, I turn and follow Jonah. Imani probably just needs some space. Who knows?

Two Guardians casually wander around the center of the village. They almost look off duty, laughing and tossing remarks between them like a game of catch. Matching Jonah's stride, I fall in beside him, pulling my hood down further. He is aware of their presence but does not rush. *Please don't see us.*

"The next alley on the right—turn down it and keep going. Don't look back at them," he utters. I nod. Dust lines the narrow space between rows of houses from the latest sandstorm. Light winds tunnel through the lane, swirling the sand around our feet, picking it up and tossing it around in a one-sided dance. Amber light from inside the building reflects off it like a shimmering haze.

Jonah stops at an old wooden door, its vertical boards wrecked from the heat and years of unfavorable weather. A rusted metal door knocker hangs precariously in the center of the top half of the door. He lifts his hand to the knocker. But the door creaks open to a slight crack, not waiting for the knock. Light pours out. A shadow moves awkwardly past the now-vibrant slip of light. Propped up by a walking cane, a man pulls back the door. He grunts and moves back for a better look.

Jonah steps towards him, removing his wrap from his face. A grin breaks across the other man's wrinkled face. He throws the door open. "Jonah!"

"It's been far too long, Henry." Jonah steps in to embrace his friend. With one hand, the old man hugs Jonah and slaps him on the back. In the small living room, three wooden chairs atop a woven mat stand guarding a small wall of books, and a handful of scattered candles sit behind him. He ushers us in, and we dump our robes by the door. Odd trinkets from a long life sit amongst the books. Jonah asks about the man's family and recent life.

"So," Henry says, now looking at me, "what can I do for you?"

"Harmen is looking for his family," Jonah says.

"Well then, in that case, I will need to know a few things about them."

"What do you need to know?" I ask.

"A name would be a start," he says, smiling at me. Heat fills my face. "Sit and tell me what you know. I will see if I remember your people." His walking stick briefly points Jonah and I to the chairs, and we sit.

"My grandmother's name is Enid Starling." Eyes fixed on the old man in front of me, I hold my breath for his reaction. He shifts in his seat and murmurs "the old desert fox."

Jonah's eyes widen.

"My mother's name was Hannah Starling, later Travesci," I offer.

"Your mother is no longer alive?" Henry asks.

"No," I breathe.

"I'm sorry to hear that."

SANDS OF RUIN

We sit in silence for a moment. Henry studies my face. "Do you remember the two women from the south that traveled northwards around eighteen years ago?" Henry asks, turning his gaze back to his friend.

"You mean the two women who crossed the desert by themselves, and the young girl was with child?" Jonah asks.

"Yes."

"I remember the stories," Jonah says.

"Do you remember why they left?" Henry asks.

"Bits and pieces," Jonah says slowly, looking at me as if I am going to object.

"They went to the north to meet her betrothed. It was just stories floating around back then, but it was said that she was in love with a man here in Tabara. But that union was not to be—something about an incompatible match. Her mother and father wanted to send her to the most northern village, as far away as possible from the father of her child. But he left before she did, and I think that broke her heart. He moved on to the east, to Farno. Whether he is still there now, I couldn't tell you." Henry stops, staring at his hands. Jonah moves in his seat, letting out a sigh, looking at me.

"How is this related to finding my family?" I ask.

The two men exchange glances.

"That young woman was your mother, Harm," Henry says softly, and Jonah's gaze fixes on Henry.

"What?! I don't understand. How can that be?" Swinging my gaze between Jonah and Henry, I lower my voice to a whisper. "My parents were happy. My mother adored my father."

"No one is saying they weren't happy, or that she didn't love your father, but this is your mother's story, and part of yours too," Henry says, looking at Jonah, who is shaking his head in disbelief.

Jonah leans forward to get closer to Henry. "But that means—"

169

Henry raises his hand. Jonah goes still and turns his gaze to me.

"As far as I know, none of your mother's family stayed here in Tabara. It wasn't the best place for them to be, with all the talk of your mother's situation. Your aunties and grandfather left for Mareya, further to the south. I believe your grandmother returned to that village also after her journey to the north," Henry finishes, laying his head back and closing his eyes as if the words have worn him out.

Shallow breaths consume my lungs. My family, as I have known it my entire life, just changed somehow in a matter of minutes. Memories of my parents together run through my head. I check each one for signs of what Henry has told me. Some sort of evidence that my mother was unhappy, or that my father was not my own. I can't find one memory to confirm what he has told me. Nothing in my childhood ever suggested that Andrew Travesci was not my father.

I stand and head for the door, jerking through each dazed step out of Henry's home. Jonah's gaze follows me across the room, worry crinkling his brows, and he stands, holding out a hand as I swing the door back and cross the threshold.

"Harm," he utters.

I ignore him.

I need air.

The small lane feels like it's collapsing in on me. I stumble down the lane, bumping into the stone wall. Stars and smoke fill my vision. Rough stone scrapes my shoulder through my sleeve, and the flat paving stones hit my knees hard on impact. I stare at the ground beneath me. My father's face flips through my mind, like a revolving record of his every expression, his every mood, every memory of us together. All I can see is my father's face. I shove my hands through my hair.

Two dark shapes halt in front of my knees in the dim light.

Guardian boots. Slowly, I track my gaze up, taking in every detail of his uniform. Black boots, dark pants, black belt, grey shirt with long sleeves. His shoulders are decorated with lapels of silver. A high-ranking officer. Our eyes meet. My stomach plummets. Cold streaks of fear pulse through my already overwhelmed body. A smirk twists his face.

Fletcher.

He stands motionless, staring at me.

I rise to my feet. Every cell in my body is screaming at me to run. Instead, we stand, staring at each other in the dark alley, willing the other to make the first move. I can't outrun him here.

He lifts a hand to grab me. I back away, glaring at him.

"Don't even think about running." He inches toward me.

"Where would I run to?"

"There is nowhere you can hide." Shifting slightly on his feet, his focus doesn't waiver. "There are Guardians in every village. You don't stand a chance. Just give it up, boy."

"Why would I let you win? You are the scourge of our lands! Nothing good has ever come from the regime." My heart thunders in my chest. My shaking hands ball into fists, and setting my shoulders back, I step towards Fletcher.

His eyes flicker slightly, but he stands his ground. I lunge for him, swinging my fist around with a vicious hook. Suddenly, his face goes blank and his eyes roll back in his head as he crumples sideways, hitting the stone wall on the way down.

My fist whips through empty air.

CHAPTER 26
IMANI

I stare at his limp body on the ground. My chest tightens a little, and the tiniest of quivers flits through my stomach before heat rises in my center. Two paces behind him, Harm stands wide-eyed. My fingers whiten around the lump of wood.

"You're welcome, clean skin," I say, tossing the wood into the alley. He looks at the limp body in front of him. His face is stunned, and he stares at me chest heaving.

Something's wrong.

"Feeling better, are we?" he snaps.

I step over Fletcher's limp body and grab Harm's hand, pulling him further into the darkness, checking him over. "Where's Jonah?"

He folds his arms across his chest and holds my gaze. "Down the lane, through that door on the left." He tilts his head toward the door.

"We need to get out of here before Fletcher's officers find him, or he wakes up," I say.

"Agreed, but where to now?"

"Did you find anything out about your family?"

He doesn't reply.

Instead, he pushes past me, stalking his way toward the door. I don't follow, and he looks back. I stand, arms crossed, waiting. He turns back and just stares at me, studying my face. Confusion and hurt are etched over his own and my annoyance melts into concern.

"I'll tell you when we're safe," he murmurs.

I walk over, stopping in front of him, resisting the urge to touch his face. "Fair enough."

We turn, and I rap on the door. Jonah opens it and looks at Harm, then behind us to the limp body of Fletcher. In an instant, recognition appears in his eyes. Jonah says his farewells. Hugging his friend, he grabs two robes before closing the door quietly behind him. Robes cinched up, wraps on and hoods pulled down, the three of us make our way to the village center. We stay silent, following Jonah's lead, aware that the Guardians are here and looking for us, and will probably realize Fletcher is missing soon.

Jonah walks with no outward sign that he is worried or tense. His pace is brisk, but not panicked. He offers pleasantries to the village people as we pass by, nothing more. For ten minutes, we walk in silence, following him. Harm trails behind me, looking back every so often, checking our surroundings.

The village outskirts come up quickly, and the surrounding buildings change from stone homes to wooden buildings, built decades ago when the change first occurred. Jonah stops abruptly, and I almost slam into his back, pulling up only inches behind him. I rest my hand on my hip, which carries my knife. A woman carrying a large basket approaches Jonah, and he shifts his feet in the sand and tightens his wrap around his face as she stops to speak.

"Are you looking for someone? Or some place?" she asks. "No, we're just passing through," Jonah says politely. "Alright, well, just in case you need to know, there is a Guardian outpost behind the rocky ridge to the north. It's abandoned now, should you need to rest on your journey. Only a half day's walk, from memory. Make sure you take water; the eastern desert is particularly unforgiving," she says, shifting her basket to her hip. It is then that I notice it is full of fruits. Peaches. Common folk don't have access to fruit, nor is it easily grown in the desert villages.

She sees us looking at the fruit in her basket. "For the Chancellor's good men." She nods towards the basket's contents and then looks to the village center.

"I see," Jonah says.

The woman moves on, making her way to the center of the village. Jonah watches her as she greets the people. They seem to recognize her, but none approach her.

"Is she a spy?" I ask Jonah quietly.

"Most likely," he says, motioning for Harm and me to follow quickly.

He rounds an old wooden building and crouches down, letting out a groan as he lowers to the ground. Harm and I flank him, sitting in the sand. We lean against the building. Harm is quiet, lost in his thoughts.

"If she is a spy, or even untrustworthy, we cannot go east via the normal route. Last I heard, that Guardian outpost isn't abandoned. It would be stupid to go that way, especially now that she has seen us, and given your run-in with Fletcher. Word will be out quickly. We need to move now." He pushes up.

"Why do we still need to go south?" Harm asks.

"To find your family, and the person with that ability to change things back." Jonah looks at him, raising an eyebrow.

"Is that still necessary?" Harm utters.

What is going on here?

"Well, if we're not looking for your family, what are we doing out here?" Jonah asks.

"We find anyone left that has the ability," Harm says, irritation filling his eyes.

"What about finding your real father?" Jonah adds, turning to Harm.

Real father?

I stare at Jonah, lips parted. By the stony look in his face, Harm didn't know.

Is that what happened? His gaze drifts to my face, his brows lowering before his eyes dart away.

"Harm, are you—"

"I don't want to talk about it, Imani, just drop it."

Something breaks in my chest. I pull in a ragged breath. Nobody speaks for a moment. I stand and offer my hand to Harm. He meets my gaze and swallows. After a heartbeat, he takes my hand in his and pulls himself to his feet.

"Why don't you look in your mother's journal?" Jonah prompts. "If she was still in contact with her family, your family's or your father's whereabouts could be in there."

Harm ruffles through his rucksack, hand searching for the journal. He pulls it out and flips through the pages. "The entries start a few years before I was born, so that makes her journal around nineteen years old," he says.

I stand next to him, looking at the pages neatly filled with words. Her handwriting is elegant for someone who had minimal schooling. The lead she uses changes periodically, and I would guess she had to barter to get whatever was available near the village. I see the same names again—the ones I saw last time. I scan the pages for women's names. Towards the back of the journal, several pages are clumped together, stuck at the outer and bottom edges. Something or someone must have stuck them together. Harm runs a finger over the joined pages and pries the edges apart.

A page tears, revealing another map, different from the previous map in the journal.

"Look," Harm says, holding the journal out to Jonah. Jonah bends his head to get a better look, grasping for his glasses before sliding them up his nose.

Jonah snaps his head up and looks at Harm with wide eyes. I meet his stunned gaze and then look back down at the map. The markings are unusual, and some villages are not on this map. There are no markings of dunes or outposts. There are villages on this map that don't exist now.

"Harm, you're too young to know what this is!" Jonah whispers wildly. Why is he whispering? The look in his eyes has changed from one of surprise to one of excitement.

"What is this a map of?" Harm asks, quieting his voice to match Jonah's.

"This is a map from before!" His words come fast. "Before the change in weather, before the lands disintegrated into desert. This is a map of what our lands were like before. This map shows all that existed when seasons controlled our world. When there were trees, grass, rivers, waterfalls, lakes, booming villages, farmers, and most of all, wealth. See!" He slides a finger over the markings that indicate landscapes foreign to me.

"But why would my mother have this map?"

"I can only guess that an earlier generation of her family lived through the times of prosperity, which means your relatives were around before, during and possibly after the change. This is good. If they've lived here for decades and existed before the change, chances are someone on your mother's side may have the ability. I was hoping for this, but now we can be almost certain of it."

"So, we find my mother's family, and hopefully one of my relations has the ability? Two birds, one stone. But then what? How do we convince them to help us?"

"That we will worry about once we have found them and confirmed they are who we think they are. First things first: let's get to Mareya, without running into the Guardians," he says, pulling his wrap tight and walking into the desert sands, head down and stride strong.

Harm and I exchange an awkward look. He rips his hood back down and trudges into the sands after Jonah. A heartbeat later, with a last look at the village, I follow him. Every revelation from today whirls through my mind, like the flurry of sand that dances around my feet, and I stride into the expanse of darkened sands after Harm.

CHAPTER 27
HARM

Two days of traveling through desert dunes has done nothing for Imani's mood. Is she annoyed that she had to knock out Fletcher? I never asked her to do that. I was handling things just fine. Or is it because I won't talk to her about what Henry told me?

If I tell her what Henry told me back in the village, what is she going to think of me then? Jonah is certain that finding my family is the next step. I'm not so sure now. Things were easier when I was just finding my mother's family, with the possibility of having a safe place to hide away. Now, my arrival may not be welcome.

I'm not sure what to do or say to make it better. Things between Imani and I swing from feeling good to complicated and tense. Her moods shift like the sands. What is going through her head? I wish she would talk to me, or even just walk next to me. Instead, following her, I stare at her back. Jonah doesn't appear to notice the tension between Imani and me. If he does, he is not letting on. Maybe I'm making too much out of it.

The sands shift around my feet in swirling patterns, and I recognize their dance: sandstorm. Between the dunes is not the place to be if a sandstorm is building. Jonah stops, sheltering his eyes with a hand, trying to determine what is going to happen next. The wind is hotter than the sun, and sand ripples off every mound.

A low roar creeps towards us as a wall of sand steadily grows to our right. Jonah and I exchange an urgent glance. Imani reads our faces and takes off running towards Mareya. But it's still miles away.

We won't make it.

I fly through the dense sands. Our robes and rucksacks weigh us down. Jonah is beside me, but he falters every few steps. I stay beside him, keeping his pace. Buffeting winds slam into us, coating our faces with hot sand, our labored breathing drowned out by the turbulence. The storm surges towards us from the south, billowing and churning in clouds of spiraling sands. Shades of brown and gold fold in around us. The storm wall roars closer with every insignificant stride we take.

"Over here!" Imani yells, pointing to a rise in the rocky outcrops to our left. There amongst the spiny plants is the mouth of a small cavern. Jonah's face is flushed and blotchy, his steps slowing. I grab his arm, steering him towards the cavern entrance.

"Keep going, Harm, leave me."

"Not a chance."

Imani runs through the opening and into the darkness.

Passing through the mouth of the only refuge we have left, I keep my grip on Jonah's arm, letting him lean against me. The roaring dulls. Imani paces in a small circle, trying to catch her breath. Jonah slides down the cave wall onto the cool floor. The darkness lightens as our eyes adjust to the confined space, and mustiness and the fragrance of disturbed plants tangles in the stagnant air.

I drop down beside Jonah, and the damp earth meets my palms. Spotted underneath me is a velvety carpet of moss, as if it couldn't decide where to grow first. Fine-leaved plants flank the cave walls, loaded with small violet flowers with finger-like petals. I rub it between my fingers, and a pungent smell stings my nose. The fumes tang like a briny infused oil on my tongue.

"Don't do that, Harm," Imani mutters, sliding down the cave wall next to Jonah. "You don't know what it is."

"That is the odor of a plant called valerian," Jonah utters through raspy breaths. "It's often used as a potent healing agent. But the fumes can render you unconscious if you're exposed to it for a period. Its roots are a sedative. Best leave it be."

"We don't want to be unconscious in here," Imani utters. "Who knows what lives in these caves?"

Our heavy breathing fills the cavern. The raging blood in my head quiets, giving way to a trickle of water from deeper in the cave. It is like stars bumping into one another as they cascade over a rocky ledge, creating a melody—music originating from the darkness.

Jonah rests his head on Imani's small shoulder and closes his eyes. Above me, an uneven layered ceiling of slime-covered rock spans the top of the cave, shimmering with a watery cloak. The storm hollers outside. Sand has covered the entrance back around the passageway behind us. We will need to dig our way out when the storm dies off.

I push up to my feet and make my way deeper into the cave. Slipping on wet earth, I steady myself with a hand against the wall. Everything is cool and wet. Goosebumps slide over my skin. The darkness is lit up by tiny luminescent creatures clinging to the ceiling. They stir above me with each step. It's unlike anything I have ever seen. Water echoes from deeper in the cave, getting louder.

I pull a ragged box of matches from my rucksack and light one of the thin wooden sticks. A puck and a swoosh, and the dark space surrounding me lights up, illuminating the outline of the cave.

Moss covers the walls and most of the ceiling in a soft, green blanket. The flame bends toward the water sounds, chasing the air. The passage narrows. I turn back, and Imani shoots me an excited glance. Transferring Jonah's half-asleep head to the wall and pushing to her feet, she catches up with me.

The walls close in the further we go. Imani's breath falls into rhythm with mine. The flame reaches my fingers and peters out. I stop, sucking on my two burnt fingertips. Imani bumps into me. I fumble for another match, and it explodes to life. We tread on the slime-covered earth, careful not to disturb anything.

The end of the passage gives way to a chamber ten times greater than the cave we first entered. I freeze, and my breath halts. Light spears down from the high ceiling in multiple places, rays of the sun seeking refuge from the torrent of winds outside. The roar of the storm is only just audible over the sounds of the running water. The flame burns down in my outstretched hand, and I blow it out. Imani steps up beside me, and her gasp splits the air.

"What is this place?" she whispers.

"I don't know, some kind of oasis?"

She looks at me for the first time in hours, and I hold her gaze for a handful of heartbeats. Two small streams twine their way around a center islet, frolicking their way over pebbles and stones. Water tumbles from a spring behind the islet, running either side of it, creating two silvering paths like an elegant boundary not to be crossed. Moss covers the entire islet. A small tree with wide, glossy green leaves perched upon elegantly twisted branches stands at its center. Small white birds land on its outstretched arms intermittently, resting their delicate wings. The walls of the cavern are home to small lizards and a variety of crawling creatures not native to the sandy surfaces of the desert.

A colorful bird darts overhead with a high-pitched sound. It looks like a tiny version of the desert vultures, but much more refined and exquisite. Bright blues decorate its wings, with a deeper hue covering its downy body underneath. Its beak is grey like the silvered leaves on the spindly trees outside. Imani watches as it flits around the skies of its confined home. A wide grin grows over her face, and her ecstatic eyes follow it with acute focus.

Imani unwraps her hair, letting it tumble over her shoulders, wrapping her scarf around her waist. She holds a hand above her as the winged creature takes another pass overhead. She giggles, tracking the bird with her outstretched hand. Her dark hair bounces around her shoulders, creating a gorgeous border for her beautiful face and bright blue eyes, now full of wonder and curiosity.

She sits on a large rock at the edge of the stream. Bending down, she runs her hand through the water, going against the current. Water ripples and wakes around her hand, white spray splashing up in protest. I sit down beside her, close enough that she looks at me with a sideways glance and a crooked smile. Every part of me that was wound up tight over the last few days lets go. Water rushing, bending, and hopping breaks the silence. Neither of us speaks, not wanting to ruin what we have just discovered.

The sight of the small tree brings back the image of the forest I used to see in my dreams. Vivid green and the rough, tapered bark trunks, so tall and grand, stick out in my memory. A small lone tree on this islet makes no sense—although looking around, there is everything required to grow trees: water, earth, and sunlight. From the stories my father told me, this is the perfect environment for a tree. But why just one? How does one tree stand and no more? And how does this place exist? It is pure chance? Now visions of entire verdant lands paint themselves into existence inside my mind: streams, trees, grass, and animals other than the predatory hunters that the desert shelters.

"Hello, you two down there?" Jonah's voice sounds off, probably from the plants he was lying on. I had almost forgotten he was back at the entrance.

Imani springs to her feet and trots towards the dark passageway. I follow, searching for the matches once again. I strike a match and follow her towards the sound of Jonah's voice. Through the darkness, we carefully pick our path, trying to stay upright on the precarious floor. Imani and the walls on either side of me are the only things visible.

"We're coming," Imani calls back, her voice echoing ahead of us.

Shuffling moves toward us.

"Jonah," I call out.

"Come back here," he replies.

"Just wait where you are, and we'll find you," Imani calls back. We pick up the pace over the slimy surface, using the walls to steady ourselves as we go. Around the corner of the passage, a figure stands hunched over. The match in my hand goes out, and I hasten to get another one alight. For a moment, everything is black, and the shuffling creeps towards us. The striking match reverberates, and light spreads through the passageway once again. Imani has stopped in front of me, her body as still as stone.

A man stands inches from her face.

It's not Jonah.

CHAPTER 28
IMANI

I scan the scrawny man up and down. His shirt, almost torn to rags, hangs from his body, held on with a meager rope around his thin waist. Pants that only make it to his bony, filthy knees are frayed beyond repair. Every piece of clothing is dirty, carrying a putrid tang. His hair is long and disheveled, and his skin is so pale. Pale-blue eyes, the color of moonstone, protrude from his face like beacons. The shoes on his feet are nothing more than sandals. He stands before us calmly, leaning on a stick the same height as himself, with a dark expression.

I move a step back, hovering a hand over the hip that holds my blade. Stepping around one side, I study the man from head to toe, taking in his peculiar dress and unkempt appearance, tracking the length of his scrawny body and back up again.

He watches me carefully, and his face mellows into a slight smile. Leaning closer, he sniffs me. I lean back. Without speaking, he points to Jonah with his stick. He appears asleep, but the man's eyes have turned to concern.

I rush to Jonah. Dropping to my knees, I place a hand on his chest, waiting for the rise and fall. His breaths are too shallow. I rough him up, waiting for a response.

"Jonah, wake up!"

Harm comes to stand at my side, putting himself between me and the man with the stick. Jonah murmurs, moving slightly. The ragged man points to the soft, green plants on the ground and then points to the opposite wall, bare of growth, just simple dirt. Of course. Jonah has fallen into unconsciousness from the foliage beneath him. We grab Jonah under the arms and drag him to the dirt patch on the opposite wall, away from the sleep-inducing plants.

Within moments, Jonah's breathing picks up pace, and his chest rises and falls deeper and longer. I turn to the man holding his stick, walking over to him.

"Thank you." I rest a hand on the man's shoulder.

His eyes flick from my face to the hand on his shoulder. Harm watches every move the scrawny man makes. The man nods, then grunts softly and turns, walking away. I follow him, and he pauses, then turns to face me. He looks at me and back to Harm.

"You should get out of here as soon as you are able," he says, warning in his voice.

"But we're buried in, and the storm outside is still hollering," I say, folding my arms across my chest.

"When it's done, then," he replies. "Your friend will be okay to travel in a matter of hours. You can dig your way out."

"Who are you?" I ask.

"No one of consequence." He turns to walk away.

"Wait." I grab his arm, and he turns back, eyes scanning my face. "What are you doing in here?"

"I live here, lass."

"What do you mean, you live here? This is a cave."

"I know what it is. If you would be so kind as to be off when your friend awakes, I would be most grateful."

"What is your name?"

He stares at me. "Charlie," he finally says.

"Charlie who?" Harm asks.

"Just Charlie."

"Why do you live here?" I ask.

"I protect the oasis inside—the one you entered without permission just now." A snarl lines his voice for the first time.

"How does the oasis exist?" Harm asks.

"It's all that's left, after he changed the weather."

"He? You mean the Chancellor?" I ask.

"Is that what the people call him now?" He walks on, and Harm and I follow him.

He walks into a smaller cave through an opening in the left side of the passageway. I didn't notice it before. It is pitch dark again, and Harm runs into me. I grab his hand. His hands wrap around mine, and I hold onto them like a lifeline.

Flame flickers in the center of the darkness before us. Harm's face comes to life in the ambient light from the candle Charlie has lit. He looks straight ahead still, watching the old man's every move. He lights every candle in the cave in a familiar routine. There are dozens of them. As the space brightens with each one, his belongings come into view: collections of odd things in one corner; several musty books with water-damaged covers; a small wooden crate with what appear to be plants and wrapped-up food; a small mat with a grey blanket, lying at the back of the cave on the floor; white trinkets with beads poking out from under a makeshift bundle of rags that I assume is his pillow.

"Why do you have to protect the oasis?" Harm asks. "As far as I know, nobody knows it exists." His voice is soft and kind, as if still in shock after taking in the man's meek existence in the now boldly lit cave.

Charlie does not answer him, rummaging through a small tin box, hunting for something. Even under the oppression we live in throughout the sands, I've never seen anyone exist in a place as terrible as this. There is a look of empathy and sadness on Harm's face. The smell of dampness and mildew tangle their way around us, and I clear my throat.

"How long have you been here?" I ask.

"I don't remember how many years it has been now. I stopped counting a long time ago. All I know is that it has been an age since anyone has set foot in this cave. It's nice to see a real face—and one as pretty as yours too," he says with a grin. He moves closer, touching my cheek with his filthy hand. I stand motionless, letting him in my space.

"A *real* face?" I echo.

His fingers drop from my jaw. "When you have been alone as long as I have, you start to make friends who aren't really there. But at least I can still tell the difference between who is real and who is not."

"Why don't you leave? Is this oasis even worth protecting, at such a high price for yourself?" Harm asks.

"I have that thought often. Never you mind," he says, walking back to his possessions, "I no longer have anywhere else to go. Besides, this place is far too important to be left alone. Without it, our chances of changing things back are impossible."

Harm looks at me, and I can tell what he is thinking. The old man knows a lot about the weather changing, so he must know about the dial, the ability, the man who controls it, and how things were before. He may also know who possesses the ability to turn the dial back. Back to rains and storms. Back to prosperity. Seasons. Every inch of this parched land, back to one magnificent oasis.

"Why is this place so important if we want to change things back?" I ask.

"It holds the flora and fauna from before—some of it anyway. Some I lost years ago. I must ensure it lives on, ready for the day that we will need it to help the lands flourish once again. Even with the rains the dial can bring, without the seeds and animals, our lands can't be restored. I have been saving and storing the seeds and tending to as many small creatures as I can for decades."

"But we only saw birds, insects, and one tree in the oasis," Harm says.

"Yes, I know. It has been most difficult to keep many species alive without them eating too many of each other. I'm afraid I have failed in that aspect." He hangs his head. "But you never know; they may exist somewhere else."

"There is nowhere else," I say.

"There is more to this place than just sand and ruin. You will see, girlie," he retorts.

"Huh," I snort.

Charlie grins. "I see the young people have not changed an ounce. Should have guessed."

Harm shifts on the spot next to me. "We should get back to Jonah, our friend."

"Yes, yes," he replies with a look of disappointment.

I make my way back to the passage but Harm stays with Charlie. Their voices echo throughout the cavern.

"Can you tell me about the ability that enables someone to change the dial?" Harm asks.

"A handful of people—the Chancellor, as you call him, and his family—carried it. Also, the family of his maternal grandmother. Last I knew, they were unaware that they held the ability, it was more speculation than anything else. They have always kept to themselves. Who would want to volunteer that information, even if they had it? With the Guardians covering every part of this land, it would be a death sentence."

"Are there any of the Chancellor's family left?" Harm asks.

I'm not sure if the man would even know, being holed up in this cave.

"Only one that I know of."

"Who?" Harm asks.

Charlie sighs. "You're looking at him."

I look back at Charlie. In the dim light, I can't see his face properly. Resting a hand on Jonah's neck and one on his chest, I check his breathing before poking my way back down the passageway to Harm.

"You mean, you also have the ability? Hang on, wait—you're related to the Chancellor?" I ask impatiently.

"Yes. Unfortunately, you cannot choose your relatives. Pity. If you could, maybe I would've fared better in this life. Although, I felt partially responsible for my little brother's actions, and this is how I pay that debt." He returns to muttering to himself and wanders over to his books.

Harm follows and grabs his arm. "The Chancellor is your brother?"

Charlie turns and stares at the hand on his arm before lifting his gaze to Harm's. "My brother—or the Chancellor, as you call him now—made it his life's purpose to restore order to these lands. I don't condone the way he did it, but I understand why he did it. We all pay a price in this life; ours was losing our parents at a tender age to violence and greed. Never judge a man before you know what drives him."

"If you're his brother, why are you hiding here, and why haven't you tried to change things back?" Harm asks, getting impatient with the old man. I pick my way closer to them over the slippery ground.

"I am no match for my younger brother. Besides, it worked for a while, all the change. There was no ridiculous wealth, and almost no crime. Things were fair. That was his goal, and he succeeded."

"But now we have next to nothing, and the Guardians rule our lives. Good people die for the sake of laws and taxes. How can you think this is better?" Harm snaps. He is standing, tense, fingers curling.

"I never said what we have now is better, boy. But you don't understand what it's like to lose your entire family because of another person's vile actions." He wobbles as he clings to his stick.

"Yes, I do," Harm whispers. The low sound tears at my heart.

"What are you talking about?" Charlie says, looking at him in disbelief.

"They threw my family in the well in our village—me included. For not following the rules. I survived. My father, my mother, and my little sister did not." Tears line his eyes. I pull in a deep breath as I come to stand beside him. I watch Charlie's face as recognition spreads across it. I stare at the both of them, my stomach flipping. I should tell Harm about that day.

Moments pass as Charlie studies Harm from head to toe, as if trying to gauge his honesty. His eyes melt into sorrow and sympathy. No doubt the pain of losing his family is being dragged back to the surface, hauled through his entire body, as it is through Harm's now, and pain warps both their faces. Time does not seem to have made much of a difference for Charlie.

"I am truly sorry about your family," Charlie utters, gazing at the floor. "That is a pain that never leaves you."

I watch as Harm fights back a sob. A single tear slides down his cheek, still covered in dirt and sand, leaving a channel of moisture as noticeable as his broken heart. Charlie's head rises, and I weave my fingers into Harm's. He cycles through deep, ravenous breaths, turning to face me. Every part of me wants to hold him tight, until the pain disappears. His gorgeous face broken up by grief stares back at me.

Tightness pulls at my chest. I should tell Harm what happened that day, how I am tied to that part of his life. But guilt, fear and hopelessness talk me out of it every time I think I have found the courage to do so. I replay the Guardians standing over his family. I force down the sick feeling clawing its way through my core. I can't. I couldn't even save him by myself. I couldn't even save one person without help.

I pull Harm away from Charlie. His hand is firm around mine as he staggers where I lead. I take deep breaths before we enter the lit-up area where Jonah is now propped up against the wall, awake. It is only now that I notice the thunderous sounds from outside have slowed to a mild hum. The winds have all but died down, and the storm has almost passed.

Jonah pulls himself to his feet with a soft groan. He looks at Harm, and the exchange is one of sympathy and knowing. He heads towards the entrance of the cave and moves aside debris before shoveling away sand with his two bare hands. I follow and do the same. Moments later, Harm falls in beside me.

The sand is thick and hot, and we work quickly. Between the three of us is a small opening above one boulder flanking the cave entrance. I climb over the rock and slip outside, taking in the landscape before popping back through the opening. "Nothing much out there but sand. It looks different now, the dunes have shifted."

"We will continue using the compass," Jonah says, concentrating his efforts on making the opening large enough for him to get through.

Harm's gaze is fixed on me while Jonah is busy. I open my mouth to say something, but close it again. Jonah's voice breaks our contact. Harm pulls on his robe and shoulders his rucksack. I do the same.

"You going to let the oldest person go first then, hey?" Jonah asks, his gaze alternating between Harm and me, as if recognizing something has just changed between us. I clear my throat and wrap my hair back into the scarf, following with my face wrap. I glance at Harm before pulling myself up to the opening and climbing outside into the hot sands.

CHAPTER 29
HARM

Everything is different. The dunes have shifted, rearranged by Mother Nature like a game for the gods. Which player won? The golden sands surrounding us are now so foreign.

Jonah is walking in small circles, assessing our position and the direction of other places in our current landscape. Imani stands with her back to me. She is still, with only her headscarf blowing in the wind over her shoulder. The dunes that lie ahead of her make it impossible to miss how petite she is.

Something feels different since she led me away from Charlie. Jonah's face when he looked at us both. What did he see? Was it the same thing that I felt when she laced her fingers in mine? I didn't want to let her go. Ever.

"We should head south-west for a couple of hours to get to Mareya," Jonah says to us both, waiting for one of us to respond. Imani remains still. I shake my head, dislodging the thoughts of Imani's touch.

"Okay," I say. My body is exhausted from being awake most of the night. But staying still is not a good plan. Jonah and I head east over the sands, still unsettled from the wind and dense to walk through. I walk for a few minutes a ways behind Jonah before I look back to make sure she is following us. But Imani still hasn't moved. She stands motionless right where we left her.

"Jonah," I say. He turns around and watches to see if Imani is going to follow. She stands rooted in the sand. He walks back.

"Wait here," he says, clapping a hand on my shoulder.

He stands with Imani, speaking with her. I watch her body language, trying to understand what he is saying and how she responds. Jonah puts his hands on her shoulders and speaks to her. Imani doesn't speak now, looking away. A handful of heartbeats later, she tightens her headscarf and follows Jonah back past me. I move in behind them and follow. We walk in silence until the sun is high in the sky, and Jonah comes to a halt.

"We need to follow the compass now; it's too easy to get disoriented out here. Have a drink, and let's keep moving," he says, taking a swig from his canteen and returning it to the belt under his robe. Imani and I do the same. I try to get a glance at her face, but the wrap hides what I want to see most.

The village of Mareya comes into view over the last of the big dunes before the rocky outcrops of the east. Smoke from kitchens and the sounds of village life float across the sands to greet us. Our stride quickens when the fragrance of spices and grains hits us. The closer we get, the more tantalizing the aromas. The only food we've had in the last couple of days is bits of dried meat and stale chunks of bread wrapped in cloth. I ache for a solid meal.

Guardians patrol the village, and we are careful to keep our wraps up and hoods pulled down to conceal our faces. The village homes sit in rings, much like in the last village, and people go about their end-of-day chores. Men and women float around in groups, chatting and eating. Many more are in their homes, sitting with family for their evening meal.

After thirty minutes of searching for a spot hidden away from the watching eyes of the Guardians, we come upon a patch of sand and sparse grass behind one home towards the back of the village. Jonah unpacks a mat from his traveling bag and lies down with a groan. Imani follows and settles in beside Jonah. He watches me as I step around the two of them, wondering where to lie. Jonah gestures with a sideways look to lie on his other side, away from Imani. Not having a sleeping mat to lie on, I clear the area near Jonah of small rocks and debris and lie back.

A thousand stars blanket the sky above us as we lie silently. After a few moments, Jonah is snoring, sound asleep. I look across his resting body at Imani, who is looking up at the stars. She's a million miles away.

"You asleep?" I whisper, knowing full well she's not.

"No, Harm."

"Are you okay, Imani?" I'm afraid of her answer, not knowing what I have done to upset her. Moments pass, and still she doesn't respond. I turn back to the stars above me. At least they are still magnificent.

"I'll get over it," she replies finally.

I look back at her. "Did I upset you? Because if I did, it was not my intention."

A small sound of amusement leaves her mouth as she rolls to face me, propping her head on her hand to look past Jonah. She stares at me for several heartbeats, her face scrunched up, brows down.

"It's not your fault Harm," Imani says quietly, her gaze dropping to her hand fiddling with the strands of the sleeping mat beneath her.

"Okay ...?"

"Your family—it's not your fault. There was nothing you could have done."

"Oh."

"Things need to change. A lot of families have ended up like yours did, and more will even still. If we can find someone with the ability who is willing to help, then there is hope that we can change things for the better."

"But what if they don't want to help us? Jonah said they may not be easily convinced. A lot of years have gone by, and no one has come forward. Maybe they won't or can't help us."

"I don't know, but we have to try. Good people are dying. It has to stop." Imani rolls onto her back, closes her eyes, and looses a shaky breath. I look back at the star-dappled sky with its midnight hues above us. I miss my family, and I just hope that they are up there, together and happy.

Morning arrives all too soon. Jonah is already up and gone, his mat still where he left it. Imani is still fast asleep on her side, her dark hair resting on her shoulders and framing her face. She looks peaceful. I haven't seen her this settled for days. Sleeping under the stars must have agreed with her. I sit up and stretch. The ground underneath me is not exactly soft, and my bones ache from lying on the hard surface all night. I get up and take another minute to stretch my arms up over my head. The muscles in my back are stiff, and I bend side to side.

"You might want to robe up before you get noticed," Imani says from behind me. She's sitting up, watching me.

"I thought you were asleep." I shrug my robe over my clothes and running my hands through my hair.

Jonah returns, two small brown parcels in hand, passing one to each of us. The smell hits me before I even open it. Breakfast. Imani and I devour our food, leaving Jonah chuckling at the pace at which we consume it. It has been weeks since we started the day with a good meal, let alone one as delicious as this.

"Now that your bellies are full, we can make our way back to the tavern and ask after your family," Jonah says, looking at me while he speaks.

"You'll need your mother's journal," Imani adds.

I pick up my rucksack and double-check that it is still inside. The ragged leather-bound book sits amongst the many possessions in my bag. I will be ever grateful to Imani for retrieving my rucksack. Without it and without her, I would have probably been caught by now, or worse.

We pick up camp and throw our head covers up to conceal ourselves before making way to the tavern. The doors swing open easily, and a friendly woman greets us with a friendly expression and a nod. We find a table at the back. Only a handful of patrons grace the space at this early hour.

"What can I get for you this morning?" the woman asks, looking to Jonah.

"Ah, we're just in need of some help. We're looking for some people whom we believe live in the village."

"I can try to be of help, but I don't know everyone that lives here. Who are you looking for? And what do you need them for?" Caution lines her voice.

"Harm, show her the journal," Jonah says, nodding to my rucksack.

I pull the bound book from the rucksack and flip to the page with the names of my mother's family on it. I hold the journal up so she can see the writing clearly. She looks at the page, then at me. Her eyes track to Jonah and stay there.

"Can you tell me why you are after these folk?" she asks hesitantly, and her eyes widen as she glances back to the pages.

"The lad here is trying to find his family, his mother's side. This is her journal. That's all," Jonah returns.

The woman looks at me for more than a moment, checking me over as if checking for honesty. She walks to the nearest table, setting her tray down and pulling a chair over to us. She sits next to me, taking my hand in hers.

"My name is Gail. I have lived here my whole life, and I might be able to help you. But first, tell me your name." Her gaze returns the journal in my hand.

"Harmen," I say. "This is Imani and Jonah."

"The Guardians punished Harm's family for rebellion. He is searching for family here," Imani says, her voice straining over the last two words.

"I am so very sorry to hear that." Gail pats my hand.

"We're trying to find Harm's mother's relations, as he needs a family and a home," Jonah adds.

"How did it come about that you did not share your family's fate?"

"One of the village men saved me during the night." Imani's blue eyes burn into mine.

"You are very lucky, young man. Most people condemned by the Guardians do not survive. Count your blessings every day," she says. I glance at Imani, returning my gaze to Gail.

"Do you know any of these names?" I bring Gail's attention back to the journal, tapping a finger on the page lightly.

"As a matter of fact, I know two of those names. One is here, the other is not. This lady," she points to my grandmother's name, "is still here. She is well known and very liked, even by the Guardians. She is our healer. Her home is just on the outskirts of the village on the southern side. A wooden fence surrounds her house, with a small herb garden in front. Goodness knows how she keeps it alive in this arid place, but she does. I wish you all well, and take care." She squeezes my hand.

Flutters twist through my stomach. My grandmother is here.

Gail gets up to leave, but turns on the spot, looking at Jonah. "You are an honorable man to return this young man to his family." She smiles at him, but sadness rushes across her face as she leaves, picking up her tray as she goes.

"Well lad, no more delays! Let's head to the southern outskirts and find your grandmother," Jonah says, standing to leave. Imani gathers her belongings.

The doors to the tavern thud open. Two Guardians hover over the threshold. They search from where they stand, hands sheltering their faces to adjust their eyes to the dim light. My heart thumps in my chest, and Imani curses under her breath.

Jonah stands frozen to his spot, and I look back at the two Guardians. Blood drains from my body from the top down, and the cold prickle of fear holds me to the floor.

Fletcher.

CHAPTER 30
HARM

Jonah grabs my arm, holding me still. Stalking over to the counter, the Guardians home in on Gail, ignoring her customers. Imani throws her robe hood over her head, wrapping her face up. Jonah does the same. The tremor in my hands matches my racing heart. I grip my hood and pull it over and down.

Gail talks with the Guardians, offering them food and drink. We sneak around the perimeter of the dark tavern and head towards the door. Terrified some small noise will give us away, every step I take is filled with heavy dread. I shove my shaking hands in my pockets, breathing my way through every foot of floor we cover. The distance to the doors seems to never lessen, and we move as fast as we can without attracting their attention. Jonah leads us towards the exit. Imani walks right behind me with her hands on her belt, on almost silent feet.

Gail tells them of the goings-on of the tavern. They question her about the patrons from yesterday and this morning, asking about anyone who has come into the village over the last day or two. She retells the events from the last twenty-four hours in great detail.

"Answer the question I asked you," Fletcher growls.

"I am trying to tell you all I know. I'm not as young as I used to be, and it takes a while to remember all the details," Gail prattles as we reach the doors.

Jonah cautiously swings them open. Imani's focus is fixed on the two Guardians as she closes the doors behind us with slow movements. We slip down the closest alleyway. Jonah pulls Imani and me behind a stack of wooden crates, and we slide down the stone wall and sit in silence.

Imani rips her hood from her head, her hands now shaking, her jaw clenched and eyes full of anger. Jonah watches her intensely, not breaking his stare. A moment passes, and the Guardians walk past our alley entrance and into the next building. Imani shifts in her spot, and every muscle in her body tenses. Jonah's hands grip her arms. "Don't."

Imani's stare burns into him. Her lip curled, she curls her hands into fists, squatting in the alley.

"It won't help. They'll just find us sooner, and that won't end well for Harm. You know that, Imani." He holds her to the spot.

"Let go of me," Imani hisses.

"Not yet. It is not time yet, my girl."

"What are you going to do?" I ask Imani.

She stares at my face and releases a low, guttural growl before slumping to the ground.

"Nothing." Raising her knees up and burying her head in them, she exhales the fury away.

"What we need to do is find your grandmother," Jonah says, meeting my gaze.

"How do we do that with the Guardians hanging around?"

"Carefully. I suspect once we find her, you will be safe, mostly.

Imani and I can continue the search for anyone with the ability without you. It is too risky for you to continue with us. I will not let you share the same fate as your family, my boy."

My breath hitches, chest squeezing tight. "No, no way! I'm going with you."

Dammit.

I did not come all this way to just to sit around in an old lady's house while Imani and Jonah are out risking their necks. I am not letting Imani run around this desolate place, hunting for someone who may not want to be found, miles away from me.

"I will look after Imani, I promise. You needn't worry about that." Jonah words are soft, but solid.

Imani looks up, fire in her eyes. Jonah holds my gaze until I finally relent with a nod. I stand, offering a hand to Imani. Her soft hand hits mine, and I pull her to her feet. She meets my gaze, and we stand staring at each other for a moment before Jonah rises to his feet. Pulling our robes and wraps around tighter, we head for the southern edge of the village.

The Guardians are busy talking to people in the center of the communal area near the well. We move as quickly as we can, still appearing as if we are going about our normal duties. They are not leaving me behind. I will think of something.

After ten minutes of traveling, watching our backs, we come to a house with a wooden fence and an herb garden in front. Sands rest up against the fence, which leans outward. The home, similar to mine in Amondo, is greyed from the weather. This must be it. Pushing the small gate open, I walk into the yard. The front of the house has a small wooden porch, sporting herbs and metal chimes making a ruckus in the wind as sand drifts around the porch like children playing. I lift a hand to knock—and drop it again. Drawing in a long breath, I finally knock on the door. Removing my hood and wrap, I step back and wait.

Floorboards squeak inside the house. The door rattles from the inside, and two locks click open. The door opens with a tug as it scrapes along the uneven floor underneath it. A woman appears from behind it. She is old and grey, hair falling just short of her shoulders. Her clothes are old but well cared for. She wears clothing like Imani's, but she is taller. A Blending pendant containing a blue stone hangs from her neck, decorating her chest with other colorful fibers woven into a necklace. Her wrinkled face holds a shape I recognize, square like my mother's, and mine. She looks me up and down with pale-blue eyes framed by the lines of time.

"Can I help you, young man?"

"Yes, I am looking for Enid Starling." My heart flings against my chest. I grip the insides of my pockets with both hands.

"You have found her."

My stomach flutters. I have been waiting for this moment, this person. Now I am here, and all thoughts of what comes next evaporate. Not speaking, I draw in a breath, trying to muster the words that I need. I open my mouth, but close it again. She stands patiently waiting, searching my face. Her gaze falls behind me briefly, to where Imani and Jonah stand outside the gate.

"Why don't you come inside and sit," she says, taking my hand. Ushering me inside, she steers me to a sitting room and sits me in a chair, studying me for signs—of what, I don't know.

I sit breathing for a time before I pull myself together. She stands across from me and waits patiently for me to speak, with a small smile, as if she recognizes something in my face.

"I'm afraid I ..." I look to the floor, gripping the arms of the worn chair, trying damn hard not to choke on the words. "I come bearing bad news."

Her concerned eyes monitor my every move. "Go ahead."

"I have come from Amondo. I have news of your daughter." I

pause, gauging her response. She clasps one hand around her pendant, but her face remains the same. "A few months ago, your daughter and her family were sentenced to execution by the Guardians."

Recognition claims her face, and she falls into the chair behind her. Her breathing hastens, and she clasps her hands together, tears welling in her eyes. She plants her face into her hands and lets out a long cry. My already fragile heart splinters in two, as if it hasn't already done so before. Every sound that leaves her keening body pulls a tide of agony through me.

She rocks back and forth, breathing through whimpers. I kneel on the floor in front of her and take her hands in mine. They are soft and thin. The weight of my chest makes it hard to breathe without sobbing. Her gaze lifts to mine, and she is shaking. I wrap my hands around hers, and she sucks in a breath and sits up straight.

"And my grandchildren, they were punished also?" Enid asks, wiping away the river of tears that has claimed her face.

"Yes," I choke out, finding the next part even harder to say, a pain in the back of my throat squeezing the words back. "But one was saved."

She tilts her head, frowning. "Saved? How could that be possible? How do you know this?" Her words quicken through ragged breaths.

"Because I was there."

"So, you saw one be saved, and you came all this way to tell me. How did you even know where to find me?"

I stay on my knees for a time before answering, not knowing how to make the next sentence leave my mouth. The wooden floorboards hard against my knees, I shift slightly before responding. I look back up at her face, and she steadies herself. With her eyes studying my face, her mouth opens. She breathes in, waiting for another blow.

"I was saved," I whisper.

Her face lights up with wonder, eyes widening. "You ... you are my grandson?" she whispers, hands shaking in mine. I squeeze them gently and try to gift her a smile. A small, pained laugh of disbelief leaves her chest. She grabs my face with her hands, her eyes searching for the remaining fragments of her daughter. Tears still come, streaming down.

"Young man, you have broken my heart and patched it up all in one moment."

"I am sorry for bringing such heartbreak to you." I know exactly what sorrow I have just caused her. "I only hope that in you gaining a grandson, I can offer some small piece of happiness back to you after all you have gone through."

"You have most certainly given me that. Harmen?" Enid asks, rubbing her thumbs over the backs of my hands.

"Yes."

"Your mother always loved that name. It was her grandfather's name, my father."

I stand and push up from the chair. She stands shorter than me by a few inches. Without hesitating, she pulls me into a tight hug. "I used to tell her stories from my childhood. She loved any story with my father in it. Your mother is—" she hesitates to let me out of the hug. "Was the most loving girl I ever knew. She would be proud of you for coming here to see me. It is the right way to do things, the kind thing to do." Her eyes drop to the floor again, as if having to process this all again.

"Come and introduce me to your friends," Enid says after a while, heading towards the door. She cracks it open and beckons Imani and Jonah inside. They step through the doorway. Imani inspects every part of me, her gaze hover over my face, before lifting to mine. Jonah removes his wrap and robe and greets Enid. She looks at Jonah and Imani.

"Thank you for bringing my grandson to me," Enid says, looking at Jonah. He simply nods. Imani's face remains fixed on Enid now.

"Enid, this is Jonah and Imani."

"Hello, Enid, it's nice to finally meet you," Jonah offers. Enid tilts her head to the side, silver lining her eyes once again, and she nods and pulls in a wobbly breath. "You must come in and rest your bodies. That is quite a journey you have undertaken. I am not unaware of the consequences of helping a person who has been deemed by the Guardians as punishable. It is a substantial risk for you both. Thank you for doing that for our family."

"It was the right thing to do," Imani replies, her words softer than the look across her face.

"You are a brave young lady, Imani. My grandson is lucky to have you in his life." Enid smiles as she gazes between Imani and me.

Imani looks at the floor as a crimson shade creeps up her neck, and she tries unsuccessfully to keep her gaze from mine.

"They are both lucky to have each other." Jonah glances between us. "However, Imani and I must continue our journey from here, and since Harm is in a tough spot with the Guardians, we were hoping he could stay with you for the time being, so he is not in danger of being caught again."

Enid's delight springs over her face like a blooming desert flower after much-needed heavy dew. "Oh, that would make this old lady very happy indeed."

"Excellent, that's settled," Jonah says.

I open my mouth, and Enid's excited gaze meets mine, and I don't have the heart to protest now. I close my mouth and nod. "But you must allow me to put you up for the night, after all the trouble you have gone to for my family."

"It would be our pleasure to acquaint ourselves with Harm's family. Thank you for the generous offer," Jonah says.

Enid claps her hands together and turns to make her way to the kitchen. She looks back and ushers us to follow her. Jonah follows her, and Imani and I make our way behind him.

"You okay?" I ask, walking beside her.

She doesn't look at me. Her shoulders are tight, her eyes off in the distance. "I'm fine." Her usual fire is absent.

"You don't sound fine to me." My hand grazes hers, and she stops and turns toward me, eyes burning into mine. Her face is strung tight, brows lowered, her mouth a thin line. She thumps my chest hard with her fist, but her hand uncurls, and her fingers lie on my chest, over my heart. I hold her gaze.

"I don't want ... I mean ..." She swallows. "Never mind."

Not offering anything else, she slides her hand from my chest and turns to follow Jonah and Enid into the kitchen.

As we enter the small wooden kitchen, Enid and Jonah are already working on preparing vegetables for what appears to be a stew of sorts. They banter away, speaking of people they may or may not know. The places Jonah has traveled to and Enid's work as a healer are mulled over while they chop and slice.

Enid gives Imani and me the job of cooking the grains. We carefully cook them per her instructions. Imani seems happy busying herself with the grains, and I am happy to just be close to her, hoping that just being here, she will feel better. I wish I knew what is bothering her.

The back door slams open, and a small boy appears beside Enid, winded but excited, three long gnarled roots gripped in one hand. "Gamma, Gamma, I found some roots to catch the jackrabbits!"

Enid turns to the young boy and bends down so her eyes are level with his, grabbing his shoulders with her fine hands.

"That's wonderful, McKinlay! I will help you set your traps tomorrow."

She is just as excited. Her smile widens and her eyes light up, matching McKinlay's.

As if he has just noticed there are other people in the room, he steps back. His gaze swings between Enid and the three of us. He grabs onto her wrists, and his fingers trace a small, winged bird inked on the inside of her right wrist as he stares at the three of us. I've seen that bird somewhere before. Jonah's eyes are also fixed on her wrist.

"McKinlay, this is your cousin, Harm. He and his friends have traveled a very long way to see us," Enid explains, pointing to me.

"Hello. I'm five, you know." He puffs out his chest.

I squat down, eyes meeting his. "Hello, McKinlay, it's so good to meet you. You're going to catch some jackrabbits? Sounds like fun."

He nods furiously, and Enid laughs.

"Now, I need you to do something for me," Enid says to McKinlay.

"Okay, Gamma." Eager to be useful, he straightens and waits.

"Can you fetch Momma and Aunty for me, right away?" she finishes, spinning him around and ushering him through the back door.

Turning back, she meets my gaze. She lets out a little laugh. "You wait until your aunties see you, young man. They are going to lose their minds with delight."

I smile, but there is a pit in my stomach. I will have to break the news to them as well about my mother, their sister.

CHAPTER 31
HARM

Imani stirs the grains slowly, her elegant hands wrapped around the wooden spoon.

"They're almost done," she says.

"When did you learn to cook?" I grin.

"I wasn't always a sand rat, Harm. I have parents, and I grew up in an almost normal home." She throws me a cheeky look and shoves the hot spoon of grains into my mouth. Ha! Heat sears my mouth, and I chew quickly, covering my half-open mouth with my hand.

"Yep, you're right, they're done," I choke out through the steaming heat, and she laughs at me. Her face lit up with happiness is the most beautiful thing I have ever seen.

I pass her the cloth to pull the pot off the small wood stove, resisting the urge to do it for her, knowing that would only end with her rolling her eyes at me. She heaves the large pot from the hot burner and places it on the wooden bench in the center of the kitchen next to Jonah. The earthy smell of the cooked grains adds to the already aromatic kitchen.

Enid removes some books and other items that she uses for

preparing healing herbs from the center of her dining table. They clank together while she carries them to the small sideboard in the dining area. Dust has covered most of the sideboard, and she bends down and blows the surface to clear a spot for the bundle she is carrying.

From a drawer in the sideboard, Enid sets seven places at the table with silverware. It is old, but well cared for, still shining, without tarnish. She adds a small row of candles and two linen mats to place the hot pots on, and plates for each person. When she is done, she stands back and looks at the space. Talking to herself, she hovers around the table, double-checking each item.

"There we go, ready for lunch!" Enid says, clapping her hands together.

Jonah carries the cooked meal to the table, placing one pot on each cloth. Enid arrives with a jug of water and ceramic mugs. A small wooden plate and cup sit on the bench with food in it already. This must be for McKinlay. Waiting for the aunties to arrive, I wander around Enid's living room. Books on healing, glass bottles, jars, and bundles of herbs hung up to dry line the walls. She must have been collecting these books for decades. Fragrance hangs in the air, accompanying the fine sands that toss about on the wooden floor.

The front door rattles under a knock. Enid stops what she is doing, brushes her hands on her pants, and makes her way to the door. We follow, but Jonah and Imani stop in the kitchen doorway.

Peeping through the small opening in the center of the door, she makes certain who is on the other side. She lets out a small cry of excitement and opens the door. Two women stand before the threshold. They both meet my gaze and stand motionless, eyes wide and mouths open. Waves of blonde curls shape the face of the woman who steps towards me. The breath leaves my lungs and doesn't return. McKinlay cuddles into her skirts, and her hand automatically wraps around his small shoulders. The woman standing in front of me stares back at me.

Mother.

She is just like my mother.

Her face and eyes. Her hair. She is slightly shorter. Waves of sadness wash down my body at the sight of her standing in front of me, knowing that despite her appearance, she is not mother. She smiles at me, and tears burn, lining my eyes with silver. I press the heel of my shaking palm into my chest, rubbing the tightness that is clawing at my lungs.

"Thank you for coming, girls," Enid says.

Enid turns to look at me, her words halting as her gaze finds my face, and she walks to my side. I blow out a low breath, and her arms wrap around me in a tight hug. She whispers words of comfort as I try to regain my composure. The woman who is not my mother blurs. Enid pats my back, and I force back sobs. I wipe my hot, wet face with my sleeve.

"Is everything okay?" McKinlay's mother says, her face dropping.

Enid drops her arms and stands beside me. McKinlay runs inside towards the kitchen, squealing about the smell of lunch.

"Harmen, this is your Aunty Layla, my eldest daughter," Enid says softly, waving a hand to her daughter, the spitting image of herself, straight shoulder-length hair, thin face and frame. Layla hugs me, then steps back, watching her sister stare at me.

"And this," Enid gestures to the woman who is almost identical to my mother, "is your Aunty Tabitha." Her words come out cracked, as if she were seeing my mother standing in front of me her too.

Tabitha slowly walks up to me, studying my face.

"Hello, Harmen," she breathes.

I release a breath. My name in her voice sounds like my mother. I swallow the lump in my throat. "Hello," I say, forcing a smile.

She steps up to me, arms hanging by her sides for a moment, before pulling me into a tentative hug. My body frozen, I hold my breath.

Enid gestures for us to sit on the floor. The aunties sit beside her, across from me, Tabitha keeping me in her gaze for now. Enid's voice is low and sad as she tells her daughters the news of their sister. Her voice cracks when she tells them of my little sister. Tears run down her face again, pain etching across her face. Both women listen. Tabitha is holding the cloth of her skirt. She stares at the fabric, twisting it between her fingers as tears fly down her face in a torrent, breath chugging out of her involuntarily.

Layla sits in her spot, her face wrecked with sadness like her little sister's. She tries to be of comfort to her. Enid holds them both around the shoulders as they mourn together. Jonah stands in the doorway with Imani. Tears fall from Imani's cheeks, her mouth a tight line and her chin wobbling. With a broken moan, she flies down the small hallway and out the back door.

Jonah nods his head in her direction, signaling that I should go after her. Glancing back at the pain scrawled across my aunties faces, I rise and make my way down the hallway to the back door. Enid's house has three bedrooms, one on the kitchen side and two on the living room side, flanking the hallway. An old wooden door with gauze covers most of it, but sports a few holes from wear and tear over the years.

I dry my face on my shoulder and push through the back door. Enid has a small stone space at the back of the house. It is sheltered from the harsh sun, and there are many hanging pots and ceramic pots with various plants, herbs for healing, and some vegetables. A large pottery urn sits in the corner to my left, close to the house. The large open top holds fresh water. Two wooden benches nestled in between the plants flank the stone patio. Imani sits on the ground with her knees up, head tucked under her arms. She is still —no noise or sobs, just still.

Dropping beside her, I gaze out into the desert sands. What can I say to her? I just sit there, hoping Imani will let me in. "Imani, what's going on?"

"You wouldn't understand."

"Try me," I breathe.

She inhales slowly, but her head remains tucked. "I can't."

"Please let me help."

She looks up squarely at me, her eyes red, and tears wet her cheeks. "I should be the one comforting you, Harm, not the other way around."

"I have had longer to process it, but I guess seeing Tabitha brought it all back."

"You have lost so much," she whispers, turning to face me. I sit on the ground, saying nothing, staring at her. She wipes away her tears with the backs of her hands, and shuffles to her knees in front of me.

"You won't be losing anything else; I won't let that happen." She leans in, wrapping her arms around my neck. I sit still for a moment before folding my arms around her. She buries her head into my neck, and I hold her tight. My heart picks up the pace until it is thundering in my chest.

"I don't want to lose you, Imani," I rasp out. I have wanted to tell her that for so long.

"You're not going to. I will always be here if you need me, Harm. And when Jonah and I get back from the outlying villages, I need to tell you something." She rests her head on my shoulder. Her breathing settles.

"You can tell me now."

"I'm terri—No." She sucks in a breath. "I mean, not right now.

We should go back inside." She rises to her feet, dusting off her clothes.

"Sure." I stand and trail behind her back into the house and to the dining room. The women are all seated and waiting. Jonah and McKinlay carry the last of the meal to the table. Two seats remain empty on the far side of the table. Imani and I take opposite paths around it. I reach my seat and look at Imani before pulling out her chair. She lingers on our stare and then sits, her eyes glued to her place setting. Enid gives me a reassuring look as I take my place beside Imani.

"Let's eat, as family found and family remembered," Layla says, tears still shining in her eyes. Tabitha picks up the nearest pot and serves the grains, through a wobbly breath. Enid serves the stew. The aromatic flavors from Enid's herbs turn my mouth into a watering mess. I shovel it in. Imani and Jonah politely eat theirs, and I slow my pace, trying to remain civilized. It is not like Imani to take her time with food.

My grandmother, she is my family. Enid, Layla, Tabitha, and McKinlay are my family. A wisp of belonging floats through me. It is a good feeling after so many weeks of loneliness and sadness. Memories of my mother flip past, and I try to match her face to the features of Enid, Layla, and Tabitha. There are so many things about my mother that I see in Tabitha—Aunty Tabitha.

Enid clears her throat and starts telling us stories of the three girls when they were younger. The two sisters laugh at the memories—most of them, anyway. The day their father died and the day my mother left were sad moments for them, and it is obvious it still hurts them, more so now that they have just lost her all over again. Tabitha looks at me, as if checking me over once more before speaking. Her voice is raw and stern.

"Do you know who your real father is?"

"No. I mean, I haven't met him yet."

"Don't," she says bitterly. Enid shoots her a look of reprimand. "Why not?"

"Rupert Barlow is not someone you want to find," Tabitha spits.

"Perhaps that's something for Harmen to think about later. For now, we will enjoy the company we have," Enid says.

Jonah looks between Enid and me. "Well, this is hands down the best meal I've had in a long while," he says, shoveling another mouthful in. Blushing, Enid waves him off with her hand. Looks dart between Tabitha and Layla.

Enid stands and starts clearing the table, and Jonah jumps up to help her. The rest of us help Enid restore the table to its bare boards in no time. Tabitha wanders into the sitting room at the front of the house. I follow behind, standing next to a chair by the bookshelf. She stands running her fingers over the books and trinkets her mother has collected. Even her mannerisms match my mother's. I clear my throat.

"I'm sorry about before," she says, looking towards the kitchen, checking if her mother is in hearing range. "Your father left your pregnant mother to fend for herself all those years ago. I have hated him for so long. It was his fault she had to leave, and now, ultimately, we have lost her all over again."

I don't know what I am supposed to say, where I would start. Telling her I know what it is like to lose a sister? That wouldn't be helpful, and I know it all too well. So, I stand in silence, hoping she will tell me more.

"Your mother loved that heathen, and he dropped her like a rock when she fell pregnant. He doesn't have a decent bone in his body. If you're insistent on finding him, then I send you with some advice and a warning. Set your expectations low, that's my advice. The warning is this, do not trust him with anything or anyone you value." She pauses, glancing over to Imani leaning against the kitchen door frame. "Ever." She waits for my reaction for a moment, then turns back to the shelves.

Imani walks over and flops into the chair I'm leaning on, studying the books on the shelf. She pulls one out and blows a layer of fine dust from its aged surface, creating a cloud in front of her. She opens the book carefully, cracking the spine ever so slightly as the pages reveal the text. Running a finger down the page, she turns it, like reading, but much quicker. Layla enters the room and sits beside Imani with a look of expectation. "You have read this one before?" she asks Imani.

"Ah, yeah, a long time ago. You can have it." She holds the book out to Layla.

"I've read this one many times. Which part was your favorite?" she says, not taking it.

"The ending," Imani murmurs, shoving it back on the shelf. I stare at Imani, trying to figure out what she's up to. Then it hits me: she can't read. Imani stands and examines the trinkets on the shelf. She picks up a small glass bottle with a round stopper. Studded with gems, the bottle is a vibrant blue, almost a match for her eyes. She is studying it from every angle, turning it in her hand over and over.

Suddenly Imani rushes to the kitchen, startling Layla. Curious, I wander behind her. She stands with Enid, holding the bottle up to her. "Where did you get this from?"

"A man gave it to me for saving the life of his wife and daughter at childbirth." Her words are calm, but confusion scrunches her face with the sudden interest in her trinkets.

"What man? When?"

"It was a long time ago. I still see him from time to time. Why do you ask?"

"My mother had some just like it, a present from my father. One was missing from the set."

Enid offers her a smile, resting a hand on her arm. She glances at me briefly. "I'm sure it's just a coincidence. There are probably many sets of these around." Resting her hand on Imani's cheek briefly her hand falls and she returns to cleaning the kitchen. Imani leaves the kitchen and returns the trinket to its shelf, staring at it. We sit around in the living room, talking and reading for hours, before Layla and Tabitha bid their goodbyes.

"Well, you two," Jonah says, "tomorrow Imani and I will set out for the outlying villages, and Harm, you will help your grandmother with her chores. She is long overdue for some strong help, I'm sure." He throws a cheeky look at Enid, who retorts with an amused laugh.

"Speaking of home comforts, would you be interested in a bath, young lady?" Enid offers.

Imani's eyes light up. "That would be amazing."

I suppress a chuckle looking up from my book while Imani follows Enid down the hall.

CHAPTER 32
HARM

I wash up in the bath after Imani before making my way back to the living room. Imani hesitates in the hallway an hour later, dressed in night attire, her hair still damp and hanging around her shoulders in curls. Jonah, Enid, and I sit reading in the living room by candlelight. Imani's eyes reflect the flickering light around her. A flutter in my gut sends my heart thumping against my chest. Gentle curves that were hidden away for months under the traveling clothes send a fire through my center. I push off the chair and pad to where she stands. Her eyes are fixed on mine. Her face is flushed, and she is breathing fast.

"This was your mother's, which is a little weird," she says. Warmth flushes her cheeks. Her long, dark hair curls around her shoulders and frames her chest.

She is stunning.

Enid has lent me a fresh shirt that is slightly too big for me and clean pants. I have bathed, brushed my hair, and shaved for the first time in a week. Imani looks up at my neatly brushed hair and ruffles it up with her small hands, her face scrunching up in amusement.

"That's better. I'm not used to your hair being all neat. I like it better scruffy." Her lips grow into a smile.

"Huh, thanks." Heat flushes my face.

She stills, taking in the books as Jonah and Enid sit reading. "I may as well just go to bed," she utters and turns toward the hallway.

"Nope, you should stay." I grab her arm, resisting the urge to touch her face, wanting so badly to run my thumb over her lips and down her neck. She turns back to face me. Releasing her I move to sit on the couch and pat the cushion beside me. Pulling her hair to one side, she sits down and takes the book I was reading. She runs a hand over the hard cover, her fingers tracing the letters of the title. I watch every move she makes. Her eyes finally meet mine, and I hold my breath.

"What's this one about?" Imani asks.

"The story of Cassiopeia, a vain queen, and her daughter, who were punished by the god of the sea. It was one of Amaya's favorites. I can read it to you, if you like?"

"Okay." She leans back in the chair and closes her eyes.

I take the book from her hands and flip to the first page and start reading. Her mouth pulls up in a smile, and she looses a sigh. I settle into the chair, reading the way I used to read to Amaya before she could read herself. Jonah looks up briefly from his book, warmth and love radiate over his face. I falter on a word and adjust my focus back to the page. Every detail of the story comes alive as the words translate from the page to the steady rhythm of my voice. Imani shifts on the chair, leaning up against me. For a moment, I take her in. Vanilla and spice infiltrate my senses. She is completely relaxed.

"Keep going, Harm," she murmurs. I return my focus to the page, picking up where I left off. Between sentences, I take in deep breaths. My skin tingles where the two of us meet, her body against mine. I read another page and another, every word seeming to take on a completely different meaning from the last time I read this story.

"Looks like traipsing around the sands has worn our girl out," Jonah says softly, nodding to Imani, his glasses low on his nose. Her head is now resting on my shoulder, one arm wrapped around mine. She is sound asleep, her face soft and elegant. The steady rise and fall of the cream linen over her chest sends warmth through every inch of me.

"I'd say it's bedtime for you two," Enid murmurs, smiling over her book.

I set the book on the small side table and inch away from Imani, trying not to disturb her. Jonah and Enid exchange a conspiratorial look before going back to their books. I stand hesitating as Imani lies half curled up in the chair. Jonah offers no help, keeping his focus on his book. I should wake her up. But she looks so peaceful, for the first time in days.

I bend down and scoop her up, one arm under her shoulders, the other under her legs. Her head bobs and rests against my chest. I stand, adjusting to her small frame and weight. Vanilla and spice meet me. Jonah watches me over his book, love and knowing in his eyes for the girl in my arms.

"Night," I utter, moving toward the hallway.

"Night, Harm," Enid offers. Her smile is a mix of love and pride—the same look my father used to give me.

In the guest room, I bend over Imani's bunk, laying her on the soft mattress. She murmurs in her sleep, but doesn't wake. I pull the blanket up over her shoulders and stand, heart hammering, studying her every detail. There is no way I am letting her leave without me. That would be a new kind of torture.

I sink to the floor, resting my back against her bunk. I'm not tired. I sit, watching her sleep, running through every new piece of information I have learned since leaving Amondo, trying to piece together how to change things and not have anyone die in the process. If Charlie would just step up as Chancellor, that would end the tyranny. But he is not willing to face his brother.

I lean my head on the bunk and track Imani's breaths. There has to be something we can do that doesn't end up with more people dying. I sit there for what feels like an hour before the voices of Jonah and Enid drift down the hall. They must assume I'm asleep. Staring at the ceiling of the weathered structure, I try to make out what they are saying. Jonah is talking too softly for me to make out any of his words, and it feels as if that is on purpose. Now I really want to know what they are saying. I gently rise from the floor and creep toward the door, leaning against the door frame with my head resting on the doorjamb, trying to breathe quietly.

"There is something you need to know about our Harm," Enid says, hesitating.

Jonah is quiet.

"My late husband—he carried the gift that allowed him to manipulate the dial. Eventually, this was discovered. They took him in the middle of the night, and we never saw him again. Rupert Barlow, Harm's real father, is from the current Chancellor's family line. He may also have that gift. We hoped that a child from Rupert and Hannah would be the end of this tyranny. When Hannah became pregnant with his child, he dropped her like a hot rock and swore he never had the gift. It is possible, due to its selectiveness. But he needs to be found, and we need to confirm whether he carries the ability or not."

The chair beneath one of them creaks with the shifting of weight, and I imagine Jonah leaning into the conversation. "Go on," he says quietly.

"Hannah has passed the gift to Harm. Imani reminds me of her so much, full of fire and kindness. Hannah lived a quiet life once she realized she was bringing a child into this world, but she was a strong soul, Jonah." The words catch in her throat. "You need to find Harm's father. If he has the ability also, then our boy will have the power to manipulate the dial at whim. But it will be dormant until he is eighteen—months away. There would be no one else with ability that strong. Having the gift from both sides is a rare, but that also puts him in more danger than you know. If the Guardians find out or make the connections, he will not live long enough to even try."

Jonah breathes out a long, low, heavy sigh.

My knuckles burn, and I look down to see my hands in a death grip on the doorframe. I slide to the floor and stare at the opposite wall.

My real father most likely has the ability.

I have it.

Turning eighteen is almost another year away.

We can't wait that long.

I won't wait that long.

My hands shake and tingle. Nausea seeps through my gut and up into my throat. I throw my head into my hands, drawing a long breath. A million thoughts whip through my mind, with no hope of catching any of them long enough to make sense of what Enid said.

The moon has started its descent when I finally make my way to my bunk. On top sits a blue scarf with a note.

This was your mother's. I am sure you will know what to do with it.
Love, Enid.

In the dim light Jonah sleeps, his back turned to me, his side rises and falls slowly. I lie down slowly so as not to wake him. My only thoughts are of how much danger I have put everyone in. This entire journey has been full of risk. Jonah has put his life in peril for me. He hardly knew me when he first helped me. If Fletcher finds out what he has done, he doesn't stand a chance. Imani would lose her only family.

Thoughts of regret and anger flood through my overstimulated body. My head feels set to explode. Imani—they would hang her as a traitor to the Chancellor for helping me. Fear creeps through me, radiating from my chest to every inch of my body. If they lay a finger on her ... If anything happens to Imani ...

I sit up and pull on my boots and grab my rucksack, shoving my belongings and my mother's journal back in it. I pluck the blue scarf from the bed and throw it in too. We have to get out of here. I will not let her end up hurt because of me. I pad my way to the door, but I hesitate, wanting to say goodbye to Jonah. He lies still, facing the window. I turn back to the door.

"Make sure you take care of her, Harm," Jonah says, his voice raw.

"You have my word," I breathe. Standing motionless, I wish I could just stay, that things were different, and I could just live a normal, mundane life with the people that are my family. Imani. Jonah. Enid. Digging deep, I gather the fire in my core just ignited and step into the spare room, next to Imani's bunk. She is so still, just like the dolls Amaya used to treasure. The pull I feel towards her is overwhelming.

I kneel next to Imani, touching her shoulder. Her eyes open slowly. She takes in my face in the moonlight, then smiles like she is still dreaming. She touches my cheek. I lean into her hand as the warmth in my chest cascades.

"We have to leave," I whisper, half pulling her up.

Her smile fades, and she drops her hand. She stands up and

grabs her clothes. I turn around, and her night dress hits the floor. I swallow the lump in my throat. A heartbeat later, she grabs her things from the foot of her bunk, shoving her weapons back into the belt around her waist. With a last look at my grandmother, we head for the back door, making sure not to wake her. Imani is close behind me when I cautiously open the door and step out onto the stone patio. I stop for a moment, looking down at her. The moon lights up her elegant face, the fire in her eyes clear despite the hour.

"You know where you're going?" she whispers.

"The only place we haven't looked. Farno. We follow the constellations to the east. You ready?"

She pulls her scarf from her rucksack and twists her hair up, tying it tight at the back. "Let's do it," she replies as she shrugs on her robe and throws up her hood to keep her head warm in the cool desert night air.

CHAPTER 33
HARM

C risp air keeps us on our toes, and we make good time to the first rocky outcrop. We walk fast, staving off the cold of the night that is descending to early morning.

Hours later, one Guardian outpost stands ahead before their jurisdiction ends. The sands swirl beneath our feet as we trudge through a recently shifted dune, breathing hard. It is only going to get hotter out here, and we need to find some shade before the midday sun crucifies us.

On the southern horizon lies the silhouette of the last Guardian outpost. Hoping the distance will protect us from their persistent scanning, we keep moving, heads down. It is not long before we find a small overhanging rocky outcrop, and Imani drops to the ground, swiping her hood back before pulling off her wrap. I drain the water from my canteen and drop next to her.

With one more day of traveling ahead, Imani and I are not slowing down now. I stand and pull her to her feet, no words needed. We keep going, talking when we aren't out of breath, but the sand is hard going in these parts, with freshly shifted dunes that rise before us, one after the other, like they will never end. We stride to the top of the highest dune. The view is incredible and disheartening all at once, knowing we have so far left to go, with nothing but more dunes in front of us to the northeast.

Winds whip across my burning face. Our face wraps help a little but not enough, and I keep moving. I turn back, and Imani is still trudging along behind. Something dark and small, moving fast, catches my eye. I stand still, straining to listen. Imani follows my gaze and stands beside me, her hand up over her eyes, trying to see far enough to make out the object. The faint sound of a small motor spits and splutters through the sand-strewn winds. Imani's eyes widen and she grabs my hand.

"Run!" She hauls me in the opposite direction of the dune buggy. Letting go of my hand, she pumps her arms to propel her up the next dune. "Faster, Harm, go!"

We have nowhere to hide.

The sands and dunes only hide us for as long as we stay in the valleys. The sound of the buggy roars closer, and the men are shouting. Judging from their voices, they have seen us and are moving in closer. Imani falters as the sand wears us out at an increasing rate.

Grabbing her hand, I pull her along with me; she is gasping for breath, and her pace has slowed. She groans, pushing herself forward. We are clambering down the side of a dune when her leg gives out, and she collapses in the sand. I scramble back to her, trying to pull her up with both of my hands. She is completely out of breath now, gripping her ankle.

"No, you go." She pulls her knife out from under her robe. "Use this if you have to. Do not let them take you!" She places the knife in my hand, waving me off.

I sink to my knees beside her, eyes burning into hers. "No, no way!"

The sound of the buggy rattles toward us.

"Go," she growls, her face twisting in annoyance and anger. I push off the hot sand, shoving the blade in my pocket, and take off across the waves, with Imani still lying in the sand. My chest tightens with every step. I twist my head back. Every step away feels wrong. She pushes up to stand, limping toward the buggy, hands waving to draw their attention away from me and onto her.

No, this is not happening.

My heart overrides my head. I growl and spin back. With a handful of large strides, I am back to Imani, and I scoop her into my arms.

"Put me down! Harm, go, please leave me! Please!"

I can't respond.

I turn back and run. The knife and rucksack bang into me with every weighted step. I pick up my pace. My legs burn, but remain moving. I hold Imani tight to my chest and plow through the sand. Fire lances through my arms, and my heart threatens to burst through my chest. Imani has tucked herself into my chest and holds on to my robe with white knuckles.

The sand thins, and I pick up the pace. Rocky outcrops spot the sandy ground. Sweat pours down every limb. Loosening my grip on Imani, I twist back to see. The buggy careens around a dune. The Guardians search high and low, heads whipping back and forth, hunting for us.

My foot rolls over loose rocks rock beneath the sand, and the ground falls away from underneath me. My stomach flies into my throat, and I grip Imani tighter, bracing to take the brunt of the fall. Her head flies up from my chest, eyes wide as she realizes we are falling. I land with a heavy thud on my back, and we slide down the wall of a rocky crevice. Pain rips through my back from the jagged rock. A groan rumbles through my throat. Imani watches as my face contorts, and she pushes out of my hold, tumbling down the rocky slope in front of me, her arms flying out to protect her head.

Imani hits the ground hard and lets out a small whimper, rolling to a stop at the bottom of the crevice. She lies limp. I slide to a halt beside her, my rucksack hanging from one shoulder. Rock and debris skitter around us. The walls of the crevice are steep, the bed of it dark and narrow, and it takes a moment for to adjust to the dimness. I roll Imani over and check her. She has cuts on her arms and a gash on her head.

"Imani." I rest a hand on her shoulders.

She doesn't respond.

Dammit.

I run my hands over her limbs, checking for breaks, but the rest of her seems undamaged. I pull myself up to sit close to her head. Slowly I lift her head into my lap, push away her hood, and unwrap the fabric from her face. Running my fingers over her face, I tell myself I am checking for any injuries. Her soft, elegant face feels like lightning under my fingertips. Near her temple, my fingers meet moisture, and I lift them, turning my hand over. Blood. I pull my rucksack from my shoulder and rummage through it for my canteen and some sort of rag. My canteen is intact, but no rags.

I rip my sleeve from my shoulder and soak it before ringing it out. Gently, I clean the gash to her head, leaving the cloth draped over it to cool down the area. For the first time in what feels like ages, I breathe out and lean back onto the rocky wall of the little canyon. Gravel and debris dig into my back. I wince, not taking gaze off her breathing.

Buggy sounds rattle around above us in the sand. I wriggle back under an overhang of rock, into the shadows, pulling Imani under with me. A flutter of sand falls from above. I press my back against the wall of the canyon and hope it is dark enough that they can't see us lying here. The silhouette of a Guardian hovers above us, leaning down to see into the crevice.

"There's nothing here. He must have changed course," says a familiar voice.

Mason.

"Back in the buggy," Fletcher barks.

"Yes, sir."

They make their way back to the dune buggy, and it surges to life and heads back into the dunes, the motor noise quickly fading. I sigh and shift on the hard ground, still cradling Imani's head. The bleeding has stopped now, but a small amount of blood cakes her hair. Her scarf is half off, and I unwrap it, letting her hair fall into my lap. My back throbs, as the air in the dark crevice cools my body.

Imani's breathing is still regular, and she moves a little as I dab the wound on her head again. I remove her hair from the area now, trying to keep it clean. She doesn't wake.

"Imani," I coax.

She moves a little again, but not stirring as much as I hoped she would. I lean back and close my eyes, wincing with the sharpness in my back. I pull out my mother's journal. I have never taken the time to look at every page. I have time now.

Diary entries fill many of the pages, some recent, some from before I was born. A list of names of her family in the south fills one page. Enid's name is there. Barlow's name as well. A map of the county and surrounding villages, including Guardian outposts, covers the center spread. I keep turning. Towards the back, there is a drawing of her Blending pendant. My hand automatically hunts through my rucksack, searching for the pendant. Cold metal meets my fingers. I yank it out and stare at it. Does the stone coordinate with eye color?

My mother had blue eyes.

Imani has blue eyes.

I curl my fingers around it, glancing at Imani's peaceful face.

My stomach flutters, warming my chest. Curious, I shove the pendant back into the rucksack and keep turning the pages of the journal. With the last page turn, a small paper folded in half falls into my lap. I haven't noticed it in her journal before. A note is scratched onto the folded page, not my mother's handwriting.

Harmen, this is from your mother, for when you are ready. — Tabitha

What is that supposed to mean?

I open the letter, slowly, as if just opening it might change something. I draw in a long breath. My mother's handwriting covers the page. Tears threaten to consume me just looking at the elegant letters assembled on the page.

My Love,

You will always be my sweetest treasure. I adore you, and I haven't even met you yet. I am not sure if you know this, but you are very special. And not in the way all mothers think of their children. You have a strength inside you that no other can match. Your destiny is far greater than you could imagine. I know as your mother that this is true. You received this gift from myself and your real father— a man that did not deserve you, but nonetheless shares your blood. Find your family. Find yourself. Change the world, my darling.

Love,

Your Mother

I drop the letter into my rucksack and sit staring at the wall on the other side of the crevice. My hands push into my hair. It's me. It really is me. My mother knew, and Enid knew it too. Tabitha knew, if she read the letter. That explains why no one likes my real father. He has the ability too, and refuses to help others with it.

I will not be like my father.

I will not be a coward.

Imani's chest rises and falls gently, and a fire ignites in my core. I will not let her down. Not as long as there is blood pumping through my veins and breath in my body. She moves, rolling onto her back, groaning as her hand moves up and touches her head. Her face is pale, but she looks up at me before closing her eyes.

"Ouch," she breathes.

"Do you need to sit up?"

"Are they gone?" She pushes up off my lap.

"Yes, an age ago. They didn't see us down here in the dark." If Mason saw us, he kept that to himself.

"One good thing about falling down a hole, I guess," she says. Her spirits have fared better than her body. She runs her gaze up and down my body. "Are you okay?"

"I'll live."

What would have happened to me if we hadn't fallen into this crevice? I can't be caught, not now—not when I have only just learned who I am. Not now that I can make things right again for our people. I don't share the letter with Imani, but knowing who I am makes me feel stronger.

"It's cold in here," she says, shivering. She sits up beside me, and I wrap an arm around her. Pulling her robe around her chest, she huddles close and rests her head on my shoulder.

"It will be dark in a few hours," I say. "We may as well spend the night here. Trying to climb out in the dark wouldn't do us any good."

"You're so warm," she whispers, and I rest my head against hers, breathing her in, if only just for a while, until she falls asleep.

Dawns light creeps its way down the crevice. Imani's head is still lying on my shoulder, the calm rise and fall of her chest a steady rhythm. My back burns and my shirt sticks to it in spots, tugging with every slight movement. I arch it away from the wall. Everywhere around us is steep, jagged rock—too steep to climb out without a rope or help. I lay my head back against the wall and yawn. She stirs beside me, lifting her head.

"Hey," she says, her eyes tracking to my stiffly arched back.

"Hey, yourself," I say softly, smiling at her morning hair as she pulls away from me to stretch. Imani pulls out some bread and dried meat from her sack, offering me half. We eat in silence until she looks at me with a cheeky grin.

"What?"

She rummages through her rucksack, putting her food in her lap as she does so. "I took this from Enid's house. I rarely take things, not anymore, so don't bother getting hot and bothered about it, but I knew we would need this, and it was just sitting there on her shelf."

She hands me a rolled-up map. The paper is old and tattered. I unroll it and examine it from the top. Amondo and the northern villages are present. There are more Guardian outposts on this map, making it dated. The major landmarks are present, the rocky outcrops and the permanent dune ridges. The great wall is marked, and the prison. Everything appears to be accurate, but there are blue and brown lines on this map that I don't recognize and have never seen anywhere else. Now I have three different maps all showing different things, like these lands have lived through many periods. I chew on the bread, turning the map from side to side.

"What are these?" I say, pointing out the blue and brown lines. Imani leans over to look at the map. She traces the lines with a finger, following them over the page like veins.

She shrugs. "No clue. The wall looks different too. Maybe someone in the outlying village will know what they are."

"Possibly." I hand the map back to her.

"A more pressing matter though: how are we going to get out of this crevice?" Imani asks, looking up as if the surface is miles away, her hand shielding her eyes from the already burning sun.

"Well, finding a way up here would be a little hard, but maybe there's another way out?" I'm not sure of what will happen next or where how we will get out. I push up to my feet—and a groan of agony slips through my gritted teeth.

A gasp leaves Imani's mouth. "Sit down." She points to the spot I just rose from.

"I'll be fine, just some scrapes and bruises, nothing serious."

But her face is scrunched up with concern, so I do as I'm told and drop down beside her.

"The back of your shirt is torn, and saturated in blood," she says, her voice tender now. Imani's expression doesn't change. She gestures for me to take it off. I hesitate, heat flushing through my face. "Come on, I can't help you if you don't show me."

I let out an exasperated laugh to hide my embarrassment, but do as she says. I hold her gaze, waiting for a reaction as I pull the shirt over my head and lay it in my lap. Imani shuffles behind me. Her hand touches my back, and she traces lines across it—scars from the lashes. Breath escapes my lungs while the blood rushes through my veins. She swallows, fingers frozen on a lash scar. "You have debris stuck in your back, Harm. I need to get it out."

233

"Go ahead," I murmur, still recovering from her hand touching my back only seconds ago.

Imani repositions herself behind me with her legs on either side of me and both of her hands on my back now, as if tracing the wounds. I can imagine what she is examining. The pain dulls as her fingers touch my ragged back. I hold my breath as her fingers take in every scar. I turn back to watch. Her brows drawn, mouth pressed into a thin line, she stares at her hands as they work.

She shoots me a look that says "sorry" just as a sharp scrape flicks across my back towards the middle. It stings and pinches, and a warm trickle runs down my back. I let out a low, shaky breath. Imani's hand dives into her rucksack, pulling out an old head wrap. She rips it in two, keeping pressure on my back. Her hand appears in my lap, and a large piece of stick covered in blood and a little of my flesh rests in her bloodied palm.

"Is that it?" I ask with a mock laugh.

"No."

Imani dabs the cloth on my skin as the blood flow slows down. Coolness spreads over my skin as she rinses the wounds with what's left of her canteen.

"Don't waste your water on my back." The throbbing rises to a sting.

"It needs it." She empties her canteen onto my back. Another painful tug. I arch my back away from the sting. Another trickle, followed with pressure from the cloth. "Sorry," she whispers.

"It's not your fault."

She replies with a half laugh through breathy words. "Yeah, well."

"There was no way I was ever going to leave you behind, Imani. Please know that." I twist to face her. Blood trickles over the old scars and my back aches.

"You should have. I told you to leave me." Her eyes find mine.

"Luckily for both of us, I don't always do what I'm told," I breathe, our faces inches apart.

She turns back to my injuries, and I turn around, lacing my fingers behind my neck, staring at my lap. We sit in silence as she tends my wounds with the cloth. A splash hits my back, but her canteen is empty, lying on the ground. Her hands tremble on my back before she removes them. She is quiet. I turn around as much as I can with her behind me. Tears fall into her lap, her head bowed now.

"Imani," I whisper as her hands fly up to her face to stem the tears. Pivoting on my seat, I turn around fully and put my arms around her, pulling her into my chest. A few moments pass, and a stifled laugh escapes Imani's tortured face as she pushes back and looks up at me.

"You realize you're half naked, right?"

"Sorry," I mutter, releasing her. She doesn't move away. Instead, staring at me intensely, she rests her hands on my chest, and my body stirs in response to her touch. Breaths shortening. Warmth growing in my core.

"Don't be," she breathes. A handful of heartbeats later she pulls her hands back, moving away, and picks up the cloth and canteen sliding them back into her rucksack. Her dark hair falls across her face as she busies herself with packing up. I resist the urge to brush her hair back and tuck it behind her ear so I can see her face.

"Imani, there's something I need to tell you before we go to the outlying villages." I wish I could take the words back the second they leave my mouth.

She is still organizing her rucksack. "What is it?"

"Finding my father in the outlying villages isn't really necessary now."

She looks up. "Why do you say that?"

"I just don't think he will be of any help to us. We could ask any of the villagers about the map, and I don't know if I want to meet him anymore."

"I thought something connected your father to the ability to change the dial. Don't we need to find him?"

I look at her, not replying for a time, unsure of what to say. How do I tell her I am the one with the gift, and that we have been looking for someone who was right here all along? And what happens to our friendship once she knows the truth? She is probably expecting that person to be courageous and strong. I don't know if I can be those things.

I can't tell her.

"Well?" she prods.

"I guess you're right." It's not the right time. I'll tell her later, maybe after we find my father.

"Fine. First things first, though," she says, looking at me with a crooked smile.

"What?" I laugh, glad the conversation has shifted.

"Put your shirt back on, Harm." She throws me a look I haven't seen before that betrays her words. I push my arms through the sleeves, keeping my gaze locked on her for a moment. She ties up her rucksack and gets to her feet, dusting off her clothes and organizing her wrap. I pull the shirt over my head and pull my robe on slowly. I ruffle my hair with one hand, dislodging sand and other debris. My face has two days' worth of growth, and I can imagine the shade it has by now. Imani stands beside me with the map held out, and we refocus on the task ahead, climbing out of this crevice.

"From the looks of the map, this crevice follows the main dune ridge. If we head east, we should come across a gentler sloping rocky patch. Maybe we can climb out at that point?" I say.

"Sounds good to me ... unless you want to stay down here a little longer?" A shy smile pulls up on her pretty mouth.

"I can think of a thousand better places to be right now." Her eyes are dark and her lips part slightly. I pull in a breath, hands hanging by my side, desperate to touch her. What I want to do and what I should do are two very different things.

I turn and start the trudge through the crevice, trekking to the east. Imani falls into step beside me. She is silent, but I know that there are a million thoughts flying through her mind.

CHAPTER 34
IMANI

By the time the sun is directly above us, we have come across the rocky patch on the map. It is one of the deepest parts of the crevice and towers over us. So much for a gentler slope. The rock is cool to the touch, but not smooth like a gorge; it is sharp and jagged. We stop, trying to make out the best place to climb up. Pulling off our robes, we shove them into our rucksacks. Fear prickles through me. What if we fall from that height?

Before I can shake the thought, Harm is a couple of feet above me, climbing. He is quick and accurate. I follow, catching up and overtaking him with my lighter frame. The rock cools my outstretched hands. Small rocks and dust fall under the pressure of my feet. Harm looks down to protect his eyes.

I hold my position firmly. I can hear him breathing heavier now as we are nearing the halfway mark of the climb. The cool rock is getting warmer the higher we go, with the sun radiating down. I find each foothold and cracked, rocky edge and propel myself upwards. I look back up, seeing only a matter of feet between us and the top.

A crack echoes through the chasm as the rock under my foot gives way. A breathy cry leaves my chest as my body drops, hitting the wall. I find purchase on a small rocky ledge for one and a rotted root for the other, grinding out a curse, scrambling to find jagged rock to take my weight. Harm holds his position and releases one of his hands, searching for a way to help me. I look down. My stomach rises into my chest, and sweat slicks my palms. The rotted root gives way, and I loose a sharp cry. My stomach drops, sending my heart racing.

"Harm!"

"Hold on, I'll come up to you." Replacing his hand back on its hold, he thrusts his weight towards me, point by point.

"Hurry, my hand is slipping!"

Harm's jaw clenches as he pulls his way up to me, faster by the second. He is almost at my level. Only my fingertips grip the ledge, my other hand frantically trying to find purchase on another hold. Harm shoves his right hand and feet into holds and braces himself before grabbing for me. I reach out to him.

My hand slips.

A whimper wrings from my throat, and fear prickles through my body.

"No!" Harm's scream echoes through the crevice.

I fall, breathless, frozen, the last two days with him flashing through my mind.

He grabs my arm as I fall past him, our grip sliding up to our hands. I dangle helplessly, eyes locked on Harm's. The gap between us and the top is around ten feet. I scan the rock face for somewhere to find a hold. Harm's arm strains, and his face contorts in pain. He briefly closes his eyes, then his face hardens and his jaw sets. His eyes open, locked on mine.

A brilliant red stream seeps over his knuckles and drops onto my shoulder. His back has opened up. No … I shake my head, eyes burning and breath lodged in my throat as I lighten my grip on his wrist.

"No, don't you dare!" he growls, breathing fast. He heaves me up, lips curling, teeth gritted hard. "Find another hold!" he barks.

I find a rock to take hold of, anxious to release the weight on his body. After what seems an age of trial and error, I find another hold and press myself against the face of the rock to rest momentarily.

Harm stares at me. I stare back before briefly closing my eyes. Breathing heavily, we hang high up on the rock face. The warmth of the rocks means we cannot stay still for too long. Harm makes another start for the top, and I follow.

The rock near the top is hot under our hands, propelling us out of the crevice. We roll onto the hot sand, a safe distance from the edge, relieved to be on the surface again. We lie on the sand to catch our breath, the blinding sun reminding us that we're alive. Immediately, I don my head wrap and robe. Harm goes to do the same, but I place my hand on his arm. Without a word, I lift his shirt to inspect his back. I pull out the cloth again and soak up the fresh blood. Lowering his shirt, I sigh.

"We're going to need to treat your back. Hopefully, there's somebody in Farno. It's too dangerous to go back to Enid."

"Is it that bad?"

"Yes, Harm, it's that bad. Let's keep moving. We'll make the outlying village by nightfall." I trek towards the east once again.

Harm follows.

CHAPTER 35
HARM

We make the outlying village in good time, the sun just sinking over the horizon behind us. My gait is awkward from the throbbing spreading across my back, and my strained muscles from the fall, the climb, and holding onto Imani when she was dangling from the rock face. She leads the way into the village as we search for a place to rest and some food. A handful of men patronize one of the outer buildings, which are mostly run down. We make our way towards it.

Entering through the swinging half doors of the establishment that looks like a tavern, but with no sort of order to it, Imani and I stick close to the perimeter and head over to the woman standing behind a makeshift counter. The patrons have stopped all conversation and are now staring at us. This may have been a mistake.

"Please, we need somewhere to stay, and some food. My friend needs a healer. Is there one in this village?" Imani asks quietly.

Dizziness sways me on my feet.

"You can't stay here," the woman briskly returns, nodding to the door we just came through. "You might find a spot to rest in the healer's shelter, three doors down to the right. Be warned, outsiders are not welcome for long," she finishes and turns her back to us. Imani grabs my hand and leads me outside. The fresh air helps me stay on my feet. Now that we have slowed down, I feel cold and weak. With one look at my face, Imani props my arm over her shoulder, leading me to the healer's shelter.

When we arrive, an old man sits on a wooden chair, carving an item with a steel blade. He looks up, intrigued by our presence. Imani tells him we need a bed, food, and some help from a healer, and he nods towards the inside. Imani steers me into the building. Narrow wooden bunks, much like the one I lay on in Maryanne and Christopher's home so long ago now, line the sides of the room.

Waves of weakness threaten to take me down, and my body shivers. Guiding me to the nearest bunk, Imani sits me down and grabs my legs, swinging them up onto the bunk. Her hand cradles my shoulders and head as she lays me down on the rough cloth. She rolls me to face her, leaving my back free from any pressure and makes sure I am comfortable before leaving to find the healer. Shivering, I slam my eyes shut, defenseless against the fever that is wreaking havoc on my body.

The throbbing in my back wakes me. I try to move, and find a wet cloth on my head. I am still lying on my side, Imani lays next to me. Her breathing rhythmically presses against my chest, her head buried against my neck. A tray with food and our rucksacks sit beside the bed on a small table. I do not know what time it is, only that it is nighttime. I try to move to give Imani more room, but my back is so painful I can't. She's cold. Awkwardly, I pull the blanket over us both, hugging her tight, and breathe through the fire in my back.

A small figure moves towards my bunk, a woman who I assume is the healer. She gestures for me to go back to sleep. Willingly, I close my eyes. A warm, thin hand rests momentarily on my forehead. She leaves, and the creaking from a wooden chair is the only sound audible over the soft breathing of her many wards. Pulling Imani closer, I fade back into unconsciousness.

Voices rouse me from dreams I would rather leave behind. Imani is gone, and her half of the bunk is cold. Her rucksack is also gone. The food from last night still waits for me, and hunger pulls at my stomach. Every movement on my way to sitting up, I breathe through pain rippling over my back. The bread tears easily as I shove it into my mouth, followed by some cold broth, almost making me gag from the grainy texture.

The old woman drifts towards me. I look up from my food as she sits at the end of my bed. Her face shows a lifetime of hardship.

"You must be feeling better, young man?" she says, nodding at my swift annihilation of the food.

"Somewhat. Do you know where my friend is?" I wince at the words, they seem like not enough now.

She offers a small laugh. "She was by your side the entire time you had a fever. Never left. I think it was a long three days for her. When I told her to get out and get some fresh air, she said there was someone she was looking for. I assured her I would keep an eye on you. She has gone looking for one of the villagers, Barlow."

I stop chewing.

I've been out of it for three days?

Imani has gone where?

No!

Oh, no, no, no, no.

Not Barlow.

Imani can't go off to find my father by herself. Who knows

243

what will happen when she finds him? My face must give away my fears, as the old woman tries to reassure me that Imani is fine.

With one rapid movement, I push off the bunk. Dizziness swallows me whole, and I quickly sit back down. Bile slides up my throat, but I swallow it back. My back aches from the movement. Fear snakes its way through my chest. Imani. I push up from the bunk once more, grabbing my rucksack as I stand.

The old healer shakes her head.

"Which way did she go?"

"Not far, just a little way down the village road to the south, to the big sandstone home. Last one on the left," she replies, brows lowered in confusion.

I rush through the door and try to orient myself. The sun is so bright; it feels like a searing assault, I stave it off with a hand over my face. Making out the path through the village to the south, I head that way. It takes a few strides to stretch out from a stagger to a hurried walk.

I pass by the people of the outlying village. My head is foggy, and it feels like they are all watching me. My breathing is ragged, my body still weak from the fever that cost me three days. Time seems to drag by in slow motion, in time with my steps that pound through every aching muscle in my back.

I reach the sandstone home, its front door wide open, and my heart stops. Imani is inside. In front of her is a man my size, but older and more weathered—a version of me that has aged twenty years. The same hair, the same brown eyes. He even stands the same as me.

CHAPTER 36
HARM

Barlow sits down at his kitchen table and starts writing in a book. The smell of goat wafts through his home. The muffled calls of the animals that must be behind the house mix with the playful sounds of children. Imani stands at the end of the table, staring at him, her arms across her chest. He doesn't pay her any heed.

"I asked you a question," she spits.

"Would you like to sit down? Can I get you a drink?" a woman says, her brown eyes darting between Barlow and Imani in confusion. Her long, plaited blonde hair drapes over her chest. A small girl clings to her long skirt.

"I asked you to leave. I will not have a stranger come into my home and start accusing me of things," Barlow grinds out.

I raise a hand to knock, and the woman notices me by the door.

"Oh," she utters.

Barlow stops writing and turns to face the door. His expression goes from blank to wide-eyed in seconds. He pushes the book back and stands, taking in the reflection of himself as he tracks his gaze over me from head to toe.

"Rupert, what is going on?" his wife murmurs, wrapping an arm around her daughter.

"It's fine, Eloise. Take Min outside for a minute, will you?" he says, gesturing to the door. She looks between the three of us before nodding and guiding her daughter through the hall and out the back door.

I step through the doorway, and Imani moves to stand beside me, watching Barlow as he walks closer. The ache in my back stiffens my movements.

"You should not have come," he says flatly.

"So, it's true? You're my father?"

He halts, studying me, brows lowered. "I doubt we're the spitting image of each other for any other reason, boy." He crosses his arms over his chest.

"Now, will you answer my questions?" Imani asks.

Barlow waves an arm to the table, inviting us to sit. I move over to the table, pulling a chair out for Imani before taking one for myself. Barlow watches me, noticing every mannerism, before he sits down opposite us.

"Do you have the ability to manipulate the dial?" Imani asks, her words getting sharper by the moment. A shiver runs over my body, and fatigue comes and goes in waves.

"Yes," he says.

"Do the Guardians know?" I ask.

"One does—the one I made the bargain with."

"Which one? What bargain?" Imani hisses.

"Fletcher. I bargained for immunity from the Chancellor, to have a life and live." His voice softens with every word. Imani goes still.

"In exchange for what?" I ask.

He stares at me. His Adam's apple bobs, and he flicks his gaze between Imani and me.

"I need some air," Imani says, drifting out the front door and toward the gate.

"In exchange for what, Barlow?" I say, my heart thundering against my ribs.

He stares at me. His mouth opens, and he closes it again. I turn briefly checking Imani is still outside.

"I have it from you *and* from my mother, don't I?" I want to hear it from his lips now.

"That is correct."

"Why did you run when you found out mother was with child?" Dizziness creeps up, and I swallow as a chill runs through me.

"I left to protect you and your mother. But it seems others did not perceive my actions that way." He runs a hand through his hair. "It doesn't matter. I have time before my end of the bargain is required."

"What. Did. You. Bargain. With?" I grind out.

But I already know.

He bargained my life.

"I was your half of the deal, wasn't I?" I lower my voice.

"I'm sorry, it was either that or execution. Your mother had fled. I assumed you would stay in the north and be safe. I thought she would have hidden you from them." His gaze drops to his hands, now in his lap.

What man sacrifices his own son? Heat floods through my core and I wobble to my feet.

"It was ten years ago, boy. Things were different, and I had no intention of ever handing you in. You should not have come. You should be at home with your parents."

"My parents are dead."

His mouth gapes, eyes tightening. I spin and stalk toward the front door. A chair scrapes.

"Wait."

I hesitate in the doorway. Every muscle starts to shiver, the fever from my back clawing its way through every inch of me. I grip the doorframe with both hands. Imani stands by the gate. She jogs to my side instantly.

"You're not going anywhere in this state. What on earth happened to you?" Barlow asks, his voice low.

"Come back and sit down. I'll fetch Eloise. Her healing herbs do wonders for most ailments."

Imani guides me back onto a kitchen chair, standing beside me, either to hold me up or put space between Barlow and me. He disappears through the back door. Moments later, his wife and three children file into the kitchen behind him. Min and two older boys stare at me. Sweat rolls down my face as I shiver, hands gripping the chair seat, as each shiver sends pain through my back like shards of glass. I focus on my breathing. A mug of water appears on the table in front of me.

"You should stay the night. You are in no condition to travel anywhere," Eloise says. She rummages through her cupboard, placing small vials into a pile on the bench. A few minutes later, a paste is held out on a spoon in front of my mouth.

"What is that?" Imani demands.

"It will help with the pain and the fever. It shouldn't make him drowsy," she offers.

Imani takes the spoon, holding it to my lips. I wince and pull back, it's vile. I have smelt that somewhere before. Pungent, it burns its way up my senses. Imani shoves it into my mouth, wrapping her hands around my face.

"Swallow, Harm," she whispers.

I meet her gaze. Worry etches lines across her pretty face. I swallow, reaching the for mug to wash it down.

"Come with me," Eloise says. "You can sleep here tonight.

Tomorrow, please find the healer and have her tend to your wounds. Infection leads to blood poisoning, and that can be fatal."

Eloise leads us to a room at the front of the house. I stagger after Imani, who leads me by one hand, and I obey when she pushes me onto the bunk. Pain throbs in my back as I shift to my side. Imani stands by the bunk until Eloise leaves, shutting the door behind her.

Imani sits, resting her hand on my shoulder. She runs a hand through my hair before checking my forehead with the back of her hand. Losing a sigh, she lays beside me on the bunk.

"Nightfall will be here soon. Get some rest, Harm. I'll keep watch."

"Mm-hmm," I manage to breathe before heaviness pulls me under.

Angry words and threats pull me from the depths of sleep. Imani lies still beside me, the steady rise and fall of her chest grounding us both.

"You had no right to do that, Eloise," Barlow snaps.

"I am protecting my family, Rupert—which you should have done. That boy is nobody to us."

"Do you have any idea what they'll do to him?"

"I don't care. I will protect my babies by any means necessary. They will not pay the price for your stupidity."

"When did you tell them to come?" he says after a moment of silence.

"They will be here at daylight, if the message is heeded." The fire in her voice ebbs slightly.

The Guardians are coming.

We have to move.

But my body is exhausted.

Imani rolls into my warmth, laying her arm over mine. Just a few more minutes. Then I'll wake her, and we will leave. Just another moment, then we will go ...

"Harm, wake up!" Imani hisses. Her hands shake my shoulder roughly. "Harm, wake up, Fletcher is here!"

I crack my eyes open, immediately taking in the terror in her face. I bolt upright, groaning through the pain. She jumps off the bunk and presses a finger to her lips. And then I hear it. Fletcher's voice in the room next door. Imani pads to the door, her body shaking. She slowly flicks the lock on the door and grabs our rucksacks.

I stand, letting the waves of dizziness wash over me. Imani grabs my hand, propelling me toward the window.

"Where is the traitor?" another voice says.

Mason.

My heart flings against my ribs, sending the pit on my stomach plummeting. My breathing turns rapid. I pull myself up onto the window frame, biting down a groan. Imani drops onto the sand outside, steadying the rucksacks to reduce the noise. I clamber out the window, landing with a thud on the sand.

Imani cringes. "Harm, we have to move!"

"Just give me a minute," I gasp, gripping my knees, waiting for the dizziness and pain to subside.

"Where are they, Barlow?" Fletcher booms. A small child starts to cry. My heart skips a beat. Hell, if he hurts those little kids. The image of Min huddled into her mother's skirt flicks through my mind.

"Rupert!" Eloise cries, the strain in her voice audible from where we stand outside.

"The spare room," Barlow finally says.

The door Imani locked rattles under Fletcher's thunderous hammering.

"Get it open, now," Mason orders.

Fear prickles up my spine. I push to a stand and grab Imani's hand. "Run," I gasp.

She takes off, dragging me behind her, through the huddled goats and over short fences. After a handful of heartbeats, my body relaxes into a stride, and Imani releases my hand.

We run hard to the north, not looking back.

CHAPTER 37
HARM

There isn't much north of the outlying areas, only a handful of abandoned villages. We stop in the second village we come across, blowing out deep, ragged breaths, chests heaving. Imani looks at me, relief all over her face.

A beaten old shack sits on the far northern side of the village, and we crash against the wall of the building. After an age of not speaking, catching our breath, Imani looks at me with a look I have only seen from her once. Pity.

"Are you okay?" She almost whispers the question.

"Yes," I utter.

I want to tell her about the stupid gift and the reason Barlow's wife was so eager to hand me in; it was not just because I am an escaped prisoner. But I can't. I don't know how to tell her, without risking her thinking of me differently. I'll find a way to keep her safe and work this ability thing out on my own.

"What do we do now?" she asks.

"We'll figure something out."

"How, Harm?"

"My mother always told me there is a solution if you take the time to find it," I say vaguely.

"Well, what this time? What is the solution?" A shiver runs over her exhausted body.

"We should get inside before the cold air settles." I stand and drop a hand to help her up. She places her hand in mine, and I pull her to her feet, gritting my teeth against the pain in my back. She holds my gaze for a moment, brows drawn down.

"I need to refill my canteen," she says, tracking toward the well in the village center. I trudge behind her, pulling my canteen from my rucksack.

"Oh, no," Imani breathes. I look up to see her standing motionless over the well. I fall in beside her. The odor of the well makes me draw back.

"What happened to it?" That is not the smell of drowned bodies. Imani turns slowly, looking around the village, scanning for something.

"What is it?" I ask.

"Poison," she utters and walks silently to the southern outlying homes of the village. I follow her, taking my time, looking through the windows of the empty houses I pass. Her scream carries on the winds tunneling around the buildings. I sprint to where she stands. Her shaking hands grip the back of her neck.

The smell hits me, and I force my body to stay upright, pressing a hand over my nose and mouth. A grave. A mass open grave lies at her feet. Dozens of village people lie piled on top of each other, with scavenger birds already making the rounds, pecking out the vacant eyes of the dead.

"Imani," I utter, placing my hand on her shoulder.

She stands wide-eyed, mouth agape, not moving. "Why would they do this?"

"I don't know, but we need to get inside." I look around the

village for any movement. Nothing, no one is here, not even the
Guardians. It's not their style to hang around. They do their
damage and then let the people deal with the aftermath. I turn
away, pulling Imani with me, trudging through the sand toward
the building that looks the least derelict. This is what we have to
change—and I am the key to that. I hate lying to her. My stomach
plummets. I shift her rucksack over my shoulder, not looking back.

The door to the old home gives way under my shove, and we
walk in, slumping against the wall, my legs shaking from running
for hours and my back aching. Every half-closed wound tugs with a
sting.

"We need to find that person with the ability, Harm. This has
to stop."

"We will." My throat almost closes over with the weight of the
half-truth.

She stares vacantly at the opposite wall. "How?"

"You know, my sister fell in the village well once. Her doll had
fallen in when she was playing with it around the well. I went to
Mother to get her help to retrieve it, and she told me I could figure
it out. By the time I had run back to tell my sister, she was in the
well, screaming. She tried to reach for her doll and fell in. I was
terrified and jumped in after her, but not before yelling to the boys
in the village center to grab my father. He came quickly and pulled
us out. But while I was in the well, I thought of all the ways I could
have fetched her doll from the well and prevented her from falling
in. She clung to me the entire time, saying how sorry she was and
praying we would not drown. My whole body was on fire, trying to
keep us both afloat. Father dragged us both up with a rope he
found, and Amaya never went near the well again. Well, not until
that last day." I pause, losing a sigh. "But that's not my point. We
will figure it out together." I slump, exhausted from reliving the
well twice in my mind while sitting on the dry, sandy floor.

"I know the well you speak of. I've seen that one myself."

"All wells are the same, I'd guess." I try to keep from falling into the dark place where my grief lives. Imani gives me a small nod of acknowledgement, fingers playing with the hair that has escaped her wrap.

"Harm," she starts, then hesitates. "You must miss them."

I swallow hard to keep the lump in my throat from choking me. "Every day."

Without another word, Imani has wrapped herself around me as I sit here. I bury my head in her hair and hold her tight, forcing myself to breathe instead of crying for my mother, my father, and my sweet little sister. Amaya, I couldn't protect her. I breathe Imani in, forcing deep breaths in and out, pushing the ache in my chest further down.

Imani falls asleep still huddled into me. I lay her on the floor, sliding the rucksack under her head, then lie beside her on my side, hands under my own. Imani sleeps heavily beside me, occasionally tossing and trying to get some relief from the hard ground beneath us. The darkness is long this night, and memories float around like ghosts. With heavy eyes, sleep finds me an age later.

I wake at the murmuring beside me. Imani is talking in her sleep—angry words. I listen. Forced and final, she speaks, disowning someone who is callous and cruel. She stops for a while, then cries out. She is screaming for them to stop. When she doesn't wake up, I touch her shoulder. She spins and faces me. Her face is drawn, her eyes wide and fearful. She thumps my chest with her fists and yells at me to stop. "Stop it now!"

She is still dreaming.

I grab her wrists. "Imani."

Shaking her head, her dark hair flying everywhere, she pulls away from me, like a trapped animal.

"Imani, wake up, it's just a dream!" But she is unchanged, her arms pulling back so hard her wrists are red. I let her go. She falters back and grabs at her clothes and starts rambling something about someone no longer being her father. This is the first I have heard of her family. I listen silently.

"You are not my father, and I am not your daughter!" she growls. Her eyes are open but she is not awake. Her face is twisted. Uneven, shattering breaths force a sob with every cycle. I scan her face, and my chest tightens. She is hurting, and I can't wake her.

"How many more innocent people are you going to claim in the name of the Chancellor, Fletcher?!" she cries.

Fletcher?

Wait, what?!

Fletcher is her *father*?

The blood drains from my face. Heat from fear and anger tangle up through my body. Scanning the floor, I try to catch my breath. My hands tremble.

I lift my gaze back up.

Imani is now awake, sitting immobile, a stream of tears running rivulets down her dusty porcelain cheeks. Eyes wide and mouth parted, she grips her arms with white knuckles.

CHAPTER 38

IMANI

I reach for Harm's hand.

He pulls it back.

Pain twists my face, weight crushes my chest and tears burn. I open my mouth, but no sound comes. My breath becomes more ragged, my hands lay limp in my lap. The same dream I have had so many times. Me screaming at my father to stop. Harm stares at me, unmoving, his chest heaving.

He heard.

I can't shift my gaze from his tortured look. His eyes scan my face as if he is going through every moment we have had together. There are so many and my chest tightens further with each one of them I relive. I reach for him again, and he slides back. Sobs choke from my chest.

No.

Please, no.

He pulls in a long breath, brows lowering further. "Is that why you're here with me? Your father has you tagging along, keeping tabs on me? Is that how he found us so easily?"

My hands shake. The aching in my chest turns to a burning

tightness. "No, Harm, of course not!" The broken words rip at my heart. Tears course down his face now and I tangle my hands in my shirt, wringing out the pain.

I am Fletcher's daughter.

Imani Fletcher.

I should have told him from the beginning. I tried to, so many times. I can feel every tiny bit of betrayal that fills his face. I caused it. I close my eyes momentarily. I deserve everything he is giving me right now.

"Why have you never told me? The only reason I know is because you were talking in your sleep." He rises to his feet. "Were you ever going to tell me?"

"Please, Harm." I stand and step toward him until I am just inches away and stretch out my hand. Tears stream down my face, and my shoulders shake. His eyes burn into mine, tension racked in every muscle, brows set low, jaw feathering.

"What difference would it have made?" I whisper.

"What do you mean? Your father is responsible for the death of my whole family!"

I wince, jerking back. My heart wrings in my chest. I pull in a deep breath, but it's not enough. I can't breathe. "I'm sorry! I tried to stop him, so many times, Harm—" I sink to the floor before my shaking legs can give out.

"You are the child of a Guardian, and all this time I thought you were some sort of rebel," he seethes. A vicious laugh curls his lips and my chin wobbles.

"Not by choice. I have nothing to do with my family now, not even with my mother." Every breath is too shallow. I owe him an explanation. More than that, but it's a start.

He stands on the other side of the room, staring at me through the dim surroundings of the dilapidated house. Moonlight pierces through the weathered walls, and jagged beams light up the space between us. I will myself to steady my breath. I can fix this.

Harm takes a step toward me, anger softening to hurt. I push my way to my feet and walk to him, and this time we are almost touching. I wipe my face and lift my chin, fixing my gaze on his and setting my shoulders back.

"There's something else." I drag in a lungful of cool air. "That I need to tell you."

He just looks at me, eyes pained, face twisting, and his chest heaves, waiting for another blow.

"I was there, when you hid those boys." I searching his face. He relaxes a little, and his mouth opens, but he doesn't speak. Blood thunders through my veins. "When you were lashed, I was there." I swallow the lump in my throat. "When they executed your family, I was there." A fresh torrent of sobs claim my burning lungs. "And," I groan through a whimper and rest my hand over his heart, "when that man who looked like your father pulled you out of the well, I was there."

Tears stream down his face. He has heard me. His breathing is so rapid, eyes now burning into mine. His Adam's apple bobs, wet with tears. "How?"

My hand still rests on his chest. "I have been shadowing Fletcher for years, since I was thirteen, doing anything I could to interfere with his orders, hoping to help even just one person." His heart thunders against my fingers, I place my other hand on his chest. "So many times, I wanted to tell you. But every day that I spent with you made it so much harder." I look away, my hands trembling on his chest. "I was afraid you would hate me." He studies my face. My chin quivers, and I drop my hands from his chest and tighten my arms around my own. "I still am."

He stands rooted to the spot. I force myself to meet his gaze, guilt and agony twisting their way through my core. I take his hand

and put it over my heart. The cloth is thin from wear, and his warm hand presses down. The rise and fall of my chest rolls under his fingertips, and my heart quickens. With every thump of my heart under his hand, his face softens a little more. He bows his head, touching his forehead to mine, and I close my eyes.

"I will stay with you if you want me to, Harm, but I'll understand if things have changed between us. Please know that I am not here out of pity. I wanted to add something to your life, since you had lost so much because of my father."

He steps into my space. Every thread of my soul wants to be enveloped in him, tangling us together until we can no longer be separated. Harm places his hand behind my neck under my hair and pulls me closer. Thoughts of us being apart vanish like the sandy wisps of a dying sandstorm.

CHAPTER 39
HARM

The heat of the early morning wakes us before the sun's light reaches inside the run-down house. Imani is lying beside me, and the events of last night flood back in like salt on an open wound. Still processing the fact that Fletcher is Imani's father, mind reeling, makes my insides crawl. She was there every time he punished me—every moment that counted. And I dreamed of her before I even knew her.

Lying on the hard floor in the heat, I am torn between needing her in my life, and her intimate connection with the man who killed my family. I shove my hands through my hair, alternating between disgust for Fletcher and the insanely intense feelings I have for her. She carries strength and courage I have tried to find since living under my parents' roof.

Imani sits up, saying something, twisting her hair into a makeshift bun before tying it off with her scrap of cloth.

"What?" I say, a million miles away.

She scans my face with her deep-blue eyes, and the pull between us is instant, tugging on my core, dragging my heart along with it. Even now, it still feels right.

"I just said I'm hungry," she utters, keeping her eyes fixed on mine.

"We should start our way through the sands, towards the southern villages." I stand and drop a hand, helping her up.

We pull our traveling gear on and wrap our faces to start heading south. I am not telling Imani my full intentions, and from her demeanor, she is aware of it. She doesn't call me out on it, either from guilt over what now lies between us, or because she trusts me. I'll pick the latter on that one. My fingers twist and pull the loose thread in my trouser pocket, tightening like the knot in my stomach.

We share a little bread and save the jerky for later before we refill our canteens at the tap of the last building that has water storage before tracking toward Mareya to Enid's. The walk is easy-going, but we don't talk. Imani is still looking out for Guardians, and I now know what that means for her. Even as a wanted escaped prisoner, marked for execution, I don't have to struggle with knowing that my father is one of the cruelest Guardians to have ever worn the uniform.

After two days of walking through the hot sands and very little talking, the small lights of Mareya flicker in the distance. We track towards Enid's house on the far side of the village. I am excited to see her again, and I have a few things to tell Jonah. He is her uncle. Why didn't he tell me Fletcher was her father? He knows about the ability I possess. If he knows, does Fletcher? What other secrets is he keeping from me?

Things in the village center are quiet. People seem to be inside, not out and about going about their daily routines. Something in my gut drops like stone. I pick up the pace. Imani keeps up beside me. We round the corner and start a steady jog towards Enid's home.

Red covers her door. X. I break into a sprint, smashing through her wooden front gate and up to her door. I trace a finger across the paint. It's still wet. I bust through her door. Her home has been ransacked, with papers and books scattered on the floor, along with her many herbs and simple belongings. I stand frozen to the spot, hands shaking.

No, not Enid ...

Please, not Enid too.

Where is Jonah? I run from room to room, swinging doors open, calling out for Enid and Jonah, but the house is silent. I stride back to the front room. Imani stands there, not moving, her entire body shaking, knowing written over her face.

Fletcher.

Instantly, she spins on the spot and charges out the door.

"Imani, no!" I take off after her. Not now. She can't find him now! She is halfway to village center when I grab her hand and pull her around to face me. Sand flies from under the weight of the spin. She stares at me with eyes full of pain and hatred. "Let go of me, Harm. This ends now!"

"No, you can't find him yet. You don't understand," I plead, grabbing her other arm to keep her from pulling away.

"Why not? It's Enid and Jonah! Who next?"

"Please come back, I—" My heart tightens, as if being crushed. "It's important." I need to keep her with me, and I should have told her when I found out. I shove my hands through my hair, eyes swinging from her face to the ground.

"Are you serious? What is so important that you need to tell me right now?" she growls, tugging backward in my hands. I tighten my grip and step into her space, eyes searching hers.

"Do you trust me?"

She slackens a little.

"Do you?"

"Yes."

I let go of her, and she barges past me, back toward Enid's house.

I follow Imani a few paces behind, watching over my shoulder as I go. The Guardians can't be far away, the ocher paint is still wet. There was no gathering in the village center. We are too late—or Enid and Jonah got out somehow. *Please let them be alive.*

Imani's fuming body drapes over Enid's chair in the front room, sand falling from her foot as she jiggles it, eyes burning into me as she tracks me from across the room. She will not make this easy for me. I sit on the floor in front of her. Her gaze softens, and she swallows. My heart leaps into my throat. Inhaling, I return her gaze and try to find the right words. I can't. She is going to hate me. The beautiful face in front of me will never look at me the same way again.

"Well?" she snaps.

I loose a breath, long and slow. "Last time we were here, I should have told you this," I start, my heart thundering inside my chest. "We have been searching for the person with the ability."

Her arms fold across her chest, and she huffs out a breath. "Please tell me that is not what you brought me back here to say. I already know that."

"It was all a waste of time." I drop my gaze to the floor and rest my elbows on my legs, lacing my fingers together, and drop my head onto my thumbs.

"What do you mean? What did you find out? There's no one else left?"

"No, there is."

"Oh?"

I lift my head and search her face for any inkling of whether she is getting what I am trying so badly to tell her.

"I have it, Imani." Every word feels like lead. "Barlow knew it. I got it from him, and my mother."

She stares at me, not breathing.

Finally, she pulls in a breath.

"And he has agreed not to use it, so apart from Charlie, who won't leave his oasis, you are the last one?" She closes her eyes briefly and grips the arms of the chair with both hands. "If Fletcher finds out you're the only one left with the ability to change the dial, on top of everything else—"

She jumps up from the chair and grabs my head. Bending over she brushes my hair from the back of my neck, sweeping side to side. Her hands still. "There's a birthmark, but it's very small." She steps back toward the chair and stares at me, mouth open, breaths coming fast. "It's almost the shape of a bird, it's flying." She raises her arms, as if imitating the bird in flight. I close my eyes briefly, absorbing her words confirming who I am. The bird in flight is tattooed on Toby, and Enid. Everything is connected.

"You can't go after him, Imani. Where you go, I go, and that means he's going to have every chance to capture me again. I'm not sure I'll be so lucky next time. They will not waste time accommodating me with a cell, and any chance of changing things back will be lost."

"No, that will not happen!" She gets up and walks out the back door of Enid's house. It slams. I sit on the floor amongst the strewn about items. Sunlight pours in through the kitchen window, the almost dried ocher's chalky smell fading. The clatter of smashing pots rings up the small passageway to the front of the house.

I rise to my feet and make my way to the back door. Fragments of pots, dirt, and limp green plants cover Enid's back porch. Imani slumps to the ground amidst the wrecked pots. Pushing through the door, I pad over to her, shoving the mess away from her with my foot. I sit down beside her, rocking into her shoulder. "Hey."

She rocks into my shoulder in response.

"I don't want to put you in danger. You are the last person I have left. I wish it wasn't me, but it is. I can't change that. It will be your choice if you want to stay with me and do whatever it is we need to do to change things."

For an age, she doesn't speak.

"I don't want it to be you," Imani whispers.

I take her hands. "I thought you wanted all this to end? The suffering and the oppression, it has to end, and it's not going to unless someone does something."

"Of course, I do," she is straining to keep it together, "but that was a lot easier when I had nothing to lose."

It has been a long two days. She looks hollow, sad, and I am crushed to think that I played a large part in that. I sit next to her in silence. She rests her head on my shoulder, tears hitting my leg as they fall, one after the other.

Almost an hour passes, and her ragged breathing steadies. My heart has settled back into my chest, although it still aches for so many reasons. I trace circles on the back of her hand. "We can't stay here."

Imani gets to her feet, holding out a hand. I take it, and she tugs me up. She brushes herself off and looks back up. "We do it together. Where you go, I go." Her words are fierce, her fire returned. She tilts her head back slightly, her eyes filled with the things that she has been missing for years—love and loyalty—along with what I have seen in her all along. Determination.

I step up to her and press my forehead into hers. Her arms rest around my neck. I grip her waist and close my eyes. "In that case, we need a plan—and a good one."

CHAPTER 40

HARM

By nightfall, we are heading north, the opposite direction of most of our journey so far. We need supplies and weapons, so we head back to the one place full of no good, Trindari. It will take us a solid three days to get there on foot, so every village we go through or around, I am on the lookout for a dune buggy. No luck so far in finding one. Imani chuckles at me every time I mention driving one.

We hit Trindari with a few hours of light to spare. The plan is to get in and get out again before night sets in. Trindari is not a place to linger. I learned that the hard way last time. Walking quickly, we make our way to the village marketplace. Only a few vendors remain. An old man stands behind a stall with a handful of patrons, in deep discussion, selling the wares we need.

Imani is quick to examine the blades, laying half hidden in a wood box. Picking up a knife with a leather handle, she turns it over, then returns it to its place. The next one she tosses around with her right hand, sighting it up with a focused gaze. She digs into her pockets, pulls out some sort of old coin, and tries to give it to the vendor. He looks her up and down before accepting the payment. She offers him a half smile and moves to the vendor behind us, leaving me staring at the weapons, something I haven't considered before now.

Imani haggles over food with the lady behind me. Apparently, she is closing, but Imani is persuasive and ends up with a sack of supplies. I return my attention to the weapons in front of me. Guardians do not allow us to own weapons, so they are not sold openly. The vendor shifts around nervously as I run my gaze over them again. I pick up the blade with the leather handle that Imani put down. It is heavier than I imagined, but soft to hold, and it feels balanced, if there is such a thing.

I hunt through my rucksack for something of value to trade. Finding the compass my father gave me, I pull it from the bag. The memory of my father handing it to me rushes back, sending an ache through my chest. Fingers still curled around it, I hesitate. The man plucks it from my hand and holds it up to the receding light. His gaze flickers between the compass and me.

"I can't take this, young man. It's worth far more than that simple blade you hold."

"It's all I have to trade." I adjust the rucksack over my shoulder and it jingles.

I tug it from my shoulder and shove my hand to the bottom, finding two coins. I had forgotten all about them. I pull one out. His eyes widen as he reaches for it. "Show me."

I press it into his hand. He turns the coin over. "That will be fine. Few people have these coins anymore, they are worth more now. That one is yours." He drops the compass back into my palm.

"Thank you." I return the compass to my rucksack, along with the blade. He waves me off again and turns his back, sorting out items on a shelf. I catch up with Imani, who now has a load in her arms. I open my rucksack, and she dumps the food inside.

"Time to go," she says and turns to leave. I follow, replacing my wrap before flinging my hood over my head. Imani does the same. We walk at a quick pace to the outskirts of this menacing village, hoping to get away without recognition. The last building on the southern side of the village shelters a dune buggy. It wasn't there before, which can mean only one thing. Guardians are here.

With a buggy, we can travel faster, but starting it will alert the Guardians. I decide to take my chances. Imani shoots me a wary look, but I climb aboard the buggy, and she slides into the seat on the passenger side. I shove the rucksacks between us and hunt for the keys in the front compartment, like last time. My fingers hit hot metal, and a clank breaks my concentration. Keys. Looking down at the ignition, I grip the keys and turn.

A hand grabs mine holding the keys, and Imani's breath hitches. The pressure preventing me from turning the key steals my breath, and my heart leaps into my throat. I turn my body, like slow-dripping sap.

Uniform.

Grey.

Eventually I track to the Guardian's face. I suck in a breath, tamping the wave of fear coursing through my body. Familiar eyes burn into mine.

"Mason," I choke out, realizing the second the word escape that I should have kept my mouth shut.

"Don't. That would be a bad idea," he says flatly.

At first, I don't think he recognizes me. Then his mouth pulls into a half smirk, and a wave of fear creeps up my spine. His hand is still firmly on mine. Imani shifts in her seat, but doesn't react. Mason looks at her, lingering for a moment before looking back at me. Disappointment flickers through his gaze. "Where are you going in such a hurry that you require a buggy?"

"You really expect me to tell you?" Why is he not dragging me out of the machine through the sand back to his comrades?

"If I were you, Travesci, I wouldn't add buggy theft to the list of things Fletcher is hunting you for." He watches Imani's reaction. She doesn't move, her expression stony, taking in the Guardian standing beside me.

"All yours," I force out, moving out of the buggy and grabbing my rucksack. Imani springs out of her side of the buggy and files in beside me, scanning Mason from head to toe. He shifts his attention to her, and she stares him down.

Two days ago, he was hunting me down. Now he doesn't seem interested in taking me in. What is going on? What's changed? He stares at Imani, briefly glancing back at me. Imani offers him nothing. He jumps into the buggy. Firing it up, he plows backwards. With the shift of the gear, he shoots forward, eyes fixed on Imani before pulling his sand goggles down and leaving us in a wake of flying sand. Imani throws me a look of urgency, and we hit the dunes running south. No time to lose. We need to get as far away from Trindari as possible.

CHAPTER 41

HARM

We fill our bellies as we hash out our plan. We will go to Charlie first, then on to the prison in Etonia at the great wall where the Chancellor lives, hopefully with Charlie in tow. Our plan is risky, and I pray it's going to work. We will need Guardian uniforms and Charlie's cooperation. I am hoping Charlie can take his place as Chancellor, but I doubt Arthur will step down willingly. Our visit to Trindari was for precisely that scenario. A knot twists in my gut. We change the dial and get rid of the last person left who can alter it. The last part will be the hardest for me. Imani doesn't seem fazed at all, chewing on the last of her bread.

With wraps and robes in place, we make for the direction of the cave where we once sheltered from the sandstorm, Charlie's home and the last remaining oasis of life untouched by the cruel desert. Without the buggy, it will take us a day and a half to reach it. I am glad for the journey. Now that we have a plan, I feel like our time has a limit. If we fail, I may have numbered both of our days. A weight pushes down on my chest, and every step is burdened with thoughts of my family and the people that have helped me. This is for them—every person I have lost or who has suffered under the regime. I have to try.

Imani walks beside me silently, consumed by her thoughts. This is what both of us have wanted for so long. Now that it is here, it feels like the end of everything.

The entrance to Charlie's hidden oasis is still the same as before: an inconspicuous opening with rock and sand flanking its edges. Imani enters, and I follow her, adjusting to the dark before calling out to Charlie. For a time, there is no reply, not even a single sound apart from the haunting sounds of the recondite cave, far removed from the outside world. Finally, shuffling and grunts sound from deep inside the cave. "Is that you two youngsters again?"

"It's Imani and Harm, Charlie," I call out.

The shuffling quickens, and Imani rifles through the rucksack hanging off my shoulder, trying to find the last of the matches. A few moments later, light flickers, revealing the smiling face of Charlie moving toward us. A warm smile stretches over my face, like it has been an age since we last saw him. Warmth spreads through my body.

"Fancy seeing you two again!" His arms wrap around us both. Imani slides a look of amusement my way and returns the hug, and I wrap an arm around the frail man's shoulders.

"Well, well, two sets of visitors in one week! Hasn't this turned out to be a wonderful day!" he says, throwing his hands in the air as he leads the way into the cave.

Someone else has been here?

We round the bend to his small makeshift room, and instantly I notice everything is the same as it was the last time we were here. Imani drops onto his sleeping mat and sits, waiting for Charlie to make the descent next to her. He takes a few moments with the aid of his stick to file in beside her, and she offers him another hug.

"Has someone been here, Charlie?" I ask.

"No, no, just me," he replies, looking towards the path that leads to the oasis deep in the cave. I feel bad for asking now, he must be confused.

"No, wait, that's not right. There was the older man that you were here with before. He was looking for someone. He was hard to talk to, getting upset about her, whoever she is," he says.

Could it have been Jonah? "Do you know who he was looking for?" I ask, hoping he says it was Enid.

"Nope, didn't say, and didn't stay either."

"Charlie, have you ever left this place?" Imani interrupts. "Occasionally for supplies, but only for a few hours, never longer than a day. So, no, not in a very long time. Why would I?" His face turns grim.

"Would you come with us?" I ask.

"No, I don't know. For how long? I mean, what about all this I am protecting?"

"No one but Imani, Jonah, and I know it's here, and it's safe with us. We need your help to do something important. We would make sure you're safe." As the words leave my mouth, I feel the undercurrent of the lie turn in the pit of my stomach. I can't guarantee his safety any more than I can my own, and being a wanted escaped prisoner makes it even more dangerous if they recognize us.

Charlie stares at me, as if turning over the legitimacy of my words in his own head.

"We need you to come to the great wall and help us persuade your brother to step down or to change the dial," Imani says. "Nobody needs to get hurt, but we need your help. We're hoping when he realizes you're alive, it will help change his mind."

Breath catches in my throat. His gaze drifts between us both

273

now. I feel more like a Guardian every moment of this conversation, with the lies and manipulation.

"There is nothing left outside of this cave for me, and you are fools to think my brother would give up what he has taken," Charlie says, voice almost a growl.

"But if it meant that we could change things back?" I press.

"There is no way he will volunteer to change that dial. I certainly cannot help you, and I don't know of anyone else left to do it," he snaps.

"Then at least we can say we tried," Imani says.

"You don't think he won't just kill you too?" he says, hands turning over his stick anxiously now.

"That is a chance we will have to take," I reply softly.

"It's a foolish plan, thought up by two youngsters that don't know what they're doing." His words tremble as he looks at us both. He struggles to get up, and Imani helps him stand before he wanders into the darkness. We stay in his little cavern and wait to see if he comes back.

After a time, we rise and stumble down the dark path towards his precious oasis. As we step through the entrance, the beauty of the light-filled haven overwhelms us again. Imani wanders in, exploring the place all over again, coming to rest on the stone she sat on once before. No Charlie. I cross the water's edge into the lagoon and crouch down. I run my hand through the water just above the perfectly round pebbles lining the bed. The center is deep—deep enough for swimming, if I knew how.

Birds and insects flit around the high ceiling of the dome, and sunlight splinters its way through the jagged opening, lighting up everything with a golden haze. It's perfection. Why on earth would Charlie want to leave his sanctuary and risk his life for people he's never met? It is a world of suffering he is disconnected from and has avoided nearly his entire life.

"If he can't help us, we can find out as much as possible about Arthur. Maybe something will help," I say to Imani.

She doesn't take her gaze off the oasis, simply nodding. We still need his help with the old map.

"You two should stay here tonight," Charlie pipes up, startling us both. A combination of pride and heaviness fills his words. "So you remember what you're fighting for, because mark my words, young ones, it will not be easy, nor will it be fair." He hobbles out of the wide cavern entrance, disappearing back down the dark passageway.

Imani pads over to the grassed area and lies down, watching the birds and colorful insects that flit overhead. I lay down beside her, and we wait out the hours until the full moon lights up our surroundings. Eyes closed, I lie on the grass, which is much softer than our usual sand or rock bed. I imagine a new world with surroundings like this, but on a grand scale. Imani tosses and turns next to me, then she sighs and sits up. I return to my imaginings.

She walks down to the water's edge and I open my eyes. She runs a hand through the cool water and looks back at me, trying to see if I am asleep. Simpering, I shut my eyes.

A heartbeat later, I open them. She drags her gaze from mine and slips off her clothing—shirt, trousers, and undergarments. She lets her hair out, and it bounces off her thin shoulders and dangles down her back. My heart races in my chest, breaths shallow. The moonlight illuminates her body, every curve and every elegant limb. Her head bends back as she looks up at the beams of light piercing the ceiling above, her hair cascades down her bare back.

She looks at me, and her face is soft but serious. Her eyes meet mine for a second, and then she enters the water, one elegant step after the other, until the water is up to her waist. Warmth spreads in my core. She turns to her left and scoops up water in her cupped hands, washing her face. The peaks of her chest protrude past her arm. Imani leans backwards into the water, her ivory rounds last to enter the glassy water.

My breathing stops.

Every inch of me burns to be that water right now.

With nothing between us.

Breath returns in ragged sequence as I watch her, my chest heaving with want and an uncontrollable ache that I have been suppressing for weeks now. Entranced, my gaze follows Imani as she rises. The water cascades from her skin, and the moonlight reflects off her almost luminescent wet body.

Unwillingly, I pull my gaze from the sight of her. Not yet. Not now. With a deep exhale, I close my eyes and slow my breathing that is out of control as every fiber of my being responds to her.

The ground beside me gives under her steps with subtle crunches in the grass. A drop of water hits my face with a splatter. Imani is above me, standing next to me. Feigning sleep, a half-smile blooms on my face, and I pull it back. I grip the grass and earth on either side of me, as if that will ground this heady feeling.

When I don't open respond, she settles down on the grass, drying off with her robe and pulling her clothes back on. Then she huddles close against my side. A handful of heartbeats later, her breathing has steadied, her body relaxed with sleep. I loose a trembling breath before willing myself to sleep too … eventually.

The subtle light from the morning sun is the first sight I see, although my mind replays Imani's swim last night, a far more arresting scene. I roll over to find her still asleep. I notice the way her clothes hang off her frame, hiding her curves beneath.

"Imani," I whisper, wanting to see her face, but feeling guilty for waking her.

"Yes, Harmen," she murmurs dryly, half asleep.

I prop myself up on my elbow, lying on my side to watch her. My stomach flutters. "You never call me that."

She rolls over to look at me and props her head up with her arm, imitating my position, eyes lit with amusement. "Don't I?"

I look at the grass beneath me, examining it with my fingers. It feels smooth and fine under my touch, which only makes it worse as the vision of Imani's bare skin returns from last night. The ache resettles in my core.

"I guess we should get up," she breathes, before shoving her hand through my hair roughly and rising to her feet. I breathe out and slump to the ground, face first with a groan, helpless. Imani's laughter echoes throughout the cavern, and my heart almost explodes with the sound.

Her small foot appears beside my head, nudging me gently. "Come on, we need to talk to Charlie. He can tell us about the map. Then we can get out of here and make a start." Her voice normal now, to my relief.

"I'll be there in a minute," I say, trying to give myself a moment alone to compose myself, for the fire in my center to peter out.

When I get up, Imani is leaning against the entrance to the oasis, arms crossed, blue eyes lit up with a grin as I make for the opening.

"What?" I utter, running my hands through my hair.

"Nothing." Her face softens, holding my gaze her eyes darken. "Let's go talk to Charlie."

"You first." She holds the rucksacks, handing me the matches. I scratch one alight, and she falls in behind me as we make our way back to Charlie's small cavern. But he isn't there. We continue toward the mouth of the cave. There he sits, as if waiting for us. I have never seen him this close to the exit of his home before. Has he changed his mind?

"Morning, Charlie." Imani springs up beside him with a light hug and he returns the gesture.

"We need your help with this map Imani found." I hand him the map.

He looks over it for a time, then looks at Imani in wonder. "Where did you find this map? As far as I know, only three were ever made. They were not for common consumption. Almost a secret, you could say."

"I found it at Harm's grandmother's house."

Charlie looks from the map to me. "The only people with these maps were the last remaining persons to hold the ability to manipulate the dial. The show the passages within the wall. If your grandmother had one, she either knows someone with it, or has it herself."

Imani face is barely restraining excitement.

"What's the look for?" Charlie asks.

"Oh, nothing," she coos, blue eyes lit up and trained on me.

"I suspected as much," he says with a wry grin. "Well, now that you're aware of your ability, Harm, it is even more dangerous for you. It's one thing to be oblivious and be out of harm's way," he smiles at his little pun, "but they can use that knowledge against you, and those you love." His gaze swinging between Imani and me. He returns his attention to the map. "These blue lines are waterways, all connected with this hidden cavern, but only three remain functional with running water—under the ground, of course. And these brown lines are tunnels dug long before the turn of the weather. If they still exist, then they could be useful to you. But remember, my brother is also aware of this map and what it contains." He ends his remarks with a hug for Imani and a slap on the back for me, followed by a nod.

Imani places the map back into my rucksack, and we leave Charlie standing at the entrance to his cave. The look on his face bothers me, sadness and fear. I hope we see Charlie again. For a moment, I doubt everything we have planned and whether we have any chance of surviving this at all.

We walk for a time not speaking. Imani slips a hand into mine, and I pull back.

Not yet.

CHAPTER 42
HARM

O ur next target is the village outside the prison walls: Etonia. It is a risky move, but to get into the great wall and to the dial, we need to get uniforms to stand a chance of not getting caught. My mind races through our interaction with Mason. Something doesn't feel right.

Mason's words hang in my mind as we trudge through the sands towards Etonia. If we don't pull this off, best case scenario, they imprison Imani and me. Worst case, we both die, and there is no hope for anyone. Even if we get through our entire plan without getting caught, the remaining Guardians may very well see to it that we pay for our efforts with our lives. Imani walks, eyes on the horizon, and I keep my thoughts to myself.

Etonia is the last place the Guardians had the upper hand on me. If it weren't for Toby, I would still be there. It dawns on me that the merchant woman, Saraya, must have strategically placed her market stall in front of the small door to intercept escaped prisoners, and on that day, she helped me. Why? There is no way she or anyone else, apart from my mother's family, could know that I'm capable of changing the dial. Perhaps she does that all the time, for every escaped prisoner—a rebellion of sorts against the Guardians. I think of the image of the bird in flight on Toby's chest—the same as the one on Enid's wrist.

"Harm." Imani interrupts my deep considerations with her urgency. "Look." She points to the horizon, where a Guardian outpost stands, guarded. We are far enough away that they can't identify us, but if we travel too close, they will haul us in. We change direction, heading east slightly, hoping that our sudden change doesn't pique their interest. Two dune buggies circle around the outpost like a swarm on the defense. One of the drivers spots us and peels out from the outpost, sailing straight toward us.

We are out in the open, with nowhere to run.

Imani grabs my hand to run, but I hold her in her spot. "No. If we run, they'll know we're trying to escape them." Standing rooted in the sand, I pull the wrap tighter around my face, ensuring that my eyes are the only thing visible. Imani does the same.

"Harm, if he knows who we are, it's over for us both."

"Then let's hope he doesn't," I respond, trying to instil a little confidence in her, but failing to do so for myself.

I let go of Imani's hand as the buggy comes to a halt in front of us. The Guardian is wearing his wrap. I hold my breath, waiting. He lowers the wrap as he steps out of the buggy.

"Travesci," Mason grates. He must recognize our clothes.

"Rayner." I fold my arms across my chest. Blood thunders through my head.

Not good.

He saunters toward us, stopping in front of Imani. "Shouldn't you be hiding out somewhere?" he says, his eyes fixed on her. I force myself to remain motionless as his gaze burns into hers.

"We need to keep moving," I say.

"Yes, you do." He smirks, eyes still on Imani. She gives him nothing but mild annoyance. Jumping back into the buggy, he pulls his wrap up and slams the gear shift forward. "Don't let me find you again, Travesci." The buggy spins, spraying sand at us. He looks back with at Imani. My insides harden, and a low growl escapes my throat. Imani's gaze is fixed on the buggy, watching Mason speed back through the sand.

We walk in silence the rest of the way, the Guardian outpost seeming less threatening than the encounter we just had with Mason. I replay the scene that just unfolded, with Imani as the spectacle, and my teeth clench together while the heat rises in my body at the thought of Rayner anywhere near her.

"You, okay?" Imani breaks our silence. I can only see her eyes, and I'm glad she can't see my entire face right now.

I stalk through the sand. "Yep, great."

Imani hangs back a step. "If anyone should be offended right now, it's me."

I keep walking.

"Harm. Hey!" Her hand grabs my arm, spinning me to face her. I steady myself and look past her at the heat waves dancing across the sand.

"Look at me," she says.

My gaze stays on the sands.

"What on earth is up with you?" Her grip tightens. I stand in front of her, breathing heavily, willing myself to calm down. But I can't.

"You want to tell me what's wrong? I thought you'd be relieved it was just Mason," she says.

"I am." I wish she would will drop it. *"Just Mason,"* she says. What the hell was that? If he'd gotten any closer, he would've been on top of her. I swallow, setting my jaw, ignoring the burn rising in my chest.

"Then what is with the attitude?" Her grip is still tight on my arm, blue eyes burning into mine.

"Forget it, Imani, just drop it." Heat waves ripple past the point of my gaze.

"Ever since Charlie's, you've been acting weird. What did I do that was so wrong?" Her features tighten to match her grip.

I pull my gaze back to meet hers. I open my mouth and shut it again. She waits a moment, but I don't respond. I don't know what to say. Everything feels like it's on a knife's edge. This damn desert regime.

Me.

Her.

Us.

"Are you mad at me because of last night in the oasis?" she utters, her eyes lined with vulnerability.

"Don't be ridiculous, of course not," I breathe. How could anything about that moment make me feel angry? My heart hammers in my chest, and a stone forms in my throat.

"Then what?"

I can't speak.

Stepping closer to me, she looks up at my face, removing her hood and wrap. "Fine, I'll talk, you listen. Whatever just went on back there, I obviously don't know your history. But I know this, I'm indebted to you. I owe you, so much. And now, I can hardly breathe around you, I'm afraid of getting too close to you, even though it kills me not to. I feel overwhelmed whenever you're with me, but in a good way—like I'm finally whole. And when you're gone, I feel like only half of me is there. And it scares me. It scares me that just looking at you has such a huge effect on me, and there's nothing I can do about it. I don't want to *not* feel it. I don't want to get away from it. Just the opposite, I never want it to end. The thing that terrifies me the most is, what if you don't feel this too? What if it's just me, and you don't need me the way I need you? Maybe you let me tag along just to keep you out of trouble."

She drops her hand from my arm. "When I'm around you, do you feel anything? Or are you just this nice to everyone?"

Breaths heavy, I rip my hood and wrap off to get some air.

She searches my face. "I don't know how to live without you near me. And I don't even have a choice. The time I touched your face, when you were hanging from that pole, when your back was shredded to ribbons—" She stops, swallowing. Tears line her eyes. "That was the second I knew who you were to me. I tried to ignore it, I tried to leave, but I—"

I stalk into the sands, not far, running my hands through my hair. My arms drop to my sides, chest heaving.

Imani stands, shaking, her eyes fixed on me.

"Why? Why are you indebted to me?" I demand stalking back to her. "How could you possibly owe me anything? You've saved my skin more times than I can count! Nothing scares you, Imani. Shouldn't it be the other way around? I should be indebted to you!" I stop in front of her.

She stares at me but doesn't answer. Instantly, my thoughts fly to Fletcher. She feels responsible for what her father did to my family. She thinks if she carries his burden, she can somehow make it better. The fire in my chest ebbs. She swallows, silver lining her eyes, and she wraps her arms around her body.

"You can't breathe around me? Since when?" I stare down at her painfully. "I don't even know who I am around you. One minute, you look at me like I'm the most wondrous thing you've ever seen, and the next, you tear me down. And I let you. I *let* you. Even when you're hurting me, it's better than being without you." My hands shake at my sides. "I look at you, and not touching you is killing me. For weeks. Every day." I walk away, drawing in a ragged breath, standing with my back to her. "I have needed you since the time you went back for my rucksack. I am indebted to you, *not* the other way around."

I turn around. She is standing in front of me with a trembling half smile on her lips. I move closer and she lifts her face. With both hands, I wipe her tears away. I lower my hands, and she takes them, putting one arm around her waist, and the other hand behind her neck. My hands shake, and a small chuckle escapes from my tight chest. She lets out a soft laugh. I pull her close, so she is up against my body.

A tear spills down her cheek. "You can touch me whenever you want, Harm," she whispers.

The feel of her skin under my fingertips radiates through me. I search her face, taking her in, hands running behind her neck. Her hair runs through my fingers, and I cup her face in one hand. Her lips part, and she draws a quick breath.

"What if they use this against us?" she says, curling her fingers around my hands at her neck. "What if they figure it out and use me against you? I've been tailing Guardians long enough to know how they operate. Please promise me you won't do anything stupid if they catch one of us."

I hadn't thought of this yet, but I'm not surprised Imani has. I hug her close. "Wherever we go, we go together."

Imani pulls back a little. She releases her fingers from mine and slides her hand behind my neck, pulling my face down to hers, almost touching.

"Together," she breathes, brushing her lips over mine.

I kiss her with every moment that has led to this. Her hands trail down my neck and over my chest, curling around my shirt.

I hold onto her for as long as she lets me.

Our last night under the stars before Etonia, we settle down under a desert tree of sorts, with an old rock fireplace from previous travelers.

We lie on the hard ground, talking about our childhoods. I tell Imani about times I spent with my little sister and the work we did to pay the taxes and feed our family. She lets out a sigh and rolls over towards me.

"I wish I didn't leave my mother behind, Harm. I was the only person she had left, and I took off without thinking how she would cope." She is holding my arm with her head resting against it as we lie side by side.

"I'm sure she was happy you got away from Fletcher."

"Maybe. She was different before I left Perendi, always so tired and vague. I guess I can't take it back now. One day, I will go home. You can come with me, if you like."

The wind rustles the tree beside us, the calls of night creatures the only other sounds. I would like that ... if we are still together by then, and I'm still alive. I sit up and grab my rucksack, flipping it open, fingers hunting for the silky fabric inside. I pull it out and hold it behind my back.

"Can I show you something?" I ask.

She nods and sits up.

I point to the constellations above us, shoving my hand into the rucksack, hunting for soft fabric. "You see that pattern of five stars?"

She looks up, following my arm. "Uh-huh."

"They're called the Cassiopeia constellation, like the story I read you. But their name is not what makes them special. Somewhere in amongst those five stars is a nebula. It's like a star cloud, almost."

"That sounds pretty."

"It does. The nebula is tucked away inside Cassiopeia. It's in the shape of a heart. You can't see it, but it's always there."

Imani stares at the five stars. I curl my fingers around the fabric and pull it to the top of the bag.

"If something happens and we are apart—" I turn to face her and she rests a hand over my heart. "I'm always there, even if you can't see me."

She closes her eyes and looses a shaky breath. I drape the blue scarf, around her neck, letting it fall over her chest. She opens her eyes, almost a perfect match for the scarf, lifting the ends with trembling hands, and studies the fabric, rubbing it between her fingers. Silver lines her gaze as she tracks it to mine.

"Oh, it's beautiful, Harm." Eyes falling shut, she hugs it to her face.

"Then the two of you are a good match." I kiss her forehead, and her face blooms into a smile.

"It's decided, then." She opens her silver-lined eyes to me. "Those five stars will be ours."

I chuckle. "The Imani and Harm stars."

"Harm and Imani," she whispers, squeezing my hand. "Harmony stars."

"Harmony stars." I take her face in my hands and kiss her mouth. She slides her hand from my chest to around my neck. A heartbeat later, she snuggles her head into my chest. In this moment, every part of me believes we can change the world. If we are together, we can do anything. I wrap both arms around her and pull her closer.

The crunch of sand underfoot startles us. Imani stiffens, moving out of my hold. I scan the darkness. Nothing moves, but the footsteps are getting louder and nearer. Standard-issue boots. Imani is sitting next to me silently, her hand on her weapon hip. Mine is sitting useless in my rucksack a few feet away.

Our small fire is the only sign we are out here, and it is not uncommon for travelers to make them, needing the warmth. It was a risk—one I am regretting now. The footsteps are almost on us, and we both rise to our feet. The uniform illuminates as he reaches our miserable fire, and Imani's breath catches.

Mason.

Imani stills beside me, unsheathing her knife halfway.

"Hey, take it easy Imani, just me." He laughs with a wry tone.

Her face is stone.

He knows her name. Do they know each other?

"I didn't realize it was you, in the dark," she says, sliding her knife back down.

"You two aren't very good at staying out of sight," he says, sitting down next to our spluttering fire. His sand goggles hang from his neck and bounce on his chest with the movement. He pulls off his hat and runs a hand through his messy hair. We follow his lead and sit a few feet apart.

"Were you two in the outlying villages recently?" Mason asks.

"Maybe, maybe not, Rayner." I pick up a stick and toss in into the fire. His eyes scan both of us. Is he trying to determine if we were with Barlow? If they think we were there and Barlow let us go, he would be punished, I assume.

"Trindari is the place we have been lately. We bypassed most of the villages," is all I offer him, hoping he buys the lies I am spinning. Imani sits watching Mason, her face unmoved, examining his gear, most likely determining whether she can take him.

Mason pokes the coals with a stick. Embers spark towards the sky, and he lifts his head to watch them float upwards. I sit in silence, not sure where his loyalties lie anymore. He should have dragged us both in the first time he saw us in that buggy.

Why didn't he?

The knot in my stomach tightens. We sit in awkward silence for another minute, and he rises to his feet.

"Wait. Why are you not taking us in, Rayner?"

My heart kicks up the pace as I wait for him to answer. With a smile that never reaches his eyes, he stops and looks at me, then Imani. "Let's just say our focus has shifted recently." He walks back into the darkness. Moments later, a buggy starts up, plowing away into the darkness, fading like our pitiful fire.

Mason let us go, again.

My stomach plummets.

CHAPTER 43

HARM

Groggy, having lived through dream after dream of Fletcher last night, I roll over to Imani. Her mat is empty; she isn't there. Her rucksack sits on the sand by her mat. I sit up. Sand lays scattered over her space. Jumping to my feet, I scan the surrounding desert. Nothing—just one set of boot prints, Mason's. Nothing else. I jog out in each direction, searching for some sort of sign as to where she has gone.

"Imani!"

No reply.

A large dune to the west hides my view to that horizon, and I run up it. My legs burn, and I fall forwards as I plow through the deluge of sand. I push up and keep running until I reach the top. Still no sign of Imani, but the great wall and the prison are visible from here, nestled beside the outlying areas of Etonia. The wall runs on forever, disappearing where land meets sky.

"Imani!"

Nothing.

I spin and head back towards our campsite. A figure moves

about the fire. I run faster. With each footstep closer to our camp, the silhouette becomes clearer, and my stomach sinks further. It's not Imani. A man stands next to the fire, hands hovering over the last of the embers for warmth. He has his back to me, but I can tell who it is as soon as I recognize his ragged clothing and the stick that leans on his shoulder.

"Charlie, Charlie!"

He spins around and waves with both arms, a wide grin on his face. He shields his eyes with a hand. Happiness pours out of him as I jog up to him and wrap an arm around his thin frame. He hugs me back before pushing away.

"Harm, where's Imani?"

"I don't know. I just woke up, and she was gone. I thought you were her. Did you see any tracks on your way here?"

His brows lower. "Nothing close to your camp."

"There is no trace of her. How can she leave without making footprints? There were no big wind gusts or storms, I would have woken up." I work through every logical way she could have left. Mason's gaze as he looked her up and down when he found us replays in my mind.

One set of footprints.

He carried her.

My breath stops.

I shove my hands behind my neck. A ragged growl tumbles through my chest. Nausea flickers up my throat. "He took her," I choke out.

Charlie's eyes widen as he steps closer, his stick gripped tight in his thin, pale hand. "Who? Who would take Imani?"

"Rayner," I growl, his name raw in my throat.

"I take it that's bad?"

"Yes." Bad. For so many reasons. "Wait—why are you here?"

I ask, remembering that Charlie did not want to help us.

"I changed my mind. I know I'm an old man, but if things are going to be done, I want my legacy to at least stand a chance. I am ready to claim my rightful place as Chancellor. And helping you is my best bet that my life's work was not all for nothing. If I die trying, so be it. I chose how I spent my life, unlike the people in the sands."

"Charlie, you don't have to do this. Imani and I can pull this off. We can come and get you when it's done." But the words grind in my gut. We can do this—*if* I can find her, if I can get her back, if we can follow through with taking out the Chancellor. A long string of ifs.

"I have made my choice, Harm." Charlie pushes up on his stick to stand a little taller. "Now let's find your Imani. I'm sure she's fine." He forces a small tentative smile. He doesn't believe his own words.

"You okay to travel? It's a couple of hours through the sands from here."

"I don't exactly sit around on my hands all day, you know. That place doesn't take care of itself. Besides, I made it here and found you, didn't I?"

"Okay, let's go." I grab our rucksacks and roll up the mats. With Charlie beside me, I stalk toward Etonia.

After an hour of walking, I offer Charlie a break. We sit in the sand, guzzling water. My mind plays out every scenario that could possibly be happening to Imani right now. Imani. Mason. Fletcher. The prison. My breaths falter, and I shake my head, dislodging the thoughts clawing their way through my core.

"Tell me about your brother," I say, breaking the silence between us.

Charlie looks at me with a hesitant face but responds, "Arthur —Artie, as he was called as a child—was the little brother that

292

followed you around and copied everything you did. He was always trying to do the things I did and failing amusingly at it. Our parents adored him, but I protected him from himself, mostly. He was always impulsive and didn't always think things through fully. I guess that's what he was like as a child. How he fared as an adult, I couldn't tell you. They separated us after our parents died. We were teenagers, I was seventeen and Artie was fifteen, but still children really. We come from a long line of Chancellors. He became the twenty-first Chancellor instead of me, after I disappeared. He had always wanted that job a lot more than I did. It was all he ever talked about as a child. It was around five years later that he discovered the secret of our family gift, as some would call it. Shortly after that, he changed the dial and wiped out the crime. I guess he thought he was doing everyone a great justice.

"Another ten years passed, and he rolled out the Guardian regime. By then, I had been living in the cave for over a decade. Challenging him crossed my mind with every story I heard from people who had escaped the regime, much like yourself. I used to leave the oasis regularly, to make supply trips." He hangs his head, shuffling his stick in the sand. His gaze hangs on the horizon, not meeting mine. "Most people would call me a coward for not opposing my younger brother, especially when others were suffering. But they were dark days for me. Just after our parents died, before Arthur and I were separated, I lost my betrothed. I was working one afternoon in the fields, and Arthur came to tell me she had been killed. That was the most painful thing I had ever felt, even more than losing my parents. Your parents are supposed to go before you, but not your soulmate. After losing my Emmie— Emmaline—and the separation, I fled. And this is how everything turned out, because I was too weak to live through my grief and do my job."

"Charlie, no one would think you're a coward or weak. Your

brother should never have done what he did. None of this is your fault. I'm sorry you lost Emmie. But there is still time to make it right. You are still the rightful Chancellor."

"Speaking of the people we love, let's find your Imani, boy." Pressing his stick into the sands, he rises to his feet. I follow his lead, and we track towards Etonia. The sands whip around us like eddies in a stream, and the once deep tracks of a buggy are almost wiped out when I spot them. Possibly these are from last night? Maybe they are from early this morning? I point them out to Charlie, and we follow the set of tracks. He periodically probes them with his stick, scanning the surrounding sands.

"Harm, there's a second set about twenty feet north."

I search the sand to the north of us. Twin tracks, out and back, made by a dune buggy. Someone came back out last night. The second set is deeper and more intact than the set we've been following. My heart sinks into my stomach. He came back for her. To hand her over to Fletcher?

"Charlie, we need to get to Etonia, fast," I growl.

"Agreed."

How could he take Imani without me waking up? She would have put up one hell of a fight. Mason must have incapacitated her somehow, or he had help. The thought of Imani not being able to defend herself makes me sick to the stomach. Why would they take her and not me? Why didn't they just take me?

The last half hour of the walk across the sands feels like an eternity. Charlie has been offering hopeful suggestions, but I know they are not realistic. He is trying to calm me down as I scan every inch of the dunes, the length of the wall, and every person who wanders around it.

A few hundred yards ahead, something flat glints in the sunlight. I jog up to it. A solar plate, cracked and abandoned. From the buggy that was here last night, maybe. A small cream piece of cloth is snagged on one sharp corner. I rip it off, rubbing it through my fingers. It feels oily. Charlie catches up, taking the cloth from my grasp. He raises it to his nose and coughs before jerking his head backward.

"They knocked her out with this, Harm." His eyes pinch, and his mouth draws into a line.

I take off running, praying Charlie keeps up.

On the outskirts of the prison village, Guardians are moving around. The entire village thrums. Robes safely wrapped around, hoods over our heads, and wraps around our burnt faces, Charlie and I head for the center of the village. A crowd has gathered to see what the Guardians are displaying. There is a dune buggy in the center, and one Guardian stands on the back of it, reciting a notice of persons wanted. My name is on the list.

Great.

Just great.

Charlie grabs my hand and turns me to the building to our right. There, plastered on the wall, are sketches of Imani and me. In my hood, I stand my ground, willing the shadow of terror threatening to collapse me to stand down. Swallowing hard, I turn back to the Guardian on the buggy. It's not anyone I have seen before, just a random guy in uniform holding up the parchment with my face on it.

The village people talk amongst themselves with hushed voices. The Guardian continues to explain the need to capture the wanted escaped prisoner, who is a dangerous criminal. I look back to the poster flapping in the scorching breeze in the Guardian's tight hold. My face is still on it. Nothing has changed in the last ten seconds.

Charlie grabs my arm, dragging me backwards, away from the

spectacle and into an alley. Everything around me is spinning, and the ringing in my ears makes it hard to make out what Charlie is saying, although I can see his mouth moving. He pushes me down to the ground to sit in the shadows of the side street.

"Harm!" Charlie is shaking my arm. "Did you hear what they said?" He is panicking now. I drag my gaze to his face, which is distraught from the strain of his words.

"Harm, they have Imani." He is still shaking me.

I stare up into Charlie's terrified eyes. He has dropped his stick and is trying to make me understand. Fear prickles its ugly way through my body, and sickness takes over my stomach. Charlie sits in front of me for a time before tugging at my hands, pulling me to my feet.

Absently, I follow Charlie as he leads me through the crowds and back out of the village in a direction I haven't been before. Nothing seems real, everything is in a haze. I can't process what is happening. We are on the southern end of the wall now. Charlie is still pulling me along by one hand, his awkward gait making good time, and he enters through a small door into the wall itself.

It's dark, and he fumbles through my rucksack. The scratch of a match illuminates the space with faint amber light. Charlie puts the rucksacks on the ground beside me and rests his stick up against the wall. The potent smell of damp ground winds its way through my senses. I lose my stomach on the dark ground beside me, wiping my face with trembling hands.

Charlie places the water canteen in my hand and wraps my fingers around it. I chug water, slamming my eyes shut, trying to shake off the shadow of fear with each deep breath. They have Imani. Mason must have by biding his time until we were close enough to minimize the risk to himself, either from us hurting him or us escaping him, and him being reprimanded for it.

Charlie and I sit in silence.

He just saved my life.

"Thank you," I say through threadbare breath.

"Harm, you can't go after her. The Guardians will snatch you up in a heartbeat. That's what they're waiting for."

"I can't leave her there, Charlie. I can't." I hunt through my rucksack for my mother's journal, hoping there will be help inside its pages. I rip the old book out. As it pulls through the weathered opening, something metallic flings from the corner and comes to rest in my lap. The pendant.

Charlie looks at it, raising an eyebrow. "Where did you get that?"

"It was my mother's," I utter.

"I don't think a woman's pendant will help you now."

A woman. The woman's face from the stall floods my mind, her knowing but secretive manner. Saraya. I jump up from my spot and shove the contents back into my bag. If anyone can help me now, it's her. I jump up and stalk out the door without a word. Charlie follows, hood up and stick puncturing the sand as we stalk our way to the market stall near the wooden escape door.

The alley has changed somewhat. I only recognize some vendors from the last time I was here. The last makeshift stall still stands in the same spot, concealing the wooden door for those who are lucky enough to find it. Charlie and I enter her stall. There is no one here, and I browse the items hanging amongst the drifting scented smoke from the slowly burning dried herbs she has hanging over her counter. Charlie is turning over goods in his hands, looking at items that may have once served those in a more prosperous world. A half smile fixed to his semi-vacant face tells me he is reminiscing.

A shadow closes in from behind me. "Is there something in particular you're looking for?" Her voice is kind, but intrigued. Her familiar face carries polite friendliness.

"I need your help," I say, my hood and wrap still firmly in place. Charlie has removed his. With no one having seen him for decades, he doesn't need to hide.

"I would love to help you, son, but I rarely hand out favors to folks I cannot see, nor recall."

I pull down my wrap and lift my hood in one smooth move, knowing that I am giving myself away by doing so. But Imani's life is worth more to me than anything else, and it feels like a small sacrifice in the moment.

"Ah, I see. Put it back on," she whispers, eyes darting between the faces of the villagers passing by before landing back on mine. "The Guardians have taken a friend of mine. I need to help her," I say, scanning her face.

"Fletcher's daughter. She will have three days from the hour they caught her," she says, her face fighting the despair she is trying to hold back. She disappears behind her counter before coming back with a box.

"The only way you can help her is to infiltrate the prison. But that is a death sentence for you if they recognize you. Your friend here, as old as he is, may get away with it if he cleans up a bit. But how you get her out is another thing entirely."

She hands me the box. I lift the lid to find a uniform, complete with shoes, belt, lapels, hat, and sand goggles.

"It belonged to my late husband. They returned his things to me when he perished, by the hands of the Chancellor. I wasn't inclined to keep them, but on occasion, I'm glad I did."

"Your husband was a Guardian?"

"Yes, but no longer. I try to help those harmed by the Guardians. It's the least I can do to pay penance for my husband's sins under the regime."

"Surely nobody holds you accountable for the damage your

husband caused?" Charlie interjects, no longer silent, drifting through the stall.

"Maybe, maybe not. But I would rather spend my days helping the people of the sands than the regime," she says, pushing the box into my chest. "Now go, before they come for daily inspection. You cannot afford to linger in any place."

CHAPTER 44
HARM

Charlie and I walk back to the door in the side of the wall to regroup and hash out a plan for getting Imani back. I am not confident that Charlie can pull it off. A single female prisoner is going to be guarded well. There would be no moving her around without piquing significant interest. Could we create a distraction? What would draw out most of the Guardians? A fire, a brawl?

We have spent two days hovering around this dark hole in the wall, trying to figure out a plan that won't end with us all strung up dead, and we still have nothing. On the morning of the third day, I lie on the damp floor, breathing past the lump in my throat. If the current Chancellor were replaced, that would make way for the new one to release prisoners falsely accused. Charlie could release her.

"I'm not sure going in as a Guardian is the best way to get Imani back. But if we can get you inside, with me posing as a Guardian, we can get to Arthur, and you can reclaim your title. It's the only way we can get Imani out."

"That might actually work. Law states, at least it used to, the eldest son of the Chancellor line is to take the position. If I can claim the title, I can have her released." Charlie looks at me with a sorrowful stare. "We need to get it done before the execution."

He almost chokes on the words, and they burn as they sink in. This can't be happening. If only Jonah knew. Then Imani and I might stand a chance. But he's not here. My heart picks up the pace, flinging against my ribs. I rip my robe and clothes from my body, shoving my legs into the grey pants. Charlie hands me the shirt, and I throw it over my shoulders, slipping the buttons closed from the top down. I slide the belt through the loops and secure it with the clasp. After the boots are on and laces done up, I pull the grey hat down over my head. I pull the sand goggles into position and hope that is enough to hide my face.

Charlie watches with lowered brows, as if me wearing the uniform hurts his eyes.

"Right. I know the main entrance to the prison. We should be able to get in there," I say.

"I can lead us to the Chancellor's meeting room from there," Charlie says. "I've been inside before, when our father was Chancellor. He was there most days. I assume nothing has changed much in that old building."

"Keep your robe on, but the stick stays here."

He nods and adjusts his clothing, losing a low sigh. A knot forms in my stomach. These could be our last moments of freedom if this doesn't go as planned. We wrap our scarves around our faces.

I crack open the door and see the light fading over the village. Guardians are strolling the alleys and interacting with folks still out—no doubt asking if they have seen the criminal in the sketches hung up around the building. I slip through the wooden door with no creak from its rusted hinges. I adjust the goggles over my face, and we make our way towards the prison entrance. I flinch as a man from behind me yells at another person and laughs. A knot twists in my gut, and I force air in and out of my lungs.

After what seems an age, we are finally standing at the entrance to the prison. I pull the hat down over my face with trembling hands. Guardians come and go through the entrance. I hold Charlie's arm and walk over the prison threshold. Fear creeps up my spine, sending my stomach plummeting. Charlie stiffens next to me as we walk past the cells, his eyes widening with every step as he studies the men behind the bars. We head for the door at the end. The door cracks open as we arrive, and a Guardian walks through, face blank. His harried steps halt. "Do you have a meeting with the Chancellor?"

"Yes." I pray he doesn't ask me to remove the goggles. The Guardian steps aside, and we go through the door.

Arthur sits at a large wooden desk, writing in a ledger. His clothes are neat, a cream robe over his dark tunic and pants, trimmed with silver thread, and a ring on each hand. A glass of amber liquid sits by his books.

"Enter," he orders without looking up from his writing. "Goggles, officer."

I raise my shaking hand and lower them slowly, keeping my head down and gaze fixed to the floor. My heart flickers in my chest, so fast that numbness starts in my hands. We shuffle closer to him. Charlie's gaze is fixed on his brother, eyes strained with emotion. His hands hang by his sides, chest pumping. His mouth turns down, and his hands curl into fists.

"Report," Arthur snaps before raising his head to look at us. His gaze lingers on Charlie. With a slight tilt of his head, his brows lower, and he stands beside his desk.

"Who is this?" He nods at Charlie.

"We found him on the outskirts, sir, claiming to be the real Chancellor." I hope he doesn't notice the strain in my voice.

Arthur runs an eye over Charlie's mussed hair and dirty face. He picks up his glass from the table, and pressing it to his lips, he throws the contents down.

"Well, that is interesting, considering I am standing right here. Have you lost your marbles, old man?" He crosses his arms over his chest and leans against the desk.

"No more than you, I'd say," Charlie replies, his eyes now drilling into Arthur.

"Huh, I have no time for ill-placed humor. Officer, you are dismissed."

I throw Charlie a glance, and he wills me to run, widening his eyes with a subtle nod. For a moment, I stand rooted to the floor. If I just leave him here, they will lock him up. The Chancellor won't even take him seriously. If he recognizes his brother, he is not letting on. But if I stay, I will be the one who is discovered.

"Why are you still here?" Arthur snaps.

I nod and spin on my heels, sickness gripping my insides like a claw. I walk out the door and toward the entrance, shoving my shaking hands into my pockets. What have I done? Charlie doesn't stand a chance. The minute sunlight hits my face, I track for the door in the wall. Now they have Imani and Charlie. I am a stupid fool. I couldn't even hash out a half-decent plan before wandering into the prison. This is all my fault.

Imani.

Charlie.

My parents.

Amaya.

All of it.

Everything.

I make a quick pace back towards the door in the wall. It sits slightly ajar. I glance behind me to check for footprints in the deep sand that abuts the great wall. No boot tracks are visible, as the wind is playfully whipping eddies and vortices around like a game enjoyed by children of the sands.

I step inside and adjust to the dimmer light of our hideout. A man stands just inside the doorway. The clank of the door closing behind me startles him, and he whips around. Larger than me, he steps into my space, arms across his chest. I remove the hat and toss the goggles to the ground. In the low light, I search every part of him. He moves closer again. A distinct smell radiates from him. So familiar. Steadying myself, I close a little distance between us in the dim light. I know that smell.

Grease.

Uncle Christopher.

After a long hug and a slap to the back, I stand with a half-gaping mouth and wide eyes.

"You are a hard man to find, Harm. Luckily for you." He looks me up and down, raising an eyebrow. "Why are you here, of all places? Are you *trying* to get caught?"

"The Guardians captured my friend, Imani." I leave out my most recent failure, Charlie, and the fact that Imani is much more than my friend. I am glad for the dim light at this moment as heat creeps up my neck and flushes my face. The truth ... Although the thought of discussing Imani and I with Christopher, Jonah, or even Enid ties my stomach in knots.

"Imani? Imani Fletcher?" Christopher responds, his tone turning cold.

"You know her?"

"I know of her. Fletcher and Petria's daughter."

"Petria?" I ask, remembering the only Petria I've met, the night I stayed with her and her son. The dark hair, the face, they all match Imani's. Miles had spoken about his sister, but I just thought she was older and lived with her own family now.

"Why are you helping her? She's a Guardian's child!" Christopher snaps.

"We, I—"

"I will not let you risk your life for her. She is a Guardian's child, Harm, nothing more." Christopher's finality that rubs me the wrong way. I will not be told what do to, especially regarding Imani.

"My life is my own to do with as I choose, Christopher." I omit the uncle part. "And I will not let Imani pay penance for the actions of her despicable father."

"If you say so, boy." He waves a hand at me, done with the conversation and moves over to the wall and slides down it to rest.

"How long have you been away from Maryanne?"

"Weeks now, from when I got word that you were in the prison."

"You were coming to get me out?"

"Something like that." He hangs his head, as if the toll from the journey of these past weeks has taken its due suddenly. He is quiet for a long time.

"Tell me, what is happening here?" His words slice through the damp surroundings and echo through our hiding space.

"Imani and I have been trying to make things right again, trying to change things back."

Christopher's head pops up. "So, someone has told you, then."

He knows, of course he does.

"You could say that."

"And Imani knows your real identity now?"

"Ah, yes."

"And they have her in the prison?"

"Yes, somebody took her from our campsite three days ago."

I know where he is going with this. She would never.

"So, she could tell them who you really are, and now they think they have a way to get you to come to them?" he spits. The blood in my body is racing around like a harried animal caught in a net. Imani would never do that to me. Heat flares up my neck. Where I go, she goes.

My stomach plummets. "That is not how it is."

"I hope so." Christopher closes his eyes and exhales. "For your sake, and everyone else's."

The overwhelming notion that I have let everyone down yet again steals the air from my lungs. I have fallen for the very ruse that the Guardians wanted me to all along.

Imani's face, her touch, the sorrow that she has let me see, all convince me that Christopher's words are untrue. Why would Jonah and Enid have helped us and put their lives at risk if they suspected Imani would turn on us? She hates her father and the pain and suffering he has caused; she would never help him. I don't believe it.

I can't believe it.

"That is not what is happening here," I growl.

"Suit yourself. I guess we'll find out either way soon enough." He leans his head against the wall. In the dim light, the angles of his face look so much like my father's.

The prison bell reverberates through the great wall, calling the village people to the center of the prison ... for an execution.

CHAPTER 45

HARM

I fly through the wooden door as if it doesn't exist, pulling my robe over the uniform. Plowing through the dense sand, I throw my hood up. Every heavy step drags on for an eternity.

Memories of Imani flick through my mind like the pages of my mother's journal. Breathing gets harder as I turn to round the prison gateway, and I steady my gait to a walk, matching the amble of the other villagers making their way to the center of the prison keep.

Christopher files in behind me, hood concealing his face. We follow the crowd to the gallows. The large open area used for public executions is grimy and old. The stains of its previous victims are a warning to the rest of us. Pungent odors of rot and waste filter through the air. The weathered stone all but groans as the horde of people gather between its tortured walls.

The gallows platform is made from the same stone as the prison. In front of the higher gallows is a smaller platform, half as wide and half as tall. Metal spikes stand in front, a foot and a half apart, to dissuade the crowd from encroaching. The odor from the half-buried souls taken during the last execution slams its way into my senses.

A fine hand slips into mine, and my heart lightens. But it's not right. My heart plummets as I find the sorrowful face of Saraya. My breath catches; this is not a good sign. She is looking around for someone while she continues to hold my hand.

"Who are you looking for?" I breathe out.

"Toby and your friend." She returns her gaze to mine. "I sent a message to Toby. I don't know if he could do anything." Her eyes crinkle, and she squeezes my hand.

"Thank you," I murmur, my heart thundering against my ribs. The movement of Toby and another hooded figure disturbs the crowd. People move aside as they reach us. Toby's strung out gaze finds Saraya's. The second person removes his wrap and hood.

Jonah. His face is drawn as he steps closer to stand beside me, placing his hand on my shoulder.

"I am so sorry, they intercepted the message. I'm afraid it may have made things worse," Toby whispers. His words ring in my ears. I shake out my hands, trying to dislodge the tingling. Christopher's gaze moves to Jonah.

"Christopher," Jonah acknowledges.

"Jonah." Christopher returns the strained pleasantry.

The tang of fresh paint from Enid's door flicks through my mind. "Enid?" I push out, past the lump in my throat.

"She is safe. She's in hiding," Jonah says and I breathe out a small sigh of relief.

"I take it you told the boy," Christopher says, eyes fixed on Jonah with a ferocity that matches the gallows' darkness.

"Not directly."

"It's a year too early."

"We are all aware of that," Jonah says flatly.

"I have to get out of here," I say, moving past Jonah and off to the side of the crowd before dizziness can take me down and I am noticed. Jonah follows me closely.

"How do you know Christopher?" I ask, sitting on the ground next to the wall of the keep.

"We are part of the band of folks who have kept secrets from the Guardians for decades. I guess you could call us the rebels," he says, almost whispering now, his face close to mine as we crouch beside the wall. He undoes the top three buttons of his shirt and pulls it sideways. Under his right collarbone is a bird in flight, like the one Toby has, like the one Enid has inside her right wrist. A marking for those in the rebellion.

"You're not friends, then?" I ask, ignoring the revelation.

"No, not as such." He mixes a half laugh with his words as he monitors the platform, periodically checking for any developments.

"Is Enid in this group too?"

"She is your grandmother, and he is your uncle. What do you think?"

"So, Enid is part of it too, then."

"Yes, a significant part of it, although I'd never met her until the day when we found her. The only name I knew her by was Old Desert Fox. We work independently, only coming together when the need arises in our own areas."

"What does the rebellion do?"

"We keep things from the Guardians, and run interference much like Imani has been doing. And sometimes, we interfere with their orders when too much is at stake, like your Uncle Christopher did."

"When he pulled me from the well?"

"Just like then. It has taken decades to get to where we are now. We can't afford another loss to the regime at this point. We have too much to lose."

"You mean me," I utter. "But why does Christopher hate Imani?"

"He has been on your side your entire life, so I would go easy on him if I were you, Harm."

"I don't know what to do next, Jonah. What can I possibly do to save her?"

"I'm not sure yet. I was hoping Toby would be successful."

"I can't lose her, Jonah. I can't." My words fall out broken, and I rub my hands down my face. My hood falls back.

"Don't give up, Harm. There may be one card left to play." Jonah stands to scan the crowd.

"What? What do we have left?" I run my hands through my hair. Jonah pulls my hood back over my head. It has been almost three days, and nothing has happened, no one else has come. I haven't come up with anything that has actually worked.

"My sister, Imani's mother, Petria. Maybe she can talk some sense into that madman she still calls her husband," Jonah growls.

"This is not happening," I gasp, knitting my fingers around the back of my neck, hanging my head.

"Harm, look at me."

I breathe through ragged breaths. He crouches down in front of me and rests his hands on my shoulders. After a handful of heartbeats, I look up, meeting his gaze, letting the tears fall down my face.

"Imani was there, watching, trying to stop Fletcher from hurting your family. Since that day, she has been trying to help you. Imani feels responsible for what you have lost. She has saved your skin time and time again, following you, trying to keep you safe. And in the end, she is the one who will pay. She loves you, that girl. I saw that when she risked her life for your rucksack. Imani is a strong girl, but she is no fool; she knew going back for your rucksack would end badly for her, but she did it anyway. There isn't another person alive that is a match for Imani. You're it, Harm. Don't let her down. She has tried to move heaven and earth for you."

I stare into his weary eyes and see myself reflected. "I know."

Jonah stands. The crowd stirs as the doors behind the gallows swing open.

"Go back to Christopher, and stay out of sight," he says, his focus on the prison door.

I push through the crowd back to Saraya. She leans into me, wrapping an arm around my shoulders briefly. Her hair drops over her back, exposing her neck. A small bird in flight marks the skin under her hair. Christopher offers me a glance of compassion before turning his head back to the gallows. Where is his tattoo?

Two Guardians flank each prisoner. They march three men out to the gallows, up the steps to the top platform. They are weak and filthy. The last man stumbles, the shackles rattling around his trembling wrists. Barlow.

My breath stops. Barlow is being executed. When Fletcher arrived and he failed to hand me over, they must have arrested him. Mason came to our camp to confirm we were there, in Barlow's village. Hell, this is my fault too.

A moment later, Fletcher and another officer appear through the same door. Mason follows them soon after, he looks terrible. Uniform untidy, hair messy, dark circles under his eyes. Fletcher is holding a paper. They make their way to the top of the steps. Mason and the other uniform hang back, while Fletcher stands in front of the accused with the announcements. Imani is not amongst the people to be executed. A glimmer of hope drifts upwards through my heavy chest.

"Harm, they will bring her out last. Women go last." Saraya says, her voice breaking, along with my heart. She grips my hand as the thundering voice of Fletcher shatters my downward spiral of despair.

"On this day, the accused stand trial and will be executed for the following crimes. Matthew Onnerhall, the crime of treason; Nathanial Brimmerston, the crime of failure to pay taxes and fraudulent activities; Rupert Barlow, the crime of treason in the form of rebellious activities. You shall hang as punishment for your crimes. Proceedings commence." He rolls up the paper, gesturing for the men to stand forward and receive the ropes awaiting them.

Christopher's gaze swings between Barlow and me. "Harm, is that your father?"

"Yes." My heart hammers in my chest. If he is gone, and Charlie is captured, I'm the last person with the ability. The last one. A small figure in a dark brown robe moves through the otherwise still crowd, ducking and squeezing through until they reach the front. Christopher is tracking their movements. Jonah stands on the edge of the crowd, watching them approach.

The first man is noosed and walked forward. Sobs turn to pleas and screams from a few of the village people at the front of the crowd. Mason pushes the man over the edge of the platform.

Snap!

"No!" a woman screams. Her cries are smothered by the crowd.

As if uninterested in the scene in front of him, Fletcher ambles back to the door he came from. The small hooded figure, in tandem with Jonah, intercepts him, removing her hood to reveal dark waves of hair. Petria, Imani's mother. Even from this far, her face looks so similar, her hair the same. I ate at Fletcher's dining table, I walked into his home, I befriended his son and his wife. The man I have been running from since the day I was supposed to die. And now he is going to execute Imani, his only daughter. My Imani.

Because of me.

The door to the prison cracks open. Between two Guardians, a small frame is dragged through the door. A black bag covers her head, and her clothing is stained with day-old blood. Her thin legs wobble through a limp with every step. Chains joining her ankles drag on the ground.

The Guardians stop in front of Fletcher. Jonah and Petria block their path. Petria pleads with Fletcher, her voice panicked and desperate over the crowd. Returning my gaze to the person between the two Guardians, my stomach flips. My legs threaten to crumple to the ground. I strain against Saraya's hold on my arm. The next man is noosed and pushed off the edge by Mason's quick shove.

Snap!

A long, sorrowful wail echoes off the filthy stone walls as another man's life is snuffed out.

Fletcher stands face-to-face with Jonah now, and Petria pleads, waving her hands around while Jonah stares, unmoving. Fletcher dismisses his wife, shoving past her, as if what is at hand is none of her business. Jonah hangs his head, and Petria screams, begging Fletcher, trailing after him.

The Guardians flanking Imani walk to the base of the stairs, their hold fast on her almost limp body. Fletcher stops and looks back at Petria. He throws his head sideways, and his officers take Imani up the stairs. Petria falls to the ground, and her robe floats down around her, her hands covering her face. Jonah stands frozen, arms limp by his sides. My gaze drifts back to the platform. Barlow stands with a noose around his neck. For a moment, I see my father, Andrew. I let out a shaky breath.

He closes his eyes as Mason shoves him forward.

Snap!

The last of the three.

Time has run out.

Imani struggles with the stone steps, each one taking a greater toll than the last. Her clothes only just cover her thin frame. Her dark hair must be wrapped under the bag, usually it would hang past her shoulders. They reach the top stair, tugging her up onto the platform. Now she straightens, and they turn her to face the crowd.

My chest stills.

Fletcher rips the black bag from her head and her two escorts descend the stairs. Mason moves in beside her, gripping her arm. Her face is covered in blood and dirt, and trails run over her cheeks from tears. The grime from the prison makes her skin appear darker than it should. They cut off her hair. My throat closes, followed by the sting of tears. Her once bright deep-blue eyes now a carry shadows of grey.

Fletcher steps in front of Imani.

Christopher grips my arm.

"Imani Fletcher." He pauses, and the crowd gasps, as if all at once, they realize the commander is about to execute his own daughter. "You are hereby charged with treason in the form of aiding a known criminal, and the act of rebellion. How do you plead?" He turns to her, his eyes vacant and face stone under the gaze of what's left of his tortured daughter.

A small growl leaves Imani's damaged face and she spits at his feet.

He doesn't react. "Does anyone here wish to appeal these charges?" Fletcher calls.

None of the other three men were given that grace. He's trying to draw me out.

The hands around my arms tighten. I am held in place by these two guardians of my own, as my heart rips from my body, piece by piece. I sob out a groan, struggling to get free. The heat from the salt-ridden streams coursing down my face burns. Imani finds me.

Her eyes flicker like a candle holding its last light. A sad smile grows across her pain-ridden face. Her body trembles.

A last gift.

She must be terrified.

No. Please, no ...

The faces of my family kneeling in front of the well scrape through my mind. The helplessness I felt. Helpless against the Guardians. Helpless to save them. Helpless to save Amaya.

"I didn't think so," Fletcher growls.

My hands ball into fists. I pull against Saraya and Christopher's hold, letting out a moan.

With a shove fueled by hate and power, Fletcher moves Imani to the ropes. Mason still clings to her arm. Her hands are tied in front, and her head hangs. This time, Fletcher does the rope. Imani's chest is heaving as she searches to find me in the crowd again, body trembling. A ragged cry falls from her lips as our eyes meet.

Fire rips through my core, burning its way through my body. I am *not* helpless now. A guttural, raw growl thunders from my chest, and I slam into Christopher. Saraya yelps, trying to grip my arm again. I stagger forward, putting space between us, weaving past several people before Christopher has time to react.

"Oh, Harmen," Saraya cries.

I don't look back.

"Don't you dare, boy!" Christopher yells, shouting for me to stop, to stay out of it. He shoves past people, cursing as he tries to reach me. I pick up the pace, but each step feels agonizingly slow. Every breath burns. I push my way through the hot bodies that fill the space between Imani and me. Either side of me blurs, my focus fixed on her. Imani's gaze tracks me through the crowd.

Fletcher is watching, waiting.

I push past the last of the people between Imani and me, stopping in the front row. Only the platform and spikes stand between her and me now. She stares at me with eyes wide, shaking her head subtly, pleading with me to stay still.

Fletcher returns his attention to the rope and motions for Mason to hold it tight. His expression pales as he obeys, taking up the rope with shaking hands. Fletcher nods to him. Mason hesitates, staring at Imani.

Hood over my head, I slide sideways between the spikes and step onto the first platform.

"No!" Imani breathes.

Fletcher stands, arms crossed and chin tilted up, waiting to see who is under the hood. Mason releases her, lifting the noose from her neck behind his commander's watch, his hands are shaking. Imani drops to the platform and crawls to the edge, chains dragging. Her cold, trembling fingers find mine. A lump forms in my throat, stealing my voice.

"You can't be here, you shouldn't have come!" she sobs.

I squeeze her hands in mine. "Imani," I choke, and trace a trembling hand over her swollen, tear-stained cheek. "What have they done to you?"

"Run, please, run!" Tears stream down her face as she shoves my hands back, letting them go, eyes pleading with me. But we both know it is too late for that.

"No," I growl, sucking in a breath. I grab her hands again, holding them tight. "Where you go, I go, remember?"

Her face crumples, and she moans, shaking her head. "Harm," she whimpers through sobs, "he will kill you."

"I will not lose you, Imani." Her forehead falls onto our entwined hands and hot tears drip from my jaw. "We will get through this, together."

"How?" she chokes, lifting her head. Her eyes widen, rapidly scanning my face.

Fletcher lands on the platform beside me. He grips my shoulder, tugging me away from Imani. My fingers trail from hers. Under my hood, I wait. His burning stare meets mine, and he shoves my hood off my head with one hand. The crowd is silent, every set of eyes homed in on my face. Imani strangles another whimper.

"Let her go, Fletcher. You've got what you wanted."

Pure hatred twists his face and he steps into my space. "I told you back in Amondo, you don't make the rules, boy. We do."

Imani stares at us both. How many times have I stood in front of him? How many times has he threatened the life of the people I love? He spins me around, gripping my arms behind my back. I stay focused on Imani, who is nearly breathless. She kneels, her hands tied, wide eyes following every movement.

A thud followed by sharp pain in my ribs sends me crashing onto the sand beside the platform. I cough, and blood fills my mouth. Fletcher yanks me to my feet, shoving me towards the small door into the prison. I turn my head to face Imani. She crawls to the end of the platform, catching my gaze. Mason stands unmoving, his face altering from vacant to pained before stilling, stunned.

I will not let her die for me.

I will not let her go alone.

We came to save our world, but now, just for now, I need to save her.

Fletcher shoves me past Petria. Her eyes widen and her hand slaps over her mouth, recognizing me instantly. "Oh, no!"

We reach the prison door. I freeze before the threshold.

My heart pounds. I turn back to face Imani. "Imani, I—"

She rocks back on her heels, tilting her head sideways, face twisting. "I know."

Mason shakes his head. Coming to life, he pulls her to her feet and drags her in the opposite direction. Imani recoils, pulling backward. He tugs her forward, and she stumbles toward him, her knees hitting the stone.

I strain against Fletcher's hold, releasing a groan.

Fletcher shoulders me through the door.

Darkness greets me.

CONTINUE THE STORY...
TAP THE IMAGE TO KEEP READING!

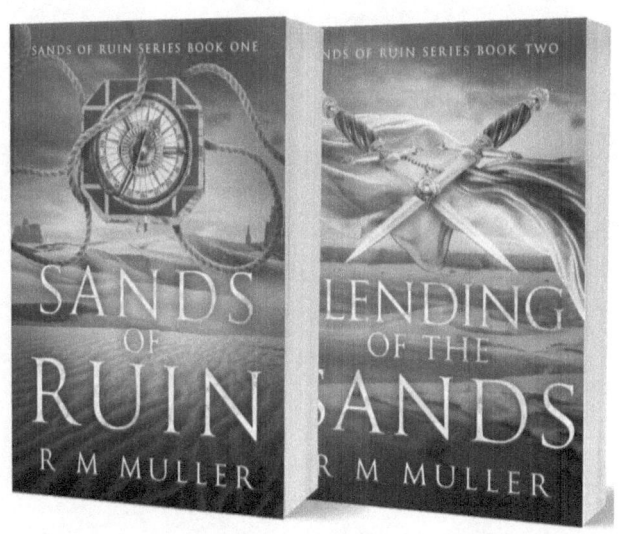

SANDS OF RUIN SERIES BOOK TWO

BLENDING
OF THE
SANDS

R M MULLER

ACKNOWLEDGMENTS

Nothing challenges your mettle like writing a novel. And it shouldn't be done alone! So here is my list of thank-yous in no particular order ... Shellah, thank you for challenging me to think every part of the story through and loving the concept. Louise, for reading and rereading this story and helping me make it its best. Robin, who's editing insight is greatly appreciated. Lindsey, for being my eagle-eye ... Christian, for your brilliant and creative cover design.

To all the writerly friends that have encouraged me through the journey of creating something from nothing, you are absolute legends. My patient and very grammatically correct mother, who read early editions that now make me cringe.

To my girls, for letting me bounce plot ideas and scenes around with them, and always giving me very honest (read: blunt) feedback, my four mini Imanis. My husband, who interest in books is nonexistent, but listens when I prattle on about imaginary people and places, nonetheless. And to my little brother, whose personality and friendship influenced the way I saw our awesome protagonist, Harmen Travesci.

Thank you to every reader who has found themselves on this page (and perhaps in these pages), you are truly rockstars!!

About the Author

Perched on a thin limb in a tree that had stood for decades, was a skinny, little farm girl. Her focus was solely on the scrappy notebook and pencil in her hands. Oblivious to the swaying branches around her and the voice of her mother calling her down, she scratched out a story. For the first time her imagination made it to paper, and she was obsessed.

Rose-Marie is a mother to four vivacious daughters, wife to a grazier, sister, daughter, etc. Stories and her little bunch of humans keep her alive and give her purpose every day, and the reason she spends a disturbing amount of time with imaginary people, in imaginary worlds, most days.

www.ingramcontent.com/pod-product-compliance
Lightning Source LLC
Chambersburg PA
CBHW030523120726
47904CB00005B/1591